BEFORE THE DAWN

Did a secret organization mastermind the empire of Alexander the Great?

Daneion Pelos, a peddler, physician and seller orf herbs, walks the roads of ancient Greece, Trusca and Gaul, learning and testing his skills of healing. From childhood, Daneion has been taught the uses of herbs by his grandmother, Yiayia, a physician trained by her father, a student of Hippocrates. From his mother who took the name, Honor, he learned to live for *areté*.

Daneion meets and befriends Olympias, a princess of Epirus and descendant of Achilles. She names him Wallis, and he becomes her physician, advisor and companion.

When Olympias is betrothed to Philip II. Basileos of the Makedoné, and when Wallis' grandmother Yiayia, dies, Wallis takes the first step of the hourney toward his destiny. He leaves his home in Athens to travel wilderness roads, unaware that he is being led by unsuspected and unseen guardians.

Beyond the Great Mountains in the village of Amber, north of the Danube River, Wallis meets a tribe of people with mysterious powers. These not-so-simple villagers, who call themselves The People of the Trees, adopt orphans from various Keltic tribes and teach them their skills. They enlist Wallis' aid in an ancient plot involving entire continents. He learns to fear them and their powers, and finally, to accept them.

The People lead him into encounters that challenge his sanity, but there is no turning back. No longer an innocent, he must decide. Will he accept his new world, learn and grow? Will he live on without arete? Without honor?

*Dedicated to the angel
without whom this work would have been impossible—
my daughter, Jenne Pfeiler.
to my husband, Bud, for editing,
to my son, Joe and all other family members who
encouraged me.*

*My thanks for the expert reference advice and
encouragement of members of
Ancient/Classical History forum at
http://ancienthistory.about.com.*

*and for inspired suggestions from readers,
Joy Kingsley, Walter Gourlay, N.S.Gill , Georgee
Spindler, and Judith Geary*

Before the Dawn

OF ALEXANDER THE GREAT

FAYE TURNER

Before the Dawn
of Alexander the Great

Copyright 2005 by Faye Turner
Ki-Eea Key Press
P. O. Box 818, Kingston, Tennessee 37763-0818
http:ki-eea-key.com/

First American Edition
Library of Congress Control Number: 2004098445
Printed in USA All rights reserved
Acid-free Paper

Publisher's Cataloging-In-Publication Data
(Prepared by The Donohue Group)

Turner, Faye.
 Before the dawn : of Alexander the Great / Faye Turner.

 p. : ill. ; cm.
 Includes bibliographical references.
 ISBN: 0-9762500-0-4 (hardcover : acid-free paper)
 ISBN: 0-9762500-1-2 (pbk. : acid-free paper)

1. Alexander, the Great, 356—323 B.C.—Fiction. 2. Conspiracies—Greece—To 146 B.C.—Fiction. 3. Greece—History—To 146 B.C.—Fiction. 4. Medicine, Ancient—Greece—To 146 B.C.—Fiction. 5. Hippocrates—Influence—Fiction. 6. Olympias, Queen, consort of Philip II, King of Macedonia, d. 316 B.C.—Fiction. 7. Philip II, King of Macedonia, 382—336 B.C—Fiction.

PS3620.T87 B44 2005
813.6

ONE

OLYMPIAS

The Legend of Paax

*As told by his grandson, Ul Avaal,
Head Speaker for the Temple Sanctuary
at Samothrake.*

In the reign of Vishtaspa in the land of Airan Vej where the River Daitya runs, Paax, a boy of fifteen summers, set out for High Hara to seek answers to the riddle of life. There he stayed for a year living on cheese made from the milk of wild goats.

When the mountain was consumed by fire, Paax soared upward, lifted on wings of smoke. He traveled across the world seeing mighty cities grow from small villages, mountains rise from plains, and lakes and seas empty and fill with water. Nearing the sun, the wings grew smaller and Paax descended, returning to his father Pourushaspa's house.

When he told of his exploits, his father's servant, a master of metals, made a medallion to commemorate the event, fashioning a sun and shaping Paax in the form of a bird.

Nearing the time of his death, Paax told his grandson his stories and gave him that medallion and two others laced into a belt.

"Keep them," he said, "until a man comes, a red-haired peddler." He pointed to the sunbird, the one in the center. "Give this one to him. He will be guardian to a prince."

Spitter

A little man stands outside the fence. An unseen Watcher, known since my birth, joins me. We view the man through my eyes. The man looks my way. He approaches my owner, the only ass seller in the Athens market, and opens a pouch hanging light across his shoulder. He jabs in a hand and searches for coin or barter. He draws a few coins from the pouch, holds them in his hand, and looks at me. He approaches my owner, lays the coins in my owner's hand. His pouch holds nothing more.

Paax–The One Who Watches–tells me to go with the man. The man's shirt and cloak are so thin with wear, so patched from rips, I wonder. Will he be able to buy grain for my feed? He needs someone to look after him. I suppose that will be me.

1

The donkey appeared through waves of heat rising from a dung and straw-littered pen. Untouched by the crude surroundings, she stood aside from the water troughs, head dipped, peering through curly silver hair, chewing slowly, eyes alert to the milling traffic. She caught my notice, stopped chewing, and stared at me, an inferior.

I leaned on the fence outside the pens, watching her being tended by the seller of asses. A bag of coins hung heavy from his girdle. He slung the bag forward with each step of the right foot, right hand gripping it, half supporting, half protecting it from bouncing against his leg, glancing at the shaded shelter attached to a grass-roofed hut in the corner of the yard. A woman propped open the door, a young woman, pretty. She threw out a dog, leaned against the opening, and stood watching. Above the heavy scent of donkeys, the aroma of stew and hot bread layered the air.

The man tossed hay into the troughs, lifted the hem of his dirty shirt, wiped his face, and slumped. He looked over his shoulder toward the hut, fingers finding and rubbing a sore place on his back.

Six asses remained of the day's trading. Nose down, front feet planted, the silver one glared at him through parts in her hair. He offered her a hand of hay. She snuffed and threw back her head, refusing. He reached into the barley barrel, grasped a handful of grain and held it out to her. She bared her teeth, stepped back. He laid the grain on a board beside the trough of water. She turned her head away.

And looked at me. She smiled, sharing the joke. Smiled? Asses don't smile. She looked...well, pretty, despite the need for a good washing and brushing. Suddenly I wanted to be the one who brushed her.

Never questioning my wisdom or the few obols in my pouch, I entered the pen. "How much?" I asked, eyes not on the seller of asses but following the lines of the donkey's body. I approached and she did not retreat. I thrust my fingers past her lips to check the teeth. A young jennet, she stood proud and strong in legs and back.

"You don't want the Spitter," the ass seller said. "That's what I call her because she's not worth spit. She's lazy and stubborn and she bites. Her last owner spoiled her. Let me show you another." He started walking toward a brown donkey, head hanging low, asleep.

"Not that one." His thin, lusterless coat showed more dust than hair. He looked sick. He showed no interest in anything, not even the food. Sick.

"How much?" I repeated, more firmly now. The dealer would not get the better of me. I could see he wanted to keep this ass; she added class to the pens.

"You don't want her, I'm telling you."

"Six obols," I said, "No more." The dealer spread his palms outward in resignation, said, "If you change your mind, bring her back." Leaving, leading the donkey on a rope, I looked back to see the dealer adding my coins to his bulging bag. I slapped my hand to my forehead. Would I never learn? I had given in to the oldest ploy in history, all because I was tired and hungry. I could have come back tomorrow and bought the donkey for a tenth of what I paid. Well maybe two tenths, or three...

I left Athens a few hours later, after the worst of the heat. I'd sold most of my merchandise, the women of Athens wild for chitons and girdles and gaudy beads for their festival of the harvests. I loaded my herbs and ointments, a small cut of cheese, some dried fish and half a loaf of hard bread into a saddle bag, slung it across Spitter's rump, and mounted. The donkey walked easily enough, even briskly, considering the heat. Until I got out of town.

The rhythmic swaying of the donkey lulled me, the countryside faded, and my mind soared with dreams and fantasy. I considered becoming a philosopher. Maybe I could learn at the school where Plato taught. But Plato lived simply on donations given him by his students.

I liked the richer things of life. Well, I liked them; that didn't mean I always had them. Dreaming. You know.

Between one sleepy step and the next, a covey of quail erupted from the brush on the side of the road and scared Spitter. She jerked sideways and leapt forward. I landed in the dust beneath her belly. Luckily, or unluckily as you might see it, I had tangled my hand in her rein before I fell and managed to keep hold of it. My weight, slight as it was, turned the donkey in circles, with me on the ground in the center, spinning round and round on my butt.

When she stopped I pulled myself to my feet, trying to make sense of a tumbling world. If I had not held the rein, that donkey would have been halfway to Elefsina by then. When I tried to remount she kept sidestepping me. I stamped my foot and pounded air with my fists. I looked around for a stick, something to threaten her with, but saw nothing. "Aargh!" I gasped, wanting to beat the donkey till she screamed for mercy. I didn't beat animals, but this particular animal strained my limits. Trying again, I tied her to a bush to hold her still. Then I climbed back on and leaned down to untie the rope. She threw me again. This time I didn't have the rein, and I expected her to bolt. No, I wouldn't beat her. I would kill her! She just stood looking at me as if at a child, and then snorted, looking down the road.

As jolly a peal of laughter as I could possibly imagine came from somewhere behind me. A woman, a girl, really, sat watching me from the back of a magnificent white mare. Stretched out down the road behind her were wagons and horses and people who had stopped to stare at me.

"Get that boy a horse!" she ordered, laughing.

Still boiling with anger at the donkey, I turned to rebuke her, she, a child, naming me Boy, dismissing me in a turn of a head. Boy she says, and I her senior by what must have been at least ten years. I inhaled to protest.

A young man got down from a soft-eyed mare and led her to me. "You might as well save your breath, friend," said the young man. "The princess always gets her way."

"Princess?" I asked.

"You don't recognize Olympias? Princess of Epirus? Where have you been, man? Everyone knows her."

Olympias. Of course I had heard of the princess. She was the scandal of all Hellas. 'The barbarian princess' they called her. Runs around the countryside like a commoner. Sometimes even walks barefoot kicking her feet along in the dust. Her father, the king Neoptolemus, got killed herding his famous horses. Her uncle, Arrybus, sent her away to school in Athens, trying to teach her to be a lady. Instead she set up camp in the woods and refused to take lodging inside the gates. Of course I had heard of her, but I had never seen her this close.

And no one had ever thought to mention her raw beauty.

I looked up at the horse. She blotted away half the sky. I searched for something to climb up on. Nothing available. "I'll ride my donkey," I said, turning away toward Spitter.

"Bendi, help that boy on the horse," Olympias barked.

A giant of a man with blond hair graying at the temples and tied at the back of his neck, dismounted his horse, stepped over to me, caught me beneath the arms as he would have any ten-year-old boy and threw me head first across the horse's back. I grabbed her mane and scrambled to get a leg across her, to keep from falling off the other side. Bendi laughed and slapped the mare on its rear. She stepped forward and I was riding. The princess beckoned and the horse fell into place beside her as though it only existed to do her bidding. Of course. Doing as Olympias bade seemed the most natural thing in the world.

"Where are you from, traveler?" she asked. Her voice belied her rough exterior, sounding as though she might break into song at any moment, words rising and falling like water swirling and sliding around rocks in a stream. I felt the tension in Olympias' people relaxing.

I chilled. Have you ever entered an instant where history stopped, awaiting your nod to begin its awesome game? For a moment I walked outside my body, looking up and down the road, seeing it in its entirety, past and future. It all stood frozen, waiting for me. I could still get out, I told myself. I'd just jump down off this mountain of a horse, take my donkey, and go. Spitter, by the way, now followed meekly at the end of her tether, looped around Bendi's foot. Bendi, hands free, bow slung across his shoulder loose and easy, rode point to the caravan. A long knife inserted in his girdle pointed to the rear. Toward me.

I did nothing.

Slowly the scene gathered movement and I realized that the princess sat studying me, waiting for me to speak. Umm, she had asked where I was from. I blurted, "I was born just north of Ambrakia, by the Adriatic Sea, but when my father died and my sister married, my mother and I moved east with her, across the Aegean. We lived inland from the isle of Lesvos. My sister's husband was a land owner, a farmer. My mother hated my father's people. She blamed my grandmother for killing my father. He fell off his horse..." In spite of myself I glanced down at the road so far beneath me. "...and broke his arm. It didn't heal and my grandmother sprinkled it with powdered tin to strengthen the bones, but his arm swelled and turned purple and he died..." I stopped, not because the story was finished, but because I found myself quite out of breath. I breathed.

"But you wouldn't be interested in the stories of a peddler."

Olympias laughed a little tinkling, three-noted bark that darted straight from her mouth into my heart. "Don't be silly, traveler, I love stories. So, did your grandmother really kill your father?"

"I thought so, until I went for a visit at seventeen. I stayed with her two years and studied with her. She, a *vikos* doctor, had treated my father with the best that she knew." Her best wasn't good enough. 'You must learn more, more, Tadpole,' Yiayia, my grandmother, had said. 'I have taught you all I know, all that my father and I learned from Hippocrates. It isn't enough. Study everything you see. Even the humblest event can teach. Listen to your inner voice; ask what it has to say.' She bowed her gray head and shook it from side to side. 'If I had known more,' she would always say, 'perhaps I could have prevented my only son's death.'

"No," I told the princess. "She didn't kill my father. I think my mother did it, with her incessant whining." The tale bored me. I longed to hear that tinkling laugh again. The princess was not to allow my pleasure. Not yet.

"Tell me about your mother," she said.

"My mother." I sought something interesting to tell. There was nothing. My mother was—my mother. I didn't want to think about her. When I thought of her, tangled lines of conflict arose in me. 'Areté' she had named herself shortly after my father took a second wife. It meant honor, an ideal of what a man or woman should become, a standard of excellence somewhere beyond the possible achievements of ordinary man—a standard always reached for, never achieved. Perhaps that was why my father had taken another wife.. He could never please his first..

"My mother never eats anything but onions," I said.

Olympias stared at me and looked away, asking no more.

"Every morning she eats onions," I insisted. "She likes them heated, in a bowl, in olive oil. Then for noon break she likes her onions raw, eating her fill then washing them down with goat's milk." I waited till I felt her eyes. I kept my own straight ahead on the rumps of Bendi's horse and Spitter.

"In the evening she eats the onions chopped up with a cut of goat cheese and raw cabbage alongside for color." Olympias stared at me then, lips open in disbelief. I allowed a tiny quirk of a smile. There it was. That little barking laugh. I looked straight at her then, and said, not entirely joking, "That must be it, the onions."

"Must be what?" Olympias asked.

"It must be all the onions my mother eats. When I was a boy, every time I looked at her I saw tears in her eyes."

Her smile faded. She reached out a hand as though to bridge the space between our two horses. "I'm sorry, traveler. I'm sorry for your mother, and I'm sorry for you. You must love her very much."

I must have leaned toward her, for my horse swayed in her direction, and our feet touched. Fearing that I might have offended her, I pulled back, surprised by a wash of fear such as that a deer might have felt approached by the hand of a man offering salt.

She invited me into her camp, and I went, willingly enough, feeling an emptiness inside that I rationally ascribed to hunger. I hoped someone among her followers could cook.

We camped by the river Kephisus just outside Athens, for, as I learned later, Olympias never trusted the wells in the city. Not because she believed they could be poisoned, but because a friend of hers had been raped there, collecting water for the school. Her friend had died in agony, squirming on the brightly-tiled floors of the women's quarters. An old woman had attempted abortion and killed her.

Someone could indeed cook, and the smell of rising bread soon filled the camp. I bathed in the river and spread my blanket in the shade of a tree near a tent. Weary from the heat of the day and from the activity and clamor of the agora, I dozed, waiting for a call to eat. Voices faded in and out in torpid waves. From within the small, rough hide tent nearby, I heard Olympias' clear-toned voice as she spoke to her maid, an older woman.

In response to a remark that had clearly been a criticism, she answered, "He knows his mother, Diana. That makes him *superior* to me, not inferior. I don't remember mine. Why should I send the peddler away? Besides, he is a doctor. We may have need of him some day."

Aroused by the mention of me, I fought sleep. What was she talking about?

"Who was my mother's family, Diana? If they were powerful people, perhaps they would help me."

"In Kreté," said Diana, "before we were stolen away from the Temple of the Unseen Spirits by your father, when your mother's mother died and your mother, Tanya, was named Regina, the high priest of the temple charged me with her care. I, hardly older than she, tried to comfort her. She told me I was more sister than companion. She said she remembered a name her mother had mentioned—Mivions, or Ivions, I think it was, and that her mother, your great grandmother, died in a village called Xios near Sparta. Her father offered her to the Temple of Orphans, and they chose her because of her beauty. Later the priests named her the Chosen One because the Unseen Spirits spoke to her. But I don't know if there is such a place as Xios."

"If I cannot find descendants of my mother's line, I am alone. Arrybus has taken my father's throne, and he hates me. If I can find my people, they may support me. They could shield me from Phaistos and his priests."

"Oh Myrtale," said Diana. "Arrybus doesn't hate you; he just wants you to accept him as ruler of Molossis. You don't know the grief you are calling upon yourself. You are a princess. You live in luxury."

"I am Olympias, Diana. Never forget it. Stop calling me Myrtale. I'm past my seventeenth birthday."

"I know what your name is, Olympias. I was there when you were named. Have you forgotten?"

Things got very quiet in the tent. I didn't intend to eavesdrop, but I couldn't help myself. I strained the hearing of my one good ear.

"I'm sorry, Diana," said Olympias. "How could I forget? I see your burned face every day of my life. You were the maid who dropped the lamp that started the fire."

"You saved my life," said the other voice. "Only two years old, you went to awaken your mother and father to tell them the house was on fire. That night, Neoptolemus and Tanya named you Olympias."

I pictured a great house afire, and wondered if the ancestral home in Molossis had burned to the ground. Probably not, for they said nothing of it.

"I owe my life to you," Diana continued. "Probably twice. Once when you showed Neoptolemus where I had hidden in the cellar. Then again when you wouldn't let him kill me for my clumsiness and for hiding. You clung to my legs and screamed till he told his guards to release me. Why do you think I have stayed with you all these years? I could have married. Your stepmother found mates for me, but I chose to stay with you. Yes. I know your true name, Olympias, but I will always think of you as my little flower. Myrtale."

Another silence. I imagined the two women, arms wrapped around each other, two as one against the whole world. I envied them their unity, and wished to be a part of it, knowing that could never be. I rose and stood looking into the darkness beyond the fire, still hearing her voice, remembering her quick, balanced movements.

"I'll wear the green," she said. "I think the peddler will like me in it." And she laughed the tinkling three-noted laugh. Suddenly terrified, my feet began moving toward the line holding the row of donkeys, down by the river.

Then I smelled fresh baked bread.

2

The camp slept. Time to go. I tried to climb onto Spitter's back. My legs, my buttocks, my side screamed with pain from the fall, so I just led the donkey, willing enough, now, toward the river along a goat trail. At least I hoped the narrow path had been made by goats. Wild dogs, spotted panther, and sometimes lions had been seen near here. I drew my knife and held it near my chest, pointing upward. By habit, favoring my bad ear, I looked about and behind every few steps or so, walking through air thick with the hot, dry scent of leaves and brush.

Spitter stopped and lowered her head. I grabbed her harness and pulled. She dug in her hooves and froze. Oh how I longed for my old donkey. Sway backed and slow, bristly brown hair almost white with age, he understood all the simple commands—I touched his side with my foot to turn, pulled his rein to stop, Never hard, just enough so he'd notice. Seldom did I even need to speak. I often felt so at one with him I forgot his existence. He never threw me. Not once. Never would he have made me so sore I could not ride. I had made a mistake with this animal. Perhaps the ass seller had been right. She was beyond training. If I took her back he might return my money, or part of it.

But she had such intelligent eyes. I seldom made such a mistake about animals. I stopped pulling, went around to the front and looked into those bright eyes. I would will her to obedience. Animals don't like humans to look into their eyes. She turned her head, looked off at the bushes along the river.

"All right." I said, pointing at her nose. "You do as I say or back you go…" She looked at me then, straight into the eye and turned again, looking to my right. I looked where she looked. "What?"

I smelled a camp fire and food. I parted the bushes to see. Downhill from the trail near the water, men sat around a fire, laughing, arguing, drinking. Perhaps I could bed down at their fire. A larger group would be safer from wild animals. Their voices came clearly. If I hadn't been struggling with the ass I would have heard them, even with my bad ear.

"They have women in the camp, Harkos. Some of them are old, but one I saw was just a girl."

"Can't you think about anything but girls?" Then a pause. "What did the old woman look like?"

"Oh, she wouldn't please you, and what do you mean, that's all I think about? You're the one who heads for the brothels every time we enter a city."

"Shut up, Kaelos! What did the old woman look like?"

"She was just a gray haired old woman. She had a scar on her face, like she'd been in a fire. I tell you, not pretty at all. But that bronze-haired beauty with them had enough spit for all of us."

"The color of the girls' hair, like hot coals left from a cook fire?"

"Well, yes, like that, skin like milk, and a voice that could summon Hades from his chambers."

Wonder, excitement filled Harkos' voice. "That's the barbarian princess from Epirus."

I left Spitter where she stood and crept down the hill, toes searching for quiet places in the soil through my soft doeskin boots, my toes felt a twig. I lifted the foot and placed it again and squatted lower, peeking through acacia brush tangled with wild grape vine. Harkos stood, advanced on Kaelos, hand raised to strike.

With my knife I pushed aside the vine and caught my knuckle on a thorn. Spending the next few minutes extricating my hand and knife without shaking the brush, I almost missed Harkos' words.

"We are not to touch her. She must remain a virgin."

"She's just a woman," he said. "But pretty. She would satisfy any man. What else would she be good for?"

The one called Harkos slapped the other, sending him reeling, tripping over the log next to the fire.

Kaelos sat down. Hard. Harkos stood over him.

I managed to get my hand loose, and crept a bit farther to peer through another brake. Phoenikians, both of them. Light from the fire colored their skin to something resembling old leather, tanned red. Though faces of other men remained in shadow, I counted five silhouettes outlined against a second fire. Seven men in all.

When Kaelos fell he had reached back to catch himself and laid his hand on a hot coal. Bawling, he stood, raised the hand to strike Harkos, changed his mind, brought it to his mouth, and licked it.

When he quietened, Harkos said, "She's not just any woman. The priest will pay us for her. Unharmed. You understand?"

"How would he know, if we just..."

"Can't you understand anything, Fishhead? Phaistos knows things. If he found out she had been used, we would both become chunks of charred flesh at the fall sacrifices. We have to catch her. Alone. Somewhere away from that Keltoi guard."

Backing out, looking for a clear path through the dancing black shadows of the brush, again I stopped to listen.

"How many guards were there?"

"I saw one drunk curled up against a tree, snoring." Kaelos laughed. "He held on to that jug of wine tight enough. Looked like he intended to finish it when he woke up. He was the only one."

"You didn't see the blond giant?"

"No, I saw some dogs, but they'll be asleep near dawn. That's the way dogs do."

"Then we'll wait. Get some sleep. Maybe later we can slip through, cut a hole in the back of her tent. Her guard can't watch everywhere."

Some of the other men had already rolled themselves in their blankets when I left. In pitch black darkness I bumped into Spitter's nose where she had lowered her head to watch. I groped for her halter, pulled to help me up the bank, and turned her toward camp. She led me away, placing her hooves as silently as a panther. I followed, grasping her tail and finding the path with my feet, careful to keep my distance from the sound of lapping of waves against the bank. Out of the shadows of trees and into white moonlight, I pulled the donkey to a stop.

"You knew those men were outlaws, didn't you, girl?" I grabbed her halter and kissed her on the nose. She shook her head, pulled away and laid back her ears, baring her teeth. From that moment forward, I never kissed her again.

Hurrying toward the princess' camp, I tried devising a story. I couldn't say I had left because I overheard her talking with her servant, but despite my efforts, no ready answer came. Before I saw the clearing I smelled smoke mixed with the fading aroma of stew and fresh-baked bread. I inhaled, smiled, and braved the camp.

Just as Kaelos had seen, one of the princess' guards slept beside a tree, a jug of wine curled in his elbow. Alone. I stepped clear of the woods, and something came out of nowhere to touch my shoulder.

"What are you doing out in the woods, Stickman?" said Bendi. "Gone to relieve yourself?" As he spoke he examined the donkey, noting my pack on her back.

An excuse, and Bendi had made it for me. It seemed that in my absence I had been named. Names have a nasty way of hanging on once they have been used.

"Yes," I whispered, so as not to awaken the drunken sleeper. I glanced at the tree where I had seen him a moment before. He was gone. Startled, turning back toward Bendi, I tried to speak. "I...I have a message. For your mistress."

Bendi raised his brow, a question.

"It's urgent."

The tall guard looked toward the fire and beckoned me into camp. Spitter followed, waited, and nudged her nose into a nearby pile of hay.

Olympias and Diana lay on blankets, Olympias with her head pillowed on her arm, staring at dancing flames. "*Mylitta*," said Bendi. "The peddler has something to tell you."

Olympias recovered from whatever reverie had captured her, sat up, and tucked a wisp of hair behind her ear.

"You missed supper, Traveler, but I think we can find something for you. Maybe some bread and stew, Diana?"

The maid looked at me long and hard. Gray hair dipped across her left forehead and cheek then disappeared into the folds of a braid to lie heavy across her breast. Startled by the intensity of her gaze, I could not look away from the burn scar only partly hidden by the hair. Rosy, rough hills and valleys danced in the firelight. She tossed back the braid to reveal the entire scar, glared at me, and went to find food.

I forced my tongue to move, my lips to speak. "*Mylitta*, I have learned something that you should know."

"Please, Traveler, call me by my name." A bit loudly, throwing her voice in Diana's direction, she added, "Too many people are inclined to forget what that name is!" She settled back on her elbow and looked at me. "I want you to remember it."

"Olympias?" I said, wondering. "You aren't afraid to have me speak so commonly to you?"

"I am not a farm girl afraid that the earth demons will spell me if they learn my name. Now what is it you have to tell me?"

"I chanced upon some men, seven of them, just a short walk down from your camp."

"I know. Bendi said one of them came by earlier, but offered no threat."

"I heard them talking. They plan to attack your camp."

She laughed. Not the tinkling three-noted laugh I had admired earlier, but a short, guttural bark, and my skin twitched. Who was this young girl that she should affect me so?

"Do you think me unprepared for such an occasion? Haven't you seen my dogs?"

Truly I hadn't, but I hadn't been looking, either. "Dogs? The men mentioned that you have dogs, but they assumed they'd be asleep nearer dawn."

"These men seem to know a lot about my camp. My dogs do indeed fall asleep near dawn, but Bendi and Boy rise early. They would alert us soon enough."

"There were seven of them, my...Olympias, and only two of your guards."

This time Olympias smiled. She reached out a hand and touched my arm. "You were worried, so you came back to warn me."

She knew I had meant to leave the camp. How could she know? I looked at the ground, embarrassed. Did she know why I had left? "They said something about a priest who wanted you..."

"Bendi." She hissed. Bendi emerged from the shadows, blond hair glinting red from the fire. She nodded. Again he disappeared into darkness.

"Bendi will take care of them," she said, and glanced at Diana arriving with a bowl of stew and bread for me. "Keep him company, Diana. I have things I must do. Diana watched Olympias leave and, tossing her braid, again revealing the scar, set a bowl of stew on the blanket. I took a bite of bread and looked around, wondering if the princess would be back. Diana caught my glance.

"She's gone with the guards. She has to know everything that happens."

I jerked and rose to my knees, the bread turning to paste in my mouth.

Diana laid a restraining hand on my arm. "It'll do no good to try to stop her, Peddler. She has a will of iron."

"She doesn't understand the danger," I said, pulling my arm away, chilled at the touch of the woman. I stood.

"Can you see in the dark?" Olympias and Bendi can."

◧◧◧

The darkness of tree shadows closed us away from moonlight. Songs of crickets and frogs, alerting me to the nearness of the river, rose and fell as I advanced then passed. I felt Spitter's ears swiveling forward and back, responding to sounds. Speaking to the night in deep throated huffs, she felt her way by its answers. Her breathing spaced into rhythmic thumps accenting the vibration of each hoof as it struck the ground. If not for the heat of her body, her silky curls clutched in my fingers, and the soil, damp from the night's dew, soak through my soft hide boots, I might have believed that I only dreamed that I walked, that no threat of danger to a princess had called me away from the comforting flames of a camp fire. The monotony of the donkey's movement lulled my tension. Somewhere ahead, light glinted through brush. The campsite of Harkos and his band. I could now see Spitter's long pointed ears, silver hair picking up faint highlights. I saw nothing of Olympias nor Bendi.

"Loo loo loo loo loo!" Screams shrilled the night. I froze, limbs paralyzed. Naked figures blackened by ashes, erupted from brush. They surrounded me, flowed toward the fire. A dying man screamed and coughed his last breath. Another. Another. Someone ran from the fire and thrust a flaming torch at my face, blinding me. He crashed into me, knocked my breath away, tilted me backwards. The firebrand shot high into the air, tumbling.

I slipped and fell through acacia. My feet splashed into water. I caught a branch of thorn bush and clung, tearing my hand, but hanging high enough on the bank to view the bloodbath raging beyond my fingertips. The firebrand fell beside my fingers. I recognized the thief, Harkos. Blood ran from a cut in his brow, washed diagonally into his eyes, across his nose, and into his beard. He rose from where he had fallen, retrieved the torch and ran, lighting the woods in long-shadowed, bouncing relief.

A sick weakness of fear drained me. I dragged sweat-blind eyes across my sleeve. The strain of holding myself above the water strictured my throat, swelled my tongue, cut off my breath. I released the thorn bush. My hands stripped the branch, ripping my palms. I hardly noticed the chill water soaking my boots, my pants, my crotch, my chest. Fainting, I heard a final fading cry.

"Harkos! Don't leave me."

回回回

My head ached; my stomach hurt when I moved. Eyelids heavy with sleep, I reached for a memory—feet and legs chilled, wet, dangling, face rubbing against Spitter's soft fur riding blanket, belly bouncing crosswise on the donkey's back, knowing her scent, surrendering to her gentle, swaying rhythm. And smelling blood.

I raised to my knees prepared to run. Normal camp sounds stopped me—someone banging an iron pot with a wooden spoon after stirring hot barley gruel, a puppy's yapping, the crackling of the camp fire, and from inside a tent, the voice of Olympias.

"I struck one across the eye. I think I put it out. All I could see was blood. Another screamed for help just before Bendi sliced his throat. 'Harkos!' Olympias mimicked, 'Don't leave me.' Laughter. Insane laughter. "The man I cut looked back and saw me. 'Medusa,' he yelled, running. Then a branch limb hooked his foot and dragged him down. He grabbed a burning stick from the fire and chased off through the woods." Finally, she quieted from laughter enough to continue. "He must have thought I was charmed."

"Well, that's not far from the truth," said Diana.

"You should have seen the man. His eye balls looked like duck's eggs." She laughed again.

Sounds of retching interrupted Olympias' tale. Two men lay across the fire from me, men I hadn't noticed before. Startled, still on my knees, I backed away. Bendi noticed and spoke. "Don't worry Stickman. They are two of ours. I brought them in to camp because they're sick. *Mylitta* will attend them."

"So, Peddler, you're awake," said the princess, coming from her tent. "Enjoy your nap in the river last night?" She laughed again, the three-note trill.

My heart thundered. My head spun. The dream had not been a dream. I tried to rise, seeking strength to speak. It hurt to breathe. "One of the band got away," I managed to say. "The leader. Man called Harkos. He ran into me." I tried to stand. "He may return..."

She squatted beside me, pushed me back to the ground, and wrapped her arms around her knees, face only half an arm's length away from mine. "Why did you follow us?" Blood streaked her cheek, clotting a braid dangling across her shoulder. She handed me a bowl of wine. "Your hands are bleeding."

I poured some across my wounds then drank the rest in great gulping swallows.

"Those men meant to..."

"Ha," a grunt. "Better men than they have tried, Peddler."

One of the men by the fire began retching again, face strained to the color of a purple plum.

"Not here! Away from the fire," she snapped, pointing her finger toward the woods.

"Wait, my...Olympias," I urged. "Let me take a look at him. Then I'll see to your wounds, if you wish."

She darted a glance at my face, arrogant, haughty. "Wounded? I do not rub ointment into thorn scratchès. A splash of wine will do. She shrugged. As for other battle wounds, there were none, and if there were, my people know enough of healing to care for themselves. To the man who had tried to throw up—I say tried, for no issue could be seen—I said, "What have you eaten?"

Scratches were one thing, spasms and vomiting were another.

"Just hard cheese." He retched again, and I felt his forehead. Cold as ice. Clammy. "And him?" I gestured to the other man.

"Yes, him too."

"Bad cheese," I said. "Can you get someone to show it to me?"

"Thalia!" Olympias called. "Show the... Traveler, what is your name?"

"Pelos," *Mylitta*.

"Pelos? Short for Pelopidos?"

"No," I hedged, mumbling. "For Peloros."

"Enormous?" She slapped her knee and bent double with laughter. "Enormous! Who would ever have named you that, Traveler?" With the sound of her laughter, a flock of birds came down out of the trees and lit on the ground surrounding her. One lit on my shoulder. She reached into a fold tucked beneath her waist girdle, held out millet seeds for the one on my shoulder and scattered the rest in a circle around her.

She seemed a nature goddess, blood encrusting face and hair, spreading her vitality among nature creatures.

"My mother named me," I grimaced, pushing the bird from my shoulder, hurting my hand. I turned my hands palm up and looked at them. "She says at birth, my father could hold me in two hands. 'Your second name will be Daneion,' my father said, 'you may borrow it until you earn another.'"

"Well, traveler, you need a new name, and I'd say, you've earned it because you helped us clean out that nest of filth. I'll name you Wallis."

"Wallis? I don't know the name. Why would you name me that?"

"Because...because... She laughed. "When you fell off your donkey, you were so mad." She crooked her elbows and paddled the air. "You just stood there flapping your arms up and down with your fists knotted. I feared for that poor animal's life. You reminded me of a bird that sometimes wanders over here from Egypt. They jiggle up and down and scream. Ouali ouali ouali! Ouali ouali ouali!! Oualies never miss a thing, and when strangers come near they set up a racket that would wake the ancients. 'Ouali ouali ouali,' I hear, then come out and feed them. So that's who you'll be. Wallis. You see all, and bring me news. Wallis, " she repeated.

I smiled, bearing up rather well, I thought. "Then Wallis I'll be. Just sing out Wallis, Wallis, Wallis, and I will come running to your cook fire."

"Wallis, " she said again, sobering, liking the sound. "Thalia, show...Wallis...the food stores."

I followed Thalia, a child of about twelve, as straight-hipped as a boy, but moving with a confidence most women would have envied. She led me behind the tents where camp activity bustled. At least ten women, children trailing their footsteps or babies cuddled against breasts, helped with the breakfast meal or gathered sticks for the fire. Three huge black dogs with brown muzzles watched every move made in the camp. Quiet at my approach, they rose to their feet and sniffed my legs. I stood still until they had examined me thoroughly.

"They'll never hurt you now," said Thalia, and smiled, sensing my fear. "Here are the stores. And here is the cheese. We opened it yesterday. Patchez and Thagoras took some to eat as they patrolled last night." So at least two guards had been outside camp last night, and I had seen about twenty painted warriors at Harkos' camp. I wondered how many more there might be.

I pulled away blue fabric. Blue dye colored the cheese. I rubbed some off with a finger and stuck it to my tongue. Bitter. I spat the taste out of my mouth. "Where did you get this cheese?"

"From farmers in Athens, yesterday."

"Don't buy from them again."

Olympias had followed us, curiosity at work. She said, "Throw it out Thalia, and make sure the dogs don't eat it. Have one of the boys take it away from camp and bury it." And with a half-glance at me, asked a question, clearly a test. "What medicines should I give my men, Wallis?"

"Nothing," I paused, thinking. "At least for three days." We walked back to the campfire. "Give them nothing but bread and a little water. They won't want even that, but charge them to eat even if they throw that up too. They've dried themselves out vomiting. The bread will absorb the poison. It will pass through and they'll be fine."

Olympias bobbed her head in that short, sharp acknowledgment that I came to know, a gesture that brooked no argument. "Where do you live, Wallis?"

"Wherever I can find a bed, my...Olympias," I said.

"I think you misunderstood my name, Wallis. It's Olympias, not *my* Olympias!" I said nothing. I didn't feel comfortable calling her that.

"You could stay here with us, be my physician." Her lips twitched in inner laughter. "And watch for robbers and thieves?"

Her blood-streaked chiton stiffening in the heat of the campfire, the night bird riding her shoulder, firelight dancing off gilded braids–the very air vibrated about this woman. Something beyond my keening called to me, drawing me as the call of a wild dog draws others to its kill, attracting, revolting. She warmed as an autumn sun warmed, but to stand too near...a man could burn, crisping as surely as dried leaves in a forest fire.

"I am a peddler, *Mylitta*, seldom do I lay my head on the same pillow two nights in a row."

I sensed her withdrawal, the cooling of her interest. An offer had been made, the offer rejected.

But if her advance had failed, her determination had not, being only shelved for a more cunning approach. "Then when you're in Attica, you'll stay with friends of mine. I'll have Bendi take you to them. Ana and Dimitri will like having someone near who knows medicine." Not a suggestion, I knew a command when I heard one. "But perhaps you'll return? You can check on my foolish guards who could not tell good cheese from bad." She glared across the side of her face at the guards. They dipped their noses, pretending not to hear. Failing.

I would be able to sleep beside someone's hearth, not having to pack my donkey and head for the wilds at night. I would be safe from snakes and wild beasts. And in the home of friends of the princess, I would likely see this enchantress, yet be distant enough not to burn. I closed my eyes and dipped my chin in gratitude. "It is my honor," I said.

回回回

After morning breakfast of goat's milk and barley gruel mixed with honey, Bendi brought two horses and handed me the reins to the one who had brought me into camp. "Thank you, no," I said. "Spitter will serve me just fine."

"Nonsense!" said Olympias. "Bendi will need to hurry back, and his horse likes to travel fast."

Olympias intended me to keep the horse, and I had no ready excuse not to accept the gift. "Then I thank you M...Olympias."

Again Bendi lifted me onto the horse. But as we moved away, I looked back and saw Spitter, still tied to a tree near the camp fire where I had slept. Olympias had disappeared inside her tent, and the others had resumed their activities. Standing alone, the donkey followed me with her eyes as I rode high atop the horse. Then she hung her head low to the ground, looking somehow defeated.

"I can't leave my donkey, Bendi."

Bendi nodded, made a circle back to Spitter, loosed her rope, and looped it around his bare foot. We rode out of camp and toward Athens.

On the road to Athens we met a group of young women barely into puberty, all barefoot but dressed in deeply dyed chitons with ribbons laced through braids piled high atop their heads and wearing flowers and bangles roped around their necks. We dismounted and stood aside to allow them to pass, joining cheering crowds waving at those they knew, paying honor to newfound womanhood. On their way to be introduced in the Ceremony of the Mysteries at Elefsina, some of the initiates, giggling, embarrassed, waved when they saw us watching. Thalia, Olympias' young maid who had showed me the stores, passed, smiling, ducking her head when she saw us. She did not wave, but her eyes lingered on Bendi and her head turned as she passed.

I glanced up at Bendi. His cheeks were red.

On the road running through the Thiusi gardens and fields we saw many servants cutting grain, watering animals, pruning grape vines and building yet another shed house. One saw us, hailed, and took off running toward the main house. When we arrived, double gates through a stone wall stood open. The man who had run ahead, shooed chickens aside to clear a path for us through flower and vegetable gardens.

Thus began the most lasting of my relationships, the most endearing memories, and the beginning of my understanding of what it meant to have friends. Ana and Dimitri and their son Delos welcomed me as one of their own, not unusual for them. Strangers from afar all knew the *doma* of Thiusi.

Today Ana welcomed me to her tables with a rich broth and bread baked in her pottery kiln. Afterwards she showed me through her gardens, pointing out herbs and vegetables, and–when learning that I was a physician–offering to share anything I saw that I needed. Later, she showed me to an upstairs room and bed laid with sweet smelling covers. A night pot painted with lines and flowers sat alongside. "You will stay with us whenever you are in Athens," she said, and when I protested imposing on her hospitality, she hushed me. "I could do no less for one who has saved the life of the princess."

3

Rounded hills purpling in the distance gave way to open grain fields, bare of their harvest yet gleaming yellow in the light of the high sun. I passed women with scarves tied about their heads lounging beneath grass-roofed shelters nursing their babies and eating their noonday meals, while others slung scythes to cut barley stalks and ready the fields for winter.

From the seat of my cart, I called out my usual peddlers' cry, but they waved and smiled and told me 'not today, come back later when we have more time.'

Along the dusty road, I followed overloaded wagons tilting side to side with every bump in the road, showering me with loose grains of barley in stray gusts of winds. It had been a good harvest. There would be dancing in the streets tonight.

Vito, Ana's brother and a priest of Zeus of the Lightning, had told me of ruins up the valley where I might find some old pottery vases with the insignia of Olympias' family. Autumn sun warmed my shoulders. My cart rolled easily, and I dozed. Driven to find the ruins before the cold drafts descended from the mountains late in the day, I could not stop to rest but ate the meal Ana had prepared for me and pulled a bunch of sweet but sharp grapes alongside the road. This year's harvest would make good wine. Dimitri should earn enough money from his vines to buy that new field he wanted. The temples of the gods should fill their coffers with thank offerings, and Olympias would get her share for her protection of the temples. Intrigued by the possibilities of this girl's influence, I wondered. Like the birds I had seen come down from the trees, perch on her arm and peck at the seed she held out to them, at seventeen years of age she had the people of the greatest city in the world eating from her hand. Tiny, birdlike herself, her darting glances saw everything that moved. Ana's brother had said that at spring and autumn festivals, thousands sought her blessings on the best of their flocks and harvests before releasing them for sacrifice.

Strange how everything I considered always returned to the girl. Was I in love with her? Nonsense, I denied. But, relenting, I admitted some fascination. Her vitality, her spirit drew me. And something else about her, a sense of destiny—a destiny too set by some rigid godlike hand to be touched by ordinary people—intrigued me. I shrugged. I was content. It was good to be ordinary.

I saw only one other person traveling, descending a rutted trail on the twisted slope. He stopped to watch me pass, so I thought to ask directions. The man, dressed shoulder to toe in undyed, winter woolens, sun-blackened face bristling with knotted hair never bothered by comb nor brush, waited till I came near, then, eyes boring holes in me, jerked his donkey forward. From the seat of the cart, I looked behind me, thinking to call out, but he had urged his mount to a bobbing trot, speeding away. A holy man, I thought, blinded by visions and oracles, or perhaps a mountaineer, secluded from people, a slave to suspicion weighing down his shoulders and heart. Spitter never paused, but began the climb upward as though she knew the terrain.

The roundness of hills deceptively hid gorges and canyons concealing everything beyond the plain. Shadowed from the afternoon sun and bracing downward drafts from the mountains, I shivered and dragged my blanket from the cart to wrap about my shoulders. Thirsty, needing to relieve myself, I hurried on, hoping to see shelter before dark when the cold would settle around me.

Spitter snorted, stopped. Two days on the road, never certain of my direction, and here I was, right where I wanted to be, as though some hand had guided me. We rested near a cliff overlooking a gorge. I climbed down from the cart and followed a narrow foot path leading through a gash in a boulder. One side, broken away some time in a distant past, tilted over the canyon. I smelled fresh water. Spitter must have smelled it too, for she had climbed the steep trail without slowing. I eased my way down the path taking care not to lean my weight on the side nearest the edge. It wouldn't do to slip and take a tumble. I probably wouldn't have stopped till I smashed on the rocks on the shore of the sea. A scattering of misty islands marked the shallows through the gulf toward Evi'a. Holding a shrub, I stood near the edge and let the water built up in my bladder flow, spilling, shattering, falling into emptiness on its way toward the rocks and shrubs below.

A spring burbled from the rock to the side of me. Constant dribbling had cut a bowl-shaped depression in the stone. I cupped my hands, drank, and went back to get a bowl to catch water for Spitter. Winds pushed and pulled. Fighting my way upward and back toward level ground, I broke to the clearing where Spitter should have stood, but found only raw scrapes of wheel marks where the cart had circled. The marks retraced our path upward and toward the summit of the pass. Unconcerned with the donkey's absence, I supposed she had seen that the path led nowhere and had turned around. She would be waiting for me on the downward trail. I congratulated myself on my shrewd purchase and in my judgment of her intelligence.

A gust of chilled wind tugged at the blanket I had thrown about my shoulders. I shivered and pulled it closer around my neck, searching for the occasional wheel scrape that would lead me to the donkey, the cart, my bedroll, my stores of food, my merchandise, my bag of coins in a hidden cache beneath the cart—in fact, most of what I owned. But more than that, the trail would lead me to the sturdy-legged body of the donkey. With The Spitter, I felt confident, secure, strong and able. Hadn't she saved me from those murderers? Night winds increased as I topped the rise and searched the trail, snapping and keening the limbs of pine above my head, pushing, pulling them to bow and scrape together in age-old ridicule of short-lived, warmblooded animals.

The downward trail was empty.

I searched for a cave, or at least for some protection from the winds in the rocks. They would retain the heat of the day far into the night and beyond into the early hours. Then I would be able to see where to put my feet on my lonely trek down the mountain and back toward shelter and food.

Why had I made this futile journey? Futile, yes. Stupid. Vain. Insane. I knew what that insanity had been. I had wanted to impress a princess. Her jeering laughter and words still rang in my head. "Did you enjoy your nap in the river?"

I wanted her respect. Perhaps I could win that if I found traces of her mother's family. I imagined her sharp, quick laugh. For that I had broken the habits of a lifetime and come out here where only a rock-bound turtle could feel at home. I didn't even have the consolation that I had sold trade goods, giving me some excuse for having made this trip.

Worst of all, my friend, my donkey who had saved me from murdering cutthroats, had deserted me. Spitter? Without her I would be covered over and forgotten somewhere along the river banks outside Attica now. "Spitter?" I said aloud, knowing she would not hear me, far away as she must be by now. Yet I called again, louder, to clear the cries of pine limbs creaking and squealing, heightened in my anxiety—and to clear my mind of the agony of betrayal.

"Spitter!"

"Honh, ahonh ahonh!" came an answered bray from somewhere above me. There stood Spitter, halfway up the side of the mountain, she and the cart silhouetted black against a rose-colored sky. Past rock and wire grass on no visible trail, she stood anchored against the winds, a steady, sturdy presence against the intimidating loneliness. There, waiting for me.

"Ha-onh. Ahonh ahonh ahonh," she brayed again, for certain, laughing at me. Mumbling and sputtering, breath short from the chilled exertion, I chased her. She simply started walking again, and disappeared beyond the rise.

At the top I stopped to search. Spitter waited in a barley field, freshly cut stubble pink in late day sun. When I approached, she snuffed at me, rubbing her nose on my wet hands. "I'm sorry, girl," I said. I'll go back and get you some water. I lifted the cover on the cart and began moving things around to get to her bowl. She snuffed and jerked away. I trailed, still fumbling for the bowl.

The last rays of the sun vanished, snuffed out by a high mountain plateau across the shallow valley. We melded with darkness, not the deceptive darkness of mountain shadows, but a world without even the meager light of the moon or the stars in a sky now covered with heavy clouds. I could not see the fields, nor even where to place my feet. I hooked a hand on the side of the cart, and followed Spitter. Carried on a vicious gust of icy wind, I smelled the smoke of a cooking fire.

回回回

A lone goose honked as Spitter and I walked into the yard and stopped beneath a tree in the front yard. A faint light escaping through cracks around the shutter of a single window called forth in hazy light the outlines of a hut. Smoke rose from a hole in the center of the roof. A huge flat rock sat atop to block the rain, with space left underneath to release the smoke. Someone who cared had built this hut, but the builder had not stayed around to repair the roof nor to mend the door, for a board swung loose, slapping in the wind.

Angry murmuring rose from within. In a crescendo of yowls, two cats escaped through the loose board in the door. They saw Spitter and me, shrieked, and vanished up the tree. A moment later their pounding feet crossed the roof.

The smell of rancid pork oozed from the window. The smell gathered and hung suspended in air like the aftermath of a bad dream. A baby screamed. The muffled sound of a hand being held over its mouth silenced it. I felt a presence watching us from the tree. My skin crawled, and a spot at the back of my neck screamed to be scratched. I would have turned Spitter around and made for better pastures, but here in the wilderness, there were none.

"Ho, in the house," I called. "I'm a peddler. I come with goods from the city to sell and barter. Good quality, fair trades. I seek a place to shelter for the night. May I stay in your shed?"

The door cracked open, held, then opened farther. "Peddler?" asked a woman, voice high, quavering, catching. The limb of the tree shook, acorns showered the earth around me, and a shadowy figure dropped to earth beside me. A boy, as tall as I, stretched a sling between his two hands, loaded with a rock and held ready for swinging.

"My donkey smelled your cooking fire and led us here. We are lost."

"Peddler?" The woman asked again.

"From Athens," I said. "I carry most anything you might need to buy or trade for."

"Athens. You come from Athens?" She opened the door farther. "We were just sitting down to eat." A fit of coughing interrupted. "You and your donkey must be starved. Timotheus take the donkey to the shed and get her some hay."

"What's left of the hay is for the goats," said the boy. His voice broke from low to high, signaling his youth. His jaws snapped shut. He glared at me.

"There should be enough hay," she argued, "left from…from…"

"Left from nothing," the boy grumbled. "The goats ate it."

"It's all right." I said. "I have barley, enough for Spitter and some for the family too." A gust of wind brushed my beard. The sky flared in a series of bright flashes. A long continuous stream of lightning crackled, sounding like pebbles falling on a tile roof. I judged this to be dry lightning bringing no rain. A wave of ozone scent came on a rush of wind to displace the odor of rancid pork, but for only a heartbeat. "May I bed down in your shed? Storms are brewing."

The woman reached back for a lamp then came out of the house and shoved past the boy. "If you won't show him the shed, then get out of the way, Timotheus. Have you completely forgotten the need for hospitality to travelers?" She coughed again, the dry cough that sometimes comes with dust and too little water. "No peddl..." cough, "no peddlers have been here for two summers. The boy doesn't even remember what a peddler is." She reached for Spitter's harness.

Spitter turned her head, leaned against the woman, and pushed her off balance. "Spitter will find the shed," I said, "and be grateful for a stall. She hates the lightning. She just doesn't like being led."

The woman stopped and pointed. "Then the shed's that way, around the house. I'll get you some food."

In back of the house, I unharnessed Spitter, pulled the cart beneath an overhanging roof and moved the board that blocked the stall and feeding trough so she could enter. Then I took two handfuls of barley from a sack in the cart and spread them into the trough. The woman came out with a bowl of boiled greens, a jar of goat curd and a wooden spoon. "Hide yourself and your donkey. If my man comes back while you're here he won't like it."

Timotheus squatted outside the shelter. "He'll kill you." He looked up through his eyebrows at me. "Thoron hates strangers." He still held the sling in two hands in a manner that told me he knew how to use it.

I took the bowl, nodded my thanks to the woman and sank to earth beside the boy, uncertain what he would do, but knowing he wouldn't have room to sling the rock at me. The boiled greens stirred with oat bread tasted good in open air, and with the first bite I forgot the rancid smell.

The woman looked uncertain whether she should stay or go back inside, and then the baby started crying. "Timotheus..." she began.

"Go inside," he said, but when she didn't move, he added, louder. "It's crying. Go on." Then adding quieter, almost in apology, "I won't hurt your peddler."

"Aren't you hungry?"

"I'll eat later. Save me some bread."

As soon as the woman entered the house and closed the door, the baby hushed. "He cries all the time," said Timotheus. "He screams every time there's a noise. He cries when the cats fight, and he cries when it storms."

"The lady is not your mother?"

"No. Patros brought me here four summers ago. He died. After that there were others. Thoron may be gone for good, this time. I ran him off with this. He stood, swung the sling about his head, twice, smiling in satisfaction with its whir. He let it go slack, capturing it in his hand, massaging it tenderly, and sank back to a squat. I have to take care of the place now. And her." He looked away. "But if he comes back I'm ready for him. I thought you were him. If it was, I was ready."

I thought of the man I had passed on the trail. "Is the baby...?"

"Thoron got her with it."

"She seems a gentle lady. She could find work in the polis. Why does she stay out here?"

"Her ancestors lived here. She wouldn't leave, even when her husband died. Pateros brought me here with him after Mitera died." He rubbed his nose with his sleeve, never releasing the sling, but relaxing. "I cut the barley." He held up the sling and pointed with both hands toward the field. "I cut it high to leave something to draw the goats. When they come into the fields she milks them. They're hers and they're tame, but after Pater died she turned them loose to forage. I kill a squirrel or a rabbit every now and then, and Marina gathers greens and roots from the wild. Pater traded barley thatch for a goose. The honker lays eggs, but I have to hunt for the nests."

"Has...Marina been sick long?"

"You hear her coughing? It comes and goes. If she dies, I'll go away somewhere. Maybe to the sea, and fish. Pater was a fisherman. I don't know who will take the baby."

I finished my greens and laid the bowl beside me on a rock. "You aren't angry about me being here?"

"Marina thinks I don't know what a peddler is," he said by way of explanation. "I've seen peddlers before. They used to come to the docks to buy fish from Pateros. One of them gave me parched pistachios once." He looked more sharply at me. "He had red hair, and a beard like yours."

"Where were you when the peddler gave you the nuts?"

"Pa called it Peraea, or Korinth or something."

"If it was Peraea it is on the Gulf of Korinth. Sometimes I cart merchandise across the isthmus between the Korinthian and the Saronic Gulfs. It's just a short way, but merchant ships would have to follow the sea route to the south, a long way. So they ship across land by carts and wagons. It pays good in shared merchandise. The peddler you saw could have been me. Sometimes, if I have extra, I give things to the children."

He looked more closely at my face, wrapping the sling around the back of his neck, and propped backwards on his hands. I hadn't guessed his strength until I saw his muscles ripple. "The man looked like you. Do you remember a bald boy with a hurt leg?"

"A boy said a woman shaved his head to get rid of bugs. He slipped on the docks and bruised his ankle. It swelled up, got hot and turned red. I lanced it. Was that you?"

He grinned, shifted. "What are you doing out here? We're a long way from that place."

"I'm looking for something, I don't really know what. A priest in Athens told me there were ruins out this way, with an old temple."

"In the hills. Marina showed it to me once, before she got big with the baby. I've been wanting to go back. I was afraid to leave her with Thoron here. He gets crazy when the visions are on him. He might kill her."

"Maybe you could show me the place, now that he's gone."

A dreamy look came into his eyes. "Maybe. Marina could go with us. She'd like that. We could pack some food and sleep out under the sky." He sighed. "But the baby would cry all the time. And Thoron might come back. When we got down from the mountain he'd be crazy... Well. I guess I can't go."

I heard his joy, felt his pain as though they were my own. His voice betrayed his love for the woman, his jealousy of the baby. How could I find truth in his words about the man? Perhaps Thoron, a visionary, was not the brute the boy imagined, but I remembered the man's eyes, and I chilled.

Timotheus pulled a blanket down from a shelf beside the hay and spread it on the ground inside the shed. I lifted my own where I had thrown it across the seat of the cart and did the same. "You don't sleep inside?" I asked.

"Marina won't let me," he said. "She says she doesn't want to get pregnant again, but I wouldn't bother her."

Lightning continued flashing across the sky, harmless, it seemed, for none struck. At the sound of a gentle wheezing snore, I pulled the blanket up over Timotheus' shoulders. The boy and I drifted off to sleep to the feel of wind buffeting the stone walls of the shed, comforted by the contented sound of Spitter nuzzling the hay Timotheus had given her, some spared from that reserved for the goats.

※ ※ ※

"She's going! She's going with us," called Timotheus, slamming the door and running toward the shed. "She's packing some food and milk. She wants to look for the cave where her people are buried. It's up there somewhere. You think we could strap the baby on Spitter's back? It would be easier for Marina to climb the hill."

I pulled a thick lambskin from its bindings among my furs. We placed the baby on the skin, bound the ends with leather straps tied around Spitter's belly, and left the baby's face peeking through a fold in the fur. He crinkled up ready to cry, but Marina laid her hand across the bundle and patted his belly. He quieted and watched us finish packing around him. Timotheus hooked a sack of food and a jar of goat's milk to a yoke across his shoulder, and I added cheese and figs to the supply I already carried in my underarm pouch. We planned to build a fire, so I packed my tinder box in my pack and shoved torches–sticks with moss tied on the end then dipped in pig fat–through a slot in my back pack. I filled a pouch with water to carry beneath my other arm, in case we found no water. Considering, I filed through my herbs for medicines for emergencies, adding herbs for Marina's cough. Last came our blankets, laid across Spitter's shoulders in front of the baby. Marina and he must have a place to rest.

※ ※ ※

Morning sun cleared away the overcast clouds, and fresh breezes drawn across the newly cut barley fields heightened my energy. Eager to ascend the mountain, I began with vigor, but my knee joints soon creaked like new leather sandals. We stopped to rest in the shade, and I handed Marina my water pouch for a swallow to relieve her hacking cough. "Not much," I said. "We may not find any more." I forgot my own discomfort and showed her how to hold Spitter's tail for support in climbing the rest of the way. Slipping, sliding and crawling, we made it to the crest and paused, both of us fighting for breath.

Two white columns speared the clear blue sky. Timotheus climbed the steps of an ancient temple, called down to us from the surface of silted, black and white mosaic tiles, then walked the lengths of a fallen marble column—he, a vessel filled with hot and lusty youth, the column, the bleached bone of a giant. Challenged in spirit by ghosts of fallen grandeur, Timotheus conquered not by right of siege, but simply of time gone by.

Marina prepared a bed against the warm rocks of the remains of a house, released the baby from Spitter's back and snuggled it into the blanket. "My uncle's doma," she said. "They called him Mivion." An atrium and doors defined by stones rose higher than my head. I imagined a hawk-nosed lord sitting there on a porch in the shadows of a tiled roof, looking out over rolling hills toward the sea, watching hempen sails gleam white in the sunlight. But the sea would have been closer then. Ana's brother had said the water had receded. I mentally adjusted the image, brought the white sails nearer, added a dock and peopled the landscape with workers busy loading and unloading ships. This must once have been a thriving city. Backed against cliffs above, the ruins now spread across an enormous shelf of rock overlooking the plains and the sea beyond.

A crevice broke the surface of rock. It looked like a place where water had carved a channel. "Do you think there is a spring at the top of the rock?" I asked, struggling to release a knot on my straps so I could drop my packs.

Timotheus walked a rim of laid stones, the remains of walls of a cellar of the shrine, and scurried up a shallow-cut, overgrown stair on a cliff. "I don't see anything. I'll look at the top."

Calling to me as he climbed, his foot slipped. He tumbled backward and down, into the cellar of the shrine. Talus—sand and rounded pebbles collected from countless rains, washed down the mountain to slope against the wall. The cascade caught him, broke, and carried him deeper into the hole. Attempting to claw his way back up the sides, time and again he fell back, raining more talus down on his head.

"Wait," I called. I whistled to bring Spitter near, took one of the ropes from her pack, tied one end around her neck and tossed the other to Timotheus.

"Hold the rope," I called. "Spitter will pull you up."

Timotheus grabbed the rope, I walked ahead, and Spitter pulled, but pebbles rolled from under the boy's bare feet. Pounded against the talus time and again, his elbows and nose came up bloody.

"Tie the rope around your chest," I called. "We'll have to drag you." When he had been raised halfway up the sides of the old cellar, the ground heaved. Two stones broke away from the lip of the wall and tumbled downward, one grazing his shoulder, but missing his head. The earth sank to a pit, a depth more than half his height, dropping him to hang in mid air. Spitter and I tried to pull him farther. His rope wedged between broken stones. Dangling, twisting in mid air, attempting to release the rope from the snag, he pushed himself away from the wall with his foot, but with nothing to lift his weight and relieve the tension on the rope, it did no good. We could neither pull him up nor let him down.

"Wait. I'll have to go down and get you," I said. Taking another rope from Spitter's back, I tied it around her neck. Allowing the rope to slide through my hands, I backed down the bare wall onto the talus at the bottom of the cellar, and stood considering how to pull the boy loose from his tangle.

"Hurry," he said, desperate, hurting from hanging. I would need a third rope.

"Throw me the short rope," I said to Marina who waited, watching from the higher level. I took the rope she threw and tossed an end to Timotheus. "Tie it around your waist," I said. Then I climbed up a short distance on the opposite side of the pit toward a rock projecting from the side of the cellar wall. Bracing my foot and pulling on the rope, I strained to hold Timotheus' body away from the snag. "Pull Spitter's harness," I called to Marina. She did, and Timotheus began to rise. He rose past his shoulders, then his waist. He caught the rim of the wall, lifted himself up with his arms, and slung a knee over the top. Good. I relaxed, letting myself go, and ran down the sides of the pit.

Earth opened up. A surging flow of talus swept my feet out from under me, sending me sliding downward on a cascade of loose, round pebbles. I grabbed for breath, filling my mouth, throat, and lungs with rock dust. The whishing, sliding roar drowned the sounds of Timotheus, Marina, and the baby's screaming. I landed like a throat-slit pig on a pile of talus. Pebbles continued to flow, burying me past my nose.

One eye, crusted with sand, struggled for vision in a place too dark to see. My lungs, trapped by rocky earth, screamed to exhale. I fought to move. My left arm groped openness. With that hand, I dug at the earth and rock covering my face. Then, nose and mouth uncovered, I took short, gasping breaths of dizzying air, struggling to cough grit from my lungs. A grinding pressure wrenched the earth binding me. A jolting thump shook the floor from somewhere nearby—a rock, probably. A big one. Other thumps shook me. Rocks falling. Holding my breath, I waited for the inevitable darkness of mind that would come when one hit my head.

Silence—and I lived. Left leg twisted and pressed into a tight bend, throat and lungs raw with sand, breathing air that gave no relief, I lay powerless, covered in dead earth, too weak to cough, too exhausted to call out. At least Timotheus had not been caught in the cave-in. I remembered, last, seeing him dangling above the pit, or climbing out, but perhaps only the wish fathered the thought. If he managed to get to the top he would come for me. Or not. In silent aftermath, unable to move, to think, I surrendered to death, feeling comfort in the stillness, in the darkness. Then it did not matter. Nothing mattered.

What harm done that I soiled myself?

4

I am in a strange place, in a strange time. Seven people sit below me on a platform, three in a row in front, four on a higher level behind. Four are women, three men. All wear hooded, saffron robes, and only their sizes suggest man from woman.

"We, the Seven, have gathered to choose." A man on the first row speaks. He is not talking to me, but to an audience of hundreds of people standing on carpets of red and gold and green covering the floor of a great chamber. I look more closely. A few of the people stand, backs bent, arms long and dangling, teeth protruding from slack mouth above chinless jaws, some with black and white spotted hair covering otherwise nude chests. The woven linens wrapped around their waists and tied between their legs seem, somehow, an unnecessary adornment. Others more like the seven people on the platform wait with infinite patience if somewhat lackluster attention.

White columns rise from the floor to a ceiling higher than two buildings, and hundreds of lamps make the room as bright as a sunny day. There are no windows.

No one has said the name of this place, but I know. These people are assembled in a temple called Phaistos, on the island of Kreté. I have been called to witness.

Chanting in litany, the man continues, repeating words learned from childhood.

"We will rise from our shameful degradation."

I floated closer, marveling at the sincerity and devotion that gleamed from eyes sunken beneath crude overhanging brows. They didn't know what they were saying. They didn't understand a word.

The people respond: "We will grow in stature, in beauty and strength."

Man: "We will once again become worthy of the love of the goddess, and she will return to us."

People: "We will wear the garments of sanctity."

The people sink cross-legged onto their carpets. The man stands, walks out among the people, and the six sitting with him on the platform join him, surround him.

The man continues. "We offer the best among us for the Great Mother's viewing. If we find acceptance in her sight, she will come among us, take us to her bosom and fill our hearts with gladness."

People: "Who is most perfect?"

Man: "We will choose from the daughters of the Seven, those created by the hand of the goddess. That one will be praised above the many."

People: "That many may be seen as one, to speak as the many, to live as the many, to die as the many."

The man and the six others remove their hoods. Each wears a crown made of two bull's horns swept back from the face and curling out, down, around the ears, and brushing their shoulders. "Who among you will wear our horns? Who will serve the many, accept the rewards of the many, and suffer their sons to join the goddess?"

People: Silence

"Then," says the speaker, "We, the horned ones, we who have been raised up from the animals and anointed by the Goddess' hand, we will wear the horns. You must choose from among us."

People: silence.

Speaker: "Then we of the Seven must choose a speaker for the goddess. She will be called Regina, the highest, the Chosen."

People: "To that one shall be given our offerings of gold, food, and precious possessions."

Speaker: "Through the Chosen the Goddess will speak to the many. A perfect mate will be found for her, and if the child of that union is born a male then he will be sent to meet the Goddess. If the child is born female, then that child shall inherit the voice of the Goddess."

The Seven: "We have spoken."

People: "We hear, and we obey."
The Speaker holds up a hand. In the hand he holds a copper key half as long as his arm. "The receiver of this key is our choice." He lays the key in the hands of a woman.
She kneels. "I submit."
The woman's face glows white with beauty; her hair gleams as the colors of the setting sun. I think: 'The woman is Olympias.' But she is not Olympias and I know. This is the ancestor of the princess of Molossis, the descendant of Achilles.
In the speed of a thought I leave the great chamber of the temple of Phaistos, and return to the cave. I see as though in bright daylight, the pile of pebbly sand where a man is almost completely covered. I see through the sand. The man wears a red beard, a red mustache. I know. This man is myself, but separate from me. This man is young. I am old, older than this cave. Older than this mountain. But I do not know how old I am.
I stand in the cave and four people stand beside me, two women and two men. One woman looks like Ana. She holds out an urn, half as big as she. She speaks. "Take the urn. It contains my ashes, my legacy, my commission. I have no further use for them." She faded.
The other woman, shorter, darker, said:
"Long have I waited, longing to join my mothers. I have kept vigil—vigil over nothing, for the fathers have taken away the god, Zeus, and left my people to fashion their own, a son made of wood."
The woman loomed closer, closer. I look into her eyes. They are filled with pain, with disappointment. Behind the pain I see anger. "I am Kaesa, named Salemé when I married a man from far away Persia." So she said, but, though her hair is brown, I know her eyes. I know she is Olympias.
"Nada," says the woman, "the servant of the shrine, caused the fashioning of the son of Zeus. Her husband made it with great care, carving hair, inserting teeth from the mouth of the ram we sacrificed for the consecration. He made a tiny god, no bigger than my hand for I was a child. Nada liked it so he made a larger one, not mighty nor proud, but no taller than my shoulders. The god sat, resting on his feet. Havos did not use precious stones. The high priest would not have allowed us to keep it.
"Then he and Nada found stones rolled smooth in the waters and added his eyes—eyes to see our grief over the loss of the great god, Zeus,

taken by the high priest to a great temple—eyes to heal the wounds of our village, to bind us together in common goal. 'We will feed the children, heal the wounded, marry young lovers,' said Nada, 'all under these warm and caring eyes.'

"Now since my death, even that comfort is gone, stolen, and I, no longer caring, am free to go. Nada said I would bear a son, a man who would become a great leader, but my son is dead, taken from me in war, and he, only a boy.

"On the day of her death, Nada knew my grief for the loss of my son. She gave me her combs, fashioned with great care by Havos and given to her on their wedding day. He had made them from the bones and shell of a turtle, leaving cutwork in the top so ribbons could be run through. 'Take care of the son of Zeus,' she said as she lay dying. "He will become flesh and blood. The priests will want him. They will come for him. Protect him. He is in danger.'

"But Nada was sick, and her reason was gone. Wood could not become flesh, and my own son is dead. I have no other. Still I care for the god, the son of Zeus, because I loved Nada, and because she said he will be born."

[ornament]

I am one, but I become two: one floating above looking down, and one lying below, covered by earth. From above I feel compassion for the man below, and almost, I relent.

[ornament]

Struggling against painful grit invading my lungs, I fought as a drowning man fights for life, succeeding in drawing a short, shallow breath. I coughed, ragged but relieving. Again I breathed and yet again. Easier. The killing air, trapped for centuries, now flowed fresh with air from the outside, and with it, a scent of perfume. Perfume? Here in a cave sealed for many years?

I opened gritty eyes, trying to see past tears that instantly flooded and spilled, washing little gullies across my cheek, into my beard. Moving to wipe the tears, my hands and arms came free. I wiped, but my sleeve, full of grit, only made my eyes hurt worse. My legs, screaming for movement, jerked. The earth fell away, uncovering my feet and my legs. I tried to stand, but instead, rolled, pulled backward and down a hill by the weight of my pack. I stood, crouching, balancing myself against the weight. Dusting grit from my sleeve as well as I could, I wiped my eyes again.

Finally, trusting that I could see without pain, I opened my eyes and straightened up. My head bumped the ceiling. I found myself in dusky darkness, the meager light too dim to allow an estimate of the size of the cave. I touched the roof above my space, letting my hands roam as far as I could reach. It seemed low everywhere. I dared not walk, for I feared that I might bump my head or stumble into a hole.

I felt for the torch and my tinder box, still in my back pack and underarm pouch. My hand came across dried figs packed in beeswax, and I bit into them. Trying to swallow, I coughed, spit out the bite and put the figs back. I removed one of the torches, felt for the latch on the tinder box, brought forth the striker and the lint, struck a spark, and touched it to the torch. Light of the flame filled the cave. I stood on the low side of the pile of talus that had poured in when I fell. Banking against a wall, its height, pressing me toward open air, had kept me alive.

I climbed the pile and held the torch as high toward the sky as I could reach. It did not clear the top of the hole, but I hoped the light would show through and Timotheus and Marina would see it. In the midst of silence, I tried to call, but my grit-raw throat made no more than a croaking sound. Where was Spitter? Where were Timotheus, Marina, and the baby?

I removed the water pouch from beneath my arm and turned it up to drink, discovering that in the fall, the strings tying the opening had loosened, spilling much of the water. I filled my mouth, spit, filled it again and swallowed, coughing. Without water, and if no one came to pull me from the hole, I would die.

Again I tried to call. No answer. Not even the braying of Spitter. How quiet is the world of a cave, the only noises those I made, and I could make but few. At least with the torch I could see. I would look for a stream, a pool, something. Sitting atop of the spill of talus, I aimed the torch first in one direction then another, hoping to find another way out, knowing there were none. Again and again I coughed, cleared my throat, my nostrils. Breathing more easily, the scent of perfume came again only to be washed away by air from outside. I slid to the bottom of the rock, wondering. It could not be. Until I fell, this hole in the ground had not felt fresh air in centuries, and no one, surely no woman wearing perfume could have been here. Something white caught the flicker of my torch light. I went closer to see.

Beneath a dark cavity in the cave wall, in the midst of a pile of round rocks the size of ox dung droppings, the corner of a marble slab gleamed through. Behind the pile of rocks and marble, bodies of the dead wrapped in funeral cloths spilled onto the floor. Thinking that the perfumy scent came from burial herbs, I leaned the torch against the side of the cavern, pulled away the remaining rocks that had once covered the bodies, lifted them out and lay them side by side on the floor of the cave. The scent vanished to be replaced others, those I associated with musty, dry death.

These could be Olympias' ancestors. Sometimes personal ornaments were buried with bodies, objects that could give some hint of the identity of the people, their lives, their loves. Perhaps something here would tell me. If so, it would be certain proof to take back to the princess–if I made it back at all.

I unwrapped the smaller body first. The first layer of long strips of white cloth came away easily, not the least rotted nor decayed by fluids seeping from the body. Someone who cared had ritually bled the deceased and prepared it by drying it in the sun. I unwrapped it fully, curious as to burial methods, hoping to learn something of the people who had laid it to rest.

Brittle but still pungent olive, grape and bay laurel leaves fell away with the outer layer. I found a second broad wrapping, a coarse muslin beneath the first. I unfolded the wrapping, pulling away a layer of compacted, bright yellow flowers of the mustard plant. I lay the cloth to either side of the body and opened yet a third layer, this a gauzy film of the finest linen, embedded with light-colored sand and salt forming a crust with the last of the body fluids, perfectly reproducing the shape of this body. I broke away the crust on the face, pulling away a few strands of brown hair tangled with two tortoiseshell combs. This then was the corpse of the woman who had served the shrine as caretaker. The one whose son had been killed. And these were the combs given her by the former caretaker, the one I imagined as looking like Ana. What fancies are conjured in the mind of one like me, so near to death.

I removed hair from the combs and put them into my sack, silently whispering blessings for the woman from whose corpse I had taken them, wishes for her contentment and peace in the afterlife.

The second corpse, male, had not fared as well as the woman, for the entire wrapping beneath the body had rotted away, kept wet by oozing body fluids. This burial had been hurried, no time had been spared for the ritual drying and offering of blood to the sky. No amount of care could replace these wrappings. I laid him uncovered on the bottom in the crypt, then rewrapped the woman, laid her on top and covered them both with the rounded rocks. I could not lift the marble slab to replace it in the wall. I let it lie.

On the floor beside the burial place sat a huge urn with rounded handles on either side. It looked like the urn the woman in the dream, the woman who looked like Ana, had handed me.

I held the torch above the urn and looked inside. A snake curled around in the bottom. I drew back. Then, when the snake did not move, I looked closer. A python, dead, completely preserved even to the grayed-brown spots on its back. I took the urn, returned to where I had fallen, and stood looking up, seeing only the rocks laid for the cellar. Fighting for a clear breath from a throat still raspy from choking, I called: "Timotheus. Marina." But no answer came.

Timotheus, Marina and the baby must have returned downhill. They had probably taken Spitter and gone for help. Gathering hope, I placed the urn on the ground nearby, plunged the end of the torch into the pile, and sat on the talus to wait. Taking another bite of figs, I resolved to rest. Then I would look for water. On still air, the scent of perfume returned. Curious, I stood, grasped the torch, and took the smoother path of the cave, leading downward. The scent grew stronger, drawing me onward despite the lack of fresh air.

Painted on the wall in white, figures emerged from the shadows. Three people crossed a bridge over a river, probably picturing the last journey of people buried here. Scattered elsewhere on the rock, someone had chiseled out shapes, triangles, some raised, some recessed, three large and several smaller shapes with only two sides. I knew some of the symbols. The first triangle, lowest on the wall, extended from the surface. The triangle, flat side down, meant man, woman and child. The second, above it, chiseled into rock and point side down, would be earth, moon, and sun. I followed the lines of the third triangle, the highest, also raised from the surface of the rock. Trying to decipher the meaning, I rubbed my fingers across the figure, seeking to draw knowledge, even as though from the rock itself.

The triangle, two sides longer than the first, stood on one of its short points, clearly pointing upward and toward the right, the eastern sky. Beyond its point, three marks had been gashed into the stone, radiating out from a center, suggesting a bright light. Above the triangle and highest on the wall, long curving gashes had been cut— a rainbow, leading toward the light. Ah. Birth. Life. And finally Death. This then, would provide a pathway from earth to the sacred gardens.

Afire now with curiosity, I explored the walls of the cave. On the right side I found another grouping, painted. A ram stood waiting, head in the air as though listening. A full set of horns curled back and around his ears. A man stood beside him holding a long knife. This was to be a sacrifice. I rubbed my finger over the figure of the man, again searching for secrets in the rock. No smear came away with rubbing. Next to the man, on the left, another figure had been drawn, the same man, same horns, but smaller, another and another, one figure beyond the other, as though marching in single file toward the man holding the knife at the right.

Each figure grew smaller until I came to the figure of a woman, painted as tall as I, larger than both man and ram, but faint. Someone had tried to scratch her out of the rock. Still the figure could be seen, if only by the indentation of the scrape marks. In her arms she held a child with horns. Beneath the figure, I read words, still legible.

"*He comes. The Son of Thunder.*"

I remembered a day in the agora as a child gone shopping with my grandmother, a raving man had grabbed my cloak when I came near, whispering what seemed now to be a multiple of reverberating echoes. Dizzy, I lost account of time. Now, as then, I heard his raspy voice. Had he really spoken, or did he speak even now, as I read his fated words? I struggled to remember. Too difficult.

I examined the figure of the woman holding the child, losing track of the picture in my search and in the poor light. I dug for the stick of charcoal in my pouch, one of several I usually carried for marking signs along a trail to find my way home, or for such as this, to write or draw. I dragged the charcoal through her hair, along the lines of her face, her arms, her breasts, legs, feet. When I finished I saw that the figure of a woman and smallest child filled a space, and that the woman's second hand did not quite touch the child, but pointed to him. I laid my hand on the child as she seemed to direct.

A grinding sound arose from the stone, vibrating my arm and making it itch all the way up to my shoulder. Curious, I pressed harder. With the opening of the door the sweet scent I had been following overwhelmed me. Light headed, not sure of my footing, I grabbed the edge of the stone wall and leaned, looking outward into the center of a well. Walled with rounded stones, a stair spiraled downward.

I put a foot on the first step, testing it. It held. I brought my other foot forward and saw that I would have to bend low and hug the wall to balance my weight. This stairwell had been designed for people shorter than I, probably women, with smaller feet.

At the bottom, a pool of water glimmered. Fantasy fought with reality. It seemed as though I dreamed, and dreaming, flying, dying. I don't know where my will resided but I descended farther until I reached a level where I could dip in my goatskin and fill it with water. From deep inside the water, blue light shone. It grew, waving, rippling, rising to the surface. The light crawled up the sides of the well, up my arms, and reached for my neck. Terrified, I hurried back up the steps, stumbled through the opening and fell, sprawling, sending my torch flying against a wall. Too addled to stand, I lay watching the blue light crawl across the floor and walls, illuminating everything in blue, no source, no shadows cast. In wonder I stood and crouched beneath the hollowed out ceiling. The light had not harmed me. Instead I felt strength flow through my body. Encouraged, again I looked through the opening and gazed below. The surface of the pool rippled as though disturbed by a breeze or a movement in the earth. Even as I watched, the pool grew more agitated, and the rock against which I leaned vibrated.

Hugging the wall to keep from falling, I stepped back into the cave. Streams of blue light forked from the ends of my fingers, and with every movement, even to breathe, I crackled. The cave ground quivered. The walls vibrated like the purring of a cat. My skin numbed. My swallowing, my breathing grew easy, my steps light. I felt gloriously alive, more than ever in my entire life. Not trusting the muscles in my legs, with uncertain steps I returned to stand beside the pile of rocks upon which I had fallen, and looked toward the hole at the top of the cave wall. The blue light flooded the chamber, climbed the hole to the top and shone through into darkness.

The remaining talus that had collected in the cellar above me, quivered, rolled downward, rained through the hole, bits of detritus stinging my face and arms. The pile on which I had fallen, grew. When the rain of pebbles stopped, I climbed the pile, and with effort grasped the edge of the hole. I thought to climb out and then remembered that I had left behind the urn with the priestess' ashes. I eased back into the hole, lifted the urn, climbed to the top of the pile, set the urn on the floor outside, and pushed it as far as I could reach to clear space for me.

Standing outside in full blue light I saw that most of the talus had been shaken down the hole, a hole that I now saw as a square doorway leading to the underground level and revealing steps that climbed the sides of the cellar to the top. In the passage of time, the steps had formed shelves for the accumulation of talus that covered the doorway. The door may have been a swinging stone, opening in the same manner as that with the picture of the woman and the boy. In the first rush of rock, it must have fallen inward and probably now lay at the bottom of the pile in the cave below.

The blue light brightened, drawing my attention upward. The two columns left standing from the old temple now glowed blue, and in the same manner as the light that even now forked from the ends of my fingers, it spread talons of light flaring away toward the heavens. The countryside shone as bright as day, all blue light.

The stair cut from the wall gave me barely enough room to place one foot at a time. I tried to climb, and saw that I could do it, but when I tried climbing with the urn, it overbalanced me.

The rope with which I had pulled Timotheus away from the ruined remains of the wall of the cellar to free him, dangled over the edge. Imagining Timotheus removing it from his waist and dropping it, I wondered why he and Marina would have left me down in the hole. Had they seen this as an opportunity to rob me? How could I so misjudge people? They had even taken my donkey, and probably, even now were sorting through my merchandise in the cart. But I had the urn, and I could get my merchandise back. I decided to use the dangling rope to tie around the throat of the urn and pull it up after I got out. I jerked the end of the rope. It would not come. I jerked again, harder. Perhaps they had tied it to something, leaving it dangling so I could pull myself out. But surely they thought I was dead since I had not answered their calls.

I pulled hard, testing my weight. A bare foot slid out over the edge. And then another. Two legs stuck out and then slid farther, bending at the hip. They hung suspended for a moment. Then, in a rain of talus, a body slipped from the upper level and fell on me, knocking me to the hard rock floor of the old basement. I scrambled, shoved it aside, reliving the choking sensation of my first fall. I got to my knees and looked down at the lifeless body...of Timotheus.

5

Timotheus lay on his left side, face down and against the rocks. Already chilled from night winds, his right arm stretched out, stiff, reaching. Caught in the crook of his little finger was the leather strip of his sling, empty. I rolled him to face the sky, and adjusted his neck to its natural position. Beneath a dented forehead filled with dried blood, eyes open, glazed with gray dust, he stared at nothing. Marina would not have done this. It could only be that Thoron had returned, killed the boy and taken Marina, the baby, and Spitter.

Somewhere far away a baby cried. I cuddled the boy in my arms and crooned the song of death, my toneless voice a mockery of Yiayia's clear soprano. In the haze of blue light, Timotheus became, not the corpse in my arms, but the living, laughing boy who walked the fallen column of the ancient temple—act become prophesy, time declared victor. So this was where he would lie, in the cave below those awesome columns.

I would bury the boy in the grave where I had found the other bodies. It seemed right, but I would not bury the sling, Timotheus' only possession, with the body. I hung it around my neck, giving it a jerk to settle both the sling and my own resolve. The weapon would perform one more task in honor of Timotheus. I owed him. I pushed him through the door into the underground room and buried him with the other bodies, carefully restacking the rocks so nothing could find him to defile the body, and then, with the rope I had removed

from Timotheus' leg, I pulled the urn to the top and looked around me. Nothing more to do except....
    I tested the length of Timotheus' sling, swinging it round and round above my head. I collected several stones for my pouch, judging each for size and shape, spit on one, the most perfect, polished it on my shirt sleeve, placed it in the leather sling and wrapped it with my fingers. Hanging the ropes over my shoulder and under my arm, I hefted the urn onto the other side, and descended the mountain. Noticing color returning to the landscape, I looked back toward the standing columns. Blue light receded, faded down the columns, disappeared into earth.
    "Good-bye Timmy," I said. "Sleep well."

回回回

    The scent of dust stirred by my feet rose from the path. No winds, no rain. The dark clouds had passed us over. How had Marina survived out here for so long with no well? Water from the spring I had found on my journey into the valley would not supply fields, animals and humans with any but killing scarcity, and it had to be transported. Even now, finishing the dwindling supply I had brought from the well in the cave, I knew I would soon be craving water.
    The donkey I had seen Thoron riding probably helped to carry water from the spring, but then the donkey would also have needed to drink between trips. Timotheus had said he cut the barley. He must also have spent a good part of his day hauling water.
    I thought of the well in the old city. It would be as hard to get to as the spring in the mountains, but with some exploration, a spring from the same stream might be found in the shrubs and rocks at the foot of the bluff, hidden from view if it reentered the earth nearby. Spitter could smell it, as could I if I came near enough. If a conduit could be built, the water could be funneled nearer the hut. Once I had rid Marina of Thoron and got Spitter back, I considered searching, perhaps laying stone for a channel.
    As mistress of water, she would be queen of her lands, servant to no man—proud, as the women of her family had been proud. The steps leading down to the well had been designed to admit only women or children. Even I, small as I was, could not safely ascend those steps carrying a filled jar. The picture of the woman holding the child had been scratched from the rock, a gesture of hatred for women—women

holding great power, judging from the size of the drawing on the cave wall. Only one answer came to mind. Women had controlled the city, and they had done it by controlling access to the water. They had held a city in bondage to their generosity. They might even have decided who lived, who died as a result of their dispensations.

Some man had found their underground pathway, had seen and destroyed the painting. But, apparently he had not discovered the pressure point that opened the door to the well. If that man had been me, I might have concluded that the women conjured the water from the rock, and I would have hated them more for my inability to do the same.

I approached the hut from behind the shed, thinking first to see about Spitter, hoping to quiet her before she brayed, attracting attention from Thoron. "Quiet, girl," I said from behind the shed. "It's me." But when I looked, only Thoron's donkey waited, eyes glazed, dry and puffy for lack of water. I turned my goatskin upside down and dripped the last of my water into his bowl. He drank it, searched for more and whuffed, disappointed.

Seeing us climb the bluff, Thoron must have hurried, leaving his donkey without care, arriving there shortly after us. Time enough to catch Timotheus pulling up and over the wall of the cellar.

My cart, contents turned upside down and scattered, waited beside the donkey. I felt beneath the cart and opened the compartment I had built to hide my more valuable pieces of merchandise and my coins. Safe. I could see nothing else taken from the cart, so Thoron must have been looking for metals.

The broken door of the hut hung ajar on its hinges. I peeked inside, and the cats scattered. Except for their scent, it smelled empty. I saw nothing of anything Marina had carried uphill. Thoron had taken Spitter, Marina, the baby and all she and Spitter had carried, and vanished, apparently leaving Spitter's and his own donkey's cart so he could move faster. An entire night's lead on me he might have taken, but he had not, at first, run, for I had heard the baby cry after I found Timotheus. He must, even then, have been here at the hut, searching for my coins.

I went back to the shed to survey the remains of my cart. I could have pulled the cart alone. It was not that heavy, but one thing remained certain. The ass would die of thirst if I left him here. I repacked my merchandise, snugging the burial urn down among the furs, hitched the donkey to the cart, and began my homeward journey. I would fill my bag and water the donkey at the spring at the top of the hill. Doubtful, but possibly he could make it back to Athens. Where are you Spitter?

Following the well-worn path uphill, the ass lifted his nose to sniff the air. He quickened his steps. Knowing the way, he hesitated not at all on approaching the spring.

"Honh, ahonh ahonh," Spitter's bray split the clear morning stillness. The ass broke into a run, jerking the cart ahead of me. Tired as I was from lack of sleep, the exhaustion of the night taking its toll, I too ran. At the peak, heaving for breath, I found Marina and the baby lying on bare ground. Alert, I searched the clearing for Thoron, thinking ambush. Seeking shrubs and low outcrops of rock for cover, I squatted as low as possible, Timotheus' sling taut in my hand and loaded with the special stone. I searched the rocks towering above the spring path. Why hadn't Spitter come to me, and why hadn't Marina called? For that matter, why wasn't the baby crying? What had Thoron done to them—and where was Thoron, now? I crept nearer to look at Marina. She and the baby lay, bound and gagged, Marina's arms locked in place around the child.

"Sh!" I whispered, and released Marina's gag and bindings. She tried to stand, lifting the baby with her. She crumpled.

Again Spitter called, this time from beyond the pass and nearer the spring. Perhaps Thoron waited, using Spitter as bait, expecting to hit me when I emerged through the pass. "Where are you, girl?" I whispered. "And where is the man?" With no other choice, I inched through the rocky outcrop, sling loaded, nostrils flared to detect the acrid scent of the man as I knew him from the trail.

Spitter stood alone, not far from the spring, a rope anchoring her to a knotted shrub. Nowhere did I see Thoron. I scoured the rocks above and behind me. No one could have climbed those sheer vertical cliffs.

I untied Spitter, rubbed her jaw, drew my fingers through her curly, silver mane, and scratched behind her ears. For an instant, she suffered the caresses then pulled away and picked her way downhill toward the spring. Of course, she would be thirsty. So was I, for that matter, for I had given my last to the ass. "Wait here girl," I said, when she neared the end of her tether. None too certain of the sloped edge, and still dizzy from my stay in the cave, I tied one end of a rope around her neck and the other around my waist. I passed, went to the spring, grasped the rock and bent to drink from the pooled water. Just beyond my knee, on the edge of the cliff, I saw the broken shrub. I eased nearer the edge. On a shelf below, Thoron leaned against the rock, leg twisted in an impossible angle. He must have fallen, trying to get water. But surely he had made this trip many times. He would have known to be cautious. Spitter brayed, lifting her nose in the air and dipping it—up, down, up. Long and loud, she brayed. Thoron's donkey answered her, and the baby cried.

Who says donkeys can't talk? Spitter had pushed Thoron over the ledge with her head. How could I blame her? "Good thinking, girl," I said. Mumbling a warrior's plea for courage and accuracy in battle, I prepared to sling the rock. Let Timotheus' spirit guide my hand in certain justice. Thoron's bushy black hair marked my target. I began my swing. A long time since I had aimed a sling, but the skill, the feel of the rock whirring around my head, returned in all its deadly accuracy. Whir, whir, whir...

Arms wrapped around my waist. The woman pulled me. I tilted, tripped over her and tumbled, rolled toward the chasm, slid over the sloped edge and jerked to a stop, snatched from the fall by the rope I had tied to Spitter.

Rope tight across my chest binding my lungs, I sputtered, trying to call. Legs and hips dangling, I struggled to speak. "Back, girl. Back." Spitter stood, not backing, but braced against my weight. "Back," I found breath to whisper. Still she stood, as solid as the eternal rocks around her. Legs thrashing empty air, I managed to grab a small shrub. Grasping both ends of the sling in one hand, I used that same hand to reach for the root, and pulled myself upward.

The rock I had loaded into the sling slipped free, skipped down and over the edge to crack against the rocks of the beach far below. I brought my knee to the top and pushed. It slipped. I tried again. It must have been like this that Thoron had caught Timotheus—defenseless, unarmed. But this time Thoron could hurt no one. With heart-stopping effort I pulled again. Up, over the edge, I rested, arms and legs spread against sloped rock, grasping life with every inch of my body.

Daring not to relax anywhere except high in the pass, I collapsed against a boulder. Moving my arms a greater effort than I could manage, I rubbed my shoulder sleeve against my face to clear my eyes of dust.

Marina stood looking away at the sea, unaware of the screaming child. I lay on my back and looked up at her profiled against a darkening sky. She didn't know what she had done. She couldn't have known—and still act to protect the murderer.

"He killed Timotheus."

She stirred, found her voice, leaned against a rock and tucked the child to her breast. "Timotheus would have killed him," she said, words slurred, mouth and lips baked as dry as bread. "The boy ran off all my lovers. He wanted me for himself."

"Thoron left me in that hole to die! He took my donkey, he beat you, he tied you and the baby here, so you couldn't move, and you help him live?"

She looked down, dragged her fingers through the baby's hair. "He's the father of my son," she said.

So what could I do? I had choices. Certainly, I had choices. I could take Spitter, hitch her to the cart and leave this place, leave Marina and the baby, and leave Thoron on the side of the mountain. Yes. That is what I would do. Just leave. Let her work out the problem to the best of her ability. She deserved nothing better. If the same blood flowed through her veins that flowed through those of the women of the ancient city on the mountain, she would manage. She would manage very well. I stood to leave.

The other choice would be to pull Thoron back up the hill and set his broken leg.

"Get a drink of water," I said. "Water the animals and fix us something to eat. I'll get him." Mumbling, cursing my weakness, I prepared the ropes. Knotting them together to lengthen them, I left one end tied around Spitter's neck, and made a loop large enough to slip down over the big man's shoulders. Saying nothing, I dropped it over the edge and onto Thoron's head. If he did not put his head and arms through the loop, I could do nothing. It would serve him right for what he had done. Perhaps he would be too stupid to understand.

He knew. He fitted it over his shoulders, and I walked uphill. Spitter followed. Thoron rose.

When Thoron saw me he cowered, holding his arm across his eyes. Relenting, I walked back to help him over the edge. He mewled like a hurt animal and pushed away from my hands. I looked at my hands, wondering. The blue light of the mountain still sparked, forking from my fingers. The big man feared me. Me. I stood back and still he whimpered. I stood back further. He pulled himself up and over the edge.

"Son of Zeus," said Thoron, whispering. Broken leg forgotten, he knelt, bumped the ground with his forehead again and again, moaning, bringing blood to run down his face. Marina tapped his arm to give him food. He ignored her.

"He saw the blue flames on the mountain. He thinks you called up the fires of Earth Mother to avenge the death of Timotheus."

"Command me, Son of Zeus," he said, words a stream of mumbles, mixing like the blood, tears, and snot running together, flowing down his face and blending with the mass of black hair covering his face.

"I am not divine," I tried to say, again relenting. "But I am a physician. I will set the bones in your leg."

I gathered my tools—wine for cleansing, comfrey root to reduce swelling and to heal, and clay to mix with water to wrap his wound and to stiffen the break. Showing Marina how to brace his shoulders, I pulled on the ankle, felt a snap as the bone fitted into place. In all this time, the man gave no sound, not even to moan. But when I reached to pull him to his feet, he pushed away. I sighed, stepped back and said. "I buried Timotheus in the hole." I did not tell them of the others with whom he lay, and, hoping somehow to preserve its sanctity, I did not tell them about the well and paintings. I fingered the combs in my pouch. This woman had no right to these, the gift from the dream women. I would give one to Ana and one to Olympias. Whether the figures had been real or only born of ancient, poison air, I owed my sanity, and somehow my life, to them.

I hitched Spitter onto her own cart, loaded my gear, filled my water pouch, took some of the cheese and bread Marina had laid out, and left the mountain, never, I hoped, to see it again. In the final turn before trees and rocks hid the pass, I looked back. Black clouds shrouded the hill, lowering even as I watched. A moment later, nothing could be seen. I hurried, trying to stay ahead of the chilling downdraft pushing at my back.

Shrugging my cloak more closely around my neck, I imagined the warmth of the fire in Ana's hearth. The thought of her bread filled my mouth with water despite the dryness of the land. This time on returning from my journeys, I would snuggle into a warm bed and let the voices of happy people lull me to sleep.

Again I fingered the combs in my pouch. I also had something to show for my efforts, though I could say nothing, ever, about how I had found them, pulling them from the shed hair of a corpse. The girls would think me a ghoul. Heh heh. Ah oooooh eeee!

※※※

"This is the urn you found in the cave?" Ana touched the urn where I had tied it onto Spitter's back, getting ready to take it to Olympias. Bendi sat his horse, impatiently flexing his toes, itching to kick his horse, to head it back in the direction of Olympias' camp. Ana ran her fingers around the throat, tracing the wavy gold line. "It can't be old. This is one of my designs."

I laid my pack across Spitter's back. "I found it in a cave. A grave site. It hadn't been entered for ages. The air was dead. You could not have been born when it was sealed."

"I'll show you." She fled around the house.

"We must go," said Bendi. I have left *mylitta* alone too long."

Watching Bendi move off toward the gates, still, I waited. I called to Ana, but she did not hear. She must have gone into her shed where she mixed clays and paints ready to fire pots in the oven outside the house.

"I have to see about her, Bendi. Go ahead, I'll come along soon."

I went behind the house and followed the path down to her workshop. She came from the hut to meet me, holding an urn, similar to the one I had tied onto Spitter, but smaller.

"See? Still warm from the oven." She handed it to me, showing me the wavy gold line around the throat. "The same. Exactly the same."

"You must have seen the old urn yesterday, when I brought it in."

"I made this before you left for the ruins. I only fired it while you were gone. It was shown me in a dream." She said the words as a challenge, daring me to disbelieve her.

"Did you see something like this in your dream?" I showed her the combs I carried in my pouch. I found them there too." Ana reached for a comb, touched it and jerked back. "Many times. I also dreamed of a man. He made them, gave them to me for my wedding." She left no room for doubt.

My hands trembled. The combs slipped from my fingers. I stooped to pick them up.

As in the cave I lost track of reality, not knowing where I was, when I was. The visage of Ana faded to be replaced by another. Hardly knowing what I said, I muttered. "In the dreams, what color was your hair?"

"Light, almost yellow," she said.

I looked at her more closely, examined her eyes. They were the same as the woman who had given me the urn.

"You were in the cave. You gave me the urn. You said you had no more use for it, nor for the ashes inside." I lifted the urn down from the pouch on Spitter's back. "See. Ashes. Beneath the snake."

"I have been here, the whole time," she said. "I have gone nowhere. How could I put my urn in the cave? Only now have I designed it."

She spun and returned to the house. I watched her go. I hadn't intended to rouse her anger. Needing to apologize, I took a step to follow, to explain that this had been my dream, but her manner warned me away.

Women. How much did they keep hidden from the knowing of men? I don't like not knowing things. I rode the entire distance to Olympias' camp without hurrying Spitter. I needed time to think about this. Time alone.

6

"How did you hurt your leg?" I asked Olympias, bandaging a blue and swollen ankle.

"I was worried about Plise. I couldn't find her." Her throat choked; she coughed. I pressed my hand against her hot forehead and pushed oily hair back from her face.

"Your sister, Plise." I said. "She is lost?"

"She may be dead. I don't know. She rode her horse into the sea. The horse came back; she didn't."

"Why...?"

She sighed, taking the breath as though wearied even to think. She pushed herself to a sitting position and then slumped back against heavy pillows. "Plise was in love with Havin. Havin Ru of Larissa, of the family Aleuadai. He was a distant cousin, and his family and ours have been friends for a long time.

"I watched them. Plise and Havin's son. From a porch of the house of Ru. They stood on the rock wall at the edge of their gardens. Plise tried to put her arms around Havin, but Havin pushed her away. He was a very shy man, and wouldn't have wanted his friends to see them embrace, and he was still grieving for his dead wife.

"Havin's son didn't like Plise. I think he must have said something to her. When Havin walked away, his son stayed and yelled "Barbarian whore" at Plise. She shoved him and he fell over the cliff onto the rocks at the edge of the sea.

"It took a long time for the servants to climb down and bring the boy back up. His head was crushed. Plise ran around screaming and waving her arms. That night Havin took poison and killed himself.

"When Plise heard about Havin she rode her horse into the sea. Maybe she swam back to shore, I don't know. She could still be lying out there, somewhere on the beach." Her voice firmed, grasping at a straw of hope. "I've heard that sometimes people can float in the sea for days until they get washed to shore. She could be there, trying to keep her head above water."

Olympias was near death herself, from the wound. The fever had crept from her leg to burn in her forehead. For some reason I never in my entire life came to understand, a simple wound becomes dangerous in a grieving person. 'First we attend the body,' Yiayia used to say as she instructed me, 'then we heal the spirit.' How could we heal this child-woman's spirit?

So I treated the wound, and when she was able to walk and ride a horse, we returned to the rocky beach where Plise had ridden into the sea, but we didn't find Plise. Tired and hungry, we finally gave up, and stood looking, searching the sea. Boats were everywhere. She might have been picked up. But neither Bird nor I believed it.

"Arrybus, my uncle, claimed that my father had fits of rage like Plise. He says when my father was out of his head with anger, his horse kicked him because he had been beating it, and then he died when the wound became sickened. I don't believe it. I didn't know Neoptolemus until I was about nine years old because I was kept by the Selloi priests until then, but when I returned home Neoptolemus was good to me. I sat beside him when he gave audience to the people. I know he never beat his horses and he never allowed his slaves to beat them either. He was a healer, and the gods spoke to him."

We were different, this child and I, though similar in some ways. She had been tutored in a life of luxury, by her father, a king and healer, even as I walked the roads with my Yiayia, a physician, surviving by taking gifts of bread from strangers.

As though knowing my thoughts and feeling my humility, she said, "I am no one. I may not claim my heritage from my mother as Chosen of the Gods. The priests have replaced me with a pretender, and many of the people support her. My mother's legacy to me burdens me with responsibility, yet I may not try to claim the rewards of it lest I risk being murdered in my sleep by priests of the Holy Island. Many who do not understand, think me insane for claiming to be the true daughter of the Regina of Kreté."

We returned to the covered stone porch where Olympias had watched Havin's son fall to the rocks below, and stood looking out over the sea. Black clouds moved into the distance.

"Arrybus holds the dowry left me by Neoptolemus. He will release it only if I wed a man of his choosing. If I wed, and if I have a child, I will lose my rights as the God Chosen and my child will inherit. The horned ones will kill me if they can, just as they killed my mother."

Out of mists left hovering over water still choppy and dark grey, a full rainbow arched the sky. I pulled her into the crook of my arm, willing her to soften, needing to lift her as I had been lifted by the blue light of the caves of her ancestors. I pointed toward the sea. "Look, Little Bird, " I said. "See the rainbow?" She looked, uncaring.

"You are that rainbow. After the storm is over, in the years when you come into your powers, your light will shine even across the seas." I spoke with assurance. It felt right. She leaned her head against my shoulder, softening. I thought I had helped her find some measure of inner peace, but her gesture meant patience, not hope.

"How naive you are, Wallis." She touched my nose, then ran her forefinger through my beard, teasing, smiling a wispy twist of the lips. "No one gives me anything. I survive only by my wits." She pulled away and stood straight, head high, once more the royal, the moment dismissed. "The rainbow and the storm are inseparable. If I am to be the one..." She shrugged. "Then I am also the other."

A stony faced, matronly woman dressed in severe and formal white stepped out of one of the doors to the house. "You are not welcome here, daughter of Neoptolemus, sister of the nameless one." From the porch on the next level up I heard muttering. "Whore, barbarian, impostor!" Then other voices, hardly more than whispered grunts, took up the chant. The sounds raised the hair on the skin of my arms. Desperately I wished for my knife, now tucked inside my bags on Spitter's back.

Bendi, tall and attentive, stepped up beside Olympias. I hadn't noticed him standing at the end of the porch. Empty space suddenly filled with armed men, burdening the air with tension. The two men with the woman in white seemed to wilt and shrink away, though neither moved. Diana stepped between Olympias and the woman, dipping her head just a fraction of an inch and briefly closed her eyes. "Good evening Altera," she said, and slowly raised her head, never looking at the woman's face. "May I express my grief on the unfortunate death of your brother and your nephew?" Her words lent formality in her obvious deference.

The woman stiffened, preparing a rebuke to a servant for supposing such intimacy, and then, looking past Diana at Bendi, changed her mind. She dipped her head in a quick, impertinent jerk and offered, "The vigil dinner is prepared. My brother's—Havin's—spirit will be honored if the family of Neoptolemus will join us." She had evoked the name of the deceased of both families. Formal indeed, though as cold as death, she had acknowledged the blood connection between herself and Olympias.

Olympias jerked, and shoved Diana out of the way, moving to respond. This time I surprised myself by stepping in Diana's place. Imitating Diana's deference, I said, "My lady Olympias of the Clan of Snakes, descendant of Achilles and daughter of the king Neoptolemus would be honored to attend, and asks, most kindly, for your permission to bathe and dress before dinner."

Startled, Altera acknowledged my presence, examining my face as though wondering at the effrontery of a stranger. Yet she replied graciously, even nodding a head slightly in Olympias' direction. "Your request is well met, stranger. Travelers are always welcome in the household of the Ru of Larissa. My attendants will prepare baths for you. Turning away she walked back into the house. Her carriage radiated a stiff and purposeful grace.

Olympias stood frozen in place after the woman's leaving, fists clenched, body ridged, face as dark as the black clouds so recently disbursed. Her entire group paused, unmoving, shadows ready to leap at a whispered word to Bendi. I feared for the life of the woman, Altera, and all her party. Finally Olympias leaned forward. She placed her feet, one before the other, and climbed the steps toward the house.

回回回

Traveling home, Olympias rubbed her stomach. It seemed the princess' anger had raised its doddering, infant head and rode along the road with her, a silent, dark specter weighing her down, compressing the spirit to a narrow band of sickly, reddish brown. I asked for her health.

"Just a stomach ache," she said, straightening her back. "It'll go away as soon as I can lie down and rest." Not yet strong from the wound on her ankle, the events of the day had robbed Bird of the last of her strength. She had done as I often did; she took the pain and moved it to her stomach. Anger, full-grown, can turn, become one's destroyer. Yet some know the art of transforming anger into strength. Bird's manner was not one of fear nor defeat, but of determination.

Lost in thought, I left the caravan near Spiros and headed for a wooded area that stretched away from a bog to seek an herb I knew that would help her. When my eyes focused on my surroundings, my head hurt. It seemed I sought to take upon myself all the pain of another, and failing, my body protested. '*Sorry, Yiayia,*' I whispered in the silent, secretive voice I reserved for my grandmother. It cleared my thinking. '*My efforts to heal Olympias' spirit almost worked. If only she had allowed it, we might have brought peace.*'

'*A bit more time,*' Yiayia answered. '*More practice, more knowledge, more, more, more...*'

I dug into the shoulder pouch for the bag of headache herbs. My fingers came away with crumbs. I had given my last willow bark to a sick boy Olympias befriended on the road.

Palo

Light from village windows, warm, yellow light spills out and floods black puddles of rain water. Sometimes the lights blink from shadows made by people walking between the windows and their lamps. The old man's windows never blink. I wait, hoping his light will blink, that his door will open, then I will run to the door and the old man will give me bread and, maybe, cheese. From the house next door to the old man's I hear a young man's laughter, hard, dry. I hear a woman scream, scream again. I see the windows blink, and blink, and blink. Then the door opens, the woman runs out screaming curses. She goes to the old man's house. I wait. The old man must be asleep. The window only blinks once; the woman comes back out carrying a lamp. She goes to a house down the street, and calls. The door opens and another woman comes out. Together they go to the old man's house.

Light from the old man's window gets brighter from both their lamps. Then the women come out and go to the first woman's house. The first woman doesn't want to go in. The second woman bangs on the door and screams for the man to open it. The man flings open the door and yells, keeps yelling, but steps back and opens the door wider. The women enter. Light from the windows blink and blink and blink. Then the man and the two women come out with a bundle and some long sticks under their arms. The sticks look like hoe handles. The three go to the old man's house.

They come out again, the man leading the two women, a blanket slung across the hoe handles, the man carrying the front end of the two handles, the women carrying one end each. Something bulges on the blanket thrown across the hoe handles. I can't tell what it is; they've put another blanket on top. It looks heavy.

One woman carries a lamp. They go into the woods, just a body's length from where I lie hidden.

"We can't just leave him in the woods, Miron. It's not decent."

"Well, what do you suggest? Move him in with us?"

"And have him see you beating me?"

"It's all right," he said, voice softening a bit. "This is what I did with my father, and later with my mother. It won't be long before he's gone. He'll hardly even notice it, sick as he is."

"Then put him by the stream. He can at least get water if he gets thirsty."

"Be quiet woman! If he gets no water he'll die sooner. Best all the way around."

I trail along behind to see where they're going. "This is too close to the house," the woman whined. "When he starts to smell we'll have to come back out and move him again."

The man grumbles, keeps moving up hill, trampling through briars, catching branches on his shoulders. The branches swing back and slap the woman in the face. She grumbles. He growls. She hushes.

They lay the old man by a rotting stump. The old man never opens his eyes. The man stomps back down the hill. I dodge out of his way behind a bush. The woman smoothes the blanket across the old man, puts her hands on her hips, turns, shoves the other woman back toward the village. "You'd better stay at my house tonite," said the other. "In this mood he might kill you, lay you out here beside the old man."

The first woman mumbles, "No, I haven't made his supper. He'll come looking for me."

Sounds tell me they're out of the woods. I hear two doors slam. I look down at the old man, wait a few minutes, thinking. No more bread. No more cheese. How will I get food?

I touch the old man's face. It feels hot. I pull down the blanket, touch his chest. His whole body is hot. I take the blanket off. The old man sighs. It is a good blanket. One of the woman's best, I think. I roll the blanket, tuck it under my arm, and return to my sleeping place. I am well hidden. Stay dry, most times, even when it rains. I have rubbed the ground smooth, hollowed it out with my body. I spread out the blanket, lie down. The blanket is soft, still warm from the old man's heat. I pull it around my body. Rain spots the earth around me.

Why was the old man so hot?

7

I left Olympias' caravan, entered Spiros, and continued down the trail between huts and lean-to shops. Never thinking about what I actually carried in my cart, I called in singsong voice words learned from a tradesman long ago. It made no difference whether or not my cart held the items. It was the song people were accustomed to hear.

"Come buy," I called. "I have woolens and dyes from Phoenikia, spices from far away Kyrene, glass from Egypt, boots from Etruria. Come buy, come buy." But no one came out of the closed and silent doors. "Come see the ivory figurines from Ethiopia, spices and ointments from Arabia," I called, breaking at the end with a yawn. I looked for a place to sit and rest, but the earth, still wet from the early fall rain, offered nothing inviting. I shivered, not from the cold, for the winds carried warmth from bogs surrounding the village. I hunched deeply into my cloak, cheerless stirrings echoing my footsteps, hurrying me through the streets and past silent huts toward the woods.

A dirty face peered at me from beyond the peaks of a waste dump. A boy, not more than ten years old, a child gone wild. I called to him and he vanished.

The brushy woods thickened at the edge of the huts, making it difficult to pass. I searched for a path and found a small one. Old ruts from ancient cart wheels still dented the earth, but no carts or horses had been through recently. I didn't remember the path, but then weeds grow so fast. Spitter and I pushed through scratchy branches and climbed toward the tall pines. The brush thinned, and the shaded ground in the pine woods lay smooth and pungent with pine straw.

A bare foot disappeared behind a tree. That would be the boy.

"Ho, Spitter," I called in much too loud a voice, imitating an actor as in a drama. "It must be around here somewhere. This is where I found it last year." I raved about demons and woods elementals, hoping to make the boy think me crazy. Perhaps he would be curious enough to investigate. I stooped and scrabbled around in wet, dead leaves, grumbling. "It was here, I know it was here. Right here beneath these trees. Maybe it got covered over with leaves. But it was. It was here." And as I bent over I watched for the boy from between my legs. I saw him again–standing out from the tree as far as he dared–to see what I was looking for.

Not really seeing where I walked, Spitter and I eased along, playing the game with the boy. I stumbled over what I thought was a root, caught myself, and looked to see what had snagged my sandal.

A hand dropped away from my ankle, gnarled and old and covered with dark brown and mottled spots. I knelt to look into knowing eyes that watched my every move.

"Ho, Spitter," I said, voice softened. "Let's see about this man." I touched his forehead. He tried to raise his head, to press his face against my hand. My fingers came away sticky with old, cold sweat. "You shouldn't be out here, father. You should be home on your nice, warm mat." I stroked his arm, felt his pulse. It fluttered, stopped, reluctantly started up again. "Haven't been here long, though, your shirt is dry, except where you've wet on yourself. Let's get you back home. Your people will be worried about you. Where do you live?" He let his head drop back, closed his eyes. "Hmmm, agh. Hunh." He sighed, tried again. "E-e-rros." He strained to point his eyes toward the village. Spiros. I tried to help him stand, wrapping my arms around his chest, lifting him. His legs wobbled, crumbled.

"We'll get you home, old one. Won't we Spitter? My strong, young donkey will pull you as easily as you carried baby lambs when you were a boy. Is that what you did in the old days? Care for the lambs?" Again he struggled to speak. "Ph–ph–ah poe-y."

"A poet!" I answered, interested. "Then we must get you well. I want to hear you recite your poems. What is your name? Maybe I have heard of you."

His eyes rolled back in his head, showing only whites. He shuddered, jerked. Lay still.

Again I felt his pulse. Reedy, rolling, it felt like a tiny stream of water passing beneath my fingers.

I pulled merchandise, bags and boxes from the cart and laid them on the ground and then lifted the man, bone thin and as light as a bag of feathers, onto the cart, easing him down onto soft wool cloaks and lamb skins.

We headed downhill, and when we reached the first of the huts, I stopped and knocked on the door. No one answered. I pounded the door with my fist. Still no answer. I whistled to Spitter to go on to the next hut, looking behind as we walked away. A curtain dropped back into place where someone had been looking out, and I yelled again, louder.

Finally a man stuck his head out the door and said, "Get away. Get away from here, and take that old man with you. We have nothing to do with him!"

"He's sick," I said, my temper for once overcoming diplomacy. "He needs help. Where does he live?'

The woman came to the door. In apologetic mumbles, she answered, "He has no family. We took him to the woods to die. The nature spirits will look after him." She eased shut the door. Inside, the voices of the man and woman raised. She wanted to take the old man in, the man refused.

I looked an apology at the old man slumped on the floor of the cart, hand drooped across his chest. He opened his eyes, once again clear, understanding, and drawing forth great strength from somewhere within, pointed back toward the woods. What could I do?

I took him back, stopped the cart and lifted him, half carrying, half dragging him downhill to a small stream. There I laid him on the ground, dipped the hem of my shirt into the water and bathed his face. Then I cupped water in one hand and held his head with the other, to drink. Exhausted, he blinked once, slowly, and then looked upward at me. Eyes speaking his gratitude, he sighed, shuddered, snapped shut his jaw, and lay still. The pulse in his wrist slowed, stopped. The eyes stared at nothing. I pulled down the lids with my fingers, whispering a blessing in the words of Yiayia. "You have done, well, old father. Go to your peace."

I would not leave him here for the wild dogs to chew. I planned to put the man on the cart then go back for the bags, thinking I could carry both him and the goods, now that I wouldn't have to be careful for his comfort, but when I looked back to where I had piled the bags, I saw the boy rummaging around in the pile, head buried in one of the bags. I crept nearer, and grasped him by a naked shoulder. He tried to bolt clutching two apples in his hands, but I held him tight, snapping him back and off his feet.

He squirmed and wriggled, but his slight body labored against hands and arms practiced with lifting merchandise bags and boxes and, at times, people too ill to lift themselves. Finally he quieted, and reluctantly handed the apples back to me. "Keep them," I said. His eyes narrowed and his brow furrowed.

"Why would you give them to me?" he asked, voice thin and high betraying a tender age but with cunning a thousand years old.

"Because you're hungry," I said, "and because you can earn them, if you're willing to work. I would see that you have food to eat, a place to sleep. I could use a smart young man like you to help me."

"What would I have to do?" he said, eyes darting this way and that, watching for an opportunity to break free.

"Well, for one thing," I said, pointing toward the stream, "you can help me take that old man to the hills for burial." The boy turned the right side of his face toward me, then toward the old man lying beside the stream. He looked at me sideways again, calculating, one eye squinted.

I waved my hand before the squinted eye. "Can you count my fingers?" He turned the right side of his face toward my hand, and shrugged.

"Five," he said in a manner that accused me of senility.

I covered the eye he had turned toward me and asked, "Now, how many fingers?"

He jerked away to see my fingers, then frowned. "Five!"

"Um humm," I said. Blind in the left eye. That explained why no one had taken him in. "So you can count. Can you count money?"

"If I had any money to count." The one good eye glared, defiant, unafraid.

"Then you can help me trade my goods," I said, pulling him down the sloping bank toward the stream. "Here, grab one of the old man's legs and help me lift him. We'll have to carry him to the cart."

"You'll need the cart to carry your load, won't you?" In truth, I had thought to pile them all on with the old man, but now it seemed disrespectful.

"I'll come back for them later."

He tossed his head in the direction of the village, flopping his hair away from his face. "They'll steal them."

I smiled. "Then what would you have me do?"

"Take the bags, leave the old man."

Ah, hard case. A vision of a laughing Delos, Ana's son, flashed before my eyes. How different these two were. "What is your name, Boy?"

He shrugged. "Boy."

"Then, Boy," I said. "We must first get you a name. Otherwise if I call you 'Boy' when we're in the city, I'll be swamped with boys come running to see what I want."

"You'll take me to the city?"

"Of course. Where else do you think I sell my goods?"

He bobbed his head. "Then what is my name?"

"We'll call you Palo," I said. "It's almost like my own name, Pelos, but I won't be needing that anymore. I have a new name too. A princess has named me Wallis. Now what do you think about that?"

"Wallis, " he said. I nodded yes.

"The villagers will steal your trade goods."

"Hmm, yes, the villagers." I sighed. It seemed I had more to do than just bury an old man.

"Maybe we can hide the load. Where would you suggest?"

He looked around, his one eye scanning the forest more completely than I might have done with two. Then he looked up, and pointed. "There."

Heavy shrubs crowded an overhanging rock. "There?" I said, not certain where Palo pointed.

He nodded. "Behind the bushes." He motioned me to follow, and showed me a narrow path leading to the top of the rock. We followed the path upward. The shelf rock projected from the hill at a spot about twice my height, and when we reached the top I saw a clearing behind the shrubs. A woven blanket, neatly rolled, lay inside a wooden box, and beside the blanket, a measure of cloth, filthy and torn. Acorns and chestnuts spilled from the edge of a chipped pottery bowl. The boy's home. Squatting, I looked out through shrubs toward the wooded area. I could see past the edge of the woods and onto grass-thatched roofs. Palo must have seen me pass through the village and had run to hide behind the dump to watch what I would do. He had seen my loaded cart and staked me for robbery. I looked at the boy, and he looked away, suddenly shy.

"This will be a fine place, Palo. I think the trade goods will be safe from the villagers." *'But I'll have to watch my new partner,'* I thought.

Together we moved the bags to the ledge then pulled the old man onto the cart. How would I bury him? Below a thin layer of soil the ground became rock, but on my previous visit to find medicine herbs I had noticed caves in the hills circling Spiros. All the better. The old man could follow in his ancestors' footprints; he could be buried within the bowels of Earth Mother herself.

The whim of modern man decreed that tombs be placed above ground. I thought it a whimsy created by craftsmen to convince clients to buy their services and to provide walls to accept their fanciful painted creatures. And of course, the bigger and better the tomb, the more quickly consciences could be eased, sins forgotten. I stretched out beside Palo in his little hole and we shared his blanket. Time enough in the morning to bury the old man. He would suffer nothing more.

The cave I chose overlooked a spring, the head of the stream by which the man had died. The stream carved a shallow crevice in the rock, gathering volume and momentum on its way toward the village.

Palo, Spitter and I stopped in the cool dimness of the entrance. I lifted the body from its soft bed and laid him in the entrance of the cave. The hole opened slightly, then slanted downward into dark nothing, wide enough for a body. Palo and I pushed him as far as we could reach and felt him sliding downward and away. A few seconds later we heard a sound from below as the falling body hit solid rock. I backed out of the hole, stood, and sighed. A proper burial, returning to the Mother one of her own. No wild animals would be able to get to him there. Would that I be so fortunate when it came my day for the journey through Hades, and hopefully, to pass on into the gardens of the immortals.

"A waste," said Palo.

"Why?" I asked.

"The body of the old man would have fed the birds and ants and little animals for a long time."

"And wolves and wild dogs and lions," I answered, and it would have smelled up the woods. Where would you have slept then?"

Palo glanced sideways at me, blind eye squinting. "You don't like wild animals, do you?"

"They have their place, I guess."

"You hate wild things. You're scared of them." His one good eye glinted, knowing. I had thought to teach this homeless waif, and it seemed I had something to learn as well.

"And you're not, I suppose," I said. "Not afraid of the wolves, that is."

Palo shrugged and turned away from the cave. "They don't bother me," he said, leading the way back down a short grade toward the cart. When we returned to Palo's hiding place in the woods, my cache of trade goods were gone. The ground showed shuffling and dragging. They had even taken Palo's blanket. Dismay vanished in rising anger. I glared toward the village. Probably the same people who had turned the old man out to the wolves had taken them. I clinched my fists, prepared to fight.

Palo stared at me, then at the huts. His eyes compressed; tears squeezed through. Did he care so for my loss?

"They knew." The words came out in a guttural groan. "All the time they knew about me. They even knew where I slept." His voice rose, approaching a keening howl. "And no one but the old man ever gave me even a piece of bread."

Anger for my own loss dissolved in the sight of the boy crying. Tears from eyes both blind and sighted cut rivulets through the grime smeared across his face.

I sighed, letting my anger go. There is no accounting for the pettiness of people. My trade goods seemed unimportant compared to the wounds this child had suffered.

"The trade goods are gone. But I can still find the herb I came here searching for. It was here someplace, I know it was. It grows on the stump of an old pine tree. It's gray and dry, and crumbles when I crush it. Where in the name of the sainted Hippocrates can it be? I bent low and scrabbled through the leaves with my hands, kicking sticks out of my path, swaying forward and back, moving in the general direction where I had seen the fungus last year.

"Now where was that blessed fungus?" I grumbled. I know it was here someplace."

Palo stood watching me but did not move. "We could get your merchandise back."

"What?".

"I know where the slaver keeps his wealth."

"Slaver?"

"He brings people home, sometimes. The pretty girls. Then he takes them back. They are tied with heavy ropes. I never let him see me. He would catch me. Make me a slave. But he knew where I was. All the time he knew. He could have taken me any time he wanted to. I just wasn't worth his trouble."

His good eye measured me, no longer wet with tears, but calculating. Cunning. No wonder he had tried to run. He thought I was a slaver.

Words failed me. Perhaps I was too late. The child, hardly more than a baby, had already been ruined.

"I am no slaver, Palo. I trade things like pots, jewelry, and cloaks. I buy from people who have more than they need and I trade them to others for things they don't have. I do not sell people. I do not take slaves." I hoped he believed me. It seemed of world shaking importance.

"We can get your merchandise back," he said.

I stood, hands on hips. "And how might we do that?"

▣▣▣

We waited till afternoon, Palo showing me how he cracked acorns, boiled them in his bowl and mashed them to eat. Then, during the time of afternoon rest, with Spitter and an empty cart, I drove slowly past the houses till we were out of sight and pulled donkey and cart off the rutted trail into the woods. Standing in darkening shadow, I examined the road and checked both ways for any travelers. No one. "Stay here girl. I'll be back in a while." Spitter lifted her head to bray, and I caught her nose. "Shh–hh. Quiet girl. Don't give us away." She lowered her head, snuffed and pressed against my leg.

▣▣▣

Palo waited behind the house of the slaver, and hissed when I crawled through brush. I went toward the sound.

The man banged the back door shut, went toward the dump, and squatted. Soon an odor arose. He wiped himself with his hand, dragged it on the ground, went toward a large flat rock, and slid it aside. He looked into a hole, then, deciding, climbed down. He stood up, holding a digging pick, one I had carried in the cart for when the wheel got stuck. He turned it around and around, held it up to see in the darkening light, then put it back, mumbling to himself. He climbed out, slid the rock back, and went inside. In a moment I heard a spoon banging on a pot and smelled food.

"They're eating," said Palo. "Now."

"It will be dark soon. We'll wait."

"No. When it's dark the woman will come out and use the dump. And it'll be too late. We'd need a light. It has to be now."

We crawled nearer the hole, and the boy and I slid back the rock. It rested on other rocks below ground level. I climbed inside as I had seen the man do, and lifted my things. Palo hurried through the woods carrying it piece by piece until we had emptied the hole. He seemed particularly happy to retrieve his blanket. I pulled out my box of surgical instruments, each piece purchased separately and at great cost. The man thought he had a treasure in the digging pick, when he could have sold these for many times more. One day rusting in this hole, they would have been ruined.

Finished, we returned to the cache and watched through branches to see the woman come out and go to the dump. Later we heard her scream. I rose to run to her aid, but Palo dragged me back with a hand on my ankle. "They do this every night. You can't stop him. He has the right. She's his slave."

I could not just sit and listen. "I'm going to find the fungus," I whispered. I crawled away, and, with the light of the moon shining through the trees, I found the old stump with the moss growing on it, picked a handful and stuffed it in my pouch, wondering if picking it at night would make any difference in its effectiveness. When I returned, the light had been put out. Still Palo held me back when I would leave, and we waited until smoke stopped coming through the hole in the roof. I heard snoring.

"We're safe."

I went back uproad and returned with Spitter and the cart, glorying in the fact that I had recently oiled the cart wheels. Silent, stealthy, we repacked the merchandise and rode out.

Beyond the village, Palo said. "I know you're not a slaver. You're not much of a thief, either." He slumped, dozing, sitting upright on the seat of the cart, and then crumpled until he rested his head on my leg, and began snoring gently. We rode through the night, approaching the princess' camp after dawn. I reproached myself for my foolishness. Bested by a woods sprite. He had not stolen from the man before, because the woman gave the old man food. Palo was a thief and a good one. A thief with honor.

I thought about chewing some of the herb for my headache, but I no longer needed it. My head felt fine. I felt fine. My chest swelled to bursting. I felt like singing, but I'd wake the countryside with my caterwauling.

The world knows I can't sing.

We neared the tents, and Bendi stepped from behind a growth of shrubs, no longer startling me. "Ho, Stickman!" Glancing at Palo, he grinned. "How's your love life?"

"Love life?" I asked. He nodded toward the boy beside me. Palo snorted, protesting the disturbance.

I shook him awake. "This is Palo. My new partner."

Palo came awake rubbing his eyes, saw the guard, long blond hair pulled back and tied showing the livid scar across his jaw and the long, brass knife inserted beneath his waist girdle. He jumped to the back of the cart, huddled behind me, and tried to become invisible.

"It's all right, Palo, this man's a friend. He serves the princess I told you about." Palo relaxed, but not much. All the few years of his life, his suspicion of people had served to keep him alive.

"I need to see the princess," I said to Bendi, still hesitant to say her name aloud.

"She's resting, Stickman. Her stomach hurts."

"That is why I must see her, Bendi. I have something to ease her pain."

After Bendi came Diana. I repeated my explanation and finally got through the opening to Olympias' tent. I stood for a moment at the door, eyes growing accustomed to the dimness. Diana found Olympias' mat and touched her. "I am not asleep, Diana. I was just thinking about today. Where did the physician go?"

"He is here, Myrtale. He says he has something for your pain."

Olympias raised to her elbow. "Wallis?" Her eyes beseeched me, narrowed, turned cold. "Go away Peddler. Get out of my sight. And don't come into my camp again!"

Thinking her delusional, I went closer and dared to touch her forehead. Hot. "You have pushed yourself too hard, Little Bird," I said.

"You had no right interfering in matters that did not concern you," she replied, grabbing her stomach and trying to stifle a groan.

Ah. Now I understood. "You are correct. I had no right butting in. Please forgive me." I rubbed a cool hand across her forehead, pushing back hot, dry hair.

"There would have been bloodshed," I explained. "Little incidents cause big wars. You cannot change the whole world, you know, at least not in a day's time."

Relenting, she sat up and lay her head on her knees. "I know, I know.

But who else is there to do it?"

"I will help, if you will let me," I said, overcome with a rush of sympathy, then overwhelmed at the enormity of my offering.

She searched for my eyes, shadowed by early morning light. "I believe that you would, but what can you do?"

"For a start, I can ease the pain in your stomach."

"It is only my term," she said. "It will go away." And that might be all that would be necessary, I thought. With her own strength renewed, no one would guess her feminine weakness.

I gave the little bag of fungus to Diana. "Brew it for tea, Diana, but use only a pinch, and make only a single bowl. Too much and our princess will sleep for a week."

A short time later Olympias sat before the fire, eating barley gruel with appetite, talking about the day's events, shoulders relaxed, face at peace.

"I missed you Wallis. Where did you go?"

"I left the train to find the herb. It was near a village called Spiros." I told her about finding Palo and the old man and about how the village had turned the old man out, how Palo and Spitter and I had taken him up to the cave for burial, and then about how my trade goods had been stolen, and how we got them back. "That is a village without honor."

"I never liked slavers. Bendi was a slave. My father, Neoptolemus, freed him. He chose to stay, to serve me, to train my guards. Where is the boy?"

"He sleeps near Spitter, down by the stream."

"Has he eaten?"

"I took him food, Myrtale," said Diana, coming up to us from out of the shadows. I knew I should be used to her ever-present attendance by now, but I still jumped.

Olympias saw my surprise and motioned Diana away. She disappeared behind folds of the tent, but I had no illusions that she had left our company. When my eyes adjusted to the dimness, she had returned and sat on a stool near a pile of bedrolls.

"Where did you find the urn?" Olympias asked. I had forgotten the burial urn. "It has my family's emblem on the throat, a gold band and olive leaves. A dead snake was inside, lying on the ashes. We store a person's ashes in jars, and sometimes put their most precious objects on top. The snake must have known the pot, and crawled inside."

"I found it in the ruins where the family of your mother's brother lived, in the hills just north of Attica. I thought you might like to have it. I found this as well." I searched to the bottom on my pouch, drew out the two combs and handed one of them to Bird. I would take the other back to Ana. Maybe, another time, she would be more open to receiving it.

Hardly looking, Bird took the comb and stuck it into her hair. "An uncle!" Her face quickened in interest. "My mother's brother?"

"That is what Ana's brother, Vitos, told me. That your uncle had lived in a village now gone to ruin. He told me that he died leaving a sister and two servants. They moved away when the roof collapsed. The ruin is in the hills above a farm where I went to trade. I found them, and found the urn and the comb. They were in a cave. The earth collapsed. I fell...."

She interrupted.

"You say he left a sister?" Excited now, she pressed me further, laying her hand on my knee. I weakened in the scent of her. "Do you know if the sister still lives?"

"She is dead," I said. "But her daughter, Marina, still lives at the foot of the mountain below the ruins. She has a child. She knew nothing about your mother."

Her countenance drooped, but then hope renewed. "Vitos has the sight. He is as good as my mother was. When you see Vitos again, ask him, Wallis. Ask him if he knows anything about my mother."

My gifts meant nothing to her, and in the sensation of the moment I forgot I had come near death to obtain them for her. Yet my heart swelled with joy of the sound of my new name coming from her lips. Not traveler, not peddler, not even physician. She called me Wallis.

Later, walking beside Spitter and Palo on my way back to Athens, one hand on the boy's shoulder, the other holding the side of the cart, I told Palo about the cave. It seemed the right thing to do. I saw belief and trust dawning in his one good eye. He saddened with the mention of Timotheus. "His mother and father died? Then he was alone too. Like me."

"He was older than you, and he had Marina." I didn't tell him of Marina's dislike of him. I let him think what he would.

"I have Timotheus' weapon." I whistled Spitter to a stop and found the sling. "You might like to play with it. You can kill rabbits and squirrels to eat if you get hungry. He looked at it, felt the leather sling. "I'll show you." I spun it in an arc over my head and low to the ground. You put a rock here, see, in the pouch, and then you release one of the ends. It throws the rock." He took the sling and hung it around his neck, just as I had seen Timotheus carry it.

"Were the people in the cave sacrificed?"

"No. But they were holy people, honored in death. "I don't know whether they died separately or at the same time. Since the woman with the urn was not with them, but burned, she must have been their mistress. And then there's the snake. Holy women sometimes keep snakes, for what reason, I don't know."

"And the man with horns. Who was he? A priest maybe?"

"The words beneath the drawings said 'Son of Thunder.' A god maybe."

"What was the blue light?"

"I don't know. I've heard that sometimes the blue fire is seen flashing from the tips of ships' masts. It shoots up and connects the ship with the sky. And I smelled perfume. It was strongest at the well. Some streams smell like that, and I've heard that the place of oracles in the Temple of Apollo in Delphé smells like that." I shrugged away chills. A great gap remained between knowledge and understanding, the knowledge evident, the understanding, hidden. "I just don't know."

8

When I pause to remember, I can still smell, still feel the moisture of the leaves soaking through my leather pants as I sat on the ground beside a fire Bendi had made near Olympias' camp. Why did this particular evening, this particular fire make such a lasting impression on me that even now, I recall it in vivid clarity?

Troubled by the troubles of our princess, Bendi and I had decided to walk and talk. We walked long past the hour for dinner, seeing hardly a soul in the deep woods on the path above the waterline of the swelling river Kephisus. For most of the day we had huddled inside Olympias' tent, hearing crashes of lightning strike nearby trees. It was a time for telling stories, for peeling away the layers of unhealed sores to reveal still-wounded and tender tissues in the soul. Olympias told us her story.

"I remember my mother. Her hair was as bright as the autumn sun. Little curls twisted out of her hairdressers' pins and brushed against her cheek. She laughed, and I knew she was happy. We went outside the house to play. She ran and jumped as though still a child herself. The maids and guards all stayed at a distance, taking their ease under the big oaks, laughing, telling stories all their own.

"It grew late, and the servants went inside to prepare dinner, but mother and I stayed outside, out where the air was sweet and clean smelling—not like the house where people lay dying with plague.

"The water in Lake Tecmon glistened with the reflection of evening lights, and my mother held me in her arms and wrapped her sleeves around me to keep away the late-day chill. 'Tanya,' I heard my father call. 'Come inside, it's dangerous out there without the guards.'

"It was awfully quiet, but my mother held me closer and called: 'In a minute, husband, we'll be in soon.' Then we let the time draw out, dreading the return to the doma and the scent of sickness. My mother pointed across the lake toward Mt. Tomaros.

'See there, Olympias. That is where the sacred oak of Dodona grows, there on top of that mountain. The story goes like this:

'Once there was a great flood. The waters rose and rose, and people who had gathered food for the winter, piled as much of it as they could carry onto their wagons and went up the mountain. Whether this mountain or another, the storytellers do not know, though they suppose that it may have been far away.

'They walked up the mountain as high as they could, but still the waters rose. So they tied young tree saplings together and piled their food and water onto the rafts. They floated for a long, long time. Finally, when the great waters receded, they saw the peak of Mt. Tomaros. It looked like an island in the midst of a world covered with water. They paddled there, and got off their rafts, all the time praising Zeus for letting them live.

'Despite the flooding waters, a single oak tree stood, and the people dedicated that tree to Zeus, for He had prepared them a shade for the blazing heat that came after the rains.

'Forever afterward, priests who called themselves the Selloi swore never to wear shoes again in honor of the sacred earth where Zeus had landed their rafts.

'They named the place Dodona for the priestess, the Spirit Speaker who lived there, and they built a shrine in honor of the god. Later, young women, women like me who hear the Pythoness, waited there to communicate the messages of the gods to man. It is a very holy place.'

My mother paused, and when I looked up at her, waiting for her to continue, she whispered: 'They are coming Lympi. Phaistos and his minions are coming. They want to take me back to the temple. I don't want to go. Oh. No. They are here!' She tried to leap up but caught her foot on her gown and we both fell. She scrambled to get me off her so she could stand, but her feet just got more tangled. Then finally she got free. She stood up and grabbed me and started screaming and running toward the doma. It was a long way to run, and some men stepped out from behind the trees. One grabbed me, and another hit my mother over the head with his axe. She didn't make a sound. She just fell to earth and blood pumped out of her head and ran down her neck, soaking her white gown.

"Big, rough hands held me so tight I couldn't move. A man clamped his fingers across my mouth and nose so hard I couldn't breathe. The more I fought, the tighter the arms clutched me. Suddenly the great arms relaxed, and the man fell to the ground. Then I saw our guards attacking the murderers. I rolled free and ran to my mother. She didn't answer when I called to her. The air stank with the scent of hot blood, and women were screaming. Vahna, my maid, snatched me from my mother's breast and carried me into the house. I remember looking over her shoulder as we ran.

"The cold hard eyes of a man looked back at me, standing still, not fighting. Everyone towered above him, but even so, I could not have missed seeing him for he drew my eyes as the color red draws bees. He wore a robe of yellow that gleamed like gold in the setting sun, and on his head he wore a crown of golden horns. My mother had told me of such a man. She called him Phaistos." Olympias shivered. "Even now I see his eyes locked into mine when I close them in sleep.

"The maids packed my clothes and some food and we left the doma. They harnessed the horses to the wagons and talked about going toward the village for protection, but I screamed at them. "No. Take me to the mountain, to the Selloi. They'll look after me." So that very hour, the servants reloaded the food and bags onto horses and we rode out toward Dodoni. I was not yet four years old, but they obeyed me as they had obeyed my mother. On the way, a shepherd and his son shared milk from his goats with us, so we didn't go hungry.

"My father said he would come for me, but he didn't come for a long, long time. He sent messengers to tell me that the plague had wiped out most of the village, and I was safer in the mountains.

"Then, when I was about nine years old, the Selloi said I should return home. The gods had a very special job for me to do. So the servants took me home.

"When I got there I learned that my father had taken a new wife. The servants called her 'The Doll' because my father petted her all the time. The Doll was the one who had kept him from sending for me. But I found time to spend with my father, because I liked the horses, and that was where my father spent his days. He raised horses and trained them for soldiers to ride into battle. He believed the cities to the south and east would be needing them to make war on the Persians. They were growing restless with the taxes the Persians were making them pay on everything they bought or sold.

"So I learned to ride. I learned to talk to the horses so they would know what I wanted without using a rein or a stick." Here she laughed that little three-noted laugh I loved so. Looking straight at me, she said, "and that's when I learned to ride the horses standing up."

"Phaistos." I reminded her. "Your mother mentioned Phaistos. Is that the priest who had your mother killed?"

She dipped her forehead, yes. "He bears the title, Phaistos. He is the horned speaker at the Temple of Unseen Spirits on the island of Kreté."

My dream inside the cave flashed before my eyes. Again I witnessed the giving of the key by the horned speaker to Olympias' ancestor, as he said: "If the Chosen be female, through her mouth the goddess will speak to the many." The horned speaker had also said that if the chosen were male he would be sent to meet the goddess. That had to mean he would be sacrificed. I chilled.

"My mother told me of the Horned Speaker. He is a strange man. Short, muscular, he can use both hands equally well, and with both those hands he clutches his anger to his breast and never releases it. My mother was chosen of the unseen spirits to carry their blessings and powers, and when she died, by tradition, those powers were passed on to me, her only child."

If my dream in the cave had been of a real event, and Olympias' mother, Regina, were the Chosen, Olympias would be the daughter of the original Chosen. Regina had been stolen away from the temple and had borne Olympias. That meant Olympias was the Chosen, and if she had a child–any child–they would get rid of her. The princess, like her mother, would die. The order seemed to be, until she gave birth, to capture her, or, after a baby was born kill her and capture her baby.

"Phaistos can use both hands equally?" I asked, to ease the tension growing in my belly.

"Yes." Bendi laughed. "So he can cause twice as much trouble."

In the ease, the quiet of the moment, we laughed and sipped our wine.

"Phaistos wants me," she quieted and continued, voice a dead monotone. "He wants to take me back to the island temple where he can unlock and control the powers I inherited from my mother. Here she looked away somewhere into an unforgotten past. "My mother never had a chance to teach me how to call the unseen spirits. I can sense things, but I never know which is real and which is imagined." Her attention returned to us, still troubled.

"The priests could have taught me to use my mother's talents, but then I would be their puppet, just like my mother." Her voice hardened and grew so cold the air of the tent chilled. "So they installed an impostor, and told the people she was me, returned from the mountains where I had gone to escape the plague. But many people know me, and knew the impostor was not me, and they support me. The rest hate me. They think I am lying about being the Chosen by rite of birth, the Chosen's only child."

When she hushed we realized the storm had quieted, and, released from the crowded tent, Bendi and I went walking. We found ourselves there, sitting on the damp earth discussing Olympias.

"We must help her, Bendi," I said. She thinks she's so strong, that she can take care of herself, but she doesn't know anything of the world except her own back yard." But how could we do that? I had no idea where to begin.

"I have heard of a man," said Bendi. "He lives in the far south. In Lakonia, by the gulf. I've heard seamen speak of him. He owns a fleet of merchant ships with wealth enough to back a movement against the priests' power. His name is Tibbelouios."

"Can you go to see him, Bendi, ask him for help?"

"I can't leave the princess now. Phaistos knows where she is. He'll come after her. You will have to go, Stickman."

The thought of visiting a stranger and asking for aid appalled me. Peddling I could do, tending the sick, natural. But asking for money? I sighed and agreed. Some things a man has to do.

רורור

The journey south would take months. I went to see to my grandmother before I left. Yiayia lived alone near Phoenikia in her little cottage built atop the rocks overlooking the Adriatic Sea. Her indigo eyes, now rheumed to the color of curdled milk, drew me within reach as withered arms pulled me close, to know me through my touch, my smell, and to sense that I understood her need. Hair once braided into links of burnished gold—now limp, liquid silver—fell across her brow. I brushed stray locks back from her eyes then traced the swollen blue veins on her still strong hands.

"I'm fine, Tadpole," she said from her bed, beneath the single window. "I'm here where I need to be. Unless you have found the cure for old age, let me be. Davos will see to my needs."

"Uncle Davos is ill, Yiayia. He can't even see to his own."

"What is wrong with Davos?" she started, raising to her elbow, searching my face as though her hooded eyes could see.

"The seizures. They're much worse now. And when he falls he can't get up without help. His daughter comes by to help, but she fears that will soon not be enough."

"I know of an herb to help him," she said, leaning back on the goose down pillow. "It grows in the lands of my father's people, north, near the great River Danube. If only I could get it for him. A pretty flower it is. An underground vine. It hugs the floor beneath the oaks. I would know it by the single black berry that shoots up from the middle of four, broad leaves shaped like a water pad."

Having heard of it since boyhood, I knew the plant through her telling, and always the description ended with a sigh, "But it's too far away. I don't travel now as well as I used to."

"I know, Yiayia. When I go that way I will bring some back for you and for Davos." I promised then, just as I always promised.

When I had told Ana of my grandmother's blind and feeble efforts, spilling the tea she insisted on brewing and serving for herself, Ana had thrown up her hands in exasperation. "Daneion! Bring your grandmother here. We have plenty of room, and I will enjoy the company."

So to laments of leaving her deep well untended, and to promises that I would come to see that it stayed clean and covered, we left Yiayia's house, Spitter's cart loaded with herbs she had labored to gather and dry, collecting them by their scent and taste. Many I could use, though some, I knew, had long flaked into uselessness.

Ana prepared a corner for my yiayia near the door of the great room where family and friends gathered to visit. She would feel the stirring of a breeze and hear voices from the kitchen, imagining that her own hands had brewed the tea made from special herbs. Ana served her always, not trusting the efforts of any of her most efficient servants. For that I will always love Ana. I left the house with my yiayia's voice ringing in my ear. "You must go north, Tadpole. North. To claim your inheritance."

"Later, Yiayia," I had answered. "This time I must go south. A friend needs my help."

9

Spitter's nose pointed the ship south into the Gulf of Saronikos, body straining forward against her tie-down ropes. Palo stood alongside grasping her mane, steadying himself against the slap of the waves, the rise, fall, shudders and jerks of the vessel. Sea mist sparkled in their hair, joining the two in cosmic alliance.

Palo's shoulders, once so thin his bones poked out at odd angles beneath his shirt, now swelled the fabric with muscle, and the shirt flapped high onto his thighs. He would be taking the eye of women soon. I had no complaints about his willingness to work, nor his enthusiasm for learning. No longer need I lift and pull at the merchandise. Before I could think of packing, the goods would be loaded, Palo waiting for me to gather my herbs and medical tools for our forays into the lands outlying Attica. Now if I could just teach him the joys of cleanliness.

Our journey would take us into the Myrtoum Sea and around the lower peninsula into the Gulf of Lakonia, not a difficult voyage, I had been assured. As viewed from the docks our ship had seemed worthy enough–clean, standard mortise and tenon joining, mast topped by a long yard arm built of strong acacia and supporting a new hempen sail gathered to hooks below. On commissioning our transportation, I overlooked the owner's apology that we must travel with pigs penned on the stern deck, stock intended for farmers in the south. Happy enough to pay the few obols required for passage, I reasoned that the animals would be no problem. I should have listened to the owner.

For three days, my stomach heaved with every swell of the waves.

On the first day out, I opened the lunch Ana had packed for Palo and me, to find I could hardly chew, much less swallow. Every bite tasted of pig dung. Farther south, breezes freshened, grew warmer, gentler. Escaping much of the stench, I felt some better and practiced my speech to Tibbelouios.

Nothing worked. Why would he, a respected and wealthy citizen of Lakonia, owner of a fleet of merchant ships, wish to see me, a poor peddler, a one-eyed peasant lad and a donkey? No reason. Still, I had cleaned and rubbed dry my best linen mantle and oiled my finest sandals, trimmed my hair and beard and brought along my best, scented body oils. I had washed and brushed Spitter till her silver hair gleamed like new money, and for Palo, grumbling all the way, I splashed with the milk of white clay, scrubbed him with an ox hair brush, shoved him into a tub of warm water, lifted him out pink and clean, dried him, smeared him with olive oil, scraped him down with a cleansing strigil and trimmed his hair and nails. In my bags I packed new clothes and sandals for him, garments suitable for presentation in a powerful household.

Nearing the harbor of Kyphanta on the coast of Lakedaemonia, whirlpool waves formed beyond a cragged promontory. The ship entered the swirling waters, lifting and dropping in chaotic bumps and slides. My belly convulsed. Gagging, struggling to maintain balance, I weaved to the side, longing to spew to the wind what little I had eaten. I must have turned several shades of green, but all without issue.

Sailors pulled on halyards to roll the sail around the yard arm, point it toward the sky and tie it off. Oarsmen strained to overcome the force of the current swinging us wide, tossing us into a small bay, then dragging us back out to sea. We broke free of the current and drifted into harbor. Lines were thrown to naked slaves, and we docked in the blackened hollows of a sheer cliff to lie lengthwise against a seawall, ours the only vessel.

A few huts, homes for the dock slaves, huddled one against another in a narrow band at the foot of the mountain, beginnings and endings lost in piles of loose rock and sea shells. Cracks stuffed with dried seaweed, roofs laid with leaves of palm, the huts differed hardly at all from drift washed against the shore or fallen from the cragged peaks above.

To the left, south, along the inland sweeping coast, the beach broadened. A few shops lined the sea road, and, farther up the mountain, thin streams of smoke rose from cook fires of huts hidden among rocks, date palm and fig trees. We were to remain overnight here and then leave for ports south with the dawn. The ship would round the coastline of the cape of Malea and dock in a northern port in the Lakonian gulf. The captain urged us to leave the cart aboard and to return after eating, for sleep. I thanked him as well as my queasy stomach would allow, but declined, intending to depart these accursed decks never to board a ship again.

Barrels and boxes were brought from below, and squealing pigs were herded down the ramp. Palo hitched Spitter, and, dragging back on the cart to slow the descent down the ramp and onto the dock, I wobbled ashore, slipping in pig dung.

I thought, once on land, my stomach would be still, but the shore road to the village took up the challenge, rising and falling to match the waves pounding the seawall and tilting my balance with every step. Palo led Spitter toward the well for water, and I reeled in to an open shelter, roof canopied with palm leaves. The weathered and peeling sign said, 'The Black Olive Tavern.'

In cool shadows, as far from the street as I could get, I staggered through barley husks covering the earth, slumped onto a bench at a table and tried to speak words to the keeper that would get me a cool glass of goat curd. In the street, two burly men grabbed another man dressed like a farmer, and pulled him away from his family, a woman and two children. Screaming, the man's family tried to follow, but a third man blocked their path. The boy broke free and ran after the men and his father. Another man caught him and tossed him over the seawall into the water. Pulling himself up, water streaming from his head, he held onto the rocks with an arm and elbow, balled his remaining fist and shook it at the departing backs of the capturers, spitting curses that curled my toes.

"What did that man do?" I asked the tavern keeper as he set my bowl of goat curd before me on a rough-hewn log table.

He shrugged. "Tried to avoid the tax collectors. It happens around here all the time."

A muscular body shadowed the street side of the open shelter, features black against the glare of light. The noisy room fell silent. The tavern keeper looked up, stiffened, then relaxed. Moving between the newcomer and me, he smoothed his apron and brushed away an imagined crumb, face rounding into an unctuous smile. I watched from beneath the keeper's elbow.

The man entered farther. I recognized the one who had kicked the boy. "How can I be of service, sir?" asked the keeper.

"Did a man and a boy come in here? The boy led an ass, silver hair, pulling a cane cart." I shrank.

"I saw no one. No one except my regular customers."

Several of the other people watched, but none spoke. "Keep your eyes open," said the man. "They owe taxes. There's a reward in it for you." He departed, dragging his gaze across every patron in the tavern, memorizing faces, clothes, but missing me, head lowered behind the innkeepers rounded middle. I wiggled my toes, smearing one across another still wet with pig dung.

Bowl hardly touched, one patron licked wine from his lips and left the tavern through another side. Barefoot, clothed only in a zomata tied about his hips to wrap his manhood, he glanced back at me. Straggly brown hair streamed over his eyes and a wispy beard caught on his shoulder. A goat herder, I decided, but peculiarly pale for these southern parts, and taller than most. Probably evading taxes himself. The entire countryside must live in fear. Spoons banged on pots near the cooking fire. Talk, growling, and laughter returned to normal.

"From here to anywhere it is several days travel over rough land and mountains," said the tavern keeper, as though no one had interrupted. "Will you be heading south with the ship?"

I felt both befriended and vulnerable. So easily could he have given me up to the collectors, should he have decided against me. Still, this whole affair left me with a vague feeling of helplessness. I chided myself for doubting.

"South," I said. "By land."

"Toward Lakonia?"

I hesitated, not wanting to tell my business. "To buy medicines," I filled in the gap. People like to be answered with reasons. Sometimes they volunteer news.

He nodded, satisfied, watching Palo enter from the rear. "You will need food for yourself and the boy, for your journey."

Eating a sweet cake with honey and nuts, Palo sat at my table. "Woman at the well gave it to me," he said. "She was nice. Told me to give you a message. Said watch out for the priests. She said they know about us."

"Priests. Here? How...how would she know, and how could they?"

"That's what I asked her. She just looked away and shook her head.

She had a bird in a cage. She let it go and it flew straight into the sky. I asked her what she did that for, and she gave me this cake. She said, 'we all have to eat.'"

He broke a piece for me and I tasted. Quince cake. That was the first bite I had eaten on the entire trip that hadn't turned against me. "What did releasing a bird have to do with eating?"

Palo shrugged, crammed a big bite into his mouth and managed a muffled answer. "I don't know, but she makes good cakes."

The keeper set a basket onto the table. It smelled of bread, cheese, dried fish and fresh garlic cloves. "Better to have good light to travel those goat trails," he said. "You can bed down in my shed."

The shed joined the tavern by a single reed wall. Palo fell asleep resting his head on a bag of barley, but I leaned against the wall, listening to the pounding surf, grateful to be on land that had finally quit rocking. Letting my mind drift, I identified sounds. A cat rustled the hay and cuddled near my foot, an owl called and hushed. Voices sounded from across the tavern near the cooking fire.

I decided to see if the keeper had more goat curd. A full belly would help me sleep. I went to see, crossing beneath the tavern shelter and heading toward the fire.

The tavern keeper sat on a stool near the fire peeling roots for tomorrow's stew pot, and another man sat nearby eating parched almonds. The scent made me hungry. I would ask for some. The men's conversation stopped me.

"Who do you suppose he is?"

"I think he's an agent from some rich banker from Athens."

"What makes you think that?"

"He came from Athens, didn't he? He must be carrying something valuable; the tax collector was looking for him. They want something bad enough to publish a reward. Did you see how he was dressed? No common farmer."

"Think we ought to warn him? They'll get him when he boards the ship tomorrow."

"No need. He's not going on with the ship. He says he's heading across the mountain."

The man with the almonds yawned. "I'm sleepy. You need help with the fire?"

"No," the innkeeper also yawned. "I'm finished here. I'm going to bed too."

Too late to ask for food, I turned to go, and a figure slipped past me in the dark. I smelled him before I saw pale skin as fire light flashed briefly across his face and shoulders. Moving easily, his bare feet hardly stirred the crunchy barley husks. He stepped from beneath the shelter at the back, circled around and came in from the street side.

"Got any more of that stew, Mathisos?" he asked, voice high, whining. "I missed my supper."

"You've had plenty of time to get in here and eat, goatherd. I'm headed for bed. The stew's cold, but there's a little left. You can dip your own, and you'll pay for it like everyone else."

"I always pay. I brought you fresh goat milk yesterday. The cream alone should buy a little bowl of left over stew."

Back on my mat, I relived what had happened. The man had heard what the tavern keeper and his friend had said about me. But why the stealth? They had said that the tax collector would catch us when we boarded the ship, but that we would be heading out in the morning by land, not sea. A sudden jolt of understanding sat me up on the mat. If the woman at the well were correct about the priests knowing about me, the 'tax collector' could very well be their agent. If the goatherd turned us in for the reward the priests' man had promised, he would have highwaymen waiting for us somewhere along our trail south, probably in the mountains. I wished I had lied to the tavern keeper, told him we were heading north. No help for that now. I pulled on sandals still wet from washing off pig dung, and shook Palo.

"Wake up, Palo. We're leaving."

Instantly awake, he hitched Spitter to her cart. I dipped deeply into the barley, filled Spitter's bag, placed a few coins nearby for pay, and we left. Trusting our progress to sounds of the surf and to reflected starlight from silvered waters, we headed south as planned, hoping that, leaving early, we would miss any traps. The landscape awoke in the eerie whiteness of a full moon rising.

"Keep your sling handy, Palo. We're likely to run across highwaymen." He found the sling in his bags, picked up pebbles washed smooth in the sea, and began practicing, proving himself accurate. "Throw a little harder," I said. "You couldn't kill a squirrel like that."

"You can if you hit him in the right place," he said. "I used to throw rocks at wild dogs. I put one's eye out. He never came around again." His next throw hit a rock too far away for me to see. The sound echoed back a half count later.

Our path steadily elevated, veering west toward a dip in the mountain. The terrain became rough, the path more twisted as we climbed. The first rays of morning sun found us high in the hills, facing a solid wall of rock. No pass.

I should have expected this. Goats don't need passes. Considering our choices, I whistled to Spitter to stop. She sniffed the wind, looking first to the north, then south, and jerked ahead. Palo and grabbed the top rim of the cart to pull back, both skidding. Spitter pulled cart, Palo, and me right up to the wall. Only on approaching the rock did we see a trail emerge, a break between two vertical cliffs with sweeping overhangs. On a dry river bed of wide, water-smoothed slabs of rock choked with sand, we followed land never touched by direct light of the sun. In air heavy with earth smell, it led us through mountain peaks we could never have climbed.

Beyond the pass we emerged into light. Pressed into a section of sand kept wet by an underground spring, I saw a single bare footprint and the mark of a cloven hoof. The traveler and his goats could not have passed here long ago, for the sand holding the print of the goat still stood high between the claws.

"Wait here, Palo," I whispered. I slipped aside from the river path, climbed the slope to the right, and looked out over the valley. No sign of goats anywhere, despite the distinct scent.

"Up here, peddler," said a quiet voice. It came from atop a huge flat stone. The goatherd lay on top, invisible to me except for a few strands of brown beard and fingertips gripping the edge of the stone. "You're as noisy as a flock of geese."

He peered over the edge, exposing the greenest eyes I had ever seen on a man.

"Where are your goats?" I asked.

He lifted the cane lying beside him and showed me the end, a perfectly carved cloven hoof. "A gift from Pan." Seeing I didn't share the joke, he admitted. "I carved it." He turned it round and round in his fingers. "Pretty good, wouldn't you say?"

Not entirely disarmed, remembering the secrecy of the man from last evening, I blurted, "What are you doing out here?"

"Admiring the view. See?" He pointed north. A creek lined with brush followed a deep-cut path through the valley. In single file, three men and a donkey trailed the creek side, heading our way.

"Priests' mercenaries," he said, "They're after you. You were supposed to be on the ship; the owner would have shielded you. He's a friend. He told me to watch out for you. When the tax collector offered a reward, I went to collect."

At my startled look he hurried on to say, "I told him you would be traveling by land so he wouldn't be watching the ship." He laughed. "I even got paid, see?" He reached downward to dip into the fold of his zomata and brought out three coins, extending them to me in the palm of his hand. "Three obols. If you are worth any reward at all, you're worth a drachm. Acteon kept the rest for himself, and sent these jackals to trap you at the pass. I gave them a long route. Serves them right. The collector should have paid me more. When I learned you were not taking the ship, I went to warn you." He shrugged. "You were gone."

Unbelieving, I asked, "How did you get here ahead of me? And how did you know I'd come up the hill to find you?"

"Goat trails all over these mountains. I took a shorter path. It crossed the ridge, near the docks. When I got here, I went down to the river bed to leave you a sign. If you were smart enough to leave Kyphanta early, you'd be smart enough to judge sign. If you didn't, you weren't worth saving. Give me your sandals."

"My sandals?"

"I'm barefoot," he said. "See? I need your sandals." I carried more sandals in the cart, and the man deserved a reward for his warning. I removed my sandals and handed them to him.

"Better get your cart and donkey out of sight. They'll be here soon."

Barefoot, I picked my way back down hill, shaking my head in confusion, trying to understand what had happened. Only after leaving the lookout did I realize the goatherd's hair showed yellow at the roots. It had been dyed with walnut husks, and that, some weeks ago. With those green eyes, he had probably dyed his skin as well, but it had worn off.

After a brief explanation to Palo, we hid Spitter and the cart in an alcove that forked off the trail, then gathered more stones for the sling on our way to the rock where I had discovered the goatherd. It seemed a good enough lookout.

When we arrived, the goatherd was gone. I searched the rocks and looked below to check the progress of the hunters. The goatherd stood talking to the men. He waved his arms wide, pointing toward us on the hill. I ducked my head and shoved Palo down, even as he tried to tell me, "That's the man I saw at the well. He was sitting on the wall beside the woman who gave me the cake."

"The man he is talking to is the thief, Harkos, the one who planned to attack Olympias. The princess and her men got to his camp first and killed everyone in his band but him. Olympias wounded him but he escaped. The goatherd has betrayed us. He's telling them we're here. Get your sling ready, boy, and if they head our way, aim your first rock at the goatherd." I grumbled. "He cheated me out of a perfectly good pair of sandals."

The men tied their donkey, removed long knives from their girdles, held them ready in their hands and headed for the river bed pass. "Not yet," I said. "Wait till you're certain you can make a hit. The goatherd knows we're here, but he doesn't know you have a sling."

Clutching several rocks in my hands, ready for reloading after Palo's first shot, I tensed, waiting.

"What are they doing?" asked Palo. At the place where the old river bed had flowed, the men stopped and examined the earth. The goatherd gestured toward the sandy bottom and pointed across the valley toward the trail up the other side. The men began arguing. Despite my poor hearing, I caught a few words.

"No. Not going that far. Acteon didn't pay me enough...."

"...across the mountain," said a voice that sounded like Harkos. "Catch him...dark, after he makes camp... ...asleep...easy.... Be slow...cart loaded...won't know we're...tell Acteon to pay you more when we get...."

"That thief Acteon would starve his own mother." I heard that part clearly enough.

"Acteon will pay," said Harkos, not loudly but with a conviction I could not dismiss. "Phaistos wants the peddler bad enough to set us up for a lifetime." Why would the priest want me? Surely not because I knew where Olympias was. He would already know that, from Harkos, and what would it serve him to kill me? Perhaps the high priest wanted to hold me hostage. Did he think that would draw Olympias out?

The other two men wouldn't budge. Harkos threw up his hands and turned back toward the donkey. "...then you'll go without pay. I'll take all the gold myself."

The other two men looked at each other then ran at Harkos. One climbed his back; the other dived, hitting him at the knee with his shoulder. Harkos crumpled, came off the ground, long knife swinging, charging. The men leapt back, shielding themselves with their arms to stop Harkos' advance, then turning to run. Glancing over their shoulders to make certain Harkos would not sling his knife at their backs, they stopped to remove their packs from the donkey. Beyond knife-throwing distance, they both shook their fists at Harkos. Harkos laughed and beckoned to the goatherd. He came. Harkos loosened the string on a coin bag and held it out to show.

"...wife, sons..." I heard the goatherd say. "....can't leave....goats need milking...."

"Argh, get on ... coward. ... do it myself." He mounted the donkey. The donkey, not wanting to go, looked back to where Spitter waited, and began braying.

'Don't answer, Spitter,' I prayed, willing her to hear me across the river bed. *'If you ever obey me, ever at all, obey me now.'*

Harkos beat his donkey with a stick, dismounted, pulled him into the stream, up the other side, and headed across the narrow valley. If that had been Spitter, he would have gone nowhere. At the foot of the upward trail, the donkey brayed once more, relented, and began the climb. Harkos mounted, and they disappeared behind rocks and brush. Knowing how far one might see from high on the mountain, I kept Palo still. Then together we slid off the rock, ducked our heads, and returned to the river bed. All the way, cutting my feet, I suppressed curses.

The goatherd handed me my sandals, eyebrow raised, lips twitching into a smile. There at his feet, in perfect impression, sandaled footprints and two cartwheel tracks crossed the sand bed. No longer the whining beggar I had overheard at the tavern, he asked Palo: "Would you really have hit me with a rock? Show me how good you are with that sling. It could be helpful along the trail."

And thus we set out. Spitter led, I walked alongside the cart, just behind the wheel on the right, my left hand resting on the side, and the goatherd and Palo followed. Palo practiced the sling until the goatherd pulled out his flute and began playing. Truly a master, I began to believe the goatherd to, indeed, be on intimate terms with the great god Pan himself. Surely they had walked the trails together—sometime, somewhere, a goat and Pan in eternal duet.

The goatherd gave Palo the flute and showed him where to place his fingers. A few false starts later, Palo found a tune he liked. He played that same tune the rest of our journey toward Lakonia. We stopped to bathe in rivers we crossed, and ate from caches left by the goatherd along the trail. How he knew we would be coming this way I did not ask, and he did not say. We never saw Harkos; the goatherd had led us along an alternate trail to avoid him.

On the crest of the hill beyond the tiny village of Kasya, we stood looking toward the sea. In the harbor, fishing boats and merchant ships drew near to the shore. Sails, gleaming orange in the last light of the day, flapped wildly, struggling to escape their tenders' hands. Then, furled, masts pointed at the sky, the ships seemed unbearably noble.

The goatherd pushed windblown, blond hair back from his face and behind his ears. The baths had washed away the last of his color, revealing skin as pale as mine, but despite the oils I gave him, he still smelled of goats. He pointed. "There. That is the home of the ship merchant." The many-leveled house spread across and down the slopes toward the sea.

With no good-byes, he turned away, toward Kasya. "But who are you?" I called. He looked back once and waved his stick before hurrying on.

"We will meet again," he called, and leapt a stone fence, disappearing.

"Why….." I tried to ask, as he hurried away. So many questions. Why had he accompanied us? Why had he dyed his hair and skin? If he were not from around here, how did the tavern keeper know him? How did he know the goat trails so intimately? It seemed that, unless it served some obscure purpose known only to the goatherd, he would never be one to explain. I could believe in him or not. It made no difference to him. None at all, but despite the smell, I would swear the man to be more than goat herder.

"The woman at the well called him Dolius," said Palo.

"Dolius only means shepherd." I said. We parted, the goatherd toward the village, and Palo, Spitter and I along the road leading downhill toward the doma of Tibbelouios.

Again I practiced my introduction. The nearer we came to the sprawling mansion, the more hopeless became my petition.

10

"My master sends his regrets," said the maid, a girl in the first bloom of womanhood. Skin, dark from the sun of the south, and black hair wild with the winds from the sea, the girl, though not beautiful, moved in grace and smelled of springtime flowers. "He cannot see you today, but you are welcome. He asks that you stay the night as his guests, and take dinner."

"Your master is Tibbelouios?" I asked, and when the maid dipped her chin, yes, a gesture I thought incredibly graceful, I continued. "We have traveled a very long way to see your generous master, and our mission is of greatest importance. Is there no way to see him?"

"Please understand. My master would greet you personally were he able. But his daughters lie ill, perhaps unto death. He fears to leave their room."

"Ah," I sighed. "But of course I understand. Perhaps I may be of service. I am a physician."

"My master refuses to call for medicines, but he is so worried. Another lady came into the room. "Who is it Daphnei?"

"A visitor, *kiria*," the girl replied, "a physician." The woman came to the door, opened it wider and looked at each of us, then glanced in the direction of the daughters' room.

Not a young woman, she wore her years well, standing straight, poised but not stiff. Her dress of finest linen brushed her body in a stately, alluring grace. Her graying hair lay in perfect waves pulled back from her face and pinned in a bun on her neck. "We will see you," she said, "whether my husband wishes or not. Please, come in. Daphnei, make them welcome. I will call my husband."

Daphnei led porters into the room laden with steaming bowls of water. I sat, removed my sandals, and plunged my feet into one of the bowls. Then, with a hot, wet towel from Daphnei, I rubbed my face, arms, hands and neck, surprised by the amount of grime picked up in half a day's journey.

"I am Mara," said the woman. "My husband agrees to a short visit and asks that you come to him in my daughters' bedroom. I have promised him that you will not stay long. I will bring you wine, and perhaps you would like cakes?" Refreshed by the atmosphere of the house as much as by the foot and towel bath, I felt fortified for the coming interview. I followed Daphnei down a wide hall floored with pebbled mosaics and lined with marble sculptures, through a columned door and into the interior garden. A wave of flower scents greeted me. I sighed.

Daphnei smiled and was suddenly pretty. "Myrtle," she said. "Beneath Kaela's window." I looked in the direction she pointed and saw several small shrubs, completely overshadowed by the flashy beauty of numerous other plants, some of which I recognized, some of which I was certain only grew this far south. Myrtle, of course, I knew. What visitor to the lands of Hel has not seen, not smelled the fragrance of Myrtle?

"You said these grow beneath Kaela's window. Does not the other daughter also like the scent?"

Daphnei laughed aloud, and the sound, formed against the quiet splash of the fountain waters, startled me. "Both the daughters are named Kaela," she said. "That's so the spirit that inhabits the two of them will remain centered, not scattered."

Kaela's room faced the south, but high windows allowed little light. Even those were shuttered. Now here, on a tiled verandah just outside their door, I smelled the sickness, and my immediate concern for the girls took control. I approached their bed even before I spoke to Tibbelouios.

The girls' shadowed figures stirred restlessly. Long, black hair cascaded limply across their pillows. Soft moans and whimpers escaped their lips. They looked exactly alike. I could not tell one from the other, except that the bruised look beneath the eyes of one were more deeply purple. I pressed open this girl's lids and stared into lusterless, brown eyes, circled by puffy red tissue. Thick tears drained across her cheeks.

I pressed my hand to her brow and drew back, stunned at the dry heat, the fever, burning the life force from her body. She would not be able to sustain such an attack for long. Prickles of red rash had begun to emerge, peppering her skin like red ants on a goat's carcass. "How long has she been like this?" I asked,

"Since yesterday," said Tibbelouios. "The sickness came upon her shortly before the noonday meal. It was sudden, as though brought by fast winds from the sea. Then her sister was taken during the night."

"I have medicines that will ease their distress," I said. "It's too bad I could not have been here sooner, but I was delayed. Quickly, we must give them the medicine. Will you help me? I will go for my bags."

"No," said Tibbelouios. "We must not."

"I assure you, I have seen this disease many times before. The medicines I have will help them heal."

"It does not matter. One of them must...must die." He crumpled to his knees beside the bed and wept, face smothered in the sheets on his daughter's bed.

A man of means, the hands of Tibbelouios, gnarled and knotted from killing work, grasped and released the bed cover, again and again. His face, not handsome, strong jaw jutting and square, nose long, broad and generous, inspired respect. Sensuous lips had long ago given way to muscular tautness. The whole face would have been expected on a common laborer except for the forehead stretching high and wide above black, thick, even luxurious brows and glittering black eyes, eyes too bright, too keenly observant to be cast into shadow. The beard, now graying to white, fit snugly to the line of jaw, neither too short nor too long for comfort and dignity.

I had come to this house to plead the case of a princess—and plead with whole heart I would—yet at this moment, in this man's presence, my mission paled. I knelt beside the man, one knee to the floor. "Your girls need not die," I said. "Hear me. My medicines can cure them."

"I have no choice," he said, and looked away, down to the floor, then back to me. His voice broke. "Do you think I would allow either of them to suffer one moment longer than necessary if I could stop it?"

"The priests have decreed this," said a frigid voice from the door, and I looked up at Mara. "They have said that one of them must die, even if we must kill her." Her face opposed the submission of her husband, hardening to the texture of stone, and no hint of softness remained in her rigid body. Her lower lip curled back to reveal uneven teeth, and almost, I could hear the growl of a wolf in her throat.

Stunned, I rose to my feet and looked from one to the other. One of the girls spoke, the one whose illness had not yet consumed her.

"We are a single spirit, the priest says. We will never know fulfillment so long as we have two bodies." Then exhausted from the effort, she allowed her head to droop back to the pillow. "After I am dead my father and mother can give my sister the medicine." The child could have been no more than eight years, yet her manner suggested maturity and resignation, not defeat. This was a being who would never understand the word.

I slumped to a stool beside the bed. A shared spirit. Yiayia had told me of such a thing. A group of villagers had kept her away from their children, fearing, she said, that she would report to the priests that a number of their children were duplicates. But she had seen the children playing when the parents hadn't known she was near. On investigation she learned that it was believed that the twins, sometimes even triplets, shared a common soul. They thought alike, spoke as one, even shared thoughts to the point that often no words were necessary between them.

"That was nonsense," my grandmother had said. "I could see differences everyone seemed to miss. Some of the children were right-handed, some left, one had a deformed foot, turning in instead of straight–little things like that. But I saw the result when priests learned of the many sets of duplicate children. I watched a ritual murder, unable to do anything but curse the hands that held the knife."

Even now I remember the horror, the frustration on my grandmother's face. Her anger renewed itself in me. I must take care, for it is a pride of mine that I hold the beliefs of others to be inviolate.

"If they are not treated, both may die," I said. "Is this what the priests have decreed?" I pressed on before the grief-stricken couple could find time to argue. "It would seem to me, ignorant as I am, having lived for much of my childhood across the Aegean, that such children would be blessed of the gods, and should be revered for their excellence."

"Are such children allowed to live in the colonies?" A studied frown suggested he might consider moving to such a place.

"I have never heard of any such being slain," I said. Truth. I had never heard of it across the sea. Of course I didn't mention the many other atrocities I had seen committed in the name of religion.

"Then, possibly, they are not doomed to an eternal life of division?" His mottled face began to clear and he looked up at Mara. Could this thing be avoided?"

"Why don't we try and see? I will give them both the medicine." I released a breath I hadn't realized I held. "I can't guarantee it will work. If they live, it is the will of the Great Spirit, and if they die..."

But I knew they would not die. I knew.

"The priests will come. They will see that the girls still live," said Mara. Then they will kill one of them."

I had no love of priests. As a boy, after my father died we had nothing to eat. My mother took us to the temple to ask for help. The priest, a short, round-faced man with the grease of roast lamb smeared across his cheek (I knew for I smelled it from the kitchen), turned us back.

"Go away." His small, round eyes could have frozen a goose. "We have no money for women and children who are able to work to pay their own way." As it turned out, he was right, and his decision probably started us on our way to recovery, for soon my sister married a man of wealth from across the sea and my mother and I went with her. But never again will I respect the sacred robes worn by holy men who do not offer help when it is needed.

"If they live, I will adopt one of them," I offered. "I am not married, and I would like to have a family, especially a family with one of them a daughter from this house. The priests need never know."

The Kaela who had spoken turned onto her side. Her eyes opened and she watched me. I saw peace, even joy written there. She looked at her father and nodded.

"We will do it," decided Tibbelouios. "Get your medicines."

My visit with the family drew out into weeks. I made ointment to rub into my patients' skin for the rash, and three times a day I brewed tea made from the leaves and flower of the yeta, a plant that grows freely along the countryside—tall yellow blossoms topping furred green leaves—and instructed the maid, Daphnei, as I worked.

"The plants are there for the taking," I said. "It is as though they ask to be used, raising their bright yellow heads high to look into the sun and to call to me as I walk by. Give yeta any time the throat and lungs are sore. It will soothe and ease the breathing. Add to the herb, eyebright, for the girls' eyes are weepy and red and they hurt from the light when I try to open the shutters to their room." I showed her the herb growing in the fields near the house, a flower about the height of my knees—small, lacy, purplish-green foliage displaying pale pink blossoms striped with deeper pink leading into the throat of the bloom.

Eyebright was past its season farther north, so I gathered an armload to dry for my pouches.

Later Daphnei showed me a place on a verandah shaded by long-limbed oaks where I could tie my precious bundles to dry. An easy learner, she charmed me with her willingness to help, her fresh, sweet scent warming me as we walked the paths through fields and foothills. I thought perhaps she enjoyed my company too, for often she stood so closely little wisps of curl brushed across my arm.

Mornings began at the bedside of the twins. I always found Tibbe there before me. I had begun to call him by his familiar name. Such circumstances as we shared did not fit well with the more formal address. Indeed, he seemed like the brother I had never had, and he called me Pelos. That is a Greek name," he said, but you are not like any other Greek I have known."

It was true, here in the Peloponnesus. Only in Thrakè had I found others with hair of orange, like mine. Perhaps in that land north of the Aegean, a foreign race had migrated and settled? It was an interesting puzzle.

"The Kaelas are from Mara's first marriage," he said. The family of her first husband believed that if the children shared a common name, their spirits would rejoin at death and enter paradise as one whole being." He smiled and chucked the one in the bed on the left under the chin. "It gets confusing sometimes. Mara calls "Kaela," and they both come running, and if one does something wrong, both get punished."

"It's always her," they both said at once, each pointing toward the other, and laughed. Tibbe and I laughed too, until tears came into Tibbe's eyes. Yes, they were healing.

"They need new names," I said. "How about Yetah for this Kaela? That's from the flower that made you both well. It would serve to link you in the book of names," I reasoned, "for it has healed you both. Then we can name the other," I said, putting my hand on hers, "oh, say Shah, for you are now separated, though you are closely joined by love and relation. Yet each of you are your own souls, free to pursue your separate life courses."

Slowly the smiles faded. "The priests will come," said Yetah. "They will not let both of us live."

"I will go with them," said Shah.

"And then the joy for us all would be forever gone," said Mara, who stood beside the door, as was her way when Tibbe and I dressed the twins' eyes, bathed their faces and rubbed ointment into their skin.

"Have you forgotten my promise?" I asked. "I will take one of the girls with me. Then the priests will think she has died."

Tibbe laid a hand on each of the girls' arms. "But which one shall it be!" I cannot bear to part with either of them."

"Let's get breakfast," I said. "Perhaps an answer will come to us."

We ate quietly, reflecting, and when he was done, Tibbe set his drinking bowl down firmly. "I don't think the priests should have any say in this."

"What can we do?" asked Mara. "We are helpless in the power of the gods."

"The gods?" I asked. "Or merely men who have misused their positions as representatives of gods?" When the stunned silence drew out, I continued.

"I know one who has rebelled against this power," I said, and some of the temples in Athens are backing her. They provide her with money so she can fight the priests of Kreté."

"Who is this woman?" asked Tibbe.

"Olympias of Epirus."

"Olympias." said Mara. "But it is the fault of that woman that any of this is happening. She speaks the words of the gods to the priests, and they know of our every movement."

"The seer of the Temple of Unseen Spirits at Kreté is not the real Olympias," I said, and told them of Olympias' mother, the Regina, being stolen from the temple. "It is for the princess' sake that I have come so far south. Aboard a ship," I added, "which I hate so much."

"But you have come on the wrong ship!" said Tibbe. "You will return aboard my finest. My captain will see that you are served royally, as a great physician should be served."

I groaned. "A ship is a ship. Can your captain stop the swaying, the rolling of the sea?"

Tibbe chuckled. "You'll see. All ships are not alike. And I have a little surprise for you. Something I discovered when I sailed my first ship as a cabin boy. Daphnei, bring Pelos some of your honeyed ginger. You'll see. This will ease the sickness."

"Ginger? I know of ginger, but I never knew it would help the water sickness."

"Then consider this my gift to you. You have given so much to us."

"If Olympias is free," said Mara, and not an impostor, then we must help her, my husband. If she is the Chosen, the true voice of the gods, we must hear her."

"Olympias speaks for the people, it is true," I said. "Though many of her followers believe her to be the true Chosen, I can only see her as a very courageous young woman, one who has been severely wounded in the spirit by the wrongs done her by the priests."

"I have come to respect you, Pelos," said Tibbe. "If you believe in Olympias, so do I. When she gathers her army to fight the priests, my ships will carry her, the fruits of my fields will sustain her, and my people will bear her spears and swords."

෴෴෴

It came time to leave, and for the last time we gathered on the covered porch, Tibbe, Mara, Daphnei, Palo, the twins and I, all clutching our cloaks against the brisk winds from the sea.

Daphnei kissed my forehead, and I allowed her to step away, despite the longing in my arms to leap from their sockets to embrace her. Mara knelt before me, took my hands in her own and kissed each of them. "Without you, we would be in mourning now, not for just one of our daughters but for both of them."

Tibbe led Shah to me and put her hand in mine. "My daughter shall be your daughter," he said, voice breaking. He put his arms around her, holding her tight. It was as I had thought. Shah, the bright-eyed one who had offered to give her life for her sister, was Tibbe's favorite.

"Perhaps...." I said, and paused.

"Yes?" asked Tibbe.

"I have no home of my own," I said. "I travel from here to there, here to there, all the time. Palo and I get along very well, but..."

"Because she is a girl?" said Mara, then fearing that I would change my mind about making her my daughter, she said, "Shah could cook for you, gather your herbs... There are many ways a daughter would be useful." But all the time she spoke her eyes bathed her daughter's face.

"Oh," I said. "That is true, that is true. Yes, a daughter would be of great help to me...when she is older." Then, as though the thought had just occurred to me, I suggested, "Maybe...maybe you could keep her here with you, hide her from the priests, just until then? You could see that she is trained in all the womanly arts, perhaps teach her to read? She could keep my books, to tell me how much money I have earned in the buying and selling of my merchandise."

"But," said Shah, "if the priests find me, they will kill me."

Tibbe's quiet, hard anger trembled the air. "No one will kill you," he said. "I will not let them."

A new Tibbelouios stood straight, free of fear for his daughter's lives, free of the superstitious power and oppression of the priests. My task now complete, I knew the worth of my coming. This man would fight, not just for Olympias and her cause, but for himself.

"Then it is settled?" I said. "Shah will stay with you until she is older?"

Shah's legs, still weak, gave way. She slumped to the couch. Mara and Tibbe sat beside her. "It is settled," they answered, both with their arms around the child.

॥॥॥

A flat boat waited on the beach to ferry Palo, Spitter, and me to a sleek ship anchored offshore in deep water. True to his word, Tibbe had assigned his finest vessel to our use for our return journey.

Boarding the ramp of the flat boat used for loading, we were able to see above the heads of milling people and beyond canvases hung for shade above carts and vendors gathered to hawk their wares near the boarding dock. I caught sight of Harkos.

Stunned, I laid my hand on Tibbe's shoulder, and nodded in the man's direction. "That man is a murderer. He is in the pay of the priests of Kreté. If he comes to your house keep the twins out of his sight."

"Which man?" he asked, but Harkos had disappeared into the crowd.

"He's gone. If you see him you will know him by the scar of a slash through his left eyebrow, put there by the blade of *mylitta* Olympias. He is named Harkos."

Tibbe gestured to two men waiting on the dock, and they came, Tibbe whispered to them, and they hurried away. "If they see him, the murderer will not survive to report to the priests. On my oath, he will not leave the docks this day. Not alive."

The flat boat pulled out. Palo jerked my sleeve and pointed. The scarred face of Harkos watched us, peering from behind a vendor's loaded cart. Not only did he know we were here, he knew of Tibbe. He would guess the mission of Tibbe's men to hunt for him. I grabbed the shoulder of the pole man pushing the cart away from the docks. "See that man...." But again Harkos had disappeared. I believed in the vow of Tibbelouios, but I knew the strength of the adversary. Harkos would surely follow us. Though Tibbe would not allow him aboard any of his boats, the wealthy ship owner did not control all the traffic on the sea. How powerful was the network of spies deployed by the priests? No doubt their ships docked everywhere, perhaps even alongside ours.

📿📿📿

In Athens, near the doma of Ana and Dimitri, my footsteps slowed. The house was dark. Quiet. What had happened. Was someone sick?

Two men dressed in formal chiton, embroidered himations wound about their shoulders and waists, stood outside the door to greet me.

"*Kiria* Ana, asked us to meet you," one said. I recognized him from a group of friends who sometimes met with Ana to plan distribution of foods to the children of the community without families.

"What is wrong?" I pushed past him and into the main room, overheated with bodies standing around, murmuring quietly.

"The Sivya Bei," he followed me inside and caught my arm to slow me. "Your grandmother. She is passing."

"Yiayia?" Impossible. The immortal Yiayia could not die. I looked at the man, daring him to speak again such a lie. He did not speak, nor did he look away.

Trembling I followed a path through the room lined with people. Yiayia rested amidst unaccustomed splendor, gifts brought from all across the country. I entered the alcove where Yiayia had waved good-bye to me when I left, the breezeway now closed, the air heavy with incense. I approached her bed and reached for her hand lying extended to greet me, eyes unseeing, lips unable to speak, not even to groan.

"It happened soon after you left, Daneion," said Ana, coming from another room and handing me a warm wet cloth for cleansing. "She spasmed, then lay still. Since then she has not spoken, and could move only the hand of one arm." She clasped the hand and whispered in Yiayia's ear. "He is here, most beloved, Sivya Bei."

I fell to my knees beside the bed and kissed the hand. How cold. I covered it with both of mine, still warm from the cloths brought by Ana. "I am home, Yiayia. I will make you well. Where do you hurt?" I touched her forehead, dry, cool. She opened her eyes and looked in my direction, though I knew she could not see. Her fingers squeezed my hand, then went limp, and she ceased to breathe.

Spears of light formed through a veil of my tears. Astonished, I opened my eyes wide and saw a glowing mass about her head. "Yiayia?" I breathed out the last of my air, and in wonder watched it connect with the glow, merge and disappear. Ana laid her hand on my shoulder. "She is gone, Daneion."

Ana and I laid her among the herbs in Ana's garden, between the house and the wall. The plants grew lush and green forever after, even in the driest of seasons.

That night, after the crowds were gone, the house remained quiet, servants moving about on bare feet, none speaking lest they disturb my rest, I lay still, neither sleeping nor awake on a couch near Yiayia's bed. What had she said before I left for the south? "You must go to the lands of our people. In the far north. You must claim your inheritance."

What inheritance?

11

In Dimitri and Ana's animal shed, Palo moaned and turned over when I harnessed and packed Spitter with travel gear, so I left him asleep in the loft. Grateful for her light load, Spitter clattered out the gates and across the cobblestone parking field onto the dusty road. I followed, eating dust, calling her to stop and wait. Passing neighbors' houses, windows lighted. "What's the rush?" A chorus of calls trailed my back.

"My donkey is running away!" I answered. After that I used my breath to run.

At the city gate's guard shed, I pulled a grumbling man from his sleeping blanket.

"All right, all right," he grumbled. Isn't the day long enough for you?" He stumbled from the shed, tying on his shirt. "I've been up all night letting drunken farmers through to return to their wives and children before sun rise. What's so urgent you can't leave me to my few minutes of rest? Oh. It's you, Daneion. Go back to sleep, Polydamus. Daneion and I can lift the bar on the gate. Do you happen to have any ointment for sore feet? Take a look here, blisters."

I had no time for blisters. "I can't look at your feet now, Kalais; I'm on my way to Olympias' camp." But Kalais had already slipped off his sandal and, dancing on one foot, held the other up to me like a horse waiting for a shoe.

Polydamus came from the shelter stretching, scratching his rear. "Mine are blistered too. Procopios had us patrolling the outer walls six days straight. If he weren't a cousin I'd never put up with that. We're gate guards, not soldiers. He's trying to attract notice, to get money from the council. Talks about how valuable we are, first line of defense against invaders, that kind of nonsense. Thinks people will leave bigger tolls if they hear of it. Scarce chance of that. Without the kindness of merchants and beggars, we'd starve to death. Look here, Daneion." He lifted a bare foot. One of the blisters bled. "That ointment of yours better be good."

What could I do? I loosened a pouch from Spitter's pack and removed a small jar of ointment. Olympias had found it soothing when her ankles were bruised. Maybe it would help blisters. I pulled the reed stopper, dipped in a finger and smeared it onto Kalais' blister.

"You're headed for Olympias' camp, huh? Didn't know she knew of you. Ouch! Be easy will you? That toe is sore. The princess comes through the gates every now and then, and she always has her woman toss me a coin or a bit of food. You'd never think the woman was just a maid the way she acts. You'd swear it was her own purse. Then she tries to stand between me and the princess. Glares. She thinks I'm beneath the notice of a royal. Diana, I think they call her." He chuckled. "She's scared of me. Maybe I should just jump the old crone. Can't you just hear her screech." He laughed so hard he lost his balance, tilted, and hopped to stay upright. "Now that would be the day when I'd be so hard up I'd want the likes of her. Huh. That'd be the day, all right. But she does what the princess says. She tosses a coin."

From what I had seen of Olympias, she always tossed coins to the populace. How much did she really care about their welfare? Perhaps it was only that she cared so little for wealth.

"No, we should turn Procopios loose on the maid, Kalais," said Polydamus. "If he can keep us hoary old gatekeepers working our feet to purple mush he can get her off hers. Ha ha."

Kalais joined him, neither of them hurrying. They slid the wooden gate bar, as long as either of them and thicker than one of their thighs, through its iron brackets and to the side. As soon as light showed through the crack, Spitter shoved the gate open with her nose and bolted for open countryside, pulling me after her, hanging onto the rein. I couldn't get close enough to mount, nor would she slow when I called. We left the brothers standing in the dust, howling with laughter.

Beginning the climb uphill, Spitter slowed enough for me to mount. Relieved of the breathlessness of running, my thoughts returned to my grandmother, her stories echoing in my mind—Yiayia singing for the sick, walking with me to gather herbs, teaching, explaining, warning of the dangers of improper use of the gifts of nature, all crowded forth, flooded in the memory of her woodsy scent. "Why did you leave me, Yiayia?" I whispered. That old, blind healer had wanted something of me, something she could not voice. I never understood what. Now her need nagged at me like a fly on a sore. What do you want, what do you expect of me, Yiayia?

Spitter stopped dead still in the middle of the road. The scree of a hawk turned my eyes to the sky. The hawk dived, clutched a mouse in its talons and flew to a tree. It sat there, bold as you please, staring at me, eating. Clutching the mouse against the limb with a foot, it pulled it apart with its beak, gulping until it disappeared. The mouse's head dropped to the ground beside me, discarded, unwanted.

Was this Yiayia's answer? That all elements—even war—must be attended, woven into the fabric of life? I hurried on toward Olympias, heady with the thoughts of righteous battle against the army of priests, and at the same time so weak I recoiled from the sight of the death and dismemberment of a mouse. Who knew what terrible violence I would be setting in motion? Still, violence must be accepted. The oracle of the hawk and mouse led my way. Death rides the shoulders of life.

I would tell the princess of my plans, ripping them piece by piece from the fabric of my dreams. Dreams only, they were, but I pushed blindly on, arguing that only in dreams are empires built. A long and bloody process it would be, but however difficult the details, Bird and I would work them out together.

We would recruit warriors. Bendi and his men would train them in the manner of his people, the fierce Keltoi of the far north. They would organize a force even to make Phaistos tremble. We would form a coinon of farmers, merchants, and craftsmen to supply food and weapons, and they would sail the seas on the ships of Tibbelouios. Phaistos' domination would come to seem foolish child's play.

Delphé, the city of gods, would back Olympias as soon as they heard of the rebellion. Vitos, Ana's brother, would lead the temples in Athens, and the gentle, barefoot Selloi priests of Dodona, though not so wealthy as those of Delphé, worshipped the princess, even since childhood. They, of course, would follow.

Doubt nagged me. What chance could farmers have against warriors? Sons of ruling families are trained for war from birth. The royals were not friends of Olympias. They hated her for her arrogance, her refusal to follow their lead, her insistence on being recognized as an equal, despite the disregard of her family.

Then—I compromised—we would build a secret network of common people. We would train teachers, cooks, seamstresses, fishermen, money lenders, farmers. Farmers and goatherds were everywhere. We would send them behind walls as spies, working for the princess and against Phaistos.

Whispers travel faster than shouts. Phaistos' power would erode, for these loyal people would report back to centers that would relay its information to Olympias and me. Each foray Phaistos sent would be met by a new kind of soldiers—soldiers disguised as laborers, peddlers, gamblers. Yes. Gamblers and tavern owners would be ideal for this work. The list went on, gathered from many I already knew. Kalais, the gate guard, for one, and whatever Kalais decided, the families of gate guardians would follow.

Never seeing the browning fields and distant snowcapped peaks, so full of glory was I that I saw the world as fresh and promising as spring. Filled with a newfound zeal, a heretofore unrealized sense of lust for power, for righting the wrongs of the world, I walked into Olympias' camp.

And into another world.

Smoke from at least twenty cook fires stretched heavenward. I could not see them all, but ranging even across the hills, they marked the skies. Pots of soup enough to feed an army hung simmering. Strangers milled in and out, seemingly without direction, babbling nonsense, yelling orders and insults. Wagons lined the fronts of many rows of tents, and vendors sorted wares at tables set up within hailing distance of Olympias' site. Women knit intricate paths through the smaller tents, many carrying jars on their heads. I saw glimpses of seamstresses pulling bolts of cloth, embroidering and stitching.

Olympias' hounds worried the feet of half-grown men, tearing savagely at the air just inches away from the ankles of posted guards. In the distance I heard stomping and shouted commands that could only have been of men training for war. I saw no sign of the old tanned-hide lodgings of the princess. In a high place overlooking the river stood a brilliantly-bannered and edged tent, three times as large as the old, with several secondary supports surrounding a taller, centered pole. From inside, women's voices joined into a cacophony even Apollo could not have deciphered.

Guards speaking a dialect of Hellené mixed with Illyrian that could only have been Makedonian, crowded the door, holding twelve-foot pikes across the entrance.

Dazed, I left Spitter with other donkeys and horses tied to ropes near the river, and climbed the hill to Olympias' tent. Instantly the pikes crossed my path, barring my entrance.

"I am here to see the princess," I said. "Surely this is Olympias' tent?"

"Who are you, and what is your business with the princess?"

"My name is..." I started to say Wallis, but somehow that sounded trite in these surroundings. "I am the physician, Daneion," I finished, "and the princess is expecting me."

"No one sees the princess without clearing through Antipatros," said a young, black-haired man, gesturing toward the plains beyond the river. "And he's busy now, seeing to the training of the princess' troops."

"This is a favored friend of Olympias," came a voice from behind the guard. The man started, just as I would have done, had I not recognized the head of the blond giant, Bendi.

"I have my orders," replied the guard, somewhat stiffly, and a trifle embarrassed.

"Your orders have just been changed, boy," said Bendi. Between the guard's elbow and hip, I glimpsed a flash of light off Bendi's polished knife, a weapon I knew he wore, but had never before seen him draw. The man jerked. Stiffened. I supposed the knife had nicked his back.

Just that moment Olympias stepped from behind a tapestry that served as a baffle to hide the interior of the tent. "Wallis? Is that you? Bendi, stop keeping my messenger. We have things to talk about."

Messenger. I was a messenger? Repelled by my reception, almost I turned away, but Olympias grabbed my arm and jerked me into the tent. With a flick of her fingers, she dismissed her maids. Skirts went flying, leaving only a brief memory of something pink vanishing into a curtained alcove. "Outside!" screamed the princess, and the tittering chatter behind the curtain quieted.

"Wallis. " Olympias grabbed me around the neck with both arms, then pulled back to look into my face. "I couldn't find you. I looked. I sent messages to Dimitri and everyone I could think of. No one would tell me where you were." Her voice broke, grew hard—as though any sign of weakness infuriated her. "I only got your message a week ago, when I returned from Samothraké. It is too late to raise forces against Phaistos."

Too late? "What happened, Bird?"

"Arrybus has ordered me to marry." She flung away a scrap of lace she had been stretching between knotted fingers.

My legs, my short, bowed and bony legs, turned to hot butter. I looked for a pillow to sit on, found none. My knees gave way, and I collapsed to the carpeted floor, trying at the last minute to make it seem intended.

"What have you done?"

"What have I done! Wallis, Arrybus plotted against me. He convinced the Council of Elders of Molossis that I should be married." She jumped up, retrieved a delicately scribed vellum scroll, unrolled it and flung it at nothing in particular. I caught it.

'I am sending three portraits by the messenger who carries this missive,' it said. 'You must choose one of them for a husband. If you refuse to marry and produce an heir, you will be written from the rolls of inheritance. This is my right according to law.'

"It shows how certain he is that he can move me at his will." She lifted a cut of wood, smoothed and painted with a portrait. She handed it to me. Bardyllis, the king of the Dardanoi, silver-hair swept back from high, narrow forehead above black penetrating, intimidating eyes, stared back at me.

"Arrybus has the audacity to present this man to me. He and my father fought all the days of Neoptolemus' life. With every harvest, Bardyllis and his hordes of Illyroi invaded our villages demanding a share. They did nothing to feed and clothe themselves, but lived off the bounty taken from my people. I have seen families who could hardly feed themselves and their children hand over their stores of barley, woven linens, hand-crafted tools, anything they could find just to buy their lives from Bardyllis and his blood thief, Agis. Offering me to this man shows his cowardice. He sent two other portraits, one Philip of Makedon, the other not even a citizen. A banker. He would sell me to a banker, to pay his debts."

"Wallis, I am more certain than ever now, that Arrybus killed my father. Oh, he is so well admired by all the intellectuals of Hellas. 'A real scholar and philosopher,' they say. 'The study of his historical scrolls alone could busy a learned man for years.' But I know him for what he is. First he cozens the Council of Elders into making him co-ruler with my father on the pretense of adding strength to Epirus' armies to fight the Dardanoi and the Illyri, led by the same Bardyllis he offers me to marry. Then—hardly a year after the council presents him—my father mysteriously dies of a wound from a horse. A horse, Wallis, when Neoptolemus lived most of every day of his life on horseback. No horse would ever kick my father.

"The Council has set Alexandros, my brother, on the throne, and Arrybus is his regent. Do you see Arrybus' plan?" I must have looked bewildered, for she explained. "Wallis, Alexandros is five years old. A child. As Alexandros' regent, Arrybus may do as he pleases. He will remove me from the rolls."

"You are a priestess. By law you may not be forced to marry to inherit."

"That is what I told him. Father said the choice was mine. I could marry or I could follow my mother's way as a priestess. He said a life without a family and children would be a hard one to follow, but still, it was my choice, as it was never the choice of my mother.

"Arrybus sent copies of the law. Law? Neoptolemus never acknowledged such a law! 'By the law of Molossis of Achilles,' Arrybus says, 'women are women, priestess or not. We have no rights except those granted us by men.' Still, the people are loyal to me."

She dragged a stool from the circle where women had gathered for spinning, dropped it beside me and sat on it as though she were squashing her uncle. "When I was fifteen summers, Arrybus told my father I needed to be educated if I were to serve as priestess. So they sent me away to Athens to be schooled. He only wanted me out of the way so he could take the throne."

"You don't know that for certain," said Diana, entering the tent from the rear. "Such words will only get you into more trouble. Arrybus is in power now."

Olympias continued, voice unbroken, as though Diana had not spoken. "Arrybus maneuvered me into this. I have been away from Molossis too long. I should have seen it coming. First the death of my father, now this...this ultimatum, as though I were no one. No one, a woman subject to the whims of her guardian. If this had been my father's wish, I would have been married years ago. I would have been the first wife of the Makedoné prince. He has wanted me since our first meeting at Samothraki, more than five years ago. The succession of our son, if we had one, would have been undisputed.

"I sent word to him. "With my dowry of gold and warriors that Arrybus will be forced by the elders to pay, Philip agrees to go to war against Bardyllis. Then we will take back my throne in Molossis." Quiet, hard, she might have been discussing whom not to invite for dinner. "I will grind that intellectual genius' ashes beneath my feet and kick them to the wind. Well will he regret the day he forced me to this."

"Little Bird..." I said, managing an opening, "Bird," I coaxed, moving nearer and touching her cold arm, rubbing warmth, life, back into it. "Don't you see? Philip is in league with your uncle. Philip marries for power, for gold, for land. He has three wives to prove it. He and Arrybus have struck a deal. Together they have maneuvered you into this."

"I had no choice. Arrybus has cut me free of my people. Without a throne, without my armies, I am at the mercy of the priests of Kreté. They will kill me, or worse, take me captive to the Temple of Unseen Spirits." Drained, face flaky white, but struggling for control, she continued. "While you were away I went to Samothraké. Philip and I made a contract of marriage.

"His first wife, Phila, a princess of Larissa, hides in her chambers, never seeing anyone except her family, and not allowing Philip into her apartment. Another, a princess of Illyria died leaving him with a daughter. The last is Philinna, my cousin, the daughter of Altera, sister of Havin of the house of Ru. You saw her when we looked for Plise. Philinna is simple. She knows nothing about ruling the women's quarters, and much less about advising a king."

Her face softened. "Philinna is a child. She loves to dance. She spends hours twirling before the servants beside the fountain. Quite beautiful. I have heard that she is pregnant, but Philip has promised that if I give him a son, my son will inherit. Inherit, he says. Ha. What is there in Makedonia to inherit? Philip can barely hold the throne. At least three contenders threaten from all sides to displace him. He is up to his eyebrows in debt. Pella is so far out in the wilderness few of the citizens of Athens even know where it is. It's a state of woodsmen and farmers, so wretchedly poor they struggle to the death just to pay taxes. They pay taxes to everybody. The Illyri, the Persi, the Atheni."

Philip wants the friendship, the power of the temples that will come with me. At our wedding I will become the First Voice, the bride of Dionysus."

Through the fog that drowned my mind and past the pounding

thunder of my heart, her words finally penetrated. I fought to breathe. She spoke of contracts, plans already decided. In her mind all other alternatives had been dismissed.

What of our—my, I amended, *plans?* "Philip is known for his false promises," I said, grabbing for points of argument.

"I know of Philip's cunning." Chilling words, hard, humorless. "I did not accept his promises without protecting myself. I made him swear oath before the altar of sacrifice before being accepted as an initiate into the Mysteries. He will suffer the wrath of the King of the Dead if he betrays me." Finally an impish grin broke the harsh lines grooved into her brow and around her eyes, releasing the trilling laughter I loved to hear. "And if ever I have seen fear on any man's face I saw it on his as he heard the priest's conditions for swearing fealty. If he defaults on any of his initiation oaths he will walk the lost trails of darkness, forever barred from eternal light and life.

"I will return to Samothraké in the spring for the wedding, performed during the second half of the Initiation. Even now Philip and our armies go to meet Bardyllis. He has trained three thousand of my men in the ways of the Thebans. That's more than half his own forces. More will join him because of our alliance. My officers hold choice commands. When Bardyllis is defeated, Philip will defend my rights of succession of the Epirus throne, whether or not I bear him children."

"You must not give him his heir too soon," I hurried to say, fighting bitter disappointment. "Once you have given birth, you will have lost your bargaining power. He will have your dowry and a son. He will no longer need you." *And you will still be prey to the priests*, I added, silently. *Philip and his entire army will be unable to protect you.*

She shrugged. "He has agreed to recognize my status as priestess. I don't have to lie with him if I don't want to. He said having me as wife would be enough. He isn't interested in me anyway. Servants of Antipatros say the king is more interested in boys. He only wants my dowry."

She faced me again, cold. Composed. "The contract is made and sacrifice has been burned and celebrated. I have to go through with it." Her brows knit and her eyes squinted.

"Wallis, why didn't you tell me where you had gone? I needed you."

"I didn't tell you, and I wouldn't let Bendi tell you. I might have failed."

She stomped the floor, but on the thick carpet her foot made no sound. Angrier, she balled her fists and came at me. I shielded my face with my arms, but let the blows fall. "Don't you think I have a mind, a will of my own? How dare you make moves you don't see fit to tell me about! If I had known I would never have agreed to marry. I wouldn't have needed Philip's protection, and Arrybus' threats would have meant nothing to me!"

"I didn't know, Bird. I didn't know if Tibbelouios would help. I almost didn't even get to meet him."

She quieted and slumped to her stool.

"But I did see one of your old friends. He was sent to kill me."

"Friends? Wallis, my friends would never hurt you and my enemies wouldn't dare. I would hunt them to their deaths."

"This was not a friend you would care to see again. He still wears the scar you laid across his brow."

"Harkos."

"Harkos. He is an agent of Phaistos. I don't know how the priest knew, but he sent Harkos to waylay and kill me. Phaistos has powerful allies, Bird. His agents control the coasts and much of the interior of Lakonia. Only with the aid of a goatherd did I escape to the town of Kasya, and to the home of the ship owner.

"It was only after I had healed his daughters of their illness that I could even ask for his support for you. In his gratitude, he granted my petition. His resources are yours to command, if command them you will..." I left the words to weigh the air, intending that they defy erasure. I waited, but the words had been lost before they left my lips.

"It is too late," she said at last, voice hollow, face wooden. "Before the Oxherd of Sitos, the God of One, I have sworn on my word as Chosen. According to the faith, at the moment a woman takes the oath of betrothal, that woman dies. Until I am reborn in the spring, I do not speak with my own voice. I belong to the god. I must do as He wills."

"Bird, this is insane. No one owns you. Only you can grant another control of yourself. Declare it, princess. Be Olympias, Chosen of God, the voice of Demeter." But Bird had laid about herself a shell of detachment that Athena Nike could not have broken. She really believed this. I must find a way to draw her out of this soulless negativity, or she would truly die. Sustained only by the energy of her anger, when that anger waned, or when she learned of Philip's talent for deceit, she would waste away. This woman's passions flooded her over and past the challenges met by other women, yet even she was vulnerable. I had seen her weakness when she faced the sea, searching in vain for her sister.

What draws a woman most? What thread pulls her forward when all other hope falls away?

"Bird. Do you want children?"

Caught off guard, she looked suddenly weak, vulnerable. "I don't know. I didn't think so. All I wanted was to restore my mother's rank and get the old religions to recognize my status as Chosen. Now...I need something, Wallis. I need something to hold onto. Maybe a baby. Maybe a son. Maybe a future king."

"A child, then, but not right away. Hold him in your heart, before you hold him in your arms. Till then, I am your friend, little bird. You can hold on to me."

For a long time she looked at something past my shoulder. Somehow I felt that I was being measured, judged, and found wanting. I should have told her of my mission south. I had lost her forever.

In the voice of a stranger, she said, "Friends are good, Wallis, but I have no choice. I am marrying a king."

Had she screamed, spit, thrown things, I could have reasoned with her. I did not know this remote, detached alien.

᎒᎒᎒

My sense of direction tumbled away like a dried leaf caught in the wind. Of the next two days, I remember nothing. I would not allow myself to think about the reason for my madness—I wished to erase any thought of the woman who had ordered my thinking for the past three years. Unaware of the jellied state of my psyche, an image of the princess had made a path for my footsteps, roused me from sleep at daybreak, tucked covers about me at night. Where was the independent peddler who had strutted through life, glorying in his freedom, friend to all and bound to none? No land. No king. No clan. Pelos—a nobody, as the world understands it, but one arrogantly proud of his autonomy—his only commitment being to gather the world about him, squeezing from his encounters the essence of life. "I honor all people, all cultures, all gods," I once boasted, "but I am chained by none." What a laugh. Without a wink of her bright hazel eyes nor a toss of her bronzed curls, a woman had stripped me of my will. Who could I blame? A slave, I had given myself freely.

First Yiayia had deserted me, dying. Now Bird, marrying. I had been dumped high and dry. No one cared. I began to see myself in a different role. No longer the hawk, my blood had been spilled without mercy, my limbs torn apart, my head discarded to the ants. Captured, ripped to shreds, I wanted only to disappear.

So I ran.

~ ~ ~

Late, long past time for poor peddlers like me to go home to their wives, to their single accommodations in crowded inns, to their tents outside the city, or to roll into blankets beneath tables in the agora to await the break of morning and the return of customers to browse their wares, I sat drinking with my old friend, Leon of Kreté, in his otherwise empty tavern. I crowded, belly against the table, arms surrounding a deep red pool, a bowl of wine, and stared past its surface into mysterious depths.

"Won't you have something to eat?" asked Leon. "You're wasting away. How about a bowl of goat's curd, a piece of cheese, some bread?" He held fresh baked bread somewhere near the end of my nose.

I cared nothing for his entreaty. Mind clouded with the fog that refuses marking of time, I relived years since meeting the princess.

'I have a new name, Leon,' I had said that day after meeting Olympias. *'No longer will I be Pelos Daneion, the Enormous Borrowed named me by my parents.'* I chuckled.

Leon mumbled nonsense. "A message came from Ena," he said. "Her husband is dead, killed by a horse."

'The princess, Olympias, has given me a new name. She calls me Wallis.'

"I thought it was a good match. The son would inherit the lands, the stock, the gold of a rich and powerful man, a chieftain. Now it seems her husband has died, and Ena wants to come home."

"What?" I asked. "More wine."

"You remember; you helped us pack the wagons, to send her north to marry," he said, pouring. "You gave her fabric fit for a queen to be sewn for her wedding *chiton*."

Fit for a queen. I heard the words, but they meant nothing.

'You're coming up in the world, my friend,' Leon had said, and I had grinned, shy, but believing. *'Be careful she doesn't sacrifice you to the gods at spring planting time.'* How we had laughed. How my heart sang. I had been noticed by Olympias, princess of all Epirus. There was not a soul in Athens who had not petitioned the little princess for her blessings on their harvests,

the selling of the harvests, the preparing for the dinner table the fruits of the harvest. "Olympias the Mother of Harvests!" they cried, and she only a girl, a tiny one at that. How warm the memory. To share with friends. To share with Leon.
'I am no different than I ever was, Leon, people are born who they are. That's not a power dispensed by kings and queens.' Yet like a pig placing his neck in the trap for the slaughter, without volition I had placed my soul into the hands of this girl.
"She wants to come home. The messenger said she has a child, a daughter."
Who cared whether I sold fabrics, or broches, or cups? Such a childish waste of time, peddling. A princess had need of me. I saved her life from a band of thieves.
"What can I do? I cannot leave the tavern, and there is no one I trust to send for her. No one but you, old friend."
I found your mother's family, Bird. I brought you a burial urn.
"I will give you Rocky, my donkey, and his cart for you to bring her back. If you will, you can keep them both. A gift from me to you, my old friend."
But I see a picture on the wall of the cave. It looks like a sacrifice. Like a warning revealed only to me. A member of your family is being sacrificed, Bird. That's why the priests of Kreté want you. They want to sacrifice your first born son. You must not marry, Princess. You must not give birth to a son. They will kill him. If not at birth, then later, when he is a man.
"It's a long way, I know, but your grandmother is dead. She will not object to your traveling."
If you marry, little bird, if you have a boy, you and your son will be killed. If it is a girl she will be taken away.
"So will you go and get her for me?"
Meaningless sounds broke through the fog in my mind. "Ena. You want me to go get Ena?" I stared into my bowl. It gleamed pink, mostly water. Leon had served me bowl after bowl of wine diluting it more and more as he talked. The traitor. How could he, a friend, do this to me? I had sought to lose myself in dream. Instead I found myself sober.
"She has no one, Daneion. She lives in the midst of barbarians. People who collect heads and hang them on their walls. What will they do to her, now that she has no husband to protect her?"
"Ena. She is in Tergesté?"
"Yes."

"Her husband is dead?"
"Yes."
"She has a daughter?"
"Yes."
"I wonder if she cries all the time. Like Ena."

Leon burst out laughing, and I laughed with him. When we finished, we both had tears streaming down our faces. We wiped with our sleeves and then laughed some more, Leon, no doubt because I had recovered my sense of humor, and I, relieved somewhat of the burden of tragedy. My Yiayia was dead. My bird was being married, and not to me.

"I won't be needing this bowl of water," I said, face as straight as I could manage. "You can feed it to the pigs. I am thinking of taking a trip up north. Something Yiayia wanted me to do. She wanted me to find an herb, to help my uncle, Davos."

"How far will you have to go to get it?"

"To the River Danube. That's where it grows, where Yiayia was born."

My grandmother, my Uncle Davos and our train had traveled that route once when I was a child, though not all the way to the Danube. I barely remembered it, but things Yiayia told me then still ring in my ears. The resonance in her voice, musical, vital even in those few months before she died at eighty-seven, still rings in my mind.

"Where did our people come from, Yiayia?" I had asked, short legs pounding earth, trying to keep up. I knew the story, but wanted to hear it again.

"Just north, beyond the Danube," she said. "Most of our people followed the rivers south; my father followed them west and found the sea. We built boats and tracked the coast line of the Adriatic until my mother picked a spot. 'Here,' my mother told my father. 'Here we will build our hut. No more will we suffer the ice and snow, and be forced to fight for our lives with every breath. Here beside the sea, in the land of abundance, where vineyards grow and where fish leap from the water into our hands.'" Yiayia laughed. "Mother thought the world existed to please her whims. Even the fish. But it did seem that when she followed father down to the sea, his boat always came back filled." She stopped and placed her hands on my shoulders.

"You must visit those lands some day, to learn from the wise people of our clan."

"How will I find them? How will I know them when I see them?" She sighed. "No need to find them, Tadpole. "They'll find you." But I was not content with such an answer. "How will they know me?" I asked.

The silence drew out, and almost, I gave up listening for an answer, but finally she said, "There are people in our village who have the Knowledge of the Oak. They do not ask questions, and rarely do they give answers, caring little about the comings and goings of ordinary people. But if they decide to notice you, they will know how to find you. Indeed, they will even cause you to come to them."

Leaving, I said over my shoulder to Leon, wiping up spills around my bowl. "I will stop by Tergesté." My hand on the latch moved with certainty, and the room stayed perfectly still. "I will see about our little Ena."

How could I do less for such a friend? Yet even to such as he, I could not reveal the depths of my sorrow. I could not tell him I was losing the only light left in my world.

My little bird had tossed me away—a crumb of bread for her birds, a coin for the gatekeepers.

TWO

PEOPLE OF THE TREES

1

Does anyone ever forget hurtful things? I never do. On that day when Palo and I with our two carts and donkeys left Athens and headed for the far north, I sought to put distance between myself and a wound too sore to examine, too raw to heal.

Approaching the market in Larissa, I scanned the cobblestone square. In bemused industry I set up my wares beside the fountain, beneath the very chestnut where the old beggar swathed in filthy folds of hempen rags once babbled wild-eyed-nonsense at me. As though still a child visiting the market with Yiayia, I heard again his broken whisper as hooked fingers clutched at my clothes, drawing me near his face, withering me with sour breath.

"He comes. The Son of Thunder."

"Who is the Son of Thunder, Yiayia?" I asked, each time, with every visit to the market. My grandmother always said, "Poor man. He is ill. He forgets who he is. The walls between his worlds have crumbled."

The air of the marketplace bloomed with an elusive wave of energy, charging my limbs. Streams of unrelated events, scents and sounds flooded my senses. I rubbed my arms, feeling myself one with the beggar who had babbled of people, times, events that no one except he could see or know, pleading with intense whispers to people who cared not to listen. Just as suddenly, the stream of energy passed. I jerked up the stack of woolens I had just laid out to view.

"Let's go, Palo."

Without selling even a string of beads, we left the land of the Aleuadai. We passed farmers slaughtering pigs, sheep and chickens, taking advantage of the cold weather to keep the meat from spoiling. Stone fences surrounded fields crowded with herds of brawly goats tied near their watering troughs—goats brought down from the mountains for the winter, their breeding season, to keep them from mating with their mountain cousins and reverting to the wild. Hot clouds of breeding scent merged with smoke from charcoal braziers in lodges built for curing. I breathed deeply, savoring the scent of home. Did they cure meat like this in the far north?

We continued across the Laetheus, the river that cut a pass through the high Pindus and west toward the Adriatic. That pass led east to Phoeniké by the sea, where every man stood tall, strong, browned black by the sun and sea air, and where every woman's countenance sang with spirit, with courage, with fire. Phoeniké, the old home place of Yiayia and my uncle, Davos. I needed to see Davos, to tell him about Yiayia's death. On my return from the north, I would journey south to the cities of the Adriatic and into Ambrakia where he now lived with his daughter. When I saw him I planned to give him the herb as Yiayia had instructed.

On a visit the summer before, when I had gone to get Yiayia and take her to Ana's home, Davos had met me at his door, pale and weak, a bit of drool from breakfast tracing a path down his chin.

"A seizure?" I asked, touching his shoulder. He brought a hand up and laid it on mine, love flooding his eyes.

"A small one, Daneion. Nothing for you to be concerned about."

"I have searched for a cure, Davos. I have found no one who knows what causes your seizures. Most just say it is punishment by the gods, but I know better. You have wronged no one to deserve punishment."

A brief, wan smile broke the insensate calm of his lips. "Now how would you know if I have sinned? You come to see me so seldom, I could have blasphemed every god on Olympos and you would not know."

I laughed. Though but a shadow of himself, for a moment he stood tall and proud, the same man who, on our trips to the Bosporus visiting the City of Beggars, had walked as though he wore wings on his heels. He had taught me the power of a smile, and I had listened into the morning hours as he told tale after tale of his youth and exploitations. It seemed he had bedded every pretty girl from the river Danube to Kreté, and each had cried to see him go.

Along the journeys, he and Yiayia huddled, arguing about this or that herb and this or that illness. Yiayia had never found a cure for Davos and his daughter's seizures. 'It is passed from parents to children, parents to children,' both agreed, but what was 'passed' neither of them knew. I watched as each new child was born of Davos' beloved wife to see if it would also be afflicted.

"Why don't we have seizures, Yiayia? You and my sister and I?" but when I asked, she would just turn aside her head as though seeking an answer and finding none.

"It could show up again, any time," she finally would say. "Perhaps your children, or children's children. I just don't know. I keep looking for answers, but the voices are quiet."

"Voices, Yiayia?"

She touched her eyes, her ears. "The voices that you do not hear, Tadpole, for they sound only in my head."

"Why can't I hear them?" I would ask, over and over again, feeling excluded from a magical portion of life, but Yiayia always smiled and got a faraway look in her eyes. "It is not a blessing, little son of my son. Sometimes the visions come with headaches." Then she would look deeply into my eyes as though searching my soul. "You have the gift of healing, Daneion. Be grateful that you are well and strong. Much of the pain you will suffer will not belong to you, but to those you serve. You can do much good in this world of sadness."

"I will, Yiayia. I promise," and she would pat my shoulder, ending our talk.

Yes, I would take the herb to Davos, if only to complete my grandmother's need. *If* I found it, and *if* I returned from far jungles and swamps inhabited by nomads and savages likely to loose arrows at any stranger passing through. Palo and I could lie bleeding, helpless in some unnamed swamp, flies festering our wounds, easy prey for wild animals and buzzards, and no one would ever know. I sighed. If only living were as easy as dying.

೨೨೨

We entered the Pass of Tempé, the gap between Mount Ossa and the sacred mountain of Olympos that would admit us into the lands of Pieria. The River Pinios lay like a sunning snake curling the sacred mountain. In the near distance the mountain seemed suspended in the sky, a trick of the layered mists. Though I am not a superstitious man, I gazed in awe as shiver bumps raised the hair on my arms. Palo, quiet, practical Palo, gazed as raptly as I. Pretending lack of interest, I gestured him onward thinking it unwise to dwell on the secrets of priests. Together we moved into the stream of traffic traveling north toward the land of lakes.

On the sixth day of journey we entered the village of Monostir. As usual I set up my cart in the market place to show my merchandise, expecting little this windy, cold day, but we could exchange news with the local folk and replace our used supplies. Few good roots, vegetables and cured meat lay on the vendors' carts and market shelves.

"Soldiers bought it all," said a man, peering through a tangle of grey hair. A wispy beard brushed his skinny chest and clung to the girdle of his ragged and patched shirt. Crook clutched under an arm, he fingered my woolens and browsed through my cheeses. A goat herder, no doubt, from his scent, probably out of the nearby hills.

"Soldiers?" I asked, replacing and restacking the woolens. "In this weather? Who is foolish enough to put troops on the road this time of the year?" Foolish indeed, I might have asked. Was I not also on the road?

"Philip of Makedoné," he replied. "War. They're probably forming up now. Up on the plains south of Lake Prespa. I came to Monostir for supplies. I'm going on to watch the show."

Another man, reedy of stature, shorter than the first, and younger, darted a look at me and peered into my cart. "Philip sent me for grain for the horses. They'll be needing plenty before this day is done."

"The armies are large?" I asked.

"Philip has conscripted every man who can carry a spear or shoot an arrow or ride a horse. Anywhere from the Kambunian mountains in the south to the high Haemus in the north. And Bardyllis got everyone north of that. Soldiers are crowding that field like crows on a dead cow. Philip says he will beat Bardyllis so bad he'll never think of raiding his territory again. He says he'll set boundaries to last a thousand years."

"You like Philip?" I asked, thinking perhaps I had misjudged the man, that perhaps Olympias' fate was not such a bad one.

"He's a real warrior. I think I'll have some of your dried figs, there," he said, offering in exchange my choice of sisal rope or an undercured bag made from a goat's belly. I took the rope. "Philip learned to fight under Epaminondas when he was sent as a hostage to Thebes," he said between bites. "Just a beardless lad. Epaminondas was the greatest general who ever lived. Philip has only about half the men of Bardyllis' army, but my money's on him. Not that anyone agrees with me. They say Bardyllis has been fighting all his life, better than ninety odd years. Philip is still a boy." He finished the figs and sucked his fingers.

"Do Bardyllis good to get beat for a change. They've been raiding those fertile plains of Emathia any time they took a notion for too long to count, but they let the lowlanders own it so they'll work the land. That way Philip's the one to pay taxes to Athens, not Bardyllis. It's not right, you know. The Makedoné have the Illyri on the north, raiding their farmlands, and Athenian taxpayers waiting at the Pydna docks with their hands out every time they try to ship their lumber—to Athens, no less, so Athens can build ships. His people feel like Philip was sent from the gods just to make things right. His men love him. They'd give up wife and children, hearth and home to serve that man."

"You know him well, then," I said.

"I've seen him," he agreed, "and I've heard talk about him. His servant is the one who sent me for grain. Philip makes his men feel like he's one of them, you know. Drinks and brawls with them in the street just like a spear soldier." He shook his head from side to side, grinning, looking as though he'd like to say more, but had just run out of superlatives.

"Me and my friend Orvon are headed back that way. We just came into town for supplies. You're welcome to join us if you want."

"I'm going that way," I said, and covered my load with a double canvas, for it looked like rain.

We made a formidable caravan on our way north—Orvon, the goat herder, Gisesi and his cart loaded and heavy with grain, Palo, Spitter, Rocky, and I. Orvon, the crusty goatherd said little, but round, bright black eyes hinted of secrets I longed to share.

"Who do you favor?" I asked, pressing, when he did not answer.

He nodded. "Philip will win."

"He's the better general?"

"He's no general at all. Never was. Parmenion will do his work for him."

"Parmenion?"

He sighed and turned away. We walked for a while, and I had almost forgotten my question when he spoke again, but he still didn't answer my question.

"Philip's mother's army is fighting alongside Bardyllis. She switches sides like an old woman turning her backside to the fire. I used to work for the family. I watched her, Eurydice, and her lover Ptolemaios, before Amyntas, Philip's father, died. I heard stories..."

"Stories?" I urged, fearing that the old man had lost track of his thoughts. I needn't have worried. He had just been gathering breath.

"Old Amyntas, late seventies, died in his sleep, they say, but I have my doubts about that. He left the throne to their son, Alexandros the second, but Eurydice's lover, Ptolemaios, had Alexandros killed. Caught him unguarded at a folk-dancing exhibition. Ptolemaios would have taken the throne as regent for Eurydice, but the other sons of Amyntas stood in his way to power. Perdikkas, the second son, was still a boy, so Eurydice backed Ptolemaios as the boy's regent, and that gave them the power of the throne." He cleared his throat and spat. I handed him my goatskin containing a vinegar drink.

"Phew! What is that stuff?" He asked, gagging.

"Something to clear your throat. Armies take it along with them when they march. Refreshes them and gives them strength."

"Yes? Maybe, if it doesn't kill them first. Then when Philip started growing a beard, Eurydice feared that Ptolemy would kill him too, so she sent him to relatives in Lynkestia, but Ptolemaios found out where she sent him, and had him kidnapped. He knew he couldn't kill him; Eurydice wouldn't have stood it, so he took him to Thebes. He wanted to win favor from the general, Epaminondas. Philip was a pretty boy, and Epaminondas was a big hero then. He and his sacred band had just taken Leuctra." He paused, thinking.

I think Eurydice was scared of Ptolemaios, and she really loved Philip. You could tell by the way she grinned at him and rumpled his curly, black hair." Orvon fell silent, lost in the past.

"So what happened then?" I coaxed, and the goat herder stirred, shifted the pack on his back, took a deep breath and continued.

"Well Perdikkas, the older boy, was pretty smart himself. He saw what had happened to Alexandros and then to Philip, so he kept quiet and stayed out of their way. He liked studying. He and his teacher, Euphraos, used to hide themselves away for most of the day reading and talking. I can't tell the times I passed by the gardens when I came in from the fields for dinner at night. They'd be there together with their heads bent over scrolls till it was too late to see, and they'd have to hold a lamp for each other to read. Euphraos stayed with Perdikkas until...until Perdikkas died.

"Euphraos was a friend of Plato, you know, and old Amyntas liked to consider himself cultured, so when Plato asked him to hire Euphraos, he did." Orvon hushed, and like a cloud moving across the sun, I could sense the old man's mind moving inward. Adjusting to his pattern of thought, I waited till he spoke again.

"Euphraos kept Perdikkas safe until he came of age. Otherwise Ptolemaios would have had him killed, too. Euphraos wouldn't even let others eat in the same room with Perdikkas unless they knew how to practice the arts of geometry or philosophy. That kept any assassins at their distance." Orvon chuckled. "I don't know many killers who study geometry nor philosophy, do you? As a matter of fact, it was Euphraos who advised Perdikkas to set Philip up as governor of his own district and to give him men to train. That was after Perdikkas came of age, of course, and brought Philip back from Thebes.

"No. Philip's no general, but he knows how to work people to get what he wants. He has the Thrakians and Amphipolitans eating out of his hand. The Athenians are so confounded by his turnabouts they don't know whether to shit or swat flies."

"I understand Amyntas left two brothers who were claiming their rights to succession. Wouldn't they go to war against him?"

Gisesi, the grain merchant, heard my question and moved up beside us. "Not too long ago," he said, "Philip's cousin, Pausanius, convinced King Kotys of Thraké that he had legal claim to the throne, and the king agreed to finance him. Then that wily bastard Philip went to see Kotys and bribed him with a promise of timber to build his ships. So what happens? King Kotys up and kills Pausanius and gives his backing to Philip." Gisesi roared with laughter and slapped his thigh with his hand. "That was all a lie, you know. Philip can't give what Philip doesn't own. Philip has a saying: 'Deceive boys at knuckle ball; deceive men with promises.'

"Perdikkas took Philip's men with him to fight against Agis' Paonians. Philip wasn't along, he stayed home as Perdikkas' regent while they were gone. Philip had taught those men how to fight like the Sacred Band of Epaminondas fought, and yet they lost that war, and Philip lost all his men."

Again Orvon stared at nothing, eyes squinting, mouth and jaw line tight.

"What?" I asked, unable to restrain my curiosity. "What?" again I asked. Orvon sighed.

"It's over now, and what's done is done. In a way, I can see Philip's side. When the Basileos, Perdikkas, got hurt, he ran—left his men without a leader. Left them to die. When Philip didn't hear anything, he sent his servant, Kornios, to see what had happened. Kornios found Perdikkas on the trail, hurt. Euphraos was there with him, tending his wounds. When Philip heard about it, he and Parmenion went to see. Perdikkas begged his old teacher, Euphraos, to kill him. He had lost an arm and an eye. His face was cut up really bad. Euphraos wouldn't do it. He loved him, so Philip told Parmenion to put his sword through his brother's heart, and he did.

Then Euphraos got scared and ran. Philip told Parmenion to catch him, he knew too much, so Parmenion chased him on his horse and sliced his head from his shoulders as the old philosopher ran. Philip didn't grieve. He acted like it didn't matter to him at all. I don't understand how a man could have his brother killed and not care."

He hushed, and so did I, for a long time, thinking. "But how do you know of this? Wouldn't Philip have had you killed too?"

"He didn't know I was there. Royals don't notice goatherds. He passed by me on the trail going to where Perdikkas was stopped. I left my herd and followed, curious. Then I hid in the trees." He would have continued, but we broke through the hills onto a plateau overlooking the plains surrounding two large lakes.

We looked out onto death.

꧁꧁꧁

In a silence broken only by screams of wounded too stubborn to die, a few foot soldiers stumbled about the field, staggering in weariness and the sickness brought on by the sight and smell of blood. Horses with riders holding white flags on sticks made lines from both camps to begin the work of clean up. Philip's carts and horses waited on the slopes nearest us, and Bardyllis and his army waited beyond the plain. At a given signal, beneath white banners snapping in a brisk wind, each group entered the valley to reclaim their wounded and dead. The numbers seemed about equal.

"They'll need me below," I said to Palo. "Wait for me at the surgeon's tent."

"They don't have one," said Palo.

I looked. It was true. Bodies lay among the trees along the creek, on blankets, for the most part, but some on bare ground. A few men moved among them, doing nothing.

I sighed. "Then go, Palo, take Rocky and the cart to help load the wounded and dead. I'll get the tents set up."

Emptying all my trade goods from Rocky's cart onto Spitter's, and checking to see that my ointments and herbs, knives and bandages were where I could reach them, I headed down the hill toward the stream. Palo led Rocky out across the field and fell in with a long line of carts. I glanced backward toward the young king where he and his generals stood outlined against the sky at the top of the hill. Intrigued by their rigid interest, I stopped my progression, covered my eyes from the sun and tried to see what they saw.

Watching the solemn progress of the cleanup crews, Philip's carts moved slowly, ponderously. Not right. Not right at all. The carts were empty, were they not? So they could pick up survivors now, and get their dead later? They should be moving quickly, bumping, bouncing. Intrigued, I moved to the top of a knoll for a better view as all the wagons, both armies, jumbled together like vendors at a harvest festival.

Suddenly, blankets flipped back in the Makedoné wagons, and armed men jumped out.

I watched men swarm around Palo, erupting from carts all around him. The man beside Palo, an Illyrian, bending forward to help a wounded comrade stand, glanced up, too late. One of Philip's men stood above him, ax raised. Leaving Rocky and his cart, Palo fled. Philip's man struck the Illyrian's head from his body. It plopped to earth beside the wounded man. Then the soldier again raised the ax and split the wounded man's head into two pieces, splattering a wet, grey mass across the grass. That bloody scene was happening all over the field. An unholy slaughter.

"No-o-o!" I whispered, gurgled, and found my voice. "NO!" I bellowed so loud it was certain to be heard back in Monostir. But, drowned in a roar of cheers that rose from the group surrounding Philip, my voice shrank to a croaked mutter. It seemed their cheers echoed from the hills and out, across the plains. Wrong. Wrong. A sacred law, the law of the white flag had been broken. Shredded. Dishonored.

Sick with loathing, I watched bodies being piled onto our cart. Then Rocky fell into line with the other carts heading back to camp.

The carnage and the resulting roar continued until only a few Illyrian soldiers remained standing, and then Philip and his men took off riding their horses, slinging their swords, cutting down any Illyrian left on his feet, but they didn't stop then. They rode off chasing anyone who had fled. They didn't come back until next day, and then when they returned, you couldn't see who they were for the blood. They fell, sprawled out on the wet ground, and slept.

When the wagons had returned with the wounded, I couldn't find Palo. I saw him later, hammering stakes for tent ties alongside me, there, down by the creek.

The storytellers say there was fighting. They say there was killing. They say the new king, Philip II of Makedonia, was a genius of strategy. They like to tell stories of how his *hoplites* and *pesotarie* formed a wedge bristling with twelve-foot pikes, how they met a massive and solid square of Illyrian soldiers, and how, when the swords rang out, loud enough to deafen the users, the square was pulled to the right of Philip's foot soldiers, breaking, loosening the square formation. They recount with glory how then, the handsome young king, mounted on a horse of unrivaled beauty, led his mounted soldiers in a charge that, like a scorpion's tail, whipped to the left and pierced the side of the weakened giant. The once solid mass of men, now thinned in the center of their square, disintegrated as men slipped, slid, stumbled forward to replace their fallen compatriots.

The remembrancers say he took with him to that battle on the plains south of Lake Ochrid, which some call Lake Prespa, six hundred men on horses and ten thousand afoot. They say when the storm passed, Philip and his army had killed seven thousand Illyrians. I can't count that high in my head; I count by tens and sometimes twenties, giving change for coin, and I've never seen seven thousand drachmai in my entire life. But I counted the fallen that day, one by one, as I laid my hand on their hearts or felt for a pulse in their throats.

And I can add to the storytellers' tale the end of that honorless day. I can say that when the fighting slowed and each army carried the banner of truce to collect their dead and dying, this brilliant strategist, this fearlessly brave leader of courageous men, had his soldiers hide in wagons intended for the dead, erupt onto the Illyrian soldiers sent to collect their own, and slay them—annihilating them all, they say, even to the last breath of the last man. But that was not entirely true, for I tended a few who spoke pure Illyri, and I, not caring the origin of a wounded man, patched them all.

I have never had an artist's knack of painting events, but I remember the plain, where on the northern horizon, the water of Lake Prespa met sky in a single, unbroken line, and where, to my right, trembling hills huddled, watching. And I remember the color red. I remember. Heaps of red, some small, some large, once living, breathing men, now lay scattered across that red-soaked plain. Lines, x-marks, circles of red painted the field where dying men dragged themselves everywhere, anywhere to reach another hand, another face, another foot to hold onto. To this day I will not carry nor sell a cloth of scarlet.

I remember the smell of one man's fear stirred with the thickening, sickening scent of blood, multiplied by thousands as bodies were collected into one huge camp site. And I remember the scent of vomit. Puking my guts out time and again, I labored to clean faces well enough to tell whether this be Illyri or Makedonè. They all looked the same to me. Brothers, now bereft of creed, empty of loyalties, cleansed of anger. Only a look of startlement remained on their faces, faces frozen in surprise with their final dying thoughts.

Together Palo and I dragged the unwalking wounded to blankets beneath the tents and led those others, offering our shoulders to some who could not have stood without us. The surgeon who had come with Philip, grateful for the additional hands, opened his wagons to me for wine, then at my direction, set his helpers to work beating rushes found along the stream bed, making them ready to soak the blood from around wounds, to prepare them for my knife.

My herbs and ointments quickly disappeared. I sent Palo back to the village for more, pouring coins into his hand from my own bags. I cut away arms and legs smeared with their own excretion and already humming with flies laying eggs and hatching. Again and again I splashed wine into open belly wounds, till all the wine was gone, then, for the more terrible wounds, poured in my precious vinegar drink. I tucked in gut, squeezed the bellies shut, and fastened ripped skin back in place with the needles of sea urchins I had brought from the far south, the lands of Tibbelouios. Hardly hearing, I muttered a constant stream—half prayer to whatever gods might be listening, half curse for the insanity in men who could bring such things to pass—as I pulled teeth hanging loose between swollen and cut, purple lips, and put patches on eyes that would never again see the light of day.

Broken limbs—thank heaven there were some with clean, unshattered breaks—I pulled to set. I dashed salt brine into open wounds and wrapped them with pounded leaves of comfrey growing wild through the valley and brought to me in armloads by Palo and the other surgeon's helpers. I smeared sticky resin coaxed from nearby pines to seal freely bleeding wounds, and with quick-drying clay, wrapped broken legs, broken arms, and feet crushed by the hooves of horses and runaway carts. The others I cut away, hacking at bone, deafened with screams. Palo came behind me, passing out dippers of opium tea to deaden pain, pouring spoonfuls down throats barely aware enough to swallow. How could I have noticed anything but broken bodies, yet now, snatches of memory crowd in on me, bits and pieces of things.

That week saw little of the sun, heavy clouds black with rain crowding the sky and sometimes dumping their loads atop the heads of those outside the tents. I saw some such men—boys, really, for they still wore the string tied around their middles, the badge proclaiming innocence until they had killed their first wild boar. I saw them dipping grain for the horses from Gisesi's cart parked not far from mine. I thought of yelling, to tell them to cover the grain, but the dead and dying claimed my attention.

I remember one night Palo promised to stay awake and call me if I was needed. Too dizzy with fatigue to see my own hand, I laid my head on a layer of rushes and let my eyelids fall. Someone called my name and I forced my thoughts upward against a dead weight of sleep. There, bending over the man near Palo I saw a woman—a young, vibrant woman, red hair caught in curls on her neck. Startled, I looked closer. She looked like my grandmother, as she might have appeared in her earlier days, the days before my sister married and my mother and I went away to live with her. Yiayia! The woman stood holding her hand above the heart of the wounded man, raised her eyes to me, smiled, and faded away. I felt a flow of energy; tears came to my eyes and I stood, refreshed and ready to continue.

The days, stretching into eight before the camp cleared, did not end with sunset but continued into dawn. Those who could walk followed their comrades home. Those who could not, rode out on wagons or sleds pulled behind war horses.

Most of the camp had cleared, when, over the groans of the few wounded who remained, I heard angry yells, and looked up to see who could profane this tragic and somehow sacred ground with further violence.

"This grain is not fit for plow horses! Where is that vendor?" I looked up to see Philip, smeared and dirty, black hair caked with mud into a matted mass of tangles, eyes glazed and ringed with black for lack of sleep, yet still the most terrible, most formidable man I had ever seen. "Find that grain seller. I will whip him until he begs for death!"

"What's wrong, Philip?" asked one of his companions.

"Look. It's wet. Sour. Sour grain will kill a horse as quick as a sword!" He held up a hand full of grain and tossed it into the wind. It fell in a sodden thud a few feet away from me. I shrank, tried to become even smaller than I was, dreading the notice of those awful eyes.

I slipped on mud, fell behind my cart and squatted, peeking over the edge. It was then that I saw Gisesi, the grain seller, hiding under the canvas on my cart. I felt as though a cold blade had been placed against my spine. What would this terrible man do if the grain seller were found here? But he wasn't, and some other crisis demanded Philip's attention. I went to the creek to bathe, again, for I bathed constantly throughout the days of tending the filthy wounded, and when done, I drew Palo with me to hook Spitter and Rocky to their carts in preparation of moving out. We retraced our pathway south toward the Eordacus River to thread our way through mountains called by their people, The Accursed. More than these mountains had become accursed, to me. I wished with all my heart that I had not followed the trail north toward the battlefield. I wanted nothing so much as to get away from that field of doom.

In my later days, I remember that battle, though I would give half a life time to forget. And I would wish to forget the pain that, even now lances my heart at the thought. In the spring, my princess, my little bird, my Olympias would be married to this man. A man who could kill a brother—a brother who had done nothing but good for him—without caring. I wiped something warm and moist from my cheek, perhaps a drop of the drizzling rain. I felt so mortally helpless. I could do nothing to stop her. Nothing.

卐卐卐

Walking on wooden legs and clay feet, I yearned to crawl into my wagon and sleep, leaving the task of following the path to Spitter and Palo, but Gisesi, the grain peddler, was there. A short way farther down the road, Gisesi slipped out from under the canvas and disappeared into the dead, sodden gray grasses. I don't think he ever knew I had seen him.

A few minutes later three horsemen approached on a dead run from our rear. Heart thundering, I glanced at the hole in the grass where Gisesi had disappeared. Nothing. Someone could have seen the grain seller hide in my wagon and told Philip. They would be searching for him, and they would think nothing of threatening me to find him. Trapped, nowhere to hide, on foot, with two loaded wagons and unable to outrun war horses, I called to Palo to stop. A tall, straight-backed man called down to me. I recognized Parmenion, the man who had slain Perdikkas, Philip's brother. I waited, expecting my own head to fall.

"Philip wants you to come back," he said.

For a moment I froze, unable to speak. Philip had seen me. I had wanted nothing more than to become a shadow, fading to nothing in the late day drizzle. It would have been as hard for me to retrace that road as it would have been for an ox to fly.

"The basileos wants to thank you for your help."

That was all? Philip would thank me? I let go the breath I had been holding, and answered. "I have been delayed too long on my journey."

"He said you might say that. He sends you a gift for your service. He said if you wish a position in his army as chief surgeon, you will be well paid."

I recovered my voice, and without looking into the pouch he tossed me, said, "Please tell the king that I thank him for his generosity." I dared not refuse his offer, but neither could I accept. My only hope was to stay as far as I could from Philip the Second of Makedonia.

"Perhaps," I said, "when my business is completed." With added incentive for climbing the precipitous peaks ahead of us, I waved Palo on. Perhaps we could lose ourselves in the mountains before the cold-eyed general could reconsider.

2

We followed the river through dark shadows of peaks too high for human feet, and for most goats. In the cart behind Spitter, I floated through waves of troubled sleep, voices fading in and out. Palo refused to rest, but walked beside our carts, listening to conversations between fellow travelers. The travelers spoke of their army's shattering defeat, about Philip's cowardly deception. Their voices held fear, yet a kind of awed respect. Some even laughed, saying it was about time the son of Eurydice showed his mettle. Prostitutes, cooks, saddle and weapons menders, animal tenders, grain sellers and food vendors walked beside wives and children leading wagons of fallen heroes—an army of walking dead.

Palo climbed aboard one wagon and adjusted a body so that the man's arm and hand drooped over the side. A boy, about twelve years old, walked alongside, clasping the hand, carting his father homeward for burial in family grounds.

The next day we descended. Leaving the others behind, Palo and I traveled wide expanses between the sea and mountains, threading through bogs on roads firmed with rocks hauled down from the heights. Palo and I chose to walk; the ride would have jolted our teeth loose from our gums. Moving farther and farther inland to avoid the bogs, we lost sight, sound and scent of the sea. The stench of rotting vegetation and exposed human excrement replaced salt air. Occasionally, startlingly, a wave of scent from late-blooming flowers lightened our growing despondency, but I never saw them.

Two days before we reached Tergesté, Spitter veered toward the fishery docks. No amount of pulling and persuading could turn her back to the sorry roads–her destination, a flat boat docked at the landing where carts like ours descended the gang plank. Palo jumped aboard the boat and haggled with the captain for passage. I chuckled and swatted Spitter on the neck. "How did you know about this?" I asked.

I could swear she smiled, for her lips pulled back from her teeth when she boarded that boat, empty except for us. We traveled north in a winter season. That night passed quickly, for despite the continuing bump and jolt of docking at small islands and clusters of floating villages along the way, we slept.

When the ferry's route ended, we debarked onto walkways threading through flatboats. Linked together like a drunken spider's web, they formed an almost solid construction, giving way only to clearings for docking small boats and rafts hung with single, tattered sails and rolls of fishnet.

Above the usual scents of fish, octopus, squid and crustaceans, I sometimes caught aromatic waves of hot bread that made my mouth water and my stomach growl with hunger. We gathered our gear and left, brushing past drivers loading their carts and wagons onto the flatboat for the trip south. A few fishermen dropped lines over the edges of docks, but most of the villagers were women hurrying to finish their chores. Eyes of the curious followed as we passed by, but none offered aid to misfortunates caught in their midst without lodgings. We found a flat boat fitted out for market, bought supplies to replenish my dwindled stores, and bargained for strings of herbs drying beneath an overhanging shelter.

Once past the deceptive permanence of the floating village and onto a trail littered with slimed rocks, donkey patties, and mud holes disguised by ice, I began searching for a telltale dip between the peaks that would reveal a pass.

Moist, warm air from the sea collided with wintry winds descending from rocky peaks. In a few heartbeats it drenched our clothes, filled my beard, and saturated Palo's and the donkeys' hair with ice crystals. Palo still had not donned his boots, preferring to walk barefoot. I could only imagine that his stamina came from a childhood spent in unsheltered wood. How he must have suffered in those days, yet he never mentioned it. My only hint that he appreciated the comforts I was able to provide was the glow in his face when I handed him new shirts, new cloaks, new sandals and hats, or when we sat down to eat in a tavern. I sighed. I had taken so much for granted in my youth. I had been loved.

A trail cut uphill toward a deep gash through high walls of rock. Near the pass, a family of fishermen saw us coming and gestured us nearer, holding out sticks with fish still dripping juices into the flames. As we selected our supper, the mother squatted before us and held out her hands. Glad enough for the food, I found dried figs in the cart and dropped them into her hands. She bobbed her head in thanks and returned to her husband and sons holding the figs out to them. One younger man, possibly her son, winced when the figs touched his hand. I went to see what his problem was, and I saw a partially-broken fish hook caught deep in his palm. Angry red and swollen welts swept up his inner arm, and at my touch he jerked away.

"Medicine," I said, and pointed to the bag hanging from a tie around my neck. He must have understood, for he relaxed and let me examine it. I lifted a jar of wine from the cart and found my knives, expecting to have to clean them before I used them. They were shiny bright and sharp. I glanced toward Palo. He nodded. How had I ever managed without him? This boy, well short of puberty, carried the load of a full grown man. Luckily, along the road I had gathered gum from flower buds of the opium poppy, replacing that used at the lakes. I hung a kettle of water on a stick over the fire to heat, and made the man a cup of tea. When I saw his lids grow heavy, I made him a pillow with his cloak and helped him lie down, then dropped chunks of comfrey root into the remaining water for later use.

I drenched the area with wine, and with my smallest knife, slit the flesh near the hook. With pincers, I gently worked the hook back and forth till it pulled loose. Again I spilled wine onto the wound then probed to release pent up inflammation. The flow stank with putrefaction. I drenched it again and again with the wine, gently pressing till only good red blood ran free.

Satisfied, I smeared his wound with the mucusy water from the comfrey root, wrapped his arm with the last of my linen cloths and rested, leaning back against the wheel of Rocky's cart. Finally I turned to my supper. The fish had cooled but, ah, what wonderful flavor. Still, I regretted the lack of good, hot bread such as I had smelled on entering the floating village.

We bedded that night beneath an overhanging rock somewhat higher than the trail, and then next morning we ate fish left from the night before. The men had already taken their fishing boats out into the marshy waters. Again I paid the woman, but when we loaded our camping gear and started up the trail, she jumped on the seat of my cart.

"You can't go with us," I said. It will be many days before we come back this way." I gestured her off the wagon, but she held on tighter and waved us to go. Go! What could I do? I went.

Then, half way up the trail where the path narrowed to a spot hardly wide enough to get the wagons through, the woman jumped off the wagon and walked ahead of us. There, from a place hidden among the rocks, men, women, and boys hardly old enough to hold a club advanced on us. Betrayed. I thought to turn and run. I had room neither to turn the wagon nor back it.

Then the woman did a wonderful thing. She called out to the robbers. They lowered their clubs, pulled back and vanished behind the rocks. The woman gestured us onward, and then turned toward the downward trail. I caught her by the arm. She waited to see what I wanted. I reached into my cart for more figs, but she waved it away, bobbed her head, and left.

When I think about that woman, I can still see her leaving, swaying from one deeply-bowed leg to the other, throwing her arms forward to help her scoot along. A breath later, a bend in the trail, and she was gone.

The thieves followed us, coming no nearer than calling distance. Palo and I stopped in the wide place on the path through the mountain, and the followers stopped as well. They loosed a bag of dried donkey chips, and struck sparks from their tinder box for a fire.

One, a wizened old man whose knees projected from his leg bones like dried sticks rescued from the waters, and in whose beard I would certainly have found vermin, gestured us nearer. Chilled, unable to find fire stuff, we went.

Uncertain about whether or not to trust them, I unwrapped a hard cheese and offered it. In return they gave me herb-spiced water and preserved turnips. Somewhat easier, Palo and I spread our wares so the family could see, and we traded. They wanted powders of many colors used to make paint for pottery and beads, and I chose their rolls of split lambskin so soft I fondled it, squeezing it between my fingers. It would make fine shirts for Palo and me in this frigid journey north.

One woman, hardly into the age of puberty sat staring at Palo and me. Thinking it mainly Palo at whom she stared, I simply smiled and raised my bowl of vinegar tea, silently asking if she would like some.

"What are you drinking?" she asked in perfect Athenè.
"A vinegar brew I make from herbs," I said. "It keeps me strong for all the walking I must do. Would you like some?"
She held out her bowl. "Just a little," she said. I poured half a bowl for her from my goatskin.
She tasted it, wrinkled her face, and then tasted again. When all the tea was gone she held out her bowl for more. I smiled and poured it full.
"You have bought an oracle," she said. "May I see your hands?"
She reached for them then drew back, sharply. "You have seen much blood. Yet you are not a warrior. A surgeon?"
I nodded, yes.
"You are a man of much destiny, Daneion." She said my name without asking, without my telling, and with no sign of the fear I sometimes saw in the eyes of women when they said another's name. I waited.
"You are running away from that destiny. You must return. The fates of thousands depend on you." Flood gates to the core of my being burst. I wanted to spill my entire life to this girl.
"There is no need to tell me. I know your anguish," she said. An honest oracle. How else could this child know me so well?
"One thing more I must tell you, before we part. There will be a child, a boy." She drooped her head forward from a neck so thin I marveled at its strength in holding erect so long. When she raised to look at me, her eyes brimmed with tears. "So many destroyed by this boy child. Yet so many made free of life's entanglement by him. He is a son of Zeus. You will be one of his teachers. You will teach him compassion; you will help him in times of need, and he will need you as long as he lives. He will die while still a young man. He is the son of your friend. She and her son are your destiny." She released my hands, rose from her squatted position on the ground and went back to her family. I watched her go, and, full of questions, I longed to follow. When my eyes finally focused they found Palo, staring at me with new respect. To my chagrin, he knelt before me and kissed my feet.
"Palo." I said. "Get up from there. Never do that again." I sounded much gruffer than I had intended, voice hoarse with emotion the nomad girl had raised. Palo scrambled to rise and turned away, embarrassed.
"Son," I said, for suddenly he seemed such to me. "I am not angry with you." I rose and touched his shoulder. He turned, dropped to his knees and clutched my legs, weeping. I stroked his hair, and looked across at the nomads. The girl had seen. She smiled, nodded her head,

and turned away to eat her supper.

Afterwards we lay by the fire of our new friends, listened to their stories and songs, and then went to sleep against a background of quiet murmurs carried away on the sighing of night winds.

༄༄༄

Morning found us with a thin coating of snow on our blankets, in our hair, and in my beard. The nomad camp had broken during the night, but I could still smell the dying smoke of their fires. Hanging from a stick above dark coals, we found a kettle of cooling tea. Palo and I drank, not bothering to break out cheese and sausages to go with our hardened crusts of bread. We would stop early, after the sun rose, to eat a proper meal. I held the bucket for Spitter and Rocky to eat, and Palo led them to water, bubbling through a crack in the rocks. We drank, dashed water onto our faces, loaded our packs, and moved out, leaving the kettle just as we had found it. Nomads, being nomads, would come that way again.

Like a specter reluctant to give way to the presence of day, the imaged face of the girl hung in my mind. Nose pinched with cold, dark eyes wide and round, black hair falling in limp waves about her shoulders, it seemed I could still hear her speak. Yet last night, had she really said: "Your grandmother is a holy woman. She guides your steps and guards your dreams. No harm can befall you as she rides your shoulder. And yes, she was really there with you in the surgeon's tent. Be at peace. You have your greatest wish—that you may hear the voices, touch with your own healing power. Go, and rest from your pain, but do not deny your destiny."

The air of morning was too sharply fresh with the wet scent of ice melting and draining from the rocks on either side of our trail, the cries of crows circling our heads too grating on the ear, to accept the voice as anything but fantasy. Here in this rock-hard reality, surely I must only have imagined her words to me.

Palo would know. He was there. I thought of asking him, "Did she actually say...?" But how could I? Most charitably, Palo would only think me unsettled. I let it lie.

"How will we find the homestead of Ena's husband?" he asked.

I had no idea where to look. Leon had not known the location of his daughter except that she lived near the village of Tergesté. "How would

I know?" I wished to see some of the old self-confident rogue in Palo's eye instead of this hero worship I didn't know how to handle, I spoke sharply, then relented. "We'll ask in the village."

3

Unreality caused by the nomad girl lingered. I saw and felt my world as though it existed beyond a sheet of waved glass, or as a reflection seen in water. She had weakened my senses in some way I could not understand. In fear of becoming lost in dreamlike fantasy, I studied the details of my world, jabbing my stick at places to assure myself of its solidity. Gnarled clumps of brush too starved to grow entered its final dissolution, useful for nothing more than holding open the choked cracks it had forced in the roadside rock. I studied the shape of Palo's back, his broadening shoulders, his lengthening hair. His muscles rippled in perfect symmetry, and his toes pointed straight ahead, not splayed as were my own. I memorized the sound of his boots scattering the pebbles on the path before me. It was then I first noticed that he had indeed donned his boots against the cold. It seemed I must memorize everything lest my senses escape me entirely and leave me defenseless—caught in the timeless tug of that girl's eyes.

Beyond the rounded basin of the valley, buildings painted white and roofed with red tiles reminiscent of the houses of Attica climbed the sides of foothills like red and white flowers overflowing a rocky garden. Rock fences bordered yards with chickens, ducks, and pigs.

"The family of Ena's dead husband must live up that road," I said.

The land leveled slightly, and the road lanced through a small grove of willows. We stepped into the clearing beyond, to face a band of guards armed with spears. Their leader spoke in a tongue we could not understand. He tried again, speaking a dialect of what I finally understood as corrupt Athenian.

"Who are you, and what is your business here?"

I dipped my chin in acknowledgment of his question and answered, as closely as I could to his own sounds, low and to the back of the throat, almost like a growl. "We have come to see Ena, daughter of Leon of Attica. Does she live here?" He seemed to understand. The group dissolved, reformed to our sides and rear, and led us toward the center of the cluster, leaving us at the gate to a wooden fence surrounding a three-leveled house. Built on terraces, it seemed to grow from the mountain itself, winding upward from front to back. The third level broke to a flat porch spreading across the lower levels. Gaily striped canvases served as protection from rain and sun. Two men dressed in fine-grade white wool met us, exchanged words with the guards, and motioned us forward.

A woman held open the door and invited us inside, waiting with us as another woman left to call the family. The narrow hallway in which we found ourselves opened to a barn-like room with dirt floor, hardened to rock by the passing of many feet. Light speared the darkness from a window high in the ceiling, shafting downward to illuminate a tall center post. Tiny pictures spiraled upward, carved and painted into the post. The woman noticed my interest. To my surprise she spoke pure Athenian. I inquired of her as to how she had learned the language, and she said her family had migrated from Attica. Each generation of elders taught their children.

"This is our history." She touched the pole, lightly dragging her fingers across the figures as she walked around it. . "This is the post my ancestors used when they built the first house. Six times, the house has been destroyed, six times rebuilt." She pointed to the lowest of the pictures. "Ten generations." Palo and I walked slowly around the pole, following the pictures until they spiraled too far above our heads to see. "My father," she said, pointing to the uppermost picture. "My brother and his daughter stand beside him."

"And Ena?" I asked.

"Ena," she said with a look of hauteur. "Only the first born of the family are depicted here."

Rocks fitted closely together and packed with straw-filled mud formed the back wall. I touched it, wondering at its permanency. "That is the wall the first ancestor built," she said. "He built it strong to hold back the mountain. We think he may have added the white of eggs to seal it, but we cannot say for certain."

Spears, swords, and shields made of tough deer hide and bone, musty with age, hung from a wall. "The family honors each warrior by hanging his weapons here when he dies, whether by battle or sickness or simply old age. My brother's." She pointed to a blade still shiny with care. "Killed training a wild horse. He was a very good horseman, and the horse was magnificent. My brother was strong and handsome, and his daughter is beautiful." Face alight with pride, she showed no trace of grief.

I looked around the room. Stacked-and-chinked logs held high the ceiling. Timbers of hand-hewn trees radiated from the central support, and disappeared into dusty-blue mist in the center. Palo gasped, and pointed. Something that looked like human heads hung from cornice boards circling the room.

"Our enemies," said the girl, again beaming. One hundred, twenty-six." Speechless, I stared. "You are impressed, I see," she said. "From childhood, I have found strength in the courage of my family."

Frozen in horror, I attempted a recovery. "Ena?" I asked. I wanted to complete my mission and get out of here as soon as possible.

A cloud descended over the girl's countenance. "Ena is a weakling. She cries about everything. She cries about the weather, she cries about the isolation, she cries about my brother's death, she cries to go home to her father. Her home is here now. My brother's daughter belongs here with us so we can teach her honor and courage."

I risked instant disapproval. "We are here to take her home. Her father has sent his donkey and cart for her things."

"If she leaves, she leaves without Thelana," she said, rippling jaw muscles in determination. Our children are valuable to us here. Even girls have a contribution to make. I myself am the teacher of the children. They learn strength and courage from the lessons I teach them about our ancestors. I will not have Thelana learn the decadence and wasting ways of the foolish Greeks."

"We would like to speak with Ena. Will you call her, please?"

"Ena does not come downstairs." She gestured upward, sweeping her arm toward a stairway. Winding upward, the stairs rested on logs cantilevered from the walls and stopping at an opening halfway between floor and ceiling. A tall man stood watching from the landing.

"Father."

"Welcome to my home," he said. "Thera, bring wine for our guests."

She went to the door leading toward the kitchen and yelled. "Wine!" then returned to stand with us. The old man glared at her, and she retreated to the shadows.

In soft, white wool, shirt tail caught up and sashed by a dark blue girdle, the man's clothing revealed a length of powerfully-formed ankle and knee. His eyes flashed a cold, gray-blue gaze at me as he descended the stair. Feeling much like a hare caught in a trap, I thought of leaving to find shelter elsewhere. Suddenly he smiled and gestured toward couches fronting a pit dug into the floor and lined with stone. Without being asked, a servant quickly brought in fatwood and logs, carefully stacked them inside the pit, and struck a spark from tools taken from a tinder box. The master regarded the action with interest, giving it the respect of an honored ritual. "We don't usually warm this part of the house," he explained. "Please, be seated."

He fired questions. "Did you find the journey through the mountains difficult? Has snow begun to fall beyond the pass? Have you heard of the fierce warrior who leads the Makedoné?" Travelers learned to expect such questions. Feeling on more certain ground, I warmed, both in the heat of the smoky flames and to the rites of meeting.

"We had no problems coming through the pass," I said, "though a band of thieves waylaid us half way through."

The big man's brows knit in icy-blue-eyed anger. "Thieves. I'll send guards at first light tomorrow."

"That isn't necessary," I said. "They let us pass without trouble." No need to draw details. I didn't want the old woman to be hurt. "They were just hungry and looking for alms." I was not beyond an outright lie when the situation called for it. I hurried on to other subjects, saying nothing of the nomad girl, not trusting my voice to speak of her.

"The warrior's name is Philip the Second," I said, gaining his instant attention. "Yes. I was at the battle of Lake Ochrid." Tempted to tell how Philip's army had treacherously fallen upon the bearers of the wounded, an unseen hand stopped my tongue. '*Caution*,' it seemed to say. I did not yet know the intent of my host.

My mouth had opened to answer. My lips would have hung there, loose, awkward, but at that moment Thera and another maid entered carrying bowls of heated wine. Then again she withdrew to stand within earshot of our conversation.

Our host held his bowl near his nose and sniffed. "I am Tharros, the father of Sata, the husband of your Ena. So tell me about the fight. I want to hear of every move this young genius made. I may have to face him in battle someday."

"I did not see the entire event," I said. "I am a surgeon. Most of my time was spent in tents filled with wounded."

"Oh," his countenance fell. "Still, I know that he must be a great warrior to defeat Bardyllis. Surely you saw the man?"

"Yes. He is tall, almost as tall as you," I lied, for Philip was fully as tall as Tharros. "His followers are very loyal." Tharros sensed my reticence.

"But not you, right?"

"I have no feelings one way or the other," I lied again, hoping for a look of neutrality if not sincerity. "I happened onto the battle by accident, and I always help out where I am needed."

"A-hum," he said, watching me closely, and leaned back in his chair. I felt stripped naked and judged–by a champion. Still I sat quietly, without continuing. I wanted to get out of this house alive, and preferably, with Ena. Suddenly a bizarre vision occurred to me. A vision of my own head hanging by my red hair from the rafters. I must have glanced upward, for Tharros waved the fingers on one hand, and said. "Oh don't mind those old relics. We stopped taking heads when my father's father was a boy."

I dared a challenge. "If you already know what I'm thinking, why waste time asking?"

Tharros roared with laughter. He stood and pounded his hard belly, leaned low to gather breath then roared again. Palo and I just sat and looked at each other. Suddenly I was more than a little frightened. Not only was this stranger's intentions unknown to us, we must also deal with a mad man.

"Thera," boomed Tharros. "Tell the servants to prepare dinner for our guests. And kill the lamb. These guests have much to tell, and it will take time to tell it. Now!" he yelled, when Thera stood without moving. All kinds of commotion awoke within the house. Many more than Thera had been listening, waiting just out of sight. I felt tension leave the house. We would not die. At least, not before dinner.

The logs had hardly taken fire when the same servant came in and doused it with water. "We'll go upstairs," said Tharros. "More comfortable there."

The stair opened into a room leading to the rooftop porch. I gazed in wonder at the panorama spread before me. Tharros led me to the banister of the balcony, spreading wide his arms as though claiming ownership of the entire world. "My father's father built this section of the house. He hated the room downstairs. 'This is a new life for our family,' he liked to say. 'From this terrace we will worship the gods of Mother Earth and all her bounty. And it will show us the faces of our enemies when they cross the mountain.' It was from this terrace that I saw you and your son advancing."

"Your position is well defended," I answered. "You have easy access to grain fields on your terraced lands; your herds are well protected, and your water supply is secure. The gods have surely blessed you and your family."

"Yet Sata, my firstborn son is dead. Fallen while breaking a new horse. But he leaves us his daughter. She will bear fine sons some day."

Tharros, massive arms crossed against his chest stood staring at his kingdom. His presence radiated out and away from his body, enfolding the villa, the compound, the hills, the village, and my beloved Adriatic. He seemed halted in his expansive control only by the wall of white mountains on the north. Though intimidated by the man, I, an itinerant physician, dared to speak.

"You know why we have come, don't you Tharros?" I waited for him to turn his eyes downward and onto me. I wanted no mistake in my intentions. I wanted to win this man's respect and I wanted safe passage through the dominion enclosed by his will. "Ena's father has sent us to escort her back to Attica."

"I know that, surgeon."

Surgeon. Could the word, meaning something like "carver of animals" in Athens, be intended to put me in my place? It seemed our little caravan would get no safe passage from this man. I began thinking of how to warn Palo to get ready to leave. We were not wanted here. Yet the man continued easily enough.

"I have known you would come since the day of Sata's death. Ena has not been happy here. We are not as cultured nor educated as Ena, regardless of what my Thera would have you believe. My son's wife misses her homeland, her Papa, her friends. She feels the loneliness of these wild green mountains. This is not like her sun swept and rocky hills. We have no bright and witty theaters, no glittering bangles for her arms, no happy chatter of women sitting together weaving and mending." He paused to stare across the hills toward the sea. "My daughter has not made her welcome, and the other women, following

Thera's lead, have sometimes been cruel."

I released a sigh, not realizing I had held my breath. The man had the soul of a philosopher; he just hadn't visited Athens, at least not recently. He led me to a wide, wooden stair descending to the gardens. I was certain he spent much time here. We sat, he one step lower than I so we were of a similar height. "Ena was a good wife to my son, despite her longing for home. Their daughter, Thelana, fills the vacancy in my heart since the death of Arenia, my wife." He placed his huge hand on mine, and though I knew he was not pressing, it weighed with size and with power. "You must understand, I cannot allow the daughter of my firstborn son to leave." Again I tensed. Could he be playing with me? A fox and a mouse?

I decided to push ahead. The man would respect courage. "I must see Ena, Tharros. I must give her news of her father."

"Of course. I cannot prevent that. Thera," he said, not loudly, and she came from wherever she had been waiting within the sound of his voice.

Ena, her daughter, and her maid appeared on the verandah within minutes. I was certain they had been waiting, prepared. "Uncle Daneion!" She rushed into my arms just as she had as a child of six or seven. "You have come to take me home." She began crying. I took a cloth from my sleeve and wiped her eyes, just as I had done when she cried back home in Attica, whether with tears of joy, or sadness, or just plain anger. I waited for the tears to stop, and said, "You have grown so tall, my skinny little girl. Look. You are taller than I." I managed to laugh, pushing away the delicacy of the situation, intending to talk further, later.

Thelana, the child, huddled near the maid, the maid's skirts almost completely concealing her tiny face. Only her eyes peeked around. Then, curiosity drew her forward.x She came to stand beside Ena.

"Your daughter is beautiful, Ena. So like you when you were her age." I made the usual comments. Again, I had to lie. The child was indeed beautiful, but her strong jaw and heavy brow were undeniably her grandfather Tharros'. Though Tharros had been the epitome of courtesy, he would never let her go, even to the extent of having Ena killed if necessary. And me, and Palo, as well, which went without saying.

The hour grew late, and still dinner had not been announced. A servant went down to the kitchen to see why. He came back a few minutes later saying that a servant had broken his arm. He was in a lot of pain and the others were caring for him.

"You are a surgeon," said Tharros. "Will you attend him?"

"Of course," I said, and leaned over the balcony wall to call below to the garden. "My bags, Palo." Palo had been walking and examining shrubs still green with late summer rain. He scurried off to find Spitter and the cart. Tharros and I went to the servant's quarters, joined to the big house by covered walkways descending toward the fields and barns nearer the lake. The man lay on a pallet beside the door.

"We went to catch the lamb for dinner," said a boy nearing manhood. "I roped it and gave Karthies the rope to hold while I slit its throat. The lamb bolted and jerked the old man onto a pile of sheep dung." The boy bent double, laughing, struggling to continue the story. "Old Karthies held onto that rope and went skidding on his belly through the mud and sheep shit 'til he hit a log. The lamb got away and I had to rope him again. Old Karthies just won't give up, I tell you, he's bound to do or die, I tell you." All this was said between spasms of laughter. "That's why, that's why he's got mud and sheep dung all over him."

I smiled at the boy, nodded, and said, "I think I've been there before." The other servants laughed, and one said, "You? A surgeon? Surely you have servants to do such things for you."

"Only me," said Palo, grinning, "And I never slip in sheep shit."

Happy laughter went around the room, and I felt the group relax. I asked, "Will you please get water and wash this poor man? Then I will see how badly he is hurt."

The tumble had resulted in a broken forearm, probably when the man hit the log. The bone had snapped cleanly, but the arm had begun to swell badly and had turned an ugly, blackish blue. "We must first set the bone," I said. "It will be very painful."

"It's the same place he hurt it when he fell down the stairs," said a woman I assumed to be his wife. They were of a similar age, about fifty or so. "He's been drinking too much wine. Claimed it was for the pain," she huffed.

"How long since he took wine?" I asked.

"Only a short while," she said. "See, he is so drunk he can hardly hold his lips together."

"Then I won't give him poppy juice," I said. "It would put him into the deep sleep. You must hold him, here, around the chest, while I pull his wrist. And we must give him air to breathe," I said to the group who had closed into a solid wall around us. "Please, open those shutters." That done without much struggle from the man, I pulled his arm to set the bone. I wrapped it in comfrey root softened in hot water, added wet clay, and smeared it in a thick layer. "The clay and the herb will draw out the swelling," I said. "The skin is not broken. He will heal properly." Yet, in touching the man as I worked, I noticed the flaccid skin, the eyes glazed white.

"He has been with our family for many years," said Tharros, quiet until now. He had stood at the edge of the gathering the entire time, watching. Forgotten. "He has never been one to take too much wine."

"He must have broken it when he fell down the stairs," I said. "The fall in the pens just broke it again. "The wound will heal," I said, looking at his wife, "but keep him protected from hard labor." I might have said more, but the woman dropped her eyes, knowing what I had seen. "Yes," she said. "I have warned him about taking chances, but he will not listen. He thinks he is still young and strong."

"He will not work at all, until that arm is healed," said Tharros. "Thera will send another man down to do his work." A stern reprimand from the Chief of his Clan. The woman wilted under his gaze, clearly frightened. I added a note to my assessment of this man. Friend or ally? Ally, I hoped.

"You will be well paid for your attendance," he said to me.

"There is no fee," I said. "I am a guest in your house." I helped the man to a footstool, and we turned to go, Tharros standing aside to let me pass. His manner had changed somewhat as I worked. Strange, the respect some give a physician. I remembered the reverence my grandmother had inspired when she entered a town. I had also felt awed in her presence as she taught me.

"I do have a favor to ask, however?" I said, and waited, putting all my effort into climbing the rough stone stairway back to the big house, noting wryly that Tharros had no such need to conserve breath, and he the elder.

"You want Ena and Thelana to leave with you...unharmed."

I stopped, not entirely because I needed to rest, but wanting to read his expression after I had given my answer, and walking made it difficult. I dipped my chin. "I merely wanted to ask that you give me directions across those mountains." I pointed north, toward snowcapped peaks glowing in pink iridescence.

"You think to take Ena through the mountains? At this time of year?"

I felt him drawing back, incredulous—and was I mistaken—protective of his daughter-in-law?

This time I laughed. "Ena? Out in weather like that? Oh no. She'd shrivel up the moment the sun disappeared behind the mountain and the chill winds struck. No. I would not take Ena across those mountains."

He relaxed, sighed. "Then you will return. You'll pass by our house on your way home." He waited, and again we climbed. Not wishing to give an impression of weakness, I continued to climb despite my short breath in the thin air of these heights.

I didn't answer. How could I tell him I might well never return? A war raged within me, and I didn't yet know which side would win. Still I heard the words of the nomad girl "Do not run from your destiny." I felt a curse rise from my gut, and quickly stuffed it away, in deference to the dangerous man standing beside me. Finally I answered.

"I have no home. I am a wanderer. And I dislike schedules. Besides, who can say whether or not I will even make it across the mountains?" There. That should do it. I had created a fork in the path of the future. Tharros would not know which I would take, and his questions would be sidetracked.

I sat beside the chief at a long table at dinner that night. There were no couches in the typical Athenian tradition, but the room was large and airy, and the table long enough to seat the adult members of the family and their favored servants.

Tharros introduced me to his second son seated on his left. "Keo," he said. "He is a singer. He tells the tales of our family." Keo briefly dipped his chin.

"We are all grateful for your aid to my servant," Tharros said. "Karnies and his wife, Sabin, have been with us since before my father died. I would not wish to be indebted. You must at least allow me to outfit you for your trip across the mountains."

"I can't cross those mountains!" wailed Ena.

"No. No, I would not take you through the mountains, little flower." How I longed to make her a promise, to give her my word that I would return and take her home. But of course, I could not. There was a very real danger that Palo and I might not make it across the mountains. And there was my diverting ploy to Tharros, my other reason.

"You would not want to travel the roads south at this time, either, sweet Ena. Perhaps, when we return, if we return, we'll make arrangements." I had gotten past Tharros, but how could I get past this woman who had known me and all my weaknesses almost since her birth? She would immediately begin to wheedle me into submission.

And was it my imagination, or at my words did the face of Keo, Ena's dead husband's brother, light up like the sun on a summer morning? I began to build on my suggestion. "You will need a few linen dresses. You are not used to the Athenian heat. And you will need time to say good-bye to Thelana." There. I had said it. I had put the problem squarely into her doll-like hands. Perhaps it would be enough to slow her down.

"G-good-bye?" Ena stuttered. "But I must take my little girl home with me. Surely there is room in the cart for another." Her eyes wildly flashed toward everyone at the table. "I must take Thelana with me. My father has never seen her. He will be heartbroken. NO! I will not leave her here."

No one answered her. Her cheeks flushed red and her eyes brimmed with tears. But these tears, unlike others, were the stuff of which life is sustained. She would truly die without Thelana. Instantly contrite, I pushed back my chair and started to rise. Just as I had when she was an infant and suffered the fever, when she was a toddler and had broken her toe, when she felt her first loose tooth and feared that they would all drop out like the teeth of her old grandfather, and again, when she had begun her menses and didn't understand the blood, I would go to her. I would comfort her. I would soothe away her pain. I would apologize. Merciful Goddess, I would lie to her if need be to ease her pain.

Tharros laid a hand on my shoulder, and gently, firmly pressed me back into my chair. I glared at him, raging inside, tensing my muscles to fling his hand away. He patted my shoulder, and his touch, gentle, persuasive, held my motion as no act of force might have. His voice, when he spoke, echoed that gentleness.

"Ena, child," he said, and though his voice was not loud, it silenced her piercing wails, and all motion at the table ceased.

"You have been unhappy here, and I apologize for that." He flashed a long and burning look at his daughter as he spoke. Face molded in rigid hatred, for an instant Thera stared back, defiant, a mirroring of her father's own features. Then she wilted. Her rigid neck became soft, pliable. Her head drooped forward. Her eyes closed. Subject to a lifetime of submission under the absolute rule of her father, she could not stand against those terrible eyes.

"There is another way," he said. "I have considered asking for your troth." A stunned silence, a jerking of heads in his direction, a palpable shock moved from member to member around the table. I, myself, sat frozen. Yet even so, my mind raced, observing, memorizing every face before me.

"You are, as your friend Pelos has named you, a flower. A precious tropical bloom, bred and grown in the warmth of the sun. Your spirit is of light, of gaiety, of brilliance. Your smile brings joy to my heart." He paused, considering, watching her face, guessing her emotions.

I too, considered and rejected such a notion. Ena understood nothing of the violence that had shaped the nature of Tharros, his father and his father's fathers. His trials had sharpened his mind and made him strong. She would live in fear of the touch of this man. It would kill her.

It was my turn to touch his arm, and, in his softened mien he felt it, responded to it, leaned aside to hear. "We must talk," I whispered.

"Yes." He drew a deep breath as though gathering back into himself all the essence that had drifted out across the table toward Ena. Reluctantly he continued. "We will talk later."

"I have a new song..." announced Keo, brightly. "Would you like to hear?" A chorus of cheers went round the table, chairs were pulled back, and from somewhere in the kitchen I heard stomping. "Music!" they called, and from one part of the house to another, the call repeated. Amphorae of wine were brought and drinking bowls passed, even as leftover food and dishes were borne away. Someone brought Keo's lute and Keo leapt onto the table to play and sing.

His dark eyes glittered from beneath heavy brows above a sharply chiseled nose, and hard, lean cheeks reflected candle light from scores of sconces set around the room. He smiled, displaying gleaming white teeth beneath a carefully trimmed mustache. He tossed long, dark hair away from his eyes and over his shoulder. Everyone in the room came to their feet, pounding the boards of the heavy oak floor. Boom, boom, boom, the pounding grew louder in competition, dissolved into laughter and faded to a quiet tapping as each member, a participant in the music, the fire, the revelry, awaited the first strumming chords of Keo's lute.

"Where did she grow, this keeper of fire?
This soft, pink sister of gods?
How did she find us in these faraway hills,

And how can we keep her here?
A ho, a hi, a sad good-bye and our hearts would freeze in sadness."
The rhythmic stomping quieted to a soft patter of feet barely touching the floor. A girl began a high-pitched trill that complimented Keo's rich baritone voice. He faced her, smiled and held out his hand. Someone helped his niece, Thelana, onto the table and she grinned, waiting for him to continue. Palo stood near, brought his flute to his lips, and found accompanying trills to play as Keo paused. Keo laughed, strummed a few extra chords on his lute and Palo echoed them.

"Cold winter winds swoop down from the hills
And all the leaves are fallen
Yet our hearts are warm and filled with joy
As our goddess lights her fire.
A ho, a hi, a sad good-bye and our hearts would freeze in sadness."

The young girl trilled, face alight as she gazed adoringly into Keo's face. Keo smiled back, and slowly turned to face those at his back. His gaze first swept across, then returned, to Ena.

"The hard stone walls of our home will protect
From the chill of ice and snow,
Yet who will fill our home with joy
If our goddess leaves our company?"

And the gathering joined in the final line,
"A ho, a hi, a sad good-bye and our hearts would freeze in sadness."
Keo reached down a hand and invited Ena to join him on the table. With every eye in the room upon her, Ena first reached out to take his hand, smiling as only Ena could smile. Then her glance brushed across the table, and I watched the radiant smile dissolve. Gone in a wave of pain. I looked where Ena had been looking. At Thera. Never had I seen such venom in the face of a woman. Numb, horrified at such hatred, I watched as Ena's hand slipped from Keo's. She turned and ran from the room, face turned white with strain as she fought to hold back tears. When I glanced at Thera again, the hated look had vanished, hidden behind her bowl in a long, slow draught of wine. When it lowered, only a microscopic sneer at the corner of her lips remained to mark her triumph.

And, abruptly, the party was over.
As though on cue, given momentum by the turmoil raging inside the house, a storm broke. Two days we huddled inside, Palo and I placing our pallets downstairs beside the log fire to sleep, being awakened each time a

servant entered to renew the wood. In this time of reflection, Tharros, Thera, Ena and I held our peace. Though the winter snows had not yet begun, the rain washed the hills, gathered in the ponds, and the sounds of water flowing across the dams roared in our ears. I felt the wild, yet controlled energy of the storm, shivered in the brilliant flashes of lightning here so near the sky, felt the jarring quakes of thunder, and wondered yet again how people could have remained here long enough to survive and tame the elements.

It finally stopped raining, but still the clouds hung low overhead, refusing to allow the wet mountain paths to dry. Palo, two servants and I foraged the hills looking for healing roots. The servants directed me to patches where the tough, resilient herbs had grown, and helped us dig. In three more days the jars Ana had given us were filled, and the skies cleared. It was time to go.

At Thera's suggestion, we left Rocky and his cart to be picked up on our return journey. "It is the most practical thing to do," she had said. Seeing some cunning ruse in her narrowed eyes, I braced myself for her explanation, prepared to deny it. "The ice is treacherous through the hills, and you and Palo will have to watch the donkey and cart constantly."

What would she have to gain by ensuring that we returned to the house of Tharros? The only possible answer was that it would be another try at ridding herself of Ena. Knowing her ploy, I agreed without hesitation. For one thing, She was right. It would be difficult enough managing one cart. But two? I have been known to build my own schemes. How could I fault her for doing the same? Yet I did. I did not like the woman.

Amused satisfaction warmed my entire body as we pulled away from the complex. Ena stood next to Keo, and though not actually touching, I could almost swear that I saw a glow surrounding the two of them that somehow isolated them from the rest of the group, indeed, from the entire universe. Now it was up to Ena. Either she rose to Thera's challenge and claimed what was clearly being offered by Keo, or a very miserable young woman, a woman without her child, would be returning with Palo and me to Attica. Audibly, I groaned. Palo looked back at me from his place beside Spitter. I made no comment and he turned his attention to the road. The house was soon lost to our view, but I had no doubt that, from his unique view of the world, Tharros watched us on our creeping way until we disappeared into the blue mist.

4

밊밊밊 ◈ 밊밊밊

I would rather not tell you about my trip across those mountains. Even now, the vagueness with which I traveled disturbs me. If I had not the more positive energies drawn from later events to seduce me ever onward in this, my personal account of history, I would lay down my marker and leave you to your own conclusions. Yet I must proceed, for you must know that I succeeded in crossing those fearsome mountains, and I did return to fulfill my destiny. How many men may say the same?

The wheels of the cart rolled easily, softly through virgin snow, smothering the usual rattle, bump and jostle of the open trail. Quiet enough, I hoped, not to disturb the mounds of snow resting precariously on steep mountain slopes. No more immediate problems presented themselves, and I found myself replaying my last visit with Olympias.

"You are the hope of a free world," I revised. "With your leadership the evil order of power-mad pretenders could be wiped from the face of the earth. Honest people would no longer be lied to and used for the glory of scoundrels playing on the simple faith of the devout.

"You have armies, you have agents all ready and in place, waiting for your word to act. You have women with courage ready to do your bidding. You have the faithful of true priests waiting for your command. What of them? What of their needs? And," as was the case in each of my revisions, I always ended, "What about me?"

What of all the work I had done or was prepared to do to bring about a network of agents who would need only a focus for their energies. Olympias would have known in a day's time what her enemy had planned. Her armies, supplied and paid for by her thousands of adoring followers would have been a force for major positive change in the world. And yet she had surrendered her power, her autonomy, to a mere man. A 'king' of a broken throne. A breaker of promises, a breaker of wives. Had he not already broken at least three? He would take her families' wealth, use it for his own ends and leave her begging for sustaining crumbs. He would even use Olympias' influence among the templar priests who remained loyal to her. They would now obey that false leader because she had relinquished her claim to the title of priestess by becoming a wife.

Without thinking, I could see the disinterested shrug of her shoulders dismissing such possibilities as of no account. "What can I do?" she asked, in my fictitious recreations. "I am only a woman. I may not command armies, I may not even own the food I eat, except for one bag of barley seed. You know that, old friend. It is the law, the holy law as held by the councils. My power as the Holy Chosen One is hobbled by those very priests who bestowed the title on my mother." In my mind's eye she would look away, as though seeing far across the mountains to the place where her mother was still being murdered by those very priests. "They gave my mother the title, they gave power to the title, and they took it away." And then I would see her snatch back the vision and replace it with the more compelling events of the present. "I no longer have faith in the Talents," she would say. "Even if I possess them, which I doubt, I haven't the slightest conception how to put them to use." Then she would look back at me, brow hardened in cold determination. "The only thing that matters is position, wealth, and armies. And the only way I can gain any of those things is by marrying them."

How could I reach her behind that regal armor? I never stopped to examine my own motives in this matter. I never stopped to consider that I might have been using this woman, this child, really, to serve my own passionate, angry rage.

On the second day we stopped in a wide, sun-filled valley. Making camp, I found myself hurrying Palo along to do his evening chores: finding firewood, setting traps, breaking out stores—an unusual thing, for the boy never needed prodding. Finally, at the end of day, I noticed him limping, told him to take off his boots so I could see. Startled, I grabbed his foot and examined it. Blisters had arisen on the backs of both heels and both big toes.

This was my fault, not his. I had forgotten that until this trip, Palo had worn nothing but sandals in his entire life, and most of that short life had been spent bare of foot. I had allowed my anguish over Olympias' problems to unsettle me. Grumbling, cursing my thoughtlessness, I rubbed ointment on the blisters and then wrapped his feet and legs in soft wool. I knotted each just above the knee and helped him thrust his feet back into frozen boots. He wiggled his toes, nodded and went off to check a trap he had set for rabbits. What if he lost his feet? Reconsidering, I pulled more wool from the cart for myself. What if I lost my own?

The next day we traveled across a landscape empty of color except for winter grays and an occasional glint of orange on white snow reflected from brief exposures of sun. Distant hills faded in and out between tranquil layers of mist. The whole world grew silent as we climbed ever upward toward undefined whiteness. The unhurried quiet lulled my senses and soothed my mind, easing my concern for my little princess. I think it must have been at this point where I slipped into the deeper state of reverie, for I don't remember entering the clouds.

Spitter required no instruction, and Palo, long ago grown quiet, had burrowed beneath the canvas on the cart where I had told him to lie, riding until his feet could heal, cushioned among the woolens and leathers. The monotony dragged on my consciousness and then, despite my intention to remain alert, my mind slipped away, ranging far afield, floating as though suspended in the opaque white of my universe. My feet moved, following Spitter's lead, but my mind took another route.

I roused as though drawn forward from another universe to take note of where I was. Still locked into the webs of non-caring detachment, I realized that Spitter had stopped in the middle of the road. I slapped her neck. "Let's go, girl. We've a long way to go before we stop. And anyway, this is no fit camping place."

Spitter laid her ears down on her neck, looked back at me, and refused to budge. I grabbed her harness. "Are we stuck? Do you need help to pull the cart?" I moved forward, grasped the leather harness around her head, and pulled.

Ice and snow fell away beneath my feet. Hands convulsed in a death grip on Spitter's harness, I watched snow cascading away from me, plunging, bouncing, shattering into misty powder onto newly-fissured spikes of rock. Desperately I clung, swinging above nothingness. An image flashed between me and that crystalline blue nothingness and vanished. A fear-crazed trick of the mind. Fumbling for the ledge where Spitter stood, I struggled to find purchase for my boots. Fear-swollen tongue crowding my mouth, muffling my feeble cry, I croaked, "Back, Spitter! Back, go back!" But she stood firm, shoulders braced against my weight. Palo heard me, scrambled down from the cart and reached to grab her harness to pull her backwards. Slowly she began to back, and finally my body dragged upward across the raw edge of the rock.

Heart pounding beneath my ribs, limbs trembling in strain, fingers melded in frozen union on Spitter's halter, I stared into the donkey's soulful eyes. We both felt the bite of the icy abyss from which I had so narrowly escaped.

The road was gone. There was no other path. "We'll stop here," I breathed when I was able to fill my spasmed lungs with air. And Palo, uttering not a word during the entire affair, quietly unloaded the sticks we had brought with us from the lowlands and built a fire. I noticed in the half light and in the reflection of the meager flames on his face that his lips had hardened and set into a purplish pallor.

How had it been possible—if I remembered correctly—that, as I dangled above the precipice, I had seen the face of the nomad girl? What had she to do with me, and how could I resolve this? I shuddered. Too much to think about. I clutched my arms about my body and shivered, not from the cold, for already the dry sticks of Palo's fire burned brightly, hot enough to boil water for tonight's tea. I went to get our water pouches from the cart and found them frozen solid. "We should have been carrying our pouches of water next to our bodies," I said. It's frozen so hard it will take too much wood to melt it. We will have to melt snow.

Palo stared at me, incredulous. "You had body bags for water?"

I shrugged. "Tharros maid packed them for us. I just didn't think we'd need them so soon." The memory of the look Palo gave me then, will never fade.

"You have forgotten how to think," he said. "I can see the death wish in your eyes. You don't care whether we live or die."

And then a quiet feeling of resignation came over me. It would be of no consequence if I did not make it across the mountains. Palo was fully capable of getting himself and Spitter to some village where they would be taken in, for their labor. And my unresolvable conflict would be over. How free I felt! No more Olympias! Stunned at my revelation I reconsidered my reaction. If it was freedom I coveted, I was already free! I had been released the instant she had muttered those words that still rang in my ears, "I am marrying a king!" Without volition, tears ran from my eyes, joined with feathery flakes of snow and froze on my cheeks.

So, whoever had said it was freedom I wanted? Helpless as a baby, I brushed at my face and moved closer to the fire, holding out my hands to warm them, and reaching to turn the spit Palo had prepared with the carcass of a frozen rabbit he had found on the trail.

That night, wrapped from nose to tail in several woolen blankets, Spitter stood close beside us as we bundled beneath the cart. Though she did not lie down, the bulk of her body lent us warmth and comfort. Neither Palo nor I slept very well, troubled at the problem now presented to us. At first light we arose and dug out of the snow that had piled around us during the night. If there were no road, how could we proceed?

Amazed, we looked for the precipice. Only a slight indentation in the smooth blanket of snow remained where once there had been an uncrossable gap. "We can cross it now!" said Palo.

But, still shaky from the memory of my near death, I shook my head. "It won't hold us. That snow will slide as soon as we press foot upon it. We'll have to go back."

"No!" said Palo, and as though it were only yesterday, I saw the determined, set jaw that had marked the skinny waif I had first seen hiding in the woods. "I will make a bridge!" And with that he dragged out the axe Dimitri had insisted I bring, and marched off toward the trees lining the road, heading straight for a tall oak. That trunk must have been the width of two men's arm spans. Caught up in his enthusiasm despite my determination toward self-destruction, I followed. "Not this one," I said. "How would we split it? We'll get a lot of small trees and lay them across the gap. That will provide support for Spitter's hooves and for the wheels of the cart." Palo shoved the axe at me and stomped away. I looked at him, concerned for his anger, and caught just the ghost of a smile as he turned away. The little scoundrel. He had contrived this!

Tricked back into life, I slung the axe with vigor, and, when wind finally deserted me, I sat down and laughed. Spasms of choked lungs caught me. I wheezed until my injured chest relaxed, then laughed again, even harder, until I collapsed onto the pile of young trees I had cut. Resting, I smelled the vapors of fresh tea, roast rabbit, stale bread and cheese, so sharp, so clear in this thin mountain air. Spitter brayed, and I roused myself, went to fill her bucket with barley seed, poured melted snow into her water skin, and hung it on the corner of the cart seat for her to drink. She snuffed the steaming water and drew back, an accusing glint in her eye. I laughed. "Don't worry, it'll cool, all too soon, in this weather." We ate, and the food restored me. We trimmed our small trees, laid them side by side, and tied them together with strips of leather. Exhausted and nearly frozen we rolled ourselves into our blankets beneath the cart and slept. The following morning when we awoke, snow covered the saplings in an unbroken sheet of white. Though we hesitated, uncertain where rock ended and bridge began, Spitter proceeded across without urging. I had no doubt that, should any other travelers pass this way, they could also cross without danger. I gained a kind of satisfaction in that. I was not entirely helpless nor useless. I vowed that, in future, I would take care of what I could, and if I did that well enough, I would have no time nor energy to worry about what I could not.

༄༄༄

In the following days I had time to do some soul-searching, however, and I began to use it. Forced to face the simple truth, I admitted that my silver-haired ass was more intelligent than I. And my little abandoned waif, Palo, possessed a far more realistic concept of life and sense of humor than I could ever match. But, rather than sulk, as had been my bent at the beginning of this trip, I fought to accept and understand these revelations, and began a most difficult time of adjustment.

So Spitter was intelligent. I had known that, but I had never really tested her depths. I determined to learn just how smart she was. And to begin, I would teach her to obey my commands. I needed a series of signals to guide her when I was unable to pull her in the direction I wanted, either by walking beside her or pulling the rein left or right. My frustration in trying to get her to back up and help pull me onto the rock made this imperative.

"We're going to learn a new game," I told her, walking beside her head and holding lightly to her neck. "When I whistle like this," and I whistled low, "that means to turn this way," and I pulled her neck toward the left. "When I whistle like *this*," I said, whistling high, "we'll turn like this," and I pushed her neck to the right. "And when I whistle twice, like this," and I whistled twice, "we'll stop. Now to back up, I need another sign."

"Do them all," Palo said, and whistled low then high and then twice. I hadn't even known he had been listening. Startled by the concept, I agreed. "To back up, we'll do them all!" Both of us laughed until our bellies ached, I, thinking about whistling while dangling a few hundred feet in thin air, only blue-filmed mist and ice below.

Spitter just looked at us and then away. Silly humans!

We spent five days on the mountains. We faced no other dangers, and our problems were minimal. Twice, we had to dig the wheels of the cart out of ice before we could move.

On the last day in the mountains it rained so hard we couldn't see the road in front of us. Winds pushed us to and fro, howling through the canyons in deafening gales. Palo and I walked on either side of Spitter's head, holding to the shaves of the cart for balance, feeling our way down the mountain. Ice melted to slush and then to sticky, light-colored mud, and finally we could hear ourselves speak.

"Can't we stop somewhere, Wallis?" yelled Palo. I found the boy's face through the pelting rain. Wind whipped us from side to side and back and forth like a dog killing a rabbit. Palo became a dark shadow cast against the white rock bank. A dark shadow bent and creeping, staggering from one step to the next. I knew I must appear to him the same way.

I nodded. "We'll stop, son. We aren't making much progress like this anyway." But I knew the boy couldn't hear me over the wind. I whistled twice to Spitter. She ignored my command. Again I whistled, and pulled back on her harness, thinking she ignored my signal. She pulled me along like a child on a sled. "Stop! Spitter, stop!" I demanded, pulling back, but skidded along by her unbending gait, still without a sign that she understood. I had no choice. Angry, frustrated and vowing once again to sell the beast at the nearest town and get a more agreeable animal, I followed. What else could we do?

Then suddenly, for no reason that I could see, Spitter stopped. "Finally!" I muttered. I staggered around Spitter's head and clamped a hand on Palo's shoulder. "We'll stop here," I yelled. "Let's see if we can set up a tent."

We rummaged around in the cart for canvas and stakes. Spitter pulled forward, and at first I thought she was trying to travel again. I hurried to catch up to her and grasped her harness to hold her back. Again she drug me along, but for only a few feet. There, appearing before me like a phantom emerging from the solid wall of rain, was a cave.

"Palo," I shrieked. "It's a cave! Come see! And it's big enough for all of us. Even Spitter."

That night, fire banked, Palo and I lay with our feet near the warm coals. Sitting on a rounded rock, I covered my head with my arms, blanket pulled high and clutched in my fingers. Only then did I let go. I cried as no grown man and probably not even a boy would cry. I cried in relief for the ending of the hard day. I cried in gratitude for a wise young animal whose only instinct was to protect her people. And I cried in utter surrender to the fates who had brought me here, who had whipped me into submission, who had dragged me forth from my dense fog of self-pity. I cried in profound love for my friends on this seemingly endless journey. And when I had cried, I buried myself in blankets and slept. Only at the nudging of Spitter's nose did I awake, raise my head and blink, blinded by the unclouded brilliance of morning sun.

I stumbled to the door of the cave and looked out. Across, and hanging suspended above a valley spread with mists, I gazed upon the highest mountain I had ever seen. Rising to the heavens, its peaks of faceted ice and snow caught fire from the sun and radiated in brilliant spikes that hurt my eyes to see. It painted Palo's wondering face, shone on his turned up nose, glittered in Spitter's silver curls and caressed my own chest, arms and shoulders with hot shades of pink and orange. Nearby, light echoed in millions of points from coated pine needles and icicles dripping from the bare branches of frozen trees.

Neither of us spoke on that final, downward trek. We walked in a world given over to the glory of the gods. Our words would have seemed dark profanity.

I walked behind Palo who, as usual, scouted the forward trail. But as the day grew warmer, sour steam rose from our drying coats and hats. He needed a bath, and so did I.

In the foothills, Spitter found a lacy, gray-green moss, and snuffed her nose through its low-growing mounds. Nearby a herd of wild deer fed on the moss, all passing the long, wild grasses by. I followed a narrow goat-trail up the side of a hill, choosing my way carefully to avoid slippery dirt and wet pine straw, and picked one of the tiny, shrub-like growths to examine. Soft, flexible to the touch, branches spread wide to catch every available bit of sunlight, it looked like a tiny tree. I put it to Spitter's mouth and she ate it as though starved, so I picked a great sack full to save for treats along the way.

We traveled easily, and to pass the time, I practiced walking with my eyes shut, hand resting on the cart, allowing Spitter, head high and proud, to lead me.

Palo picked out tunes on his flute, and I followed along, whistling, filling in a slow strain with a treble and roll. When I whistled a three-note phrase twice, Spitter swung wide right, curled back, and again stepped onto the trail. This, despite all my effort, pulling and straining at the harness to get her to straighten out. After making a complete circle, she continued on as though it were the exact right thing to do. I pulled my hat off my head, and scratched an ear.

"Dancing for us, are you? You like that tune?" So I whistled it again, and again she made the wide right circle. I had struggled, pushed and pulled her for more than three years every time I needed her to turn in a circle. The only time she had circled willingly was the time she had thrown me from her back onto the dusty road outside Attica, the time she had bolted because the quail startled her. It was the same tune, the very same.

"All right, two whistles, you turn in a circle, but slowly, yes? I don't want to wind up in the dirt again." I would have to stumble my way onto the signs by her lead. When I snapped my fingers she lay down, and when I clapped my hands she came to me. Spitter had no difficulty at all, but times when I forgot and reached for her harness to pull her around, she would not budge until I signaled in her special way.

We came at last to a break in the evergreens walling our road and looked over a valley saturated in rising vapors. Bare of the dark color of evergreens, pink tinges of new growth brushed the tips of beech, oak, linden and birch trees.

We descended the slopes, marveling in the clarity of the air. Leveling to flat land, our cart moved easily toward a range of mountains bordering the distance. Along the wayside, snows thinned, releasing long, velvety grasses to stand undefeated against winter's onslaught. We joined a stream of carts on the road, all loaded with rich produce and tools, carrying their wares in baskets and bags of honey-gold jute. Each jaunty donkey wore a shining collar made of the fiber. A stream crossed our path. In the narrows, thick with icy slush and protesting the force of newly melting snows, it swelled to about the width that a tall man was high.

"We'll stop here," I told Palo. We would wash. We would purge ourselves of the weary miles and the negativity draining me of strength. I would put all thought of the little princess behind me. This valley, a likely place to start my new life, would mark a new beginning. Perhaps I would never see Bird again. Perhaps I would find a woman, a woman who could bake good bread. Perhaps I would open a stall beside a well-traveled road, build a hut, have children. Well, no. I wouldn't have children. I dreaded the curse that could find a home in flesh of my flesh—the convulsions that robbed people of their minds, their bodies, from time to time, the tortured fits curious to my family for which I could find no cure. But perhaps there was a woman here, someone who needed a man like me. Well, I admitted. That was unlikely. But images of home and hearth strengthened my will.

"Why stop here?" Palo asked. "We must be near a village with all these people around. Let's wait. We can get our supper there." He grabbed Spitter's rein and pulled to cross the stream.

I clapped my hands. Spitter, though usually compliant in Palo's hands, stopped, perked an ear and turned, bringing cart and Palo back to me. "We'll camp here," I said, "and we'll bathe. We'll put on clean clothes and wash our dirty ones. And we'll stay here long enough to have them dry."

"You want me to bathe in that cold water?" Palo asked, stunned.

"We'll heat water," I said.

"Our kettle is too small." He jerked the iron pot from the cart and swung it before my face. "You are mad!"

I couldn't resist. Bending low at the waist, and humping over like a simpleton, I took my stick and scrabbled through the sodden leaves beneath the trees, baying like a hound chasing a rabbit. Palo's eyes, both seeing and blind, crinkled into a grin.

"So you're not crazy. But I'm still not getting into that water."

"Find sticks for a fire," I said, as though dismissing the issue, letting him win the argument.

Meanwhile, I gathered wide, flat stones from the creek and placed them to seat our kettle. The place seemed overrun by rabbits, so many tracks had crossed and crisscrossed our trail. Palo set traps while our water heated, and soon had three, winter-skinny animals for me to clean. I skinned and gutted them, washed them in the creek and hung them on sticks near the fire. By the time I was finished, the water in the kettle bubbled happily. I lifted the pot from the fire, set it on the side of the stones to stay warm, stripped my clothes, and, whistling, waded into the water, trying to ignore the icy chill that leapt to my thighs.

The boy was right. We should have waited, but I would finish what I had begun. I dug a handful of dirt and clay from the bank, softened it with water, and rubbed it on my skin. Still whistling, I sank beneath the water and came up with mud streaming from my hair and beard, breathing white vapor as my breath met the chill wind. I dipped again and again, trying not to wince where Palo could see me. Then I came out of the stream, dipped water from the kettle and poured it over my head. Zeus be praised, it felt good.

"You're next," I said.

"No. Not me," said Palo. "I'm just fine like I am."

"You stink like a waste dump," I said. "No one will talk to you."

"They'll just have to get out of my way."

"I saw you looking at that pretty girl in the last wagon," I coaxed. "You could see her again down the road."

"Time enough to take a bath after we get to a village. Then we'll take care of the ladies."

"There's plenty of water left for you in the kettle. It'll still be warm if you hurry. It feels great!"

Stubbornly he shook his head. I loomed over him. He was not yet quite so tall as I. Silently I edged him toward the creek. He tried to dodge away from me. I cut off his retreat and blocked him with my arms. He dodged again, nearly knocking me over. Soon it became a battle, he almost as strong as I. I slipped, fell into the mud and smeared myself good, hair and beard as well as shoulders and legs and buttocks. Palo laughed. I laughed harder. I jumped up and descended upon him. Shrieking as though a pig lanced for the butcher, he ran into the stream. I trailed him in and shoved his head beneath the water. He came up gasping. I shoved him down again. Recovering, he jumped on my back and pulled me under. We rolled, laughing, fighting for air, until the water seemed warm. Returning to the fire, I poured steaming water over our heads before we scurried to wrap ourselves in blankets then look for fresh clothes from the cart.

"We still have to wash our dirty clothes," I said.

Tense with cold, teeth chattering, dismayed but resigned, he said, "We'll have to go back in."

"Oh, just to the edge, this time."

I added more wood and refilled the kettle with water for tea. Waiting for the rabbit to cook we explored the woods beside the creek. Fish jumped and scurried around cascading chunks of ice, and Palo said, "Water doesn't seem cold to them."

"Think you could catch one?"

"With my hands?"

"Sure. Why not?"

Doubting, he rolled up a sleeve and bent over the water. The next fish that jumped he slapped with his hand. It flew through the air and out onto the bank. "Good work," I said, slapping the next.

Sluggish and slow with the cold, the fish seemed ready and willing to accept our hand. A child could have caught enough for a meal. "This is truly a good land," I said. "Would you like to live here?"

"You still thinking of not going home?"

"Oh, we'd still go back to Attica. I'd get lonely for the theater and shops and old friends, but we could stay here, build a home. You know. Find a woman?"

"What about Olympias?"

I looked away. My eyes found the distant line of purple mountains, but my inner vision reviewed another sight. A vision of wagon loads of dowry treasures, wedding clothes, gaudy tents. Gaily-bedecked pack animals pulling loads of servants, all bound for a palace. "She doesn't need us now. She's in the hands of the gods."

5

A grove of linden trees broke to admit us into a small village of mud huts. Grass covered shelters stood to either side of us. Blankets of colorful wools lay beside furs bundled and stacked. Baskets of all sizes were stacked high on handhewn benches and tables, ready for transport to market in the carts and wagons we had passed on coming into the village.

Fires blazed in the communal ground. People waved us in and directed us toward tables loaded with food and drink. Flutes piped, and people circling dancers kept time by beating jars with long spoons. Spitter bolted and dodged our efforts to capture her harness. I clapped my hands, sharply, but the sound was lost in the maelstrom of other clapping hands, hooting, laughing calls. Finally, forced to get her attention with a new command, I put my fingers between my lips and whistled. Abruptly she halted, laid her ears back, and turned to glare at me, but she returned and did not resist when Palo led her to a hitching post. One of the men sitting on a log beside the fire waved. Palo went to join the musicians and dancers, digging for his flute as he approached, and I squatted beside the man who had waved to us.

"Have barley beer with us," the man said. His speech sounded similar to the dialect of Tharros and his family. He offered a bowl. Another man reached for a jar and sloppily poured. Only by holding up my hand and withdrawing the bowl did it slow the stream. "Watch it, H'ruso, you'll soak our guest with drink and none of the ladies will dance with him."

"You are the one who must watch it, Shalot, for soon you will have no daughter to console you when you run out of beer." Hoots rose from the six men in the circle, a ragged response, for to boo and hoot they must first swallow their beer.

Shalot lifted his bowl, pointed once in each of the four directions, and said. "May the gods protect my future son-in-law from harming himself and others through his clumsiness!" Everyone laughed and booed again, and the man continued. "You must pardon H'ruso, stranger," said Shalot, spreading his palms. "He has just been given the word that my daughter, Estra has decided that tomorrow is the day she will marry him." Perfect teeth gleamed when he smiled, and rosy cheeks poofed out like plums. He shrugged a brown woolen cloak closer around his shoulders to cover the bare neck and sleeves of the white linen shirt he wore beneath, a wrap clearly too fussy and thin for this chilly evening. Short, white beard fringed his chin, and the skin beneath his nose glowed warmly from recent shaving. Soft-voiced, almost feminine in manner, Shalot held command of the gathering like a wondering child holds a butterfly in cupped palms. It was enough. He turned to me, asking nothing, but clearly waiting for me to speak.

"Thank you for welcoming us into your village," I said. "I am called Daneion, and my friend, now playing the only flute in the chorus which is out of tune and off the beat, is called Palo. They knew that Palo's flute now made a real chorus where before had been only chaos, but the men saluted me, expressions of sympathy on their faces, and held their bowls out to H'ruso for more beer.

"Come and eat," called a woman, "before you are too glutted with drink to find your spoon." Again the men laughed as though uproaringly amused at her keen humor.

"Hola, Kenari," answered the man who sat on my right. "At least we know what's in the beer." Everyone laughed, she loudest of all.

"If the sweet Estra will sit beside me," called one, a boy the age of Palo.

"Come with me Boy!" laughed Kenari, waddling toward him and waving the stirring spoon like a sword. "*I'll* sit *on* you!" Boy dodged and headed for the cooking pot, holding his now empty bowl to be filled by a younger woman. She tossed long, black hair away from her face and dipped her spoon.

"First to the pot as always, Boy. Watch it or you'll be as round of belly as your friend, H'ruso." Boy ducked his head and grinned, seeing the knowing glance in Estra's eyes. "He only calls for me after he's been rejected by you," he said. "And I only come when he gives me gifts."

"That is my daughter, Estra," said Shalot. "Already she is a good cook. She can spin and weave as well as her mother ever could, and she only sixteen summers old."

I dipped my head in Estra's direction. "Your betrothed is indeed fortunate, *Kiria,* many of the young women in Attica, where I come from, can hardly boil an egg."

It was clearly the right thing to say, for Estra dimpled prettily and filled my bowl with choice pieces of lamb. H'ruso followed. Estra again dipped the spoon, and poured the meat stew into his bowl. Still he held out the bowl, and again she dipped, muttering. "You will be as round as a pumpkin before you are thirty, H'ruso, son of Berg. Not only was your father named for the mountain but he was as big as one and he was too lazy to work it off in the fields."

"I am not like my father, Estra. I have a job. I am keeper of the trees."

"Ha," said Estra, hardly a laugh of good humor. She filled his bowl and waved him away, preparing for the next, and muttering. "A god he's not, but he's a man, and can father children. I know for I've seen them trailing behind him when he goes into the woods."

"As you may have guessed, my daughter is not too happy with this marriage," said Shalot.

"Who else might I marry?" she scoffed. "Do you see any other unmarried men around here?" She returned to her task of filling bowls, but her smoky-lashed eyes lingered on me. Shalot also looked at me, interested. I felt like a fish being baited with a juicy young worm. I said nothing, and we returned to our seats near the fire.

Serving done, Estra and Kenari joined the group, and for a while only the sounds of slurping and chewing could be heard throughout the gathering, with an occasional curse from someone spitting out a bit of gristle, or someone coughing, choking from eating too fast.

H'ruso got up from his seat and moved closer to Estra, attempting to touch her leg. "We're not married *yet.*" she quipped, pushing away his hand. "Why don't you go get some more stew. That'll settle you down."

"But Estra, we'll be married tomorrow, and besides, you said I eat too much." Nevertheless, he got up to refill his bowl.

My eyes must have asked a question, for she answered: "The gods have made my decision for me. What have I to say about it? I will marry H'ruso and have a lot of children, and they will all grow up doing what we do, and that will be whatever the gods have designed for us. The boys will be keepers of the trees and the girls will marry farmers or makers of cheese or furniture or whatever."

"Is it so bad, Estra, being a maker of furniture?" asked the man on my right, the one who had taunted Kenari about her cooking.

"Yelin is the finest table maker in the valley," said Kenari, patting her husband's shoulder fondly. "Your girls will be lucky, Estra, finding a man like him."

"It's not that anything is bad about marrying a carpenter," said Estra. "Yelin is a fine man, and a very good maker of tables. But what is there to do in keeping trees? H'ruso just sits, day after day, and watches them grow."

Everyone in the crowd, listening quietly before now, laughed. "He watches for fires!" called one, and, "He shoos away woodpeckers," called another. "He caught me stripping jute the other day and chased me away," called still another, still more loudly so to be heard above the bursts of laughter.

When the laughter waned, I said. "I've heard it said that the gods form patterns for us to follow, patterns like the fences we build to hold our sheep, but once people step outside their patterns, choices become their own."

"How can we step outside the pattern?" asked Shalot. "Don't the gods guard against that? Surely they are more powerful, more all-seeing than we?"

"Yes," said Estra, shrugging. "I have no choice. I will marry H'ruso."

"Sometimes choices are given us," I answered. "Like when I found Palo living in the woods with no family to help him. I caught him stealing from my pack while I was helping an old man get a drink of water."

"A thief!" cried Yelli, and looked around at Palo. Palo kept his head down, eating.

"Yes," I said, "a thief. But he was only about ten years old when I found him, and the people of the village would not even give him food. I offered him a job with me, to help me sell my merchandise. He could have remained a thief all his life, but he made his own choice, pattern or no pattern. And here he is."

"Well, I have no choice, either," said H'ruso, returning with his bowl, and plopped down on his box. "Most of the other girls died of the fever when Estra was a baby. The rest were chosen before I got old enough." He glared around the group, daring anyone to dispute him. "I only picked her so she'd have somebody. Anybody else here interested?" He raised his voice, calling to the woods and countryside. "Anybody out there want Estra? Or maybe we have someone right here at our fire who would like to take her off my hands. How about you Daneion?" Then he glanced sideways at Palo, and slurred. "Or maybe you prefer boys?"

The crowd grew quiet, waiting for my response. Saying nothing more, I lifted my hands toward the fire trying to warm them, for the air felt suddenly chilled. It was Palo who broke the spell. He got up, pulled out his flute and said, "Spiri, would you dance for us?"

How had I not noticed? A girl, slightly older than Palo, smiled, fluffed out her hair and rose. "Play the one about the soldier going off to the wars again, Palo," she said, leading the way to the clearing. As one, the crowd followed, circling the two, and preparing to clap their hands and sing when Palo gave them the nod. Once again I was given reason to wonder at his diplomacy. But of course, Palo had been there each time Olympias' guards had called good naturedly, "How's your love life, Stick man?" leering at Palo. Always, Palo listened without rancor, dismissing their taunts.

Shalot pulled Kenari into the clearing, and soon the whole gathering danced, arms linked, swaying back and forth and side to side in a giant circle. On one side of me Kenari danced, and on the other, Estra. Forgetting the petulance in H'ruso's voice, I embraced the joyful melody of Palo's flute and, though I hardly considered myself a dancer, I found my feet moving briskly to the rhythm of his playing, dancing splendidly. Perhaps it was the natural mood of the moment, or maybe it was that Estra had a way of leading that made her seem the follower. However it happened, for each succeeding dance, I found her by my side. I danced until dizzy, both from the spinning and from the beer, and I danced until my head cleared, my feet certain and sure.

Palo wearied, and sat beside Spiri to rest. I brought from the cart one of Ana's jars filled with Dimitri's olive oil. "This is for you, Shalot, and for Estra, who has been so kind as to teach me to dance. The oil is from my friend Dimitri's grove in Attica, and the jar was made by his wife, Ana. I held the amphora, more than two hands wide, against my chest, not trusting the handles for its weight. Shalot took the jar, showed it to Estra, and set it on the table. "We have not had olive oil for many seasons," he said. "We have seasoned our grain with pork fat. Not many traders from the south come across the mountains." He banged a spoon against a jar to get attention.

"It is time for the prenuptial sleeping arrangements," he said. "H'ruso will choose a member of Estra's family to bed with, and Estra will choose a member of H'ruso's, to show good will between our families."

"There are no other members of Estra's family except you, Shalot," said H'ruso, so I guess you'll just have to put up with me tonight."

"Just stay on your side of the mat," laughed Shalot, "and I'll stay on mine."

"Ah, sweet thing!" called Yelli, and again everyone laughed.

"And you can sleep with the boy," said H'ruso looking at Estra. "He's been wanting you to notice him all evening."

"Boy isn't your family," said Estra, heated. "I will choose my own sleepmate. Kenari, will you bed with me?"

Kenari smiled and put her arm around Estra. "Gladly, little sister, if Yelli will excuse me from his bed for a night."

Arrangements made, the party broke, and each family stumbled off to lay their mats. I made my tent in the grove somewhat distant from the late night chatter and looked around for Palo, ready to retire. But Palo was nowhere to be seen. Sighing, I lay on my mat and pulled up the cover, preparing to sleep. I had no need for the lamp, moonlight flooded the yard and woods so brightly the trees cast shadows. I thought nothing of it when the tent flap opened and darkened with a figure. "About time you got here," I said to Palo. I thought maybe you were sleeping with Spiri." I chuckled, knowing Palo would not be amused.

"He *is* with Spiri," said a voice, definitely not Palo's.

"Estra?" I asked, stunned. "But you should not be here," I sat up.

"I choose my own prenuptial partner," she said, and Kenari wanted to sleep with her husband." Placing her hand on my shoulder, and leaning her lips onto my neck, she said, "Besides, didn't you suggest I step outside the pattern of the gods?"

"But," I protested. "Not with me, Estra. I have vowed not to marry." I could not bed with Estra. She could become pregnant with my child, and that child could carry the jerking sickness. I could not let this happen.

"Don't worry," she whispered, gently pushing me back. "No one knows I am here." Powerless to protest, I groaned as Estra's skilled hands slipped beneath the covers, searched for and found a not unwilling agent to her suggestions. I gasped. How could such a young woman have learned such art? Trembling, I lay back on my mat. A vat of smooth, wet warmth closed on my member, and I groaned. It had been such a long, long time. Morning would be soon enough to give Estra a potion to kill my seed.

6

High in the mountains of the people of Norikum, we paused at the crest of a hill and looked over into a valley filled with black smoke.

"Fire?" Palo shielded his eyes and searched for the source of the smoke.

"Not woods fire," I said. Foundry smoke. These are the iron mines Tharros spoke of. It's dangerous to go any farther. If guards from the mines don't kill us, that smoke will."

Spitter started forward. "Pull her around Palo; we'll find another way. Palo jumped onto the wagon and pulled the rein. Spitter ignored him, continuing over the crest and downward. I whistled the command for her to turn around. She paused as though considering, and then pushed on. The left wheel ground against the outer edge of the road and began slipping over the side and downward.

"Get off, Palo," I screamed. "She's going over!" Palo jumped for the high side, landed and rolled. The wheel crunched, caught and pulled back onto the road, Spitter's will stronger yet than the pull of earth.

At a lower grade, through layered smoke, we saw mud huts clustered near the water. Smaller, bluer streams of smoke issued from the central courtyard of a raw cut village. There were no pastures, and no sheep grazed nearby. Our feet crunched across brown mud hardened to cracked and peeling brick. People milled nearby, and mules and oxen hitched to logging traces made brutal intrusion on the forest. We drew nearer and peeled off our coats, dreading to walk on the heated ground.

Our eyes stung. Men dressed in zomatas began to notice us. I coughed. A group unloading woods bark pointed our way and paused.

Spitter crossed between two domed furnaces. From their tops, dark smoke rolled upward in oily coils. I choked, coughed, wiped my eyes and followed.

Spitter stopped near a group of men seated on boxes, rocks and rolled blankets near a camp fire. The fire reddened their bare arms and torsos, sparking light in the sweat from their bodies.

Palo lifted the canvas from the cart to get Spitter's watering urn. One man, soggy wet in the heat, mid thirties in age I guessed, from the wrinkles around the eyes, wore a shirt dyed blue and green. It sagged from broad, square shoulders. He looked up at us, turned back to say a few more words to the men seated around him, and, as though just noticing us threw out the dregs of his wine bowl, stood and approached. Longish, brown hair, bleached auburn in the sun, had been pulled severely to the back of his neck and bound. The reddened skin of his features stood in stark relief, accenting a face ravaged by the pox, badly healed. He stood a distance away from me, glaring. Somewhat taller than I, square and more muscular of frame, he rested his hand lightly on a staff, carried more for office than support.

I dipped my head, held it longer than necessary and then raised my eyes, waiting, expecting an invitation to join the group, to be offered water and wine. I was to be disappointed. I took hold of Spitter's halter, meaning to lead her back in the direction from which we had come. Spitter, nose dipped into the bag of oats Palo had hung around her neck, refused to move.

I chose another tactic. "I am a healer," I said. "Perhaps you have someone in your camp who has need of me?" At the man's hesitation, I said, "but of course, if you already have someone here to take care of such matters—broken bones, fevers, teeth, that sort of thing—I wouldn't want to offend him. I'll just be on my way."

"I don't know of anyone..." He paused. "Boy!" He beckoned to a man his elder by at least ten years. The man rose, stretched and ambled toward us. "Yah, Rufus?"

"See if anyone needs the services of a physician," he said over his shoulder. "This man here says he's a healer. He can stay."

I waited, enduring the scrutiny of smoke-reddened eyes. "You bring your own medicines?"

"Oh yes," I replied, and again dipped my head, more to stifle a sneeze than to show deference. "Perhaps, if it's no trouble to you and your village, I could forage for herbs? Different species grow here in the north than those I carry in my cart, and of course, my stores always need replenishing."

He ignored my request. "That is a fine donkey you have," he nodded to Spitter, and moved closer to her, looking her over. "Your boy keeps her groomed. Must not be easy out on these muddy roads." By this time, two other men had moved closer, also examining Spitter. I laid my hand on Spitter's muzzle, something she detested my doing. She suffered the indignity, even nuzzling my hand before jerking away.

"Palo has a way with animals," I said, "but I brush Spitter myself." Not liking the acquisitive gleam in the men's eyes, I added. "She's rather fearful of strangers. She only lets Palo or me handle her." In response to my words, as one of the men reached to pat her neck, Spitter snapped at his hand, teeth bared, missing his fingers by a breath.

"Haven't you trained her yet?" asked the man, shaken.

Rufus gestured for me to follow and led us toward the big house. "We're still working on it." I tossed back. Any thief would think more than twice, now, before he tried to steal this irascible, cantankerous, now vicious, piece of work we respectfully called Spitter.

I coughed, my eyes burned, and I sought some way to get out of this dirty cloud of smoke. I would be surprised not to find several cases of lung problems here, and vowed to move out as soon as I could get away, yet the air did seem to clear as we climbed.

The thickest of the dark smoke hovered above the lake, tendrils like an octopus attempting to crawl up the sides of the basin, recoiling when pushed back by descending air currents. Palo, coming up beside me, wiped a sleeve across his face and eyes, the sleeve coming away oily black. This would not do. I searched a place up the side of the hill behind the house, saw a shallow declivity and pointed Palo toward it. "We'll camp there," I said, "but we'll have to get water from the well."

"No need," said Rufus. "That's near a spring. You may be bothered by others spreading their pallets, but most of the men sleep in the mines. It's clearer there."

The hillside was also several degrees cooler than lower in the basin, an effect both of the altitude and the distance from the furnaces belching smoke and sparks. "That go on all night?" I asked. Rufus ignored me. "Father," he said to a man leaning against the door wiping mud from a sandal with a stick. "This is a healer. Maybe he can look at that burn on your arm."

"Sure," he said. Get yourself settled and I'll get us something to eat. Won't be much, we don't have anyone around here who can cook. It's just Rufus and me, and we don't bother much."

Though slightly stooped, Rudy stood taller than Rufus. Hair that showed red through the white in fringes around his bald head suggested the reason for his name. His forehead, naturally high, rose in a dome above heavily bushed brows. Straight-cropped, rough white beard, filled now with black flecks from the smoky fires, covered his chin. His eyes, squinting through narrow slits, glittered, and I knew that the older man had watched our ascent, taking our measure.

He replaced his sandal, ducked his head and entered the hut. Rufus went back downhill, calling names as he went, issuing orders to men who scurried to finish loading and unloading wagons, and stacking boxes near a hut. As I watched, other wagons entered the yard in the same direction from which we had come, settling themselves into a line behind the others, hurrying to finish their work before darkness fell, though with the flames showing through holes in the furnaces, I doubted that it would get much darker.

We found the spring, just above our campsite. Water flowed through a huge bowl, and Palo dipped in his hands to wash, liberally splashing the cold water across his face, neck and shoulders, clearing his eyes of sooty smoke, dousing his hair and wringing it dry. For once he didn't grumble at my demands, but breathed a huge sigh and continued to splash water onto his genitals and feet. Despite his reluctance he had begun to see the need for bathing. As he retrieved a clean shirt from the cart, I also bathed, dressed, then soaked rags to wash Spitter's eyes and clear her nose of soot. She stood still, quiet as a mountain cat basking in the sun.

Here away from the fumes, the beauty of this accursed place startled us. The sun edged the black smoke with gold light, and the two furnaces half way up the hillside glowed, suggesting an image of winking red eyes in a huge animal, sitting, waiting for the camp to sleep so it could spring, routing us all. Lake waters turned pink then black as the sun passed beyond the western hill, but the winking red eyes continued to glow.

Palo and I sat beside Rudy near a fire pit where iron bars had been suspended above the flames to hold hanging, iron pots. Coaxed into shape by an expert metal worker, the pots, still showing the artisan's hammer marks and fitted with lids, were works of art. I knew, as I saw Rudy lift one by a long rod with a hook on the end, that I was looking at the artisan. The ropy muscles of Rudy's arms and shoulders, shrunken now, with age, seemed somehow alien to the man, for I would have expected to find that chiseled nose and those sharp cheek bones mounted on the slender, ascetic frame of a philosopher or teacher, someone like Aristotle. Yet–I corrected myself in my thought–did not Socrates himself have the rough-hewn countenance suggestive of pagan savages? Still, the head definitely did not belong on those shoulders.

Rudy must have discerned my thought, for he said, "I am not an iron worker by birth. Working the ore is necessary if I am to study it. I am not very good at it; we have craftsmen here far better than I, even Rufus, though he considers that work beneath him." He nodded toward his son, climbing the hill. "Yet everyone seems to expect me to make the rules they are happy enough to follow." He shrugged. "Before I could tell them how to work it, I had to learn for myself."

"You discovered iron working without a teacher?" I could hardly credit my hearing.

"Oh, I had a few things to get me started." He never looked at me as he talked, but looked at marks he drew in the dirt with his staff. "When I was a boy I used to come up to these hills looking for artifacts. The clan stories told of a colony of mages who lived here in this valley. They all got sick and died, leaving their magic to crumble and decay. My parents tried to stop me, not wanting me to waste time proving old stories, so I came up on the pretext of fishing and gathering roots for our family. I found the ruins and worked them, rebuilding what I could, obsessed with the desire to learn what they had been used for.

"I married a woman a lot older than I." He smeared his drawings with a sandaled foot and began again. "She had a son. That was Rufus. He was about sixteen. Ten years later, we moved into these hills, built a hut, and started studying the ruins. Then my wife became ill. I was no physician, you see, but a woodsman. I couldn't save her. But Rufus and I stayed. That was two years ago."

"Did you ever wonder what happened to the iron mages, to make them ill?"

"I know what it was," Rudy said. "It had to be the air they breathed. We have already had men become sick and move away. It's much worse now than it was in the beginning."

Intrigued with his drawings, I pointed to the three circles, questioning him with my brows lifted. "You are also an artist?"

"Oh no, no," he said, worried. "I'm just trying to figure out how to relieve this valley of the smoke. He pointed to the hills that surrounded us. "At first the smoke was carried away by the mountain winds. Now it just stays here and collects. I don't know what I'm going to do. Rufus has built up quite a business, selling iron to craftsmen across the mountains, away from this place. Every day, we must hire more wagon masters. The demand grows as people learn about us." He rubbed his balding head and pulled at an ear. The only thing different now is that the forest has been cleared of trees. I think maybe that has something to do with it."

"I noticed the clearing when I came in," I said. "The trees have been clean cut. The ground has eroded, and young saplings have not come back. That's how it is in the southern lands. Few trees remain, except those that are cultivated for fruit and nuts. But the land is put to good use growing vegetables and feeding sheep and goats. Here, well, the land is wasted."

"I know. It is not the way of my clan. In my village the land is precious. It just seemed that there were so many trees here they would last forever. We didn't think about the damage cutting them would do."

"Do you need so much wood? Surely your people's huts don't require so much."

Rudy glanced up from his drawing, at first startled, I suppose, at my ignorance. Then the look became more appraising, and I sensed a decision. "The wood is used to make coke to burn in the furnaces," he told me, watching my eyes as he spoke. "Without the furnaces we could not melt the ore."

I was suddenly a stupid boy again, as when my grandmother had to explain the straightening of a broken bone. "Of course. The furnaces."

At this moment Rufus joined us, frowning at his father, and looking with decided distrust at me. Was it deliberate that he stepped on the lines drawn in the loose dirt?

"The physician and I were discussing the reasons for the sickness in the camp," he said, redrawing the lines. "I'm studying how to clear the valley of smoke and fumes."

Uncertainly, Rufus sat down beside me and looked at the drawings.

"We have cut too many trees. The smoke clings to the earth and the winds do not clear it away as they used to do," said Rudy.

"What can a stranger tell us about our business?"

"The physician comes from the far south, Boy. He has seen many great wonders. What do you think, physician? What would you do?" Rufus caught his breath as though to speak, but at a glance from Rudy, he swallowed and settled himself on a bench.

"I am but a peddler, Rudy. I buy and sell things, and gather herbs to use in the manner taught me by my grandmother who was a healer. I know nothing of craftwork." I would have left it there, for Rufus' manner shouted his doubt of me.

"Surely you have seen other mines, noticed how they have solved this problem," he urged. "I would hear what you have to say."

"Well…" I began. "The mines I have seen were not located in a bowl, like this valley, but slope downward and away, toward the sea. It seems the smoke here becomes trapped and does not blow away. Mixed with fog, it becomes deadly to breathe. Palo and I will be leaving with the morning." I felt Rufus relax. He didn't quite know what category to fit me in, I think. A peddler/physician, yes, but also perhaps a spy who would steal their secrets?

The old man let the wooden staff hang, gently tapping the ground near his drawing. "We have people in need of a physician," he said. "Would you leave them untended?"

Ah. Craftsman became politician. He had seen a weakness in me and was not above driving his point home. "It should take about a week for you to see everybody. You could stay up here, where the air is cleaner, and they could come up to you."

I understood his game. This man had more colors than a rainbow. I had spoken of leaving to put Rufus' mind at ease. Rudy spoke now for that same reason. Rufus must see that his father trusted me and wanted me to stay. Now, fully aware of the game we played, Rudy and I played it with vigor. The father needed the assent of the son. Without Rufus, there would be no trade, and without trade, the smelting must cease. I looked expectantly at Rufus. "If I may be of service… and if I am not intruding…"

Looking away toward the valley rather than at me, the younger man said, "My man said more are falling ill every day. You can stay and treat them." Then he dipped his head. It was the only apology I would get.

I shrugged. "Then how can I refuse?"

"You will be well paid," said Rudy. "You and your boy and your donkey will be fed while you are here. And," he added. "We'll rim your wheels with iron. I notice one of them is cracked. Wood doesn't last long on these roads."

I nodded. It was well that I would be paid, for I could use the money for merchandise bought in these northern lands. "You are very kind," I said. "I will begin looking at your people first light."

※ ※ ※

Rocks clattered as bindings on bags were released, dropping ore into huge troughs descending toward the grading tables.

"You see, Rudy," one man called. "I told you we'd get the better of Lehan's team. We hit a vein of ore the size of a house. It'll take three weeks to clear it all."

"Longer than that." Another laughed. "We have no idea how far back into the mountain this seam extends."

"You'll be done in half that time, I'll wager," called the one named Lehan, for you'll be meeting us coming down from the corner digs."

I heard the sound of laughter, and the thunder of rocks being slammed onto the table. "You're on." said the first, and, voices fading, two of the men went away to splash water across their faces to clear their eyes.

"Ho, Rudy," called the third man, the man named Lehan. "I finished the bracelet for Lilia. Come, see what you think."

We followed Lehan down an alley between mud huts, stepping over a board-covered ditch carrying wastes, and dodging a clothes line hung with still-wet laundry, fabric already dusted with flecks of soot. A woman watched as we passed, and waved.

"How much ore did you dig last night, Lehan?"

"Enough to pay for that sow you wanted," he called, not slowing.

In a hollow in a bank of rocks, brush and clay, Lehan's forge huddled against the cliff beneath an extended shelter of mud-chinked logs. He entered, tossed chunks of coke on a bank of embers and stirred it. A deep depression in the earth beneath his feet told of the hours he had stood here, working.

"This it?" asked Rudy, picking up the bracelet from among the other iron pieces and bits of scrap iron on Lehan's table. "Pretty," he said. "You used your new technique. How do you do that?" He handed the bracelet to me. Meant to fit on a woman's upper arm, it was about four inches wide and polished to a high gleam. It opened on two small hinges and fastened on the opposite side by a tiny latch. I held it up, trying to catch a nonexistent morning ray of light. The bracelet gleamed white, like silver, but this didn't have the feel of silver. Harder, somehow, and heavier. I turned it in my hand, following the contours of the metal with my fingers. Rudy's work was good, but this man was a true artisan. I handed the bracelet to Rufus.

Lehan leaned against the side of a post holding up the roof. "I fire the metal and hammer it on the anvil, then dip it in the water to cool and then fire it again. I cool it nice and slow. Takes longer than what I usually do. I found that if I fire it and fold it and hammer it and cool it more, it gets shinier. Do you know it won't even rust? I swear, look at this." He held a cup lifted from a shelf loaded with pieces he had made, some silvery, some black, and some red and rough with rust. He polished the cup with a woolen rag and tossed the rag back onto a peg next to the shelves.

"This is the first piece I made like this," he said, holding it up and turning it. "That was last spring, and it still looks polished."

"You have more of those cups?" I asked. "They'd sell pretty well at the market, and I'd like to take some home to a friend."

"Oh, maybe a few, I gave them to the wife, but she just set them on a shelf and never used them. She says she'd rather use the pottery bowls. You think that bracelet will fit Lilia?" he asked. "Ahner says it's too small."

"Too small," Rufus agreed. "Lilia's arm is a lot bigger than that."

Rudy laughed. "You've been watching Lilia pretty closely, have you?"

Rufus grinned, and his face turned a deeper shade of red. "I just notice things," he said.

༄༄༄

I sat for a few moments before calling my next patient. The air seemed clearer this morning than it had last night. Why would the early morning air be cleaner than later in the day? The furnace fires never went out, and black smoke continuously belched from the holes in the tops of the rounded domes. If the smoke were truly being trapped in the valley, wouldn't it remain heavy throughout? I asked Rudy as much when we broke for a meal at noontime.

"That's what stumps me," he said. "When we first began to work the ore, there was just fog, caused by the heat of the furnaces meeting the cold air here around the lake. It's always hard to see in the early morning, because of the fog, but at least, at first, we could breathe. Of course some mornings are better than others."

"I noticed a back draft from the west last night," I said. "Why didn't that clear it?"

"The smoke just moves about. These valleys are like a beaded necklace—a string of basins. The fumes move into the next basin at night, then come morning it moves back. We're breathing yesterday's fumes."

"But why don't the winds draw it through the basin and up the sides of the mountain?" I asked. "Usually, heavy updrafts toward the peaks come with the dawn, and downdrafts come when the valleys cool. It seems you have no updraft in the morning, here, at all."

"The trees," said Rudy, after a long pause. "I know it has something to do with the trees. When the trees were gone from the easy slopes around the lake we started cutting from the next valley down stream. The smoke settles there. Then in the mornings the east wind brings it back. Day and night, the fumes just trade back and forth, east to west, west to east. Now it's gotten so thick it hardly stirs."

"Yes." I said. "And the drafts curl back at that ledge up there. The smoke never gets past it." Vertical columns of rock faced the valley. Exposed ledges cantilevered outward along the top, some boulders extending like huge heads poised to fall at any moment, any one of which could have decimated the camp. Between the columns where time had eroded the rock in eight to ten-foot channels from top to bottom, heavy growth choked the gullies.

"Maybe the ledge at the top traps the smoke and holds it here in the basin. Then it has no place to go, and just sinks back down when the valley cools. The winds can't pull it through and up the east mountain because the rocks curve in and out again at the top." We sat together, thinking. I shrugged. "But what can you do?"

"We could clear the trees out of the gullies," Rudy said softly, as though to say it aloud would make him seem foolish. Taking his staff, he began to draw. Louder, said, "We could clear the trees in the cracks up the side of the mountain. The channel would allow the mountain drafts to draw the smoke up and out, through the breaks in the rocks." His eyes burned with excitement. "About here," he said, poking his map, all the time getting more excited. Then he waved the rod high in the air and shouted, laughing, swinging the rod back and forth to show the motion of the smoke. "The wind will come down through the channels at night strong enough to blow the smoke away into the west, into the next valley and the next after that. Then when the winds reverse, what's left of the smoke will blow up and out. Up, through the channels!" He quieted. "Of course, it will have to pull the smoke in from the next valley in the mornings, too. It will take a few days to get it all, and we'll be making more all the time. Still, it might work." He jabbed his stick into the ground. "We'll do it. We'll cut wood from the gullies, up the east side. We have to try something, else none of us will live long enough to make any difference."

Neither of us had noticed Rufus standing by, listening. "It's too steep," he said. "We can't get our donkeys up there to haul the lumber back down."

Both Rudy and I looked toward the mountain, but Rudy would not allow the idea to die.

"We'll use ropes," he said. "We'll suspend ourselves from the top, cutting below us. We'll cut the lower ones first. They'll slide downhill to where the donkeys can haul them the rest of the way."

"It might work," Rufus said, shaking his head. "But we will lose some men."

"Offer bonuses," said Rudy. "Tell the cutters it'll be dangerous, but tell them it'll make the air cleaner. They'll do it. We have a lot of good men here, and didn't you have to turn away work crews yesterday because you had nothing for them to do?"

"People outside will learn about this place if we hire more men. He looked at me as he continued, "The more people who learn what we're doing, the harder it'll be. We'll have to increase watchers to keep them out. Do you know how much that will cost?"

"Rufus!" said Rudy, parking his hands on his hips, and for once showing irritation at his son's pessimism. "You look for thieves and robbers behind every rock. Do you think so little of what we're doing that you think just anyone could walk in, take a look around and know all our secrets? It's taken me more than twenty years to make sense of it. How do you think a casual observer would know?"

Heated, Rufus argued, "We can trust those we have now because they have a stake in the business. Every one of them would stand to lose if someone comes in here and takes it away from us. And if bandits are strong enough they can hold us captive and make us work for them. They wouldn't have to know the secrets to make money off us. We'd be their slaves, Father." Then ashamed of his outburst Rufus bowed his head, but not before he stole a glance at me.

"My patients are waiting," I said. "I have two with teeth that need pulling, and one broken arm to check and repack. I'm finished, unless more get sick. By the way, how is your burn?" I asked Rudy.

"Oh," he said, glancing at his wrist. "It's nothing. I even forgot about it. Pain's all gone. What did you put on it anyway?"

"Secret," I said, and we both burst out laughing. Rufus walked away, grumbling at our teasing.

෴

The next morning I spoke to Rudy about leaving. He grabbed my arm as though losing a brother. "You can't," he said. "We'll be starting the channel cuts today. Rufus hired more men for a work crew last night. We're all set. It's dangerous work, and someone could get hurt." He pleaded. "We need you here. At least until the cutting is done."

So each morning for six days, Rudy met me, overflowing with plans for the day. Each day I spread my merchandise in case there should be something someone wanted to trade for, then, together, we stood on a knoll overlooking the cutting of the channels up the hill, watching the wood being chopped for the furnace fires. In a fury of activity that left my head spinning, he showed me the iron smelting works, describing in ongoing detail about how coke, made from the wood, was layered with ore, dropping the pieces down through a hole in the top of the furnaces. He told how the ore melted, blended with ash from the fire, bled through a hole in the sides of the furnaces, ran downhill underground till it emerged downhill in the next basin to continue on oven-baked pottery troughs, a natural conveyor of the soft, hot iron. Eventually, as the metal cooled and slowed, it was to be scooped up by workers, pressed into molds, and laid out like bricks while still warm and pliable. From there, except for the ingots Rudy and a few others worked into things for use in the camp, they were loaded onto wagons and readied for shipping to foundries and metalworking artisans across the mountains.

Iron was not the only business here. Rudy told me of another operation down the valley where salt was mined. It was across the hill from where we had entered H'stok, nearer the joining of the rivers. These hills were riddled with pockets of salt deposits, Rudy's discovery. Salt miners paid fees to dig and for wagons to cart it down from the mountain. Rufus used the salt mines as an excuse to explain the coming and going of carts loaded with iron ingots.

Hearing miners of one team hooting and jeering, taunting miners of another to best them in production excited me. "I'd like to see the mines," I said, one morning at breakfast. "Do they go far back into the hill?"

"About two stadia," said Rudy, "at least at this point. We'd have gone much deeper, but we had to shore up the old tunnels along the way to keep the earth from crumbling and burying us, at least for those digs that were here already. I used to explore them when I was a boy, and later, Rufus and I came up to talk about our dreams of reopening them."

"You and Rufus are close, eh?"

"Don't know what I'd have done without that boy. I'm no business man. Rufus takes to it like a fish to water. He has a natural sense of how to make money. He's no judge of men, though. I have to deal with them to keep them happy."

The next day, Rudy took me down into the mines. I wouldn't let Spitter come down; the floor was too uneven, and I didn't want her falling and breaking a leg, so Palo, fearing that the donkey would be stolen, stayed above ground with her. Sometimes I thought he should have been born an ass himself. He was certainly stubborn enough.

When we entered the door of the mine, the smoky fog vanished. The roof of the first level soared upward and away to a rounded top, a natural opening in the rock. Crates and boxes and bags lined an inner wall. "Emergency supplies," said Rudy. "If we are attacked, we can hole up in here and defend ourselves. Bandits would have to come through one by one."

The floor sloped downward on a clay-filled and smoothed ramp and into a smaller room, where beams crisscrossed and braced the ceiling. Donkeys waited there for pulleys to haul up platforms loaded with ore. After that, steep declines made ladders necessary to descend the slopes. We descended one such ladder through a hole toward another level lighted with torches stuck in the walls, the ladder shifting and popping, creaking with my weight. I touched the jointings and found that the rungs had been tied on with leather bindings. The leather could have been hundreds of years old, judging by their color and hardness.

"The ladders were here when we came," said Rudy. "Work of the mages who were here before us. They don't wear out. We're up and down these ladders night and day, and up to this minute, none have broken. Nothing rots down here. We've found bodies of ancient men, whole, perfectly preserved bodies. We covered them with grit and let them be. The men say it's their spirits that keep the ladders from rotting."

"How about you?" I asked. "Do you believe in the spirits?"

"I believe in what I can see," Rudy said, putting an end to more questions on the subject.

Rudy stopped to chat with miners, asking about their caches, spoke of how much it would weigh out when melted, and how their pay would be meted. I wandered away, picking up curiously colored pebbles, dipping my hand in greasy-looking water and rubbing my fingers together. Hardly drinkable, but good for rinsing off the worst of the dirt that clung to the ore before packing it uphill to the donkeys.

Workers moved briskly, hauling ore up from a still lower level, but there was neither bickering nor fighting and it was evident that each man knew his job and did it with vigor.

"How did you get them so organized?" I asked.

"Teams," said Rudy. "One team gets a bonus for bringing up more ore than the other."

"Do they all work for you?"

"No, some are independent. If they make a strike they come to me to make a deal. They pay me for each load they bring up."

"Well, that explains why they wash the ore before they pack them in bags for loading," I laughed. "They know you won't pay for dirt."

"If you tried lifting one of those bags and hauling it to the top," he said, "you'd make sure you weren't hauling up dirt, too. Maybe you'd like to see one of the lower levels. It goes on for about a stadia and a half."

I looked at the ladder descending a nearby hole, heard the rungs creaking long before an ascending miner got to the top. "I think I've seen enough," I said. Rudy laughed and clapped me on the shoulder. "Cautious little man, aren't you?" Following a woman miner carrying a bag loaded with ore, we returned to the upper room. A work crew had already built a fire, and about thirty of the one hundred or so men and women who worked down here, rested on bunks spread around in a circle. Two mats were laid out for Rudy and me. Rufus lay on a bunk next to ours.

Rudy sat on one and motioned me to the other. "Thought you might like to see what it was like, sleeping in the mine," he said. I looked at the door longingly. I didn't want to offend my host, but I liked my own tent and my own blanket.

"No one's going to bother that donkey of yours, Shorty," one of the men called. So I had been named again. The list of names was getting longer. "I have a whip that works really good keeping our donkeys in line. Maybe I could show you how to use it." They all laughed.

Suddenly I felt exposed, unprotected here among this rough group of men, men I didn't know, really, except for Rudy and Rufus, and I wasn't even certain of Rufus.

"That donkey saved my life a few days ago," I said, and told them the story of the rock slide I had nearly fallen into. "Spitter isn't just a donkey, she's my friend. I don't use whips on her."

Why did I feel the need to justify that ass? I had walked the edge, near to whipping her myself almost every day she had been with me. "But she is a cantankerous beast," I agreed. "Like some people I know. She's too smart to be a donkey. She's the one who led us here. Or I should say, brought us. When she makes up her mind about something, neither Palo nor I can convince her otherwise.

"I threaten to sell her, but then as soon as I do, she does something incredible, like keeping me from falling into that crevice. She stopped on the edge and wouldn't move. I tried to pull her along, and the ground fell away beneath me. When I looked below all I could see was a blue ice hole. I never did see the bottom. If my hand hadn't been holding her muzzle, I'd be a frozen corpse by now, and no one would ever have found me."

When my story ended no one spoke. All we could hear was water dripping, falling into the pond on the level below us, producing a kind of humming ring that vibrated the still air. "A-hmm." Rudy finally broke the silence. "I brought ribs and turnips, and one of the wives packed us some loaves of bread. Thought you boys might be hungry for something besides dried meat and cheese." Then he waved his arm in the air, holding a jar of wine. "Eat up, boys. We're giving the physician a royal send off."

Everyone converged on Rudy's sacks, grabbed pickled turnips by fishing them out of the jar with two fingers, and dug into the ribs, tearing them apart with their hands.

"You planned all this ahead of time, didn't you?"

"Didn't want you to go away thinking our camp had no hospitality," Rudy admitted. "You had to see the spirit of these people. Besides I have too much to learn from you. It isn't often I get to talk to someone outside this valley."

Time counted for nothing there in the blackness of the mine, illuminated only by the flickering fire and torches set on walls about the cave. Wine was passed and then again and again, and I, to still my nervousness and warm the chill of the mine, drank my share with each passing of the goatskin.

"What is it like in Attica," asked Rufus. "Is it hilly like here?"

"Hilly, yes," I said. "And the waters of the sea all around." Suddenly I felt very lonely, very homesick for those barren hills. "But there is never enough fresh water for all the needs. Wells are precious, and often run dry in drought. Streams are sacred, and some people greet the dawn beside the creeks and rivers to give thanks to the gods for letting the water run freely. Olympias says the rivers are the blood of the land."

"Who is Olympias," asked Rufus. "Your woman?" Everyone laughed, for they thought that Palo was my bedmate.

"She is a princess of Epirus," I said. "She is also a priestess. When she is in a city she leads the morning prayers beside the rivers."

"Priestess?" asked one of the men. "Does she give blessings to lonely men?" The whole company laughed long and hard. "You interested Valdo?" one yelled. Valdo shrank. His question had been sincere, not meant to disparage a priestess.

"She is not that kind of priestess," I said. "She is the daughter of the Chosen One of the Temple of Unseen Spirits at Kreté. Her mother was killed by the priests because she had disobeyed their commands, married and had a baby. Then the priests came to get Olympias, to take her mother's place at the temple, but her friends aided her escape into the mountains."

"Do you know her well?" asked Rufus.

"I treat her when she is sick," I answered.

"What is she like?" asked Rudy.

"Her hair curls around her face and glows red in the sunset. "She's a little bird of a girl. But she has more courage in one of her fingers than I have in my whole body. I'm scared to even try to get on a horse, but she..." That reminded me of an incident that still gives me the shudders to think about.

"She used to have weak ankles. I used an ointment on them, and then bound them to keep them from bending too easily. I showed her maid how to do it when I wasn't there. I gave her a pair of my boots to wear till her ankles got stronger. She's so tiny, shorter than I. Well, one day I entered her camp, and there she was, riding a horse. Standing up on his back. That horse just galloped in a wide circle while she held her arms out, like she was flying. 'Look at me, Wallis! I'm flying!' she called. I thought I would spill my water."

"You love her," said Rudy.

Embarrassed, I tried to recover balance. "Everyone loves Olympias," I said. "When she enters a noisy gathering everyone stops talking and stands to honor her. When she speaks she brings chills of joy to the listeners."

"She called you Wallis, " said Rufus. "Is that your name?" My breath caught. I hadn't meant to reveal so much to these people. Wallis was my secret name, the one only she and Palo used. "Oh, along with Stick Man," I said, "That's what her guards call me."

"She has guards?" Rufus again. I put my wine bowl down. There was something about this deep, dark place. Wine never affected me so before. I would arouse Rufus' fear. Men who are afraid, are dangerous.

"Sort of an honor guard," I said. "She is a priestess, and she is still sought by the priests of the Temple of Unseen Spirits. They want to capture her or kill her. Either would be acceptable."

There were no more questions after that, and I knew that the lonely miners, hungry for news of anything beyond their valley, would go to sleep dreaming of a tiny, beautiful maiden, flying along on the bare back of a horse. A priestess, Chosen of the Gods. And they would know I loved her.

回回回

At Rudy's insistence, we stayed one more day. The work went well, and there were no accidents; even Rudy lost interest in the project. But with only half the channels cleared, the air in the valley became sweeter. The night before I left the following morning, we sat by the fire in front of his house.

"I'd rather live outside," said Rudy. "I never wanted the house. That was Rufus' idea. He said his crew wouldn't respect him if he slept in the mine with them. And it wasn't enough to just build sleeping quarters. He had to have the biggest house in the camp, and had to build it up here, on the hill." He laughed. "That way everyone would have to look up to him."

I said nothing. I knew how much the father really cared for the son.

We looked at stars that had been invisible, hidden by smoke and fog before now. "You see that bright star, there in the east?" Rudy asked. "I grew up watching that star. It's just like one I see in the west, in the summer time. I think it's the same star. Different times of the year it shows up. In the early mornings I can see it in the east, and then it starts to travel over, heading west. Then when I see it in the west, in the evening, I see it setting across those hills. He pointed west. I think it travels around the earth."

"Around?" I asked. "You think the earth is round?"

"It's got to be. That's the only way to explain how a star can come up in the east and sink in the west. Just like the sun and the moon. Sometimes I see a red one that does the same thing."

"I talked to a ship's captain a while back. He says he can find his way by looking at the stars. He says they're not really gods; it's just that men name them so they can keep track of them better. Of course, the common people believe they're really gods. I try not to argue with them." I chuckled. "Sometimes people get right angry when they get disagreed with about their religion. But the captain didn't mention stars that go around the earth."

"I think that bright star is different from the others. Those you always see together. This one goes from one to the other. Like a messenger. Flies faster, taking the news to those others who have to stay in their own camps." He looked at me. "Like you, Daneion. You travel about from here to there. Rufus and I just stay in one place."

"That's all too much for me to learn. I'm a common peddler and simple herbsman. I know nothing about stars."

But, though Rudy offered no contradiction, I knew I would have difficulty persuading him of anything other than what he had decided. I let it lie.

The next day we packed our cart getting ready to leave. Much of our merchandise had been bought by the miners and the few women in the camp, and the cart loaded quickly. "Do you have any of those iron pegs some people like to use to make boxes?" I asked Lehan, and he went back to his shelter, returning with a large box. Inside were the cups I had asked about, and a few of the pegs. "These won't rot away," he said. "They've been dipped in kalmia earth while they were hot. I looked at one of them, turning it over in my fingers. "This looks like what I need," I said. "You have any more of them?"

"That's all I have now," he said, "but I can make you more for your next visit."

"I never know for sure where I'll be going. It all depends on that ornery ass of mine." The man laughed. He had been the one who had tried to pet her.

Then Rufus came, handing me a small casket made of polished wood. The lid lifted on hinges, and when I looked inside I found a woman's armband. It was the bracelet Lehan had shown us.

"It was too small for Lilia," Rufus said, so I traded for it. It's a gift for Olympias."

I lifted the armband and turned it in my hands. Wavy lines, engraved and polished, had been filled with some kind of blue filler. The wavy blue lines circled the bracelet. It caught the rays of the clear morning sun, and shimmered like newly-minted gold.

"The wavy lines are made by filling them with powdered calcite and then fired. They are for the water and the rivers where the priestess Olympias gives her blessing."

My breath caught and my hands shook. I had misjudged Rufus. This man who seemed driven only to fashion a fortune from the sale of iron ingots had the soul of a poet. I struggled to speak past my choked throat, finding that the discovery of the man within the brittle shell he effected had left me undone. "My lady will treasure this beyond all her other jewelry."

"I would have set it with gems," he said, "but I had nothing to put on it. When you find a gem smith, have him put gems along the wavy lines, like stones along the river."

〰〰〰

From H'stok, we headed directly north, following wagons loaded with iron. When I turned to look backward as I always do, feeling that I am leaving part of myself behind, I waved to a crowd of people standing in sunlight, bright and clear, and looked over a lake as blue as an ocean—a turquoise jewel set in patches of red and yellow, the colors of earth. And it was then that I knew I would return here again and again, despite where that pesky donkey led.

"Get up!" I called, and Palo, Spitter and I descended the mountain following a string of mules, oxen, donkeys, wagons, wagon masters and loaders, along River Traun on our way north. We descended the mountain into the darkness of storm.

7

▣▣▣ ⊛ ▣▣▣

Rain-filled clouds closed in around us, stifling even the sounds of a flute calling the wagons in the caravan onward. Winds swayed the tall pines in a terrible but majestic dance, bending them half way to earth. Palo and I clung to the cart for balance as stinging droplets of water gathered into sheets and fell, turning the earth to sooty gravy. Our clothes clung to our backs, and our leg muscles throbbed with the effort of jerking our boots loose from the mud, feet slipping beneath us with every step. Palo and I stopped and stared at a sea of writhing gray-violet mist.

The last wagon of the caravan disappeared, and the sounds of donkey bells quieted. The rain-washed trail looked no different now, than any other part of the forest, despite the tonnage of the wagons passing before us. The heavy rain ceased, but fog settled in, gathering us in swirling patches.

I don't know how long we would have waited, uncertain and lost, had Spitter not jerked the wheels of the cart loose from the mud and pulled forward onto a narrow trail leading upward. We followed it onto firmer ground, and, as the trail climbed, I lost any sense of direction. Though we moved, it seemed that we ploughed through nothing, going nowhere.

Finally, muscles taut from caution, the fog thinned and I saw that we followed a hillside road, steep banks rising on our right and a chiseled gorge dropping away to our left, how deeply, I could not tell. No heavy wagons had passed this way; the only tracks left on the moist roadbed were those of goats. Palo called me to stop.

"Listen."

I turned my good ear in the direction he pointed and stood very still. Faint bleating sounded from somewhere ahead. "A goat," I said. "Maybe a newborn. It's probably all right. Goats usually throw kids in early spring, especially the wild ones. We'll see how it is when we get closer."

Continuing on, the sounds didn't increase but seemed to localize somewhere on our right. "I'm going to look," said Palo. He slipped out of his boots and tossed them onto the cart. Barefoot, he climbed the raw hillside, fitting toes in holes caused by loosened and rolling rocks. Slipping to his knees time and again, he climbed still higher.

"I don't see anything but a few goats, Wallis," he called from a slanted ledge. "Up here the sounds seem to be coming from down there."

"Nothing down here," I called, then, "Wait." A faint scratching, tapping sound like worms burrowing into dead wood came from a pile of rocks and mud that had fallen and lodged not too far above the road. Palo had passed right over them. I climbed toward the pile, and the tapping seemed louder.

"Something here, Palo. Come help me clear away these rocks." Palo picked his way more carefully coming down than going up. Blood streamed from one knee down his mudcaked leg.

We pulled on a boulder recently broken and exposed to the weather. Jagged and rough, almost buried in clay, it refused to give way. Still the knocking continued, faster, harder. "Whatever it is, is alive," I said.

Palo found a young sapling broken by the landslide, and together we fitted an end of it beneath the topmost rock. The young tree bent beneath our combined weights, but did not break. Again and again we leaned on it, placed it in other crevices, and leaned again. Then with a sucking noise the boulder pulled free, teetered on its side and rolled away.

The knocking sounded louder, and with the knocking, came a faint bleating. Harder now, Palo and I worked the end of the tree into crevices and pried loose several smaller rocks, exposing a cavity formed between the original cliff face and a large, flat stone. Beneath the stone lay a man, head mostly buried in mud, but with an arm freed when the upper stone rolled away. He wiped away enough mud so that he could see and talk.

"I'm here," his voice wavered, high and reedy. "Do you see the kid?

He was with me when the ground fell away. Just born. The mother is somewhere close by, too."

Palo and I worked more carefully now, prying loose outer rocks and letting them roll downhill, working on and on, heedless of exhaustion. Through a crevice I saw the shepherd's foot caught beneath two stones. I reached for the pole intending to pry them apart to release him, and then a cramp froze my muscles stiff.

"A moment," I gasped, falling onto my side across the loose rubble. Then I saw it. A tiny, newborn kid, eyes wide and staring, face visible only from the angle where I lay. When it saw me it opened its mouth to bleat, but nothing came out. Again. Then it closed its eyes and stilled. I tried to reach, meaning to lift the rock blocking it from freedom. My arms refused to move.

"Palo," I whispered. "Here's the kid. Right here, beside my face."

Palo kneeled, looked, and also whispered. "Is it dead?"

"Move that rock, and we'll see."

He lifted the rock and the dull, gray light of clouded day fell across the head and shoulders of the kid. "Touch it," I said. "See if you can feel a pulse."

Questioning, he looked at me. "There, on the throat," I said.

He touched the kid's throat, stroking it as he would something precious. "Hold it," I said. "Press your thumb there just beneath the jaw, and feel the pulse."

"You do it," he said. "I don't know what to look for."

I tried to lift my arm, but it refused to budge.

"Wallis?" he said. "Are you all right?"

"Muscle spasm," I said. "Takes a minute to relax. You'll have to dig it out, son."

So he did, rock by rock, pebble by pebble until the kid was free. Then he reached beneath the body and lifted it out. Cradled in Palo's arms, the kid struggled to raise its head. It opened its eyes, bleated once, shortly, and its head fell back.

"Breathe into his mouth, Palo. Close his nose with your fingers. Pull aside the lip, and blow into his mouth. Yes," I said. "Like that. Again. Again." The baby goat's breast rose, fell, rose again, and began to breathe without Palo's help.

I tried to reach for the kid, but my arm only stirred. "Lay it beside me, here," I said. "Next to my stomach, then try again to get the man out."

Palo began digging at the rocks pinning the man, looking, with each freed rock, to see that the baby goat still breathed.

Most of the shepherd's body lay free and exposed, except for one leg remaining fastened between two rocks. "You'll have to pry the rocks apart," I said. "If either of them slips it'll crush the leg."

"What should we do?" I asked the shepherd.

"Go ahead," he said. "That rock has to come off. If not, I'll die here."

"Palo," I said. "Go to the cart and get the bag of white powder. We'll put just a pinch under his tongue. It'll ease the pain. Then you can pry away that rock."

Palo climbed down toward the cart. The cart was not there. Instead, where Spitter should have been standing, a large boulder lay, that first boulder we had rolled downhill. Loose rocks from the landslide littered the downhill road. No cart. No Spitter. Palo looked over the side of the cliff, then up the road. There she stood, calmly chewing the roadside grass. Had she moved downhill, she would have been hit by the other rolling rocks. She looked up as Palo neared and brayed. "Ha-onh. A-honh ahonh ahonh." Palo laughed aloud, rubbed her mane, jaws and neck roughly and hugged her around the neck. Spitter suffered an indignity she would never have allowed me. All this I saw from my birds-eye-view atop the rock slide. Then Palo rummaged around for the bag, and came slipping and sliding back up the mountain, two paces forward, one back, holding the bag between his teeth.

He rubbed a pinch of powder between the man's lips. The shepherd's eyes closed. A few minutes later the throbbing in his neck slowed, and I nodded for Palo to begin.

I tried my arms again, and they responded. Flexing them, drawing them up and dropping them, I ignored the pain, rolled to my feet, and grabbed the man by his shoulders, pulling him clear.

The sun had passed beyond the western horizon, leaving us cold, tired and hungry by the time the shepherd, the kid, and three other goats were freed. The man's leg dangled at an obscene angle, raw white bone and blood-choked muscle poked through red clay, exposed to the world, but he lived. The goats were dead.

"The rest of my herd is up there," said the shepherd.

"We'll come back for them." I said. "We have to get you home first." I made a crutch, cutting a branch with a t-shaped limb from an oak tree, and wrapped rags around the top for the shepherd to support himself. He tried to walk, and fell. Palo and I pulled his arms across our shoulders, then stumbled and slid downhill toward the cart. We worked him into the back, lifted the crushed leg and lay it on a blanket across Palo's box of treasures he had found on the trail.

Nothing would do Palo but that he carry the kid, gathering it beneath his shirt and tucking its head between his neck and shoulder. He carried the little goat for miles, and then stopped and handed me the kid.

"It's cold," he said. Face colorless, he turned away and continued his quick, steady pace. I lay the goat across my shoulders, holding its four tiny legs by both hands.

For a long time, walking in drizzling rain, Palo's shoulders convulsed in silent, terrible, sobs.

凹凹凹

With a bleak smile, the shepherd's wife welcomed us into her dirt-floored home, a rounded structure built of saplings and covered with skins. She added more wood to the fire on a loose, stone hearth in the center of the room, and offered us blankets so we could cover ourselves as our clothes hung on pegs nearby to dry. A trail of smoke rose and escaped through the roof, filtering through loosely laid bindings of grass. The room began to warm. Swollen with child, the woman clutched her side, squatted beside the mat, and watched me work.

I cleaned and set the man's leg, poked the tissues back into place and wrapped it with crushed leaves of the comfrey plant collected on the roadside. I patted on soft clay, smoothed it over, then splinted the inside of his leg with a board of linden wood I had cut from a fallen tree in Shalot's forest, whittling it smooth as we followed the trail toward the shepherd's hut. The scent of the linden reminded me of Estra and the fragrance wafting through night air when she had come to me. With a thrill, I wondered about her, even as I watched the shepherd's wife clutch her back and grimace with pain. Her time was near.

I pulled strips of linen from another bag and wrapped the leg. Arms trembling with fatigue and legs buckling beneath me, I collapsed next to the shepherd on the straw pallet. He groaned. I touched his forehead. No fever. From the bag lying beside us, I took a pinch more of the herb from the yellow bag and shoved it beneath his tongue, then, even as my fingers slipped away from his lips, my eyes closed.

Lost in the sounds of rain pelting the grass roof, the smoke of burning pine faded. In my last moments of wakefulness, I saw the woman on the mat beside us, knees drawn up into a fetal bend, clinching her belly and moaning.

The next day, I whittled smooth the oak limb I had cut for a crutch for the shepherd and wrapped it with wool cut from an old and ragged blanket. Ashen faced, jaws clenched, the man clung to my shoulders, placed the crutch beneath his arm and took a step, two, three. Face clammy with the moisture of effort, he would not stop when I said rest, but paused for a moment and continued. "Bella needs me," he said. "I have to learn to use this thing."

Palo returned with Spitter and the cart to the high pasture to get the dead goats and then went back to get the others. He drove five of them into a pen near the house, and, without waiting to eat, he began repacking our cart to leave.

"We can't go yet, son," I said. "We must help butcher the goats."

"No," said Palo, "I won't." He continued with the packing, working furiously.

"The shepherd and his wife will need the meat of the dead goats," I said. "Without it they will starve. They aren't able to butcher them themselves. The meat will rot."

Palo stopped, looked back at the goats, lying alongside the baby kid he had carried for so many miles. His face crinkled, agonized. "I can't cut it up, Wallis. " His voice grew high, choked. "I can't cut it up!"

"It's all right, Palo," I said, grasping him around the shoulders. "It's all right. The spirit of the little goat will not mind. It is the way of life. We live for a while and then we die. Better that our lives count for something than to be wasted. The flesh of this baby goat will lend its strength to the woman's unborn child, a child that, even now, struggles to begin his own life."

"I'll do the kid," I said. "You work with the other goats."

"No," he said, finally. "I'll take care of it." He lifted the kid from the ground, tied a rope around its legs and hung it from the limb of a tree. Then he began, pulling a blade down its belly, prying out the entrails and dropping them into a bowl, all the while wiping away his tears with the sleeve on his upper arm, turning away from the man and his wife so they would not see.

But the woman saw. Her arms rose, halfway, as though she would clutch this boy-child close, to comfort him.

And when he finished, he laid the pieces on a table by the smoke house and helped the woman and me butcher and clean the other goats. We worked throughout the day without stopping, the shepherd watching, instructing from his bench, while he kept the fires going inside the shed. When we finished we took the bowls to the spring to strip the entrails clean. Then we packed the organs in boxes of salt and quartered the goat carcasses, dropping pieces of fat into a kettle hung above a fire to render. The shepherd showed where to hang the quarters on rafters across the top of the smoke house. That night, after we had eaten from the meat of a goat, we fell asleep breathing the sweet smell of wood smoke blended with meat juices.

I woke to the sound of a newborn's cry, and Palo, saying, "Wallis. What do I do now?" Kneeling on the mat where the woman lay, Palo held the wet, sticky, blue-white baby in his two hands, the cord still stringing from the mother to the baby's belly.

"Hold him," I said, for it was a boy. I took my knife from my surgery bag, waited a moment until the cord began to pale, and cut it. "Lay the baby on the mother," I said, and tie a knot in the cord. No, not there. Tie it close to the belly. Yes. Like that." The woman moaned, the afterbirth erupted, and she closed her eyes, not asleep, for her arms held the baby close.

"Get some grease from the kettles in the yard," I said. "It should be cold by now." I smeared the grease on the baby's body, wiped away most of it, then wrapped him in a clean blanket I found on a shelf. I cleaned the woman, stuffed clean rags between her legs, helped her roll over, and cleaned her bed. Then I gave her powdered herbs rolled into pills, all the time mumbling the ritual after-the-birth chant.

"Always sing the songs, Tadpole," Yiayia had urged. "When the baby is presented, it will hear and be made strong by its welcome. The mother will hear and be put at her ease."

"You are *Derwydd*," said the woman, as I finished the verses, and, palms together, touched my forehead. "You sing the old songs."

"Derwydd?" I didn't know the word, but I sensed awe in her manner. "I am a poorly trained *vikos*," I demurred. "All I know, I learned from my grandmother, a wise woman. She taught me the old songs." I snuggled the baby into the woman's arms, brought her a bowl of water dipped from an earthen jar beside the door, and held it for her to drink.

Palo and I loaded the cart to leave. When we pulled out of the yard, the man called after us.

"We will name the baby Palo, for his hands were the first to touch him."

Palo ducked his head, but not before I saw his good eye. No longer red from weeping, a gleam sparked, and his steps broke into a dance. He pulled the flute the goatherd had given him from his shoulder pouch and keyed a note. Another. He slammed the flute against his leg to shake loose water, and tried again. Then he began to play a new, different tune. Badly.

I slowed to put distance between us.

8

The rains followed us through pasture and across flooding, swirling creeks, seeking us out even through dense forest foliage too wild to settle. For more than ten days it rained. We walked, slept, ate, and walked again in soggy, muddy clothes, never bothering to pitch a tent or build a fire, but sleeping wherever we found enough high ground to protect us from floods—rain, always rain, pelting our shoulders.

We spoke rarely, Palo and I, using hand and arm gestures to do our talking, and I, calling to Spitter with whistles.

On the eleventh day, about noon, we broke free of the forest into a clearing. Supplies exhausted, weary of the taste of raw fish and wild roots, we stood on the crest of a low hill, basking for a few moments in the light of sunshine.

"There's a house," said Palo. Too tired to say more, he trudged ahead and downhill past a grass-roofed shed toward a hut beside a creek. Outside the one-room building of rough-split logs and attached lean-to, three dogs met us. Snarling, they kept their distance, but would not allow us near the door. Finally a woman came out, spoke to the dogs and sagged against the mud-daubed doorway, waiting for us to approach.

No smoke from cooking fires issued from the chimney, and no light of lamps shone through the doorway. Her white hair hung limp and wispy, loosed from its pins. Her chewed-skin dress hung heavy with food grease and clung to her angled form.

I stopped several feet away, Palo and Spitter well to my rear. "Are you ill?" I asked, then, deciding, moved closer. "I am a physician."

"Old man. Sick," she answered, in weary monotone. "Maybe dead."

"May I see?" I asked, and without waiting for an answer, entered the door, brushing past her, through an aura of sour vomit. The man, lying on a reed pallet on the dirt floor, stank of urine, feces, vomit and wine. Even from where I stood there was no doubt. The man was dead.

"When?" I asked.

"Morning," she said. "Early. Went for water. Came back. Cold. Didn't notice. Before." A jar, still full from her last visit to the stream, sat beside the stone hearth.

"Palo," I called. "Bring in some wood, will you? The house is cold. Where should he gather wood?" I asked her. She pointed up hill, toward a grove of trees.

"You may have to cut it," I called to Palo, already on his way up the hill.

I grasped the corner of the pallet in both hands. "We'll have to take him outside," I said. "Will you help?"

She looked at me, struggling to understand what I was saying. "Here," I said, taking her hand and pulling her gently toward the corpse. "Help me pull him outside."

She jerked her hand free, put her arm across her face as though shielding it from a blow. "Ah-ee-e" she cried, and began keening, blubbering. Cries of the damned.

What had this woman suffered? I would have tried to comfort her, but her stench held me away. I pointed outside, and pushed her gently out the door. She leaned against the side of the house, still keening.

Grabbing the corner of the pallet again, I dragged the man out behind her, into the mud. Palo returned and dumped an armload of dead wood under the roof of the shed room.

"We must bury him," I said. "Where do you want him to lie?" I asked the woman, but when I saw the unbearable wildness of her eyes, I looked away. "Up there," I told Palo. "We'll bury him away from the house and uphill from the creek."

Together we dragged the man, pallet and all through the mud and up the hill. Palo went back for the shovel. We carved a shallow grave from the earth, taking turns with the shovel, and pulled the man in. Then we covered him.

We returned to the house. The woman, still leaning against the wall outside, sagged and slid to the ground. Now quiet, her wide-eye gaze followed us inside.

I found a short pole tied to another, shorter one turned crosswise. Taking it, I dragged debris and filth from the room and shoved it out the only door to the house. It splattered the woman. She didn't notice. Palo ran out the door, stopped, and flung vomit to the winds.

Pale as the moon, he came back inside carrying hay from the shed. We spread it on the floor and he went back for more. And more.

"That's enough," I said, catching him by the arm. "See? It's covered." He collapsed against the low stone wall that supported the logs of the house, leaned back, and laid his head on his arms, crossed, resting on his knees.

I sat down beside him close enough to lend my heat. After a moment, I stood, brought in the kindling he had gathered, and laid a few splinters atop dry, banked coals on a small hearth built of rounded river rocks and mortared with clay in a shallow pit in the center of the hut. I blew on the ashes, hoping for sparks. There were none. I went back to the cart to get my tinder box and returned. There, winking merrily was a small flame. "How did you do that?" I asked. "The coals were dead."

"No," he said, without looking up from the flames. "They were just sleeping."

"Sleeping," I said. "Palo, the coals were dead."

He looked up at me finally, incredibly weary. "I don't know," he said. "I found a live one."

As the flames built higher, gusting from short bursts of wind from the door, I piled on the rest of the wood, and soon the hut began to warm, pulling steam in wispy vapors from the grass nearest the hearth and sending it oozing through the straw of the roof. The woman came in, squatted, and held her hands to the fire, staring at it as though in trance. What is it about fire? I wondered, loving it. I poked it to new bursts of sparkling frenzy.

The woman stood, went out the door and around the house. She returned bringing meat cured with salt and a jar of milk, sides still wet where she had pulled it from a bog. In a second trip she brought a thick-walled clay vessel, so black from the smoke of many fires it looked like a large piece of rounded char wood, but the inside had been scraped and rinsed clean. She scattered the wood Palo had stacked and laid the bowl in the center, then filled it with water from the jar, all the time throwing glances at me, convincing me of her cunning. I looked closer. She had washed her face and hands, for drops still fell from her chin.

Finally, with a long-bladed knife, she cut the meat into chunks, and dropped them into the jar.

Remembering the roots we had dug along the trail, I left the fire long enough to get them. I washed them in the creek and brought them in. With a flourish intended to match that of the woman, I dropped them into the pot with the meat. Eyes lighting, the woman lifted a bag from atop the shelf over the hearth, loosened the draw string, poured yellow seeds of mustard into her hand and threw it into the kettle, then squatted again, pleased.

Palo, who had been watching with interest, went out and came in later with wild onions. He tossed them into the pot.

Miracle of miracles, the woman laughed. I reached for a wooden stick and stirred the bubbling liquid.

We watched the fire, each of us lost in our thoughts. When the stew was done, we ate from the common pot with carved wood dippers and talked, she in one-or two-word spurts.

"Do you have family?" I asked her.

"Son," she answered. "Comes. Sometime."

"Is he nearby? We could get him."

"Would. Come. Doesn't know. Old man. Dead."

"He would want to help bury his father?" I asked, thinking he would be a little late for that, now.

"No," she said, glancing back to where the man had lain. "Hates him. Comes. Hides. Woods...Hid, woods," she corrected, "Waited. Old man. Leave. Check traps. Trade skins."

"Where is he now, your son?" I asked, wondering who would see to her needs now that the man was gone.

"Three Rivers." she said. "North. One day." And she held up a thumb, for one day.

"We're going north," I said. "Tell me his name. I'll try to find him."

"Tivol," she said, searching to remember. "Tivol, at the tannery. Three rivers."

Well, that seemed clear enough. He could be found in a tannery at a town on three rivers. That would have to do.

When we finished eating, Palo and I spread our bedrolls on the hay near the hearth. The woman pulled a blanket down from a shelf and spread it on the floor where the old man had lain.

Thinking to tell her to spread her blanket near the fire, I touched her shoulder. She jumped, cringed, threw her arm up and across her

face as though to shield from a blow, and would hear no more from me.
Palo and I spread our wet clothes on the hearth and lay before the fire. Weary from the strain and work, we soon slept, the scent of fresh hay sweet in our nostrils.

The earth vibrated and the hay crunched. The air layered with the sudden stench of the old woman. Annoyed, I opened my eyes. The woman stood above me, both hands holding the long knife she had used to cut the meat, pointing downward.

Even as the knife plunged toward the floor in the direction of my belly, I rolled aside, bumping against her skin and bone ankles, tilting her backwards. The blade buried itself deep into the dirt. Palo was afoot sooner than I, and stood between the woman and me, pushing her away, for, having lost the knife, she already held a knot of wood high overhead, blank eyes lost in some tormented sea.

I stood, took the wood away from her, and patted the sides of her face. She drew a lungful of air, as though she had been holding her breath. Her eyes came alive and her body jerked. "What happened?" she asked. "Who are you? She looked around. "And where is the old man? Gone to collect his traps?"

We spent the rest of that night, Palo and I, explaining to the woman what had happened.

"Do you suppose she killed her husband?" Palo asked, later.

"There were no wounds," I said. "It was just his time, I guess."

Preparing to leave, I asked the woman. "Can you take care of yourself until your son gets here?"

I don't think she heard me. "Merchants come through here sometime," she said, dreaming. "The old man sometimes traded for things. He used some of his treasures from a skin pouch. It looked like rocks and shells. I saw it one day. Then he hid it from me."

"He must have hidden his wealth in the shed," I said, and I went out to look. The old man's cart had been pushed to the back of the shed, into the shadows, but I could see that it was much like mine, two-wheeled and rounded in the back, light weight, to be moved easily by hand when necessary. Made of bent wood, sides and bottom were woven with strips of leather. Unhitched from the donkey, the staves of the old man's cart rested on the ground, setting the back end up higher than the front.

Spitter stood beside the other donkey, both of them nuzzling an empty hay rack. I pulled down hay for them and checked to see they had water. It brimmed full from the rain.

Then I searched the cart, poking my fingers through rolls of dried, raw skins. I found a pouch tucked under the seat of the cart. The old man's treasure.

I handed the bag to the woman. She jerked away, letting the pouch fall to the hay at her feet. "He'll kill me if he finds me with that," she said.

Stunned, Palo and I stared at her then at each other. Palo grabbed her shoulders and shook her, yelling. "He's dead. The old man is dead! He's dead, don't you know that yet?"

I touched Palo's shoulder, to stop him. He dropped his hands and stepped away, ashamed.

"Dead," she said. "Dead? The old man is dead? What happened to him?"

Repentant, Palo began again to explain to her, but I stopped him. "It won't do any good, Palo. She won't remember it."

"What will she do," he asked. "When we're gone?"

"We must go on. We have no choice. She survives or not. We'll stop at the three rivers and tell her son. It's all we can do."

We had moved apart from the woman as we talked, and now she came near. "Don't you worry, boys. I'll be all right. I'll be just fine. See, you buried the old man. You cleaned my house and made a fire to keep me warm. My stomach is full. What more could you do?"

Bewildered, we edged out the door. The dogs, worrying bones left from the stew, didn't bark. With Spitter, we followed the trail downhill and through a rocky forest, away, toward the north. We found rabbits caught in the old man's traps, cleaned and skinned them, wrapped them in their skins and packed them into the cart.

In the evening, we broke free from the woods and into the glare of the sun setting across a river. Beside the river a platform of wood and stone had been built, reaching out into the water. A boat landing.

Palo sneezed. Scratched. "I need a bath," he said. Taking care not to smile, I gathered rocks for a hearth. Palo found sticks for a fire and filled the pot with water.

Later, bodies clean and oiled, stomachs filled, Palo and I lay beside our camp fire. "What was wrong with the old woman?" Palo asked. "How could she change like that? She seemed like a lot of different people. And why didn't she remember what we told her?"

I had been shuffling those same questions around in my mind all day. "I used to know a man like that," I said. "In Larissa. I used to visit there with Yiayia before my mother and sister and I moved to the island of Sapphos across the sea.

"His pallet lay beneath a spreading chestnut, in the center of the agora. People around the village said he harbored demons. They wouldn't come near him, but my Yiayia anointed his sores. He always reached out, trying to grab me. I dodged him, but sometimes he caught my shirt and yelled—like he was happy, happy and scared all at the same time. "He comes, the Son of Thunder."

"Who is the Son of Thunder, Yiayia? I asked, but Yiayia said not to mind him. He was just ill. 'He forgets who he is,' she said. 'The walls between his worlds have crumbled.' "

"What walls?" Palo asked.

"That's what I asked Yiayia," I answered. "She just jerked her head and looked mysterious. 'Do you think this to be your only existence?' she said. 'Your feet walk in many fields, but your thoughts keep them separate so you may pay attention to them one at a time.'

"I told Yiayia I didn't understand, and I looked at my feet and then my hands. I don't know why I looked at my hands, but I remember doing that, wondering how many pairs I possessed. Yiayia threaded her fingers through my hair. It made me feel good inside. Protected, safe. 'Not something for you to worry about, Tadpole,' she said. That's what she called me all my life until she died. Tadpole. She never finished telling me about the walls. I guess that is what was wrong with the old woman. Something, or someone, hurt her. Broke through her walls. Maybe the old man. Remember how she cringed when I touched her?"

"She was just crazy," muttered Palo. "And so are you." He rolled over and went to sleep.

Crazy. Others had called me that. I remembered scrabbling around in the leaves when I had met Palo, mumbling, "It's around here, somewhere, I know it is, hmm hmm." I would have done that again, but my humor would have been lost on the sleeping boy.

By dawn light the clearing crowded with people assembling for the ferry boat. Where had they all come from? We had passed no houses, seen no trails leading away from the road we had followed. Sensing a trading opportunity, I called, "Trade goods here. Anybody need anything?"

Embroidered fabric from Athens sold immediately, to a woman dressed in a thin, pale woolen dress girdled at the waist and hips. She fingered bone figurines I had bought in Tergesté, exclaiming over their intricate design. "What I really need is jewelry," she said, smiling, holding a tiny white goat up to her ear. "Something that would be pretty with this dress."

"My jewelry has been sold," I said. "I need to find more."

"West of the Three Rivers," said a man, standing next to her. He found my ax and hefted it, tossing it into the air and catching it with one hand. The other sleeve dangled, empty. "Good tool," he said. "Buy it around here?"

"That belongs to a friend in Attica," I said. "He sent it along with me to keep me from freezing if I needed to cut down a tree for fire wood."

"Conifers?" he asked.

"Hard wood, oak if I can find it, burns hotter, longer." Stunned silence met my remarks. Finally he said, "People around here don't cut oak to burn. The tree spirits would die." He paused, considered. "There's a village, out north and then west of here. Not too far. They make jewelry. You might find something there you like. A village they call Amber."

"What kind of jewelry?" I asked.

But the man never answered. The sound of a sheep's horn filled the clearing, a barge docked, and the people flowed up the gang plank and aboard.

I tucked my bag of coins, now much heavier, into the hidden compartment beneath the cart. "The coins are here, Palo," I said, patting the bag. He dipped his chin, point made, remembering the miserly skinner and his pouch.

Standing on the shaft of the cart and holding onto Spitter's mane, I peered over the heads of the people, trying to find the boatman, meaning to ask if he knew Tivol, the son of the old woman up the hill. But I did not have an opportunity to ask about Tivol, for with the last of the fares, the casting-off horn blew. Palo, Spitter and I followed the tow path north and west, cut by the feet of oxen pulling barges upstream.

9

മമമ ✣ മമമ

All roads, all bridges, led through Three Rivers. A thousand flavors of smoke issued from alley ways and windows along our path. The odor of decaying meat and soaked and rotting oak chips led us toward the tannery. A variant breeze erased tannery odors and brought the sharp scent of alum and salt brine from pickle vats, teasing our nostrils, testing our wills to advance. That smell vanished to be replaced by the aroma of celery, onions and garlic, only to flee against the invasion of an odor of old urine. We stood disoriented until the tanning smells returned, heavier than ever.

There, on a platform built over water, raw and partially tanned skins hung on lines. I left Palo and Spitter and approached the platform, threading through grass-roofed stalls and tables laden with articles made of leather. From among items spread on the table of one stall, I bought pouches for my herbs, harness reins and traces for Spitter and the cart, leather split and cured for writing vellum—all things I knew I could sell once I left the area. Crossing the wooden bridge, breathing the clean scent of new leather, I walked out onto the heavy, wooden boards to find Tivol. I passed more stalls and tables of leather goods on the way to the working areas of the tannery. Workers hauled water up from the river to pour into vats of skins, soaking them to soften. Raw pelts, gathered at the top and filled with water and wood chips, hung from pegs. Some of the skin bags—finished curing and minus the wool and hair—lay on the floor, waiting to be split or dried on molds of varying shapes. Men and women dressed the pelts, washing and squeezing them again and again until water ran clear before hanging them to drip. One group heated beeswax and brushed it onto leather for breastplates and greaves, molding, waterproofing and firming body armor. A few men, tall, narrow of face, all with yellow hair and muscular bodies, lounged around on benches and leaned against the railings. They all carried blades that didn't look like skinning knives. Sky-blue eyes, missing nothing, followed me, watching as I walked across the platform. Guards. Why would a tannery need guards?

I knew without asking which man was Tivol, for he had the same square face and blunt nose as the old woman, and in his approaching middle years, the drooping lines of his mouth echoed hers. Dressed only in a woolen cloth wrapping his hips and tied at a knot near his navel, his shoulders, back and chest gleamed with sweat.

"Tivol?" I asked. He looked up from his task then down again.

Whetting a long narrow blade on a stone, a knife exactly like the one I had seen descending toward my belly in the cabin of the old woman, he tested the edge with his thumb and said, "I'm Tivol." He unhooked a skin from a line where it had been left to drip, sat on his three-legged stool, and chewed a corner of the skin until it frayed. Then, grasping a layer with his teeth, and holding the other with the nails of the left hand, he inserted the blade and sawed back and forth, expertly dividing, layering the pelt. I waited, watching until he finished.

"What do you want? You want special orders, you have to see the owner," he said, waving the point of the knife toward a shelter in the corner next to the stair. He stood, walked to the edge of the platform, relieved himself, then returned and resumed his seat on the stool.

"I'm here to see you," I said.

"Eh?"

"Your father is dead." I didn't soften the news, knowing the man's hatred. "Your mother is..."

"My mother," he said, sighing. "My mother is finally free of that beast." He nodded. "I'll go get her. She's lived in the woods too long. It's gone to her head. The wife and I will make her a bed in our house. Plenty of room. Not much money, but we'll make do. When did you see her?"

"Yesterday," I said. "We buried your father."

"I'll go get her." He stood immediately and headed toward the owner to tell him he was leaving.

"Something else you should know," I said thinking his mother might not remember to tell him. "We found the old man's purse and gave it to your mother. It's enough to take care of her and you and your family, for a long time."

"The old man's treasure." He stopped, turned back. "Where'd the old goat hide it? I've been taking stores to mother for years. If not for what I gave her she would have been dead by now. I knew he had to store his wealth somewhere. When he brought pelts to be tanned, he went away counting coin."

"It was in his cart," I said, "beneath the pelts he had packed to bring for tanning."

"So there are pelts, too. Thanks, traveler," he said, for the first time looking into my face. "You need a favor, ask any time. The owner will know where to find me." He smiled, and suddenly I liked him, realizing that he could even be handsome, dressed in bleached linens or the sheer woolen fabric of the wealthy. Of course, now he would be wealthy.

Threading through tables on my way out, I passed near the owner's shelter. A group of guards stood alert. Standing in the shade, a round-faced man with balding head and heavy black beard, barked to a younger man, "Don't bother me with that! I hired you to see to supplies. If the trappers won't come up here, get bearers and go down to them. We're falling behind in our orders. Just take care of it." The owner, I guessed. "Don't stand so near the stairs," he grumbled to the guards. "You're keeping the trappers away. Hide."

A man of a different sort stood near the owner's shelter. No taller than I, so thin his ribs rippled beneath a knee-length, girdled shirt of finely carded wool, he pulled a cowled collar farther down over his face to shade hazel eyes from glare. Pale, he was, the pallor of one who rarely trespassed the lands of the sun. Slowly, as though time awaited the old man's pleasure, he tossed a fold of a cape across a shoulder and back and shifted an earthen jar hung on a strap across one shoulder. He thumped a knotted staff against the wooden floor, a short, sharp thump, and his long, wispy white beard twitched.

"You must stop cutting the oaks," he said. "The spirits of the dead are being displaced. They are wandering."

The owner sighed. "Wandering. And where are they going?"

"They are here. They follow the trail of their flesh you have cut to tan your leather."

"Their flesh," mocked the owner. "You mean the wood." Glancing at the old man's woolen garments, he added, "Don't your gods allow you to wear leather?" His voice fought to conceal a sneer. He almost succeeded. This was a man who counted his options. The woods people could cause trouble for his cutters.

"The god Tannin grants us that, to care for our needs. We don't cut down the trees. We strip a little bark. And you are using the flesh of the god to make armor for fighting men. In wars forests are destroyed. People die too young and in dishonor. I say this to you. The spirits are angry." He raised his staff and looked upward; his cowl fell back revealing a pale face, ghostly in the thin afternoon light. Mumbling, he began a singsong chant that grew louder with each deeply inhaled breath.

At a nod from the owner, the guards lifted him beneath his bony armpits and dragged him off the platform. The owner looked at me, questioning. Realizing that I had been staring, I dipped my chin, 'Good Day,' and followed the guards and the old man. They released him at the bridge to land, and not unkindly, supported him as his foot slipped on the edge. "Careful, grandfather," one said, and waited, watching till the old man joined several others, both men and women, similarly cowled and covered.

A woman in a blue-stained gown, uncowled and ungirdled, slipped an arm around his waist. He laid his arm across her shoulders and they disappeared into the crowd. It seemed the attack for which the guards had been posted, had been fought by a single old man. But surely there were others more threatening, waiting, perhaps, in the woods across the river. That would be the direction in which we were headed.

◩◩◩

"North and then west," the one-armed man at the ferry landing had said, "to Amber." The Ilz flowed north, at least for now, and the road, a good one, ran alongside. We walked the sandy road, the river Ilz on our right shedding its fading, dappled light. We had purchased no food in the city, leaving the village of Three Rivers with only the leather goods, our traveling gear, the picked-over remains of the merchandise we had brought with us, my herbs and medical supplies, a few hard biscuits and moldy cheese, and the last of Spitter's barley.

I remembered the moss I had found and saved for her from the hillside, drew some from a bag, and held it for her to nibble as we walked. We camped beside the river, just before road and river separated.

The next day, we did not stop to eat, but Palo and I munched the last of our biscuits and cheese as we walked a trail marked only by the absence of underbrush as I held hands full of barley for Spitter to nuzzle. Pine needles lay thick along our path, softening our steps as we walked, scenting the air with a moist pungency. Palo craned his neck, following chittering squirrels along a highway of their own making, through the limbs of towering pines. He squinted his eye to identify birds calling reports of our progress to cousins on the next hill, in the next valley, pointing out to me each discovery. Charmed by a subtle change of atmosphere, I paused, listening, waiting for the mood to identify itself.

When sunlight broke through the shadows, we stood at the foot of a rolling hill. Crowning the peak, a massive oak tree waited. Gnarled and twisted, it challenged mere mortals such as we to remove our shoes and kneel in humility. I shrugged away the feeling. It was only a tree. We climbed the hill and stood in quiet shade beneath spreading limbs. Some of the limbs swept earthward, touched the ground and soared upward. Dripping with silvered threads of fungus trembling nervously in the uncertain breeze, limbs twisted and turned, rejoining, binding with themselves and others to rise heavenward, forming a tortured, sensuous, lacy pattern across a clear, blue-white sky.

Palo scrambled upward along the massive trunk from a crooked limb and quickly disappeared into the tree's tangled growth, trusting the heights to the sure-footed grip of strong young toes.

I found the herb Yiayia had sent me to find. It grew on a bed of pale green moss. "A cure for the jerking sickness," she had said. "It will help Davos." How could I forget the memory, seeing her blind eyes, knowing that she sought my face, that last day as she lay dying. "A ground-hugging plant," she said, "one that branches into four large, equally-spaced leaves, forming a pattern seen as a cross within a circle." This one had bloomed, and made one proud blue-black, grape-sized berry that stretched high on its own thumb-length stem. I dug it—leaving soil embedded around the root—and planted it in an earthen jar, wetting it with water from a nearby spring.

An acorn dropped beside me, and I looked up. Palo, hands on hips, high on the limb of the oak, called. "Come on up. I want to show you something."

I snuggled the jar and herb into a corner of the cart, stepped into a crook of the limb embracing the earth, and climbed, pausing now and then to pull some of the fungus bearding the limbs of the tree and to tuck it into my pouch.

Branches erupted from the trunk in jagged junctures, making the climb swift and easy. I followed a path smoothed into the bark by the passage of many feet, and came upon an open space where limbs grew horizontally to the ground, crowding, squeezing each other together to form a cupped floor in a space about as large as the cart. An embowerment of woven limbs, twigs, and leaves, formed a dome above our heads, and lacy blue leaf shadows crawled across the floor, across our shoulders, across our arms and feet, enfolding us, melding us as one in the tree's embrace.

Facing the north, Palo showed me a knot. An interesting formation of natural projections covered with tiny fronds of moss emerged from the knee of an outward curving branch.

"It looks like a man, yet not quite a man," I said. "More like a cat, don't you think?" But Palo had begun climbing higher, and did not hear.

Intrigued, I traced the brow, the eyes, and the feline nose. The longer I stared, the more entranced I became. A face, yes, a face, but man? Or panther? The features of the face suddenly cleared. Part man, part cat, I decided. I ran my fingers along the brow, down the broad, shallow-rounded nose and under the chin. Then I found the eyes, open, fastened upon me, knowing me. Decrypting my deepest secrets.

My legs trembled, jellied, folded. Eyes never leaving the knots of wood, I sank to the floor, and, kneeling, looked up at the natural sculpture.

From this angle the face could not be seen, but had reverted to an unpretentious knot, gnarled and distorted, yet just a knot. Feeling foolish, I harrumphed, rose, checked to see that Palo had not observed my loss of dignity, and looked again. This time I had to search for the face, for having seen it as a knot, it was hard to see it any other way. Yet, there it appeared. Again the eyes found me, and the strangely compelling need to kneel overcame me again. I shook my head, squeezed shut my eyes and looked away. Palo, several branches above me, waved for me to come on up.

Shakily, I climbed, taking care to grip the branches tightly, to place my feet securely, for earth lay far below, Spitter and the cart mere toys.

"There," called Palo, and pointed to my left. A carving cut through rough bark, this time clearly a man-made design, the familiar circles-within-circles, seen on doorways of huts and shelters, embroidered on fabrics, and etched into amulets hung on strings around children's necks.

The pattern Palo showed me suggested a simple maze, and, intrigued, I touched it with my finger at the entry point and began tracing a trail toward the center. Blocked and blocked again, having to redraw, I became so absorbed in solving the puzzle that I completely forgot where I was, and only regained my senses when my finger found the path to the middle and the puzzle released me. It was only then that, in silence, I realized I had heard—or imagined hearing—voices chanting, murmuring from somewhere near my right ear.

Palo showed me another, and I climbed to see. This puzzle was drawn in the shape of the circle divided into four sections, each section opening onto a path that led toward the center, like a cross within a circle. Having worked the first, I understood the principle and began tracing my finger through one of the four sections. Here there was no maze. This puzzle seemed less a puzzle than a design repeated and repeated onto itself until a singsong rhythm began to develop. This was no puzzle at all, but merely a way to trace a path through from beginning to end, traversing each of the four sections.

Why work the puzzle? It was too easy. Just follow the paths drawn into the wood until emerging—not at the center. Not at the center, but back to a gateway leading outside the design. Why go to the bother of creating the design, it being so easily solved? Nevertheless, someone had taken great care to carve this pattern into the tree. Could I do less by not honoring it? So I allowed my finger to trace the paths, knowing where the path would emerge, yet tracing it anyway. Around and through one quarter, out, into another quarter, and so on until the final quadrant had been traced. Then, there in the center of the design, I saw the circle. I had not seen this circle before. There was no entrance. It stood inviolate, separate from the four quadrants, yet attracting them, binding them to itself. Stunned, I sat puzzling the properties of that circle.

The tree vibrated, calling me to wakefulness. My surroundings reasserted themselves. Palo had adjusted himself to the fork of two great limbs and sat staring out over the forest, disturbing my concentration in his movement. I looked again at the design.

The circle at the center of the pattern had vanished. Indeed there had never been a circle at all, just a pathway touching each of the four quadrants and then leading back toward the outer rim of the design. Bemused, I looked again, but could not find it. Determined, I again traced the paths. But this time was different. Having come this way before, I saw—not the pattern cut into the tree—but the events of my life. Bored with the simplicity of the design, still I traced, determined to again find the circle. Memories came and faded, easy like, just wandering as I traced the pattern. Then, in the center again, I viewed the whole, and a profound understanding raced through me.

I am the outer circle. And I am the center.

All this other, the four sections, are rooted, projected, from this center. Overwhelmed, I allowed my finger to be released by the pattern, yet sat there, bemused and enthralled. The pattern was my pattern. The purpose of this pattern was to show me myself. My eyes watered. I felt—empowered. I am me. Me!

Impatient to get on with this importance I thought of as life—I called, "Palo, are you ready to go down?"

"There is another one up here to see, if you can climb this high."

Of course I could climb that high. At that moment I could fail at nothing. I proceeded to show this young tree sprite that a bit of youth resided in myself as well as in him.

Near the top and on a limb no larger than my thigh, the last design, another maze, far more intricate in design than the first on which I had traced a path, awaited me. I hooked my leg across the adjoining branch for security. Clearly this had been where the artist had perched in the long hours necessary to do the carving.

My fingers reached out to trace the pattern. I heard fluttering wings. A nesting bird, no doubt, and I looked to see what kind it was, but I saw no bird. Instead, in looking up, I looked into openness. No branches soared above me. Nothing, not even clouds, separated me from clear, blue-white sky.

A trick of depth dizzied me for a moment. Not realizing which way was up, I felt myself falling, falling into that blue-white openness. I clung desperately to the branch. Like a dam just burst, images poured into me, through me. People, armies, kings and queens, faces, lives, disjointed, disunited except for a brief flash—a figure of a woman hovering within the leaves of the tree. Her long white hair and skirts streamed in transparent waves as though brushed by currents of water.

I fought to pull the images together, to make sense of the chaos. Faster and faster, they flooded my mind and soul, forcing me to gasp for reason, to fight for my own, familiar world. Suffocated, heaving for breath, I watched the flood slow to a drip and fade, but one very bright image refused to recede. I had seen myself seated on a throne, a throne not my own, for I had been dressed in the rags of a beggar.

Longing to solve the puzzle but still weak with vertigo, I tried to push away the images, to lift my hand and again try to trace the pattern. Arms frozen, bonded in fear to the limb of the tree, I could not move. Then, from a fork in the limbs below me, Palo spoke, breaking the spell. "What are they, Wallis?"

That was a question about which I wondered, myself. But, not knowing the answer, I felt a need to appear knowledgeable before my apprentice. Trying to control my quaking voice, I said, "Mind traps." I cleared my throat. "Meant to catch unwary travelers and halt their progress through the forest. And," I added beneath my breath, "this one almost trapped me."

Descending that tree, trembling, reaching with my foot for the next step down, I slowed, prepared to climb upward again. Something precious had been presented to me, and I had allowed it to slip from my grasp. Another, unvoiced possibility gnawed my reason. I had not the courage to complete a very special test, whatever that test had been. Yet, had I managed to solve that puzzle, I truly feared that I would not have emerged the same man as the one who had climbed this tree. I would have been something, someone different. Someone alien.

旧旧旧

We traveled on, and I, knowing in some part of my mind that, beyond the shading trees, the sun shone in fiery glory somewhere above me, still I could not be certain that it even existed. I knew only that I must pick up my feet and put them down, having practiced an entire lifetime performing this simple act. The road grew rougher, narrower, and curving. Wheel ruts hardly visible led this way and that through bogs cloaked by miasmic steam and around bubbling springs almost hidden by lily pads and moss. Quietness stifled me, muffling even the squeak of cart wheels. Palo fell back to walk beside Spitter and me, touching me once and again as though needing to reaffirm my existence. For whatever reason, I sighed, grateful.

Shut away from sight of the sun, my only orientation for the four directions was the moss growing on trees. If I saw no moss, I faced south. So we proceeded west, though I should not have concerned myself with minor details. Spitter never slowed and never led us through dangerous soft spots. I only needed to keep my eyes on those long, pointed ears. That I was fully able to do, except sometimes, when the world blurred, and the visions from the tree returned. So I closed my eyes, held my hand on the side of the cart, and let the donkey lead me.

Late afternoon found us under open skies on a knoll covered by waving blades of grass. Sight of the sun loosed the tether holding me in the embrace of the old oak. I drew a great lungful of sweet air and collapsed on the grass. I rolled onto my stomach, lay my head on my arm and rested, warmth of sunlight caressing my spine. The pictures began again, but these were pictures I could control, could even command. They were pictures of other carvings on the tree, carvings passed on my way down, observed but unheeded. One of the pictures was of the herb I had found beneath the tree. This then, was a sacred herb, for the puzzle of the cross in the center of a circle had been cut in its honor. Other than for calming seizures, what was its nature? How could it be used?

We stayed the night in that enchanted glen, finding roots and berries, frogs and fish in plenty. The next day we entered Amber.

வுவுவு

Climbing from dark, wet lowlands of shadowed bogs, warm, morning sun broke on our backs, and I stopped to flex muscles stiff from the night. Spitter and Palo stopped too, ending the measured squeaks of long-ungreased cart wheels. In sudden quiet, we heard high-pitched clinks of a hammer on an anvil.

Clink, clink, taptap, pause. Clink, clink, taptap, pause. A woman sang, and her voice kept beat with the clinking hammer. I put a hand on Palo's shoulder, warning him to silence, and cupped my good ear. Her voice sounded as clear as the call of the raven, lifting across the hill.

"Sacred mother, bring us light
Show us through the starry night,
Hold us gently in your hand and sing your songs
Of joy.

"Ancient wisdom stops to wait
Pausing patient at the gate
"Ten million years and more to learn your thousand songs
"Of joy.

"Many are the paths of man
"Many trace the Mother's plan
"Still we work as hope grows dim to learn your songs
"Of joy."

The clinking anvil quieted, but the woman finished her song. We topped the rise and descended the hill, entering a copse of trees on the outskirts of a village.

"Welcome, Daneion," said a woman. Without looking in our direction, she leaned forward over the walls of a well. Long, silver hair, braided to a single plait, fell forward across her breast. "I see you made it through the forest."

"You know me?"

Hand over hand she reeled in a rope tied to a filled jar, set the jar on the wall of the well, and reached for a silver dipper hanging from a fork in the tree. She dipped it in the jar and turned toward me to offer water. I saw her face. Eyes as green as shallow sea water looked into mine.

"You're the *kiria* of the tree."

10

The clearing, the well, the lady—everything wavered like images in a pond. The earth spun. I heaved, throwing my few bites of breakfast to the winds.

My hands found the stone of the well. I gripped it, solid, cold, eternal. I closed my eyes, felt only the scratchy surface beneath my fingers. Anger at my own clumsiness cleared my vision. The world settled. I opened my eyes.

Holding out the filled dipper, she ignored my distress. "Will you share truth with us?"

My legs steadied. My mouth twisted. *Truth! I would give a year of my life to know truth. Who are you? I saw you in the tree...* I thought the words but they died in my throat.

She smiled and touched her ear. A silver pendent of a tiny goat hung from one ear.

"You are the woman I met at the boat landing. You said you needed jewelry." The wife of an elder of a village, I had thought, born to wealth, married to wealthier. Now she wore only a rough, undyed, ungirdled robe, like the woman in the tree. The wind caught a hem and brushed it away from bare feet. The left foot bore a sixth toe. On the extra toe she wore a ring. "I make jewelry," she said, "I made the toe ring."

She pushed the dipper nearer. "Will you share truth with us?"

"Truth. Yes." I said, realizing, in speaking, that I had made a sacred vow, for only when I had answered did she pass the dipper to me.

"Then drink of the water of the Well of Truly Spoken," she said.

The traditional gesture of the friendship of a village, this offering of water. Villages grew around a good source of water, and whoever tended the well ministered to the people and extended the offer to strangers. The well keeper yielded power recognized by all–the need for life-sustaining water. It seemed the keeper of this well respected the virtue of truth.

Water from each well tasted different. This water, sparkling in the filtered light of the woods, embraced me with heady scent, not the dusty scent of rain falling from the sky nor the salty scent of the ocean brought to shore by breezes, nor was this the same as that I had scented coming from springs. I sipped. The flavor held me captive. I rolled it on my tongue for long and long before swallowing and taking another. It reminded me of water from Yiayia's well.

"Cover the well, Tadpole, it looks like rain," Yiayia used to say. I wondered why the well must be covered. Surely water was already wet.

"Do you cover this well when it rains?" I found myself asking. The woman's brow furrowed. I gave her the dipper and she dipped for Palo.

"Truth," Palo answered, without prompting. She nodded and smiled at him.

"Truth," she replied.

"I tend the well," she said, finally. "I cover it from the rain, I, and Ton, and Ton's uncle, Fedei."

As though summoned, a man came down a path leading through bush.

"Avi," he greeted the woman. "I see you've found our lost wanderers."

"You won't have to search for them, today, Fedei," said Avi, "They have found their way through the forest."

To me he said, "Welcome, Daneion, Palo...and, I believe, Spitter?" One hand waved in greeting. Where the other arm should have been, the sleeve hung empty. No longer surprised at this turn of events, I recognized the man at the ferry who had given me directions.

"Fedei?" I asked. "Your directions were a bit difficult to follow, but we made it through all right. I did not see you on the trail."

"We came by river boat," he answered, grinning. "Much faster. Easier."

"Yet you directed me through the forest?"

Avi handed him a dipper of water. "Truth," he said, and drank. "You found the oak? And you climbed it?" He tossed the remaining water from the dipper into the brush and handed the dipper back to Avi.

"Palo found it," I said. "Yes, we climbed it."

"And did you trace the paths of the puzzles?" asked Avi, returning the dipper to a fork in the limb of the tree. The limb tremored and two hazelnuts fell into the water. Plink, plink, I heard the splash far below. I thought I read puzzlement in Avi's face, but, without voicing her thought, she turned away and led us down the path.

"I finished only the first two puzzles," I said, and followed her toward the village.

We broke through the trees and looked over the valley. Pierced by a lone, pale stream of smoke, misty fog veiled a small cluster of round-top huts made of clay mixed with straw. Our trail entered the village and passed by a clearing shaded by a lone oak tree. Flat rocks of a size and height comfortable for seating, circled the clearing.

Across the road, a small group worked among tables and benches. A huge, domed oven and dyeing vats sat near grass-roofed shelters covering weaving looms. Tinkling and tapping sounds of hammers and chisels, mixed with the murmur of voices and occasional laughs, formed a pleasant hum with no particular pattern.

Beyond the huts, farther down the road and nearer the stream, grass-covered sheds used for sheltering wagons and for feeding farm animals lined the road.

An acorn fell on my head. I looked up. A boy and two girls, the girls as alike as chipmunks, straddled limbs in the great oak tree above the clearing. When I found them, they laughed. "Some of Ton's students," said Fedei. He sat on a three-legged stool, just inside a circle of flat stones. A basket, shallow and broad, held a pile of sheared sheep's wool. Fedei took up a wad, tucked it between his knees to secure it, and stroked it with a carding brush. "You traced two patterns?" he asked.

"I would have traced the third," I said, finding a seat on one of the stones. Fedei glanced at Palo, nodded toward a basket filled with fruit. Palo lifted a bunch of grapes.

"But as I reached for the puzzle, I heard the fluttering of a bird's wings and looked up. It caused an attack of vertigo, and I had to climb down."

"Then you didn't find the herb." He sounded disappointed. He removed the brushed wool from the carder by pushing it backward across his knee, then rolled the wool from his knee with the palm of his hand,

and pressed the thin roll into a half-filled, third basket.

"Well, yes. I found an herb," I said. "I dug it for transplanting. I hope I haven't offended you by digging it. I will put it back, if so."

"You traced two of the patterns," Avi said, coming from behind me and sitting. "You heard the fluttering of Abraxas, the Bird Who Was Not There–intense, interested. "Yet you did not use the herb. Did the god Tannin attempt to speak to you?"

"I heard no god. I saw...visions," I said, unwilling to expose my weakness to these strangers–and equally unwilling, having made a vow of truth–to lie. I longed to tell her I had seen her, there, floating between earth and sky, to have her confirm or deny it, yet I could not. She would think me insane. "Abraxas? The Master of Word and Number?"

"And of Days." she said. "Abraxas, yes. He lends his voice to Tannin, God of the Oak." I knew of Abraxas. Many in the lands of Athena thought him to be the One God, but I didn't realize his fame had spread to these people of the deep wood.

"You need tell me nothing of what you saw," she said. "Tannin speaks as he will to whomever he chooses and in whatever manner. But I am curious. Did you make sense of the visions?"

"Some," I answered. "There were too many. They came too fast."

"You should have eaten the herb as offered by Tannin," Fedei said. "She slows the voice of the god."

"May I see the plant?" asked Avi.

We rose and went to the cart where Spitter had pulled into the yard behind us. I lifted the pot and herb out of the cart and showed it to them.

"You know about herbs?" Avi asked.

"Some," I said. "This is like one my grandmother described to me. She said it would be good to give to my uncle Davos. He suffers the shaking sickness. I hoped to take it back to him. I wanted to keep it fresh for its greatest powers."

"Then you have made your choice," she said. "Knowledge of the Oak is coveted by many, but offered to few. That you have chosen to use the gift of Tannin to ease the distress of your kinsman rather than expand your own knowledge is an act of greatest generosity."

But I hadn't known about the herb, the tree, the patterns. Perhaps I would have eaten it, knowing what it would do. I attempted to protest, but she would not listen. "The gods allot, according to the necessity of employment," she said.

My bafflement must have shown, for she explained, somehow apologizing at the same time. "Sometimes ignorance will accomplish a greater good than knowledge." She would explain no more, but said, "Take the gift that has been granted you, and use it for Truth. With our blessings." Her lips pulled away from slightly protruding, uneven teeth in a shy but welcoming smile. "I will show you my herbs," she said, and pointed back up the hill.

We passed tables where people made various crafts. A boy of about sixteen years made jewelry, stirring tiny beads, some made of bone, some of amber. Finding the perfect one, he grasped a bead with tweezers made of bronze and pushed it onto a thread of horsehair. At another table, a man pounded gold into sheets. The boy took a sheet, pressed it between thumb and forefinger and rolled it into a long thin spear of gold. Then the man took the spear and wound it about a polished piece of amber, all without speaking.

"Land cannot bear to be touched," said Avi, "It is a miracle that Rork has managed to teach him to roll the gold."

"He needs a squeeze collar," I said.

"What is that?"

"I will show you," I said, and we turned away headed for her house. Palo stayed to watch.

Climbing the trail down which we had come, Avi and I took a right fork, zigzagged up, around and onto a rock shelf. The well keeper's mud-daub house snugged into a rock overlooking the village below. Grass and wild flowers had taken root in a sod roof, and had I not been expecting a house, I would have thought it only earth and stone.

Avi lifted the latch and invited me through a painted blue door. An aromatic fog of herb scents enveloped me as I stepped down two steps into a large room and stood on grayed yellow, polished chert tiles. Logs chinked with yellow mud formed the walls and rested on the stone from which the floors had been carved. A small, potbelly stone fireplace extended a few feet into the room, funneling upward to channel smoke from the room and to meld with a ceiling of sun hardened mud and straw..

Shelves, bulging with gaily-painted baskets, boxes, bags, and jars, lined the walls. Beneath the shelves, children's toys—figures of animals, carts, birds—were piled, waiting for little fingers to pick them up.

"The children come here to play?" I asked.

"The children go everywhere," she said. "Just try to keep them out. See?"

Two children, a boy, about three, and a girl, about six, brushed between us to get to the toys.

"Yours?" I asked, stooping to examine the toys they had chosen.

"Not in any sense you mean," Avi laughed. The laugh came from low in the throat, husky, warm. "These are some of Ton's students. Nearby clans sometimes leave their little ones in the forest. Usually they are crippled in body or mind. We help them if we can. Ton hears about others and goes to invite them here to learn. Veil, the girl, will probably stay. We don't know about little Doss yet. He is still too young to judge for intelligence."

Veil lifted a doll and straightened her dress. "Te saw you and Palo come," she said. "Te dreams, and then she tells me all about it." She smiled, holding the doll out to me to admire. She brushed back a braid of hair the color of an autumn maple leaf. Tiny braids gathered from hair on each side of her face and fell just forward of her ears to the line of her jaw.

"And are they good dreams?" I asked.

"Sometimes," she said. "She told me you liked hot bread and fresh goat's cream."

Amused, I said. "That's certainly true. What else did she tell you?"

"She said you miss your grandmother, and that sometimes you want to cry, but that a grown man doesn't cry." She took the doll and headed for the door. "Come on, Doss. Ton's waiting for us."

Stunned, I looked at Avi, begging explanation. Avi shrugged. "Veil dreams true dreams," she said.

"Always?"

"Always."

The scent of herbs filled me with nostalgia. Like Yiayia's cottage. I paused, inhaled, and walked toward a shelf. Painted pictures of herbs identified the contents of each box. I found one, carefully slid it from beneath another, lifted a lid, and inhaled. "Eucalyptus," I said. "Freshly dried." I ran my fingers along the boxes. "Your art work?"

"Fedei's. He paints everything."

"Pennyroyal. I have a friend who sometimes suffers from cramps. Her body resists surrendering her monthly fine of blood." I chuckled. "As a matter of fact, she resists surrendering anything, both of the earth and the heavens. Do you suppose the two traits are linked?"

"And do you suppose that if young women proved more submissive, the cramps would vanish?" Avi laughed that low, throaty laugh again.

"I think not. Who is your young friend?"

"A princess of Epirus," I said. "From a neighboring city near where I was born. By the Adriatic Sea."

"Some of the families of Keltoi went south from here. It is said that some settled near the Adriatic." Avi found two bowls on a shelf above a table, filled them with steaming water and dropped a pinch of herb into each. I lifted my face as I do when I study a scent. "Berry leaves. And perhaps fennel."

Avi smiled. "And a little hyssop. I see you are more than a seller of trinkets."

"My grandmother used to make tea like that. She made it without the hyssop—unless someone in the household suffered with congestion in the lungs and nose."

"I heard you sniffing as we walked. This will help clear you."

"Thank you. I hadn't noticed. My blankets were damp, and the ground was cold and hard last night."

I sat on a bench by the table and sipped the tea. Avi prepared to sit, paused, listening, and rose to gather herbs from the shelves. She set them on the table beside her place, took pinches of first one and then the other and combined them.

"Grindelia," I said. "You suffer from tightness and wheezing in the chest and throat?"

"Not for me," she murmured, continuing her measuring. "For Neelis, my sister. Sometimes she panics, thinking she is suffocating."

Someone pounded the door. "Avi! Neelis is choking to death." A boy's voice, young, high. "Avi!"

"A moment, Reed, I'm almost ready." Avi had begun the mixture before the boy called. She had known he would come, just as Yiayia had always known.

The sounds of labored breathing greeted us. Avi made tea of the herbs she had brought and Neelis managed to drink it. Time drew out and sounds of wheezing grew fainter but no less labored as she wearied. Her face glowed white in the light from a window. It seemed Avi's sister would get no sleep tonight.

"I have hirta," I said, hurrying away. "It will help."

"Neelis just started wheezing," Reed said from inside the hut. "She had been sweeping the floor because she thought Wallis and Palo might come for a visit. She forgot to sprinkle it with water first, and it was very dusty. Did you add the grindelia?"

"Yes," said Avi, "but this time it isn't working."

I set mortar and pestle on a stool near the hearth, dipped a fingerful of hirta spurge and several crystals of maple resin into the mortar rock and mixed it with a drop of wine. Taking small pinches, I rolled them into pellets between my palms and dropped them into a cloth bag with a laced top.

"One," I said, handing the bag to Avi. "Only one, then wait for results. If nothing happens, give another."

Avi took one, rolled it into her palm and paused, holding it near her lips and mumbling.

"You must not test it. You are not ill," I said. "This medicine would bring harm to you, but not to Neelis."

"I know the teaching," she answered, rebuke in her tone. "Where did you receive your training?"

"My grandmother was a physician. I studied with her."

"Do you know the songs?" she asked.

"I am no singer, but I will say the words for you. Perhaps you will be able to put them to music." I began.

"Canyons part the open plain,
Oceans fill them up again.
Sunlight colors leaves with green..".

Avi, humming as I spoke, continued the song.

"Mothers' tears heal more than seems.
Winter calls it all again
Canyons part the open plain."

"Why do the songs heal, Yiayia?" I once asked. "They don't make sense."

"It isn't the songs that heal," Tadpole, "and they don't have to make sense. The songs heal the healer. The patient heals himself."

"I don't understand," I said.

"Before a healing can occur," she said, "a vision of rightness must prevail. The song is meant to call to the healer's mind this sense of rightness; it is the rightness that orders the healing, a rightness the healer shares with her patient through song."

How could it be? I never understood my grandmother's words, but my herbs did their work anyway. Most of the time I did not even speak, but a discipline born of hours in my grandmother's tutelage asserted itself so that, in an irresistible flood, the words flowed through my mind as I ministered—all in Yiayia's voice.

Relenting, Avi pressed a pellet between Neelis' lips, held up her head, forced water into her mouth, and whispered, "Drink, Neelis. Swallow. I give you strength from the spirit of a wise one." Night slipped in through the open windows of Neelis' house, and bird calls ceased except for one lone nightingale, which seemed prepared to sing all night.

I settled by the door and chewed on a biscuit brought me by Reed, watching the flashes of fireflies rising like a twinkling fog from their places of hiding down near the river. I felt curiously alive here in this place of green things, and curiously at peace.

I must have dozed, for when I noticed, the silence of Neelis' breathing startled me. I crossed the room to stand behind Avi and search the face of her sister. Gone was the pallor from skin now golden yellow in the light of the lamp. A dew drop of moisture dragged down her forehead to trace a path toward her pillow. The brow, now smooth, seemed that of a child, unblemished from long days away from the drying sun.

Avi sighed. "That's it for tonight. She'll sleep till morning. Reed, go to bed. Neelis will be all right."

Reed roused from where he had lain his head on Neelis' mat. Lids drooped over eyes bulged with sleep.

"Hmmm?" he said.

"She's resting," said Avi. "Give her more of the tea in the morning." Whispering to keep from waking Neelis, Avi seemed somehow unrelated to the woman who had spoken so vibrantly only that afternoon. She reminded me of some potted plant, gone too long without water. "You made several pills. Will she need more?"

"She will need nothing, tonight," I said, "but you are in sore need of rest. Your concern for your sister has drained you."

"I will be all right. It is not Neelis' illness that has fatigued me," she said, taking my arm and leading me through the door. "We must talk."

We sat at the flower-painted table in Avi's house, the flickering light of a single candle lighting our hot milk and cold biscuit, this time layered with blueberry jam and cream from Avi's spring house.

"I have been given a vision, Daneion, known as Wallis. You make passage, a passage from the old to the new." Her voice sounded as though from far away, almost as though from another woman's throat.

"It is a difficult journey you take, and one that binds into place many events in the future, both for this life and beyond."

The scent of fear rose, layering the air with a thickness I could almost touch. In our first meeting at the river ferry, I had scented something akin to distrust from her and Fedei. Not understanding what teased my senses, and hardly thinking it worth noting, I dismissed it. Many people reacted thus toward strangers. But the scent exuding from this woman went far beyond distrust. Avi feared me! She watched, waiting. Judging. Planning her words.

Finally, she continued. "I have followed the threads of these...what shall I call them? Perhaps Divine Influences? Where you appear, things happen. You are the beacon light that signals the happenings. It is a heavy burden to bear.

"Because of your presence heads will fall, kingdoms will be overthrown, new dominions will rule."

My arms grew cold. A violent shiver wracked my limbs, and suddenly I was snatched away, no longer to sit in Avi's house, at Avi's table.

രരര

...I rode, cart wheels squishing through mud in the midst of a thousand squeaking wagon wheels, mummering horses, whispering men. The smell of unwashed bodies crowded my senses like dirty fog. Such awful, enforced silence. No songs, no whistles, no laughter. Hunger gnawed our consciousness, silent, unforgiving partners who would not sleep. Today we ride. Tomorrow we die.

A man on a great black horse pulled up beside my cart. The sick-animal sweat smell disappeared in an aura of the sweet scent of honey and cinnamon. I had no need to ask. This was the man for whom the army marched. Barely could I define his figure in the darkness, but I knew him, felt him as I felt myself, at one in motivation, in strength.

"Another hour," he whispered, leaning toward me. "Wait for us beyond the city."

"The gate will be open," I said. "Find the woman who sells the purple. Beware the man who stands in the shadows of the temple. He is an agent of Phaistos."

The man on the horse nodded. His blond hair caught light in the first tinge of morning sun. "Noted," he nodded again, in words without sound. "Forward Bukephalus," he urged, nudging the great horse in the side with his soft-slippered deerskin boots. "Stay alert, Phoenix," he said, moving away.

The scene dissolved and I stood at the foot of a great, white, mountain. Sheer, shadowless ice rose up, up, blinding the blue from the sky.

Men, like tiny bugs, scaled the sides, clinging to spidery lines—gnats caught in a web. One slip and the icy snow beneath would gorge on its victims, turning wiry bodies to clumps of frozen meat. "Stay back!" I screamed, no one hearing. "No one calls the gods to account." But my words whisked away in the keening of winds too powerful to order.

...And then I lay, spent and broken in spirit. Friends all gone, only the daughter of Palo to tend my needs. One face, fairer than all the lands to me, looked on with eyes full of pity, here yet not here. Quietly, so as not to call the wardens of this half world down on us, she removed a bracelet from her upper arm and placed it on my wrist. "You were a friend," she said. "How could anyone be more?"

Avi's home firmed, focused around me. Catching an unwilling breath, I rose, stood and paced as Avi watched, unspeaking. These were like the visions I had seen while clinging to the soaring limbs of the oak tree. Armies marching. Horses dying of thirst. A golden throne on which I, dressed in the rags of a beggar, sat, dangling my feet from a too-high chair. I wanted to run, to flee this body. To flee the images.

A strangled groan broke from my throat. I collapsed onto the chair by the table, laid my head on folded arms, the remainder of the biscuit and jam discarded beside limp fingers. The warmth of a hand covered mine. "Where can I go, what can I do?" I choked, senses straining toward this kind woman.

"Your spirit is strong. You will not falter," she said. "Be blessed with the knowledge that what you do is the course laid by the holy ancients. Your work is not to do, but simply to be. You bring changes, alternate paths, forks in life patterns. You transform others and raise them toward new levels of courage. It is not a rewarding role. The world will never know, for all the glory will be heaped on the heads of others. You labor in secret, but you are necessary."

I felt overwhelming pity weighing her words, and I sought her face for some explanation. "I don't understand," I managed to say, never thinking to wonder that this creature of the woods should know me, not only for what I was, but for what was to be. She said nothing, but kept her hand on mine for a long time.

It was good that I had dozed in the doorway to Neelis' house, for that was all the sleep I had that night. Avi laid a mat for me and went away, taking the lamp with her. I sat on the step to her back door, staring over the tops of trees in the blackened forest behind her house, listening to a chorus of frogs seemingly awakened from sleep to sing an anthem to the drums pounding inside my head.

Somewhere out there, in the dark of a dark woods night, I heard Spitter "Ha-onh. Ahonh ahonh ahonh," calling for her treat. She hushed and I knew Palo had come to offer her a bite and to scratch behind her ears. How could life continue just as always, when I had somehow lost my hold on the golden thread?

11

At dawn, that time of the day before shadows form and the world is painted pink, a man, perhaps the same age as I, came up the hill from the direction of Avi's shed. He emerged from the shadowed gloom, a tall, thin specter materializing from the trees, a phantom only just now created.

"I'm Ton," he said. "Are you hungry?" Without waiting for an answer, he passed me by and entered Avi's house. A small flame flared in the stove. He drew biscuits and cheese from his pouch, filled a pot with water from a bucket and set bowls on the table. "Neelis sent me with food," he said. "She also sends her thanks for your help last night."

He folded his long, lean body and sat beside me on the stoop, waiting for the water to heat. I welcomed his presence and leaned into it, reaching desperately for substance. Still, his solidity did little to dispel the detachment that isolated me, holding me at arm's length from reality, so caught up was I in the images of the night. The teacher did not try to explain or to bring me to my senses. He blended with the moment as a flute blends with a song, as a dream stands waiting, ready to take up residence in the world of the waking. He rose, poured hot water into bowls, added berry leaves and brought them, handing one to me. "Avi said you might need me," he said.

We ate, watching pink light chase away the blackness that saturated the valley, revealing tips of trees dotting an unending blanket. Palo and Spitter and I had come through that valley. How had we ever found our way?

"You've been out all night?"

He nodded, indicating Avi's shed.

I swallowed the biscuit and cheese and cleared my throat with a swallow of hot liquid. "Who is she, Ton? Who is Avi to walk so freely inside my mind?"

Ton examined a finger nail, cut short, square. Fingers all the same length, these hands, wide and powerful, seemed structured more for building houses, dams, and waterways, than for teaching children.

"She and I came here when we were children. Rallah brought us."

"Rallah?"

"The Administrator. He came to my grandfather's home when I was a child. He had heard stories. I told Pateros he and two others were coming, and we killed a goat in their honor. When they arrived, the goat was prepared and all the people of the Well of Ton gathered to welcome him. It was a great day for them, but a fearful one for me. Rallah wanted to take me away from my grandfather and bring me to a place of learning. They brought Avi and me here, to Amber. I was seven, Avi, nine."

"How did you know Rallah was coming?"

He shrugged. "I just knew. The villagers were frightened of me. They were glad when I left." I did not fear this lonely man. What I felt was overwhelming pity.

He nodded. "Avi said something about a...a squeeze collar?"

"For the boy, Land. Avi says he won't allow anyone to touch him."

"Land," said Ton, wondering. "Land sees everything, hears too much. Feels too much. It is more than he can bear, so he runs away, hides inside."

"Perhaps the collar will help quiet him," I said.

"There is so much he could teach me," said Ton.

"Teach you? But I thought you were the teacher. Fedei says they are your students."

"I teach nothing," he said. "It is the children who teach me with their wondering. I just play with them, to hold them here with us—to keep them from running away to join the trees."

"The trees call to them?" I asked, feeling foolish with such a question.

"The trees, the animals, even the snakes that slide through the rotting leaves and burrow into the ground, and the spiders who build their nests between the twigs. They call to Whist," he said. "And when Whist answers the call, he draws the other children along with him. He was among the trees when I found him, only about four years old, three years ago. He slept humped against the base of the oak, quite at peace. It was as though the trees had spawned and nurtured him. He could remember nothing, not even his name. So we named him Whist.

'Whist' he would say, showing us how the birds fly through the air." Ton sliced the air with his palm, back and forth. "Whist. Whist."

I cleared my throat. "We'll start that squeeze collar now, if you're ready. We need carving wood."

"The boards are in my workshop. Pine. Already split and sanded, ready for cutting."

"And we'll need sheep skins, thick with wool."

He pulled the skin of a lamb from his shoulders and handed it to me. "Fedei has more," he said. The wool, damp from early morning dew, dragged against my fingers as I caressed it

Ton whistled. Two girls, the ones who had thrown acorns at me from the tree, came tumbling from the hay loft rubbing sleep from their eyes and staring at me. One approached and slipped her hand into mine. "I'm Ovie," she said. "She's Shal." She listened as her twin whispered in her ear. "She asks, 'Who is that lady who follows you?'"

"Lady?" I said. "You mean Avi? She's not here. I don't know where she is."

Ovie giggled. "Not Avi. The other lady."

Shal edged past me and stood looking up at something. Perhaps something in the trees? Something I could not see. Then Shal smiled, and whispered to Ovie again.

"The lady says Tadpole is blind and deaf, and that we are pretty little girls." They both giggled, Ovie took my hand again, and pulled me toward the path down the hill. Several times, Shal pulled Ovie to a stop to whisper into her ear, and the two of them giggled and looked at me.

Thin wisps of smoke from morning fires layered the crisp, thin, mountain air. From a house we passed, I heard singing. A man's voice, deep and strong, brushed my skin and vibrated my spine with resonance. "Fedei," said Ton. He joined the song, and children, eight of them, flowed from various doorways, into the road, joining us as we descended toward the river. Voices, some high and sweet, others catching in their throats, boys becoming men, some as tone flat as the geese who honked around Dimitri's barn yard. Then, from the doorway near where Rork and Land had rolled the gold wire, a woman joined in. She waved, then lifted a large bowl of slops and tossed it to the winds to mingle with the grasses, to sink into earth. Dogs awoke, rubbed against our knees, and fell behind to nose through the slops.

Palo rolled from his pallet beside Spitter in the shed near the meeting place, pulled on his woolen cloak, folded his bed and tucked it inside the cart.

"Come with us, Palo," said Ovie, releasing my hand and grabbing his. "My mother has made fresh bread spread with honey."

Palo tucked in his chin. With a compressed-lips smile, he yawned and allowed Ovie to pull him along.

"I think she likes you," I said, unable to resist teasing him as he passed nearby.

"I watered your plants," he said, not looking back, not waiting for an answer.

Veil took Ovie's place and clutched my hand. "Te says you should wear the bracelet like the goddess meant you to do when she gave it to you," she said.

"The goddess?" I asked.

"The goddess, Athena," she said. "She put the bracelet on your wrist."

"You...Te...dreamed...of the bracelet?" I had believed my own disjointed images to be nightmares, dream escaped from sleep to haunt my waking and fashioned only for my torture. In one of the visions, Olympias had put the bracelet on my wrist. Olympias, not Athena, but yes, I thought. It is right. I took the bracelet from its wrapping where I had tucked it beneath the seat in the cart, next to the bag of coins. I snapped it around my wrist and latched the clasp. Olympias would wear it on her upper arm, but though I was small, my muscles were large, and my wrist would be about the size of her arm. "It is done," I said.

She nodded, a thing complete, ordered. "She will like it," she said, and hurried away toward the woman who had thrown away the slops.

"Her mother?" I asked.

"Veil has no mother," Ton said. "She died giving birth to Veil. A local clan gave her to the oaks. They say she killed her mother. Rallah found her in the forest and brought her here. Rork and Minna feed and clothe her."

Keer, the boy who had showed Palo how to string beads, led the way toward Ton's shop, a shed built downhill from the village overlooking the river. Whist, emerging from the woods where he had been sitting among the pigeons, walked with us. A look passed between Whist and Ton, but neither spoke, and I wondered.

"Whist feeds the pigeons," Ton explained. "He will let no one else near them."

Reed and Veil went with Avi, and Ovie and Shal and Palo went to get breakfast at the home of the twins. I hadn't seen the youngest child, Doss, and thought him a late sleeper. Land, the boy who would not be touched, stayed with Rork, following by his side as Rork set up their day's supply of materials for rolling the gold wire.

"Is Land one of those who came from the forest?"

"No. Land was brought to us by his parents. He's from a local tribe. They believed him to be one of the lost ones, those who are born with a damaged spirit. The agreement was that if we couldn't train him for a useful life, he would be put to death. But we sensed his spirit. We have been working to draw it forth.

Ton's workshop smelled of pine resin. Split boards awaited his knowing hands. Whist and Keer handed him tools before he asked. First tapping a bronze chisel along imaginary lines on a board, he then raised his hammer high and with a single blow on the chisel, cleaved the wood through. Then another, another, parting the board in a smooth, curving line.

How strange, how unreal the dance of his hands became, every slightest tap of the chisel parting the wood, shaping the collar into a circled hole in a rounded frame, even as I thought of the pattern and before I could give directions. I forgot where I was, what I was, who I was, becoming a dancer held captive to that otherworldly rhythm.

Keer grasped the board and held it firm as Ton trimmed away the edges, then Keer handed the board to Whist, to sand. Whist rubbed the pieces with damp sand beneath blocks of wood wrapped with hardened deer hide, the swish swish sound of sand on wood continuing a flow of hypnotic movement. No one spoke; all seemed involved with the motion of Whist's fingers.

The longer he rubbed the more I felt dislocated. The feeling disturbed me, and I stepped away, outside the carpenter's shed. The feeling vanished. I saw that Keer and Ton had also stepped away, and stood watching from the other side of the work table. Curious, I returned, interested in watching Whist work.

He held the wood near his face, almost lost in a confusion of curled black hair that tumbled to his shoulders. Long black lashes further shielded his eyes, but when I brushed his arm he looked up, dazed. A child of seven, his face blurred as I stared, eyes become black pools in an uncharted face. Weakened, I moved to where Ton and Keer stood.

"He enters the soul of the wood," said Ton. "See how it responds to his commands?" I said nothing. I was beyond my depths.

Whist continued until the piece slid like silk beneath his fingers. Ton oiled the board, and then drilled holes, one on either end of each hollowed-out half moon piece, securing one of the halves on a device to hold the piece firm.

He chose a tool—a device similar to a bow strung with a sturdy cord. With a deft, twisting motion, he wrapped the cord around an iron bar with a ball on one end and a point on the other. Then placing the point hard against the wood, he laid the palm of his hand on the ball, leaned his chest onto his palm and push-pulled the bow. The bar spun first this way then that, burrowing a hole through the wood.

To finish, he tied the completed pieces together on one end with leather string, opened and closed the half circles to check how they worked, then wrapped both pieces with lambskin. "We'll fasten it at the bottom after the head is in."

We carried it toward the work table of Rork and Land. Avi, Fedei, Reed, and Veil appeared from the village gardens, Fedei's shirt wringing wet from tilling, carrying a pick with his single arm. Avi lowered a basket of melons from her head, set it on one of the stones in the circle, and followed.

We approached Rork's work tables and Rork and Land roused from their noonday nap beneath the tree.

"We have a gift for Land," said Ton. "Wallis says it will help him feel more comfortable."

A cloud passed over, casting us all in fleeting shadow. Land jerked once, twice. If the shadow of a cloud disturbed him, how would he feel with the lambskin on the collar touching his neck? Almost, I called it all off.

"How will we get Land to wear the collar," I asked, "if we cannot touch him?"

"There is no need to touch him," said Avi. "Reed, you are only a little larger than Land. You will show Land what to do by wearing the collar first."

Ton fastened the collar around Reed's neck. Reed grinned. "It feels good," he said. "I feel....safe."

Ton released the neck piece and held it out toward Land.

Land stood beside Ton, and Ton closed the collar around his neck. A terrified expression flickered across the boy's face, then smoothed. He closed his eyes, and groaned. Ton hurried to remove the neck piece, but Land said, "No," and held the collar to himself.

Rork's wife, Minna, came from the door of the house where she had been watching. "He speaks?" she said. "Land? You understand?" I saw her, felt her body strain toward the boy, but well knowing what his terrified response might have been, she kept her distance.

Land, collar secure around his neck, smiled. She walked slowly toward him, holding out her arms. He walked into them, and clutched her around the waist. "Mama."

回回回

That afternoon Palo and I joined the children and Ton to bathe in the river. Time and time again Ton tried to teach Palo to swim, and, ignoring the laughter of the children, Palo learned that by constantly kicking his legs he could avoid drowning, but no amount of help by Ton, and no amount of demonstrating the skill by the children, could teach him the art. Palo's body refused to float. His legs sank like rocks as soon as he became still.

Afterwards, we gathered on the river bank, formed a circle around a fire where a goose roasted on a spit. We danced and sang to the music of Palo's flute and Fedei's slapping, sliding feet, and then Avi sang a song for the nourishment of the body. When she had finished serving she came to sit beside me on a log at the edge of the water.

A glint of light flashed from the bracelet when I lifted a bird's leg to take a bite.

"What a beautiful bracelet," she said, craning her neck to see the design. I unlatched it and handed it to her to see.

"Fine craftsmanship," said Fedei, from behind. "Where was it made?"

"It was made by an ironmonger," I said, "At the H'stok Iron Foundry."

"We know of Rudy H'stok," said Fedei. "A fine craftsman in his own right. See, Avi, the rivers are blue, filled with the calcite powder that changes from pink when it is fired. You bought the bracelet from him?"

"I have not enough money in all the world to pay for this bracelet," I said. "It was a gift. Rudy's son, Rufus gave it to me as a gift for the

Princess Olympias. He wanted to place white stones along the rivers, but he only had the powder."

At once interested, the children drew near. They passed it one to the other, murmuring, touching it to their cheeks to test its finish.

"The miners of Hern have calcite," said Fedei. "Are you going that way?"

"Hern is north of here?"

"On the great river Rhine," he said.

"Olympias," said Veil. She pushed between Fedei and me, insisting, "The goddess Athena."

I would have corrected her; as far as I knew, Olympias was no goddess. No goddess would have suffered as had Olympias, who lived every day in danger of her life, but Veil didn't wait for me to correct her.

"I know stories about Olympias," she proclaimed, proudly. "Once upon a time," she began, "The Chosen of God, the Regina, was stolen from her school in Kreté."

"Let Reed tell it," said Keer, sixteen-year-old voice deep and full, accustomed to directing the children. "He is the bard, and he needs practice."

"Just tell it right," Veil warned.

"I will tell it word for word," promised Reed, and began. "Once upon a time, The Chosen of God, the Regina, was stolen from her school in Kreté. The evil priest, Phaistos, searched and searched for her, but could not find her until years later, after the Regina was married to the king, Neoptolemus, and bore a daughter who was named Olympias. The princess won her name through an act of bravery, for it was she who discovered a fire in her home, caused by a servant.

"The servant hid in a closet because she feared to be punished, but Olympias awoke the Regina and her father, King Neoptolemus, and told them about the fire." Reed concluded, and I stared. Finally I stammered.

"You see what is in my mind?" I asked, no longer amazed at the gifts of these people.

He laughed. "No, of course not. I don't do the seeing, I do the telling. Ton teaches us the stories."

"And then came the slaughter of the Regina," began Veil, and again Keer interrupted. "Let Reed tell it, Veil. It is his calling."

"The evil administrator, Phaistos, learned where the Regina lived and that she had borne a child, a girl," said Reed. "Enraged, he gathered his warriors, raced to Molossis, and lay in wait outside the palace until the Regina and Olympias were exposed. Phaistos and his warriors fell upon the Regina and slew her, for when she bore a child, she became an abomination to them for her powers had been passed on to the child. The Regina was slain with an axe to the back of her head as she ran toward the house, carrying the child, Olympias. The Regina and the child fell. Olympias would have been taken, except for a servant girl, named Vahna. Ignoring the shouting and screaming, ignoring even the arrows that flew through the air toward her, Vahna snatched Olympias from her dead mother's arms and raced toward the house, to safety."

"Enough," said Avi. "We must sleep, for tomorrow we gather herbs."

I knew that Olympias led the harvest prayers each year and people from far north came to celebrate the festivals. It must be a common enough story. Ton may have learned the stories from travelers.

🏛🏛🏛

The next day, climbing a grassy hill where goat herds grazed, Avi, Ton, the children, Palo and I bumped sides with excited village dogs whose lolling tongues urged us to be off and moving. My shirt, soaked from exertion in the sun-heated day, thrilled to delicious chills beneath short, quick passings of clouds.

I stopped on pretext of resting, but really to gaze south across the valley, to soak up the beauty of lush green hills cleft by the flashing blue-white line of a river. The river Vils followed a low path through willows and along a white trail marked by groves of birch. Freed from hard winter and imprisoning ices, the stream plunged from waterfalls, splashed over rocks, and lazed through the village of Amber, finally, dashing off again to hide in solid green masses of trees. Southward, it faded in distant blue mist. Though I could not see it from here, I knew that the river joined with the great Danube to continue on its way eastward then to turn south.

Dizzied by thinned air, I braced my legs against sudden gusts of wind, seeking balance amidst intermittent bursts of sunlight and shadowed darkness—clouds spotting the land, racing across the knoll like rabbits fleeing dogs.

Arms laced through straps of the still empty, open-top herb sack, a long-handled wooden pick laid across my shoulders, I chastised myself for wasting precious daylight time, and, turning again to the climb, I bumped into Ton. He stirred, as though wakened from a dream.

"Gone. All gone," he said, and rubbed an eye with his shoulder sleeve where perspiration dripped from his forehead.

"What is gone, Ton?" I asked. Though no cloud passed over, the air surrounding the teacher felt heavy, shadowed, drowning me in a vat of sorrow.

"Oh?" he responded, as though suddenly waking. His eyes caressed the valley, a lover stroking his beloved. "Nothing. Nothing is gone. It's still here—for now."

Poor man. I had seen this type of sadness in patients, and near them, had felt the air thick as honey and just as heavy, weighing my heart. I had felt it near a mother whose baby had just succumbed to a fever, and I had felt it from a man whose wealth had been confiscated for an imagined crime against the state. Gone. All gone.

I would look for the sacred wort of peace for Ton, the herb with perforations lining the edges of the leaves. It would raise his spirits. I laid my hand on his shoulder. We turned to continue the climb.

The grass of the meadow spread thick and spongy, clipped short by grazing goats. The children had passed beyond sight now, their laughing, whispering, giggling, sounds silenced in the soughing winds. The world lay quiet.

"Watch out!" Ton said. There, a short distance ahead and above us in the pasture the children appeared. Heads tucked between knees, legs and feet wrapped tightly by interlocked arms, they rolled downhill, coming at us like a flock of geese in tight formation. Keer and Palo led, forming the point, with Reed, Doss, and Veil, on their left, Whist, Shal and Ovie on their right. All of them, laughing so hard they had trouble holding onto their legs, rolled toward Ton and me.

Keer relaxed his hold on his legs first, rolling to a stop, then stood and helped the others up.

"Keer taught us how to do that." Ovie laughed, grabbing Keer around the legs, and thrusting, toppled them both. Doss stood, fell, and stood again, looking dazedly at a world still spinning. Keer laughed, pushed Ovie away and stood, then took Doss by the arm and helped him up, asking, "Are you all right?"

Doss nodded, yes, but when Keer released him he fell again and tumbled against my legs. Palo ran a hand through brown hair clearing it of bits of grass. Grinning, he grabbed Doss and swung him into the air. "Come on, Doss, I'll carry you. Let's outrun these other weaklings."

Carrying Doss on his back, arms about his neck, Palo raced up the hill, all the others crowding behind.

Keer, limping, followed, last of all before Ton and me. "Did you hurt yourself, Keer?" I called, but he tossed his head, no, and continued up hill. Ton and I also climbed, not hurrying.

"Keer's parents brought him to us about five years ago," Ton said, "to see if we could help him straighten his foot. He has learned to walk, but still his spirit will not let him run. He suffers from a pain hidden in his past."

"Before he came to the village?" I asked.

"Before he was born into this life," said Ton. "His spirit will not let him run until he has once again learned how to crawl."

Crawl? Ton had lost me. Clearly Keer could now walk. "He is an old friend," Ton explained, which explained nothing to me. "He was a spirit of great power. He abused it. Now he must begin again, and he has been brought to us to be taught."

"There is something about him," I said, "that reminds me of an old man, a man with authority. I felt it when he chose Reed to tell the stories."

"It is clear he and Reed are bound in spirit. Reed and Keer come from the same village. Reed came looking for Keer after his parents brought Keer to us to help his leg to heal."

"Then there is nothing wrong with Reed?"

"Oh no," laughed Ton. Reed is my brightest student. He never forgets anything that is told him. His sums are always accurate, and he thinks without aid from sticks and stones. He doesn't even use his fingers. I am teaching him the stories of the Old Ones. He will keep the records for the others after I'm gone."

The Old Ones. The Wise ones? I remembered my grandmother's teachings. 'They never write their histories, Tadpole, but remember them, and tell them in songs and stories.'

Ton pointed to a grove of Beech. Avi likes to dig over there. That's where we'll find her."

That afternoon, standing inside the circle of stones, Avi and I watched Ton cut the boys' hair. Using a blade made of smoothed, slivered bone, he shaved the tops of their heads from ear to ear and forward, leaving their heads half bald. When the others were finished, Palo took a seat on the bench in front of Ton and waited.

"You want your hair cut like theirs?" asked Ton. Palo nodded, and Ton started shaving.

"I can't believe Palo would want his hair cut like that," I said. "The boy continues to amaze me."

"What is wrong with his eye?" Avi asked.

"Palo is blind in his left eye. I found him living wild in the woods. If only I could find a cure for that blindness..."

"If I may..." Avi said to Palo, and stepped nearer. Ton paused from his haircutting. She put her fingers across Palo's eye and held them there, barely touching, for only an instant. "No need for healing," she said. "The boy sees more, sees farther, sees truer with his one eye, than most see with both." She smiled and laid her hands on Palo's shoulders. "You have been touched by the goddess," she said, and kissed his shaved head. "You have the mark of the special people."

"Special how?" he asked, unimpressed.

Avi laughed. "See?" She said to Ton. "The touch does not make him swoon." And to Palo, "The day will come when I will have need of learning from you, Old One. Remember me, if you will, for I shall remember you." Palo shrugged, lifted an eyebrow at me that said, 'Old one?' and turned away, holding still for Ton to finish shaving.

"Honh, Ahonh ahonh ahonh," Spitter called, lifting her head from the barley hay Palo had piled on the ground nearby. She snuffed the air, scratching the sand of the road bed with a hoof, and eyed Avi. Avi laughed, that low, soft, husky laugh of hers, and it seemed the entire woodland across the river caught the laugh, magnified it, and echoed it back to us. "Yes," she said. "You are special, too, Spitter." And she went to the donkey, held her harness and led her inside the circle. She stepped back, and everyone laughed, applauding with a hand slapped against a thigh. Spitter, embarrassed, ducked her head, looked up at us through lashes tangled in curly, silver hair, and twitched her long, pointed ears.

Why did that make me feel good, I wondered. It was not I who was special.

That night the children told their stories from within the circle, continuing from the night before as though no break had occurred, delaying supper till the shadows were long and the depths of the old oak darkened to a purple mystery.

"Olympias was taken to the mountain of Tomarus to the Temple of

Dodona and the Selloi priests," said their apprentice bard, Reed. The priests taught her the songs and the stories, and she returned to the palace.

"Then Neoptolemus was killed, and the murder was blamed on a horse. Arrybus, Olympias' uncle, adopted by the counselors of the Clan of the Snakes to be a co-ruler with Neoptolemus, married Olympias' half-sister Troas, and claimed the throne as regent for Olympias' brother, Alexandros. He was only five years of age.

"In the summer of her twentieth year Olympias received a missive from her uncle, who said she must marry. The clan counselors supported him, and Olympias was forced to obey, lest she lose her place in line for royal succession.

"In the fall of the year, Olympias became engaged to be married to Philip of Makedon. During the time of sleeping animals, Olympias died to the world, and, like Eurydice, was taken to the underworld. In the spring, the time when the barley breaks through the ground, Olympias emerged from the ritual death and married King Philip."

Reed turned to Ton. "That's all I know. What happens next, Ton?"

"That is as far as the stories go," he said, but I could see he was trying to avoid Reed's answer. So could Reed.

"Ton. Tell us what happens next."

Ton tossed his head, No, and glanced at me. But Reed would not give up.

"Wallis is her friend, Ton. He has seen her, talked to her. He wears the bracelet of the sacred rivers."

Ton rubbed his hands together, those powerful, work callused hands, and then the hands lifted, parting in resignation. "May I see the bracelet?" he asked. I handed it to him and he stroked it as though caressing a kitten.

"And to Olympias was born a son," he said. "They called him Alexandros, which means, in Makedon, a leader of men. Now this was not Alexandros, Olympias' brother, but Alexandros, her son. Alexandros took upon himself the cloak of The Chosen, by right of agreements made between Athena and man. He possessed a keenness of mind even greater than Olympias, and he possessed the memories as given to few men. Men and boys gathered around him like bees to clover. He killed his first boar when still a child. Alexandros, The Chosen One, the Son of the Bracelet, grew to be a man, a great warrior and leader."

Son of the Bracelet? My body hummed as though stung by a thousand wasps, and I looked at the bracelet, now held, gleaming, in Ton's hands. My bracelet?

"And the time came for Alexandros to take his father's place on the throne, for Philip had arrogantly proclaimed himself a god, and put Olympias aside to take a new wife above her in rank. The people were angry, and they plotted his death. At the wedding of his daughter, an assassin killed him."

Ton looked at me, considered, and then continued. "And Olympias had a friend—the friend who had given her the Bracelet of the Sacred Rivers."

The words flowed on. I no longer heard a voice, but saw pictures. I saw myself on returning from the land of the Galli, presenting Olympias with the bracelet, helping her put it on her arm, and telling her the story of the story tellers.

"And in his twentieth year, Alexandros met with the leaders of the Keltoi people of Galli, on the banks of the river of the goddess Danu to make treaty. The king, Alexandros, said, 'I have heard that you are great warriors and that you do not feel fear.' Rallah answered, 'We fear only that the sky will fall on our heads,' and in so saying he swore a vow not to go to war against Alexandros till the sky falls, which is the first part of the Gallic, three-part vow of peace."

Ton's throat tightened, he gulped, and his forehead wrinkled. He squeezed shut his eyes, then shrugged. "We must wait to tell the rest of the story," he said, "for too much depends on decisions that must be made, and the Muse has stilled my voice." He handed the bracelet to me, and when I touched it, a thrill shook my fingers, washing through my arms and down my body, the words, 'Son of the Bracelet' echoing in my mind.

※ ※ ※

We stayed four days with the people of Amber. Fewer would have denied me the pleasure of their company too much. More would have held me captive in that little village for the rest of my life.

I knew I must leave, but questions remained. I had first heard the clink clink of hammer on anvil, and I had seen and recognized the black smoke of an ironmonger's fire, but I had not yet spoken to the fashioner of iron. The house and shop of the ironmonger and his wife sat away from the central village, and across the river Vils. He had never joined with us at our evening meals, though his wife sometimes came and sat talking with the women.

"I would like to speak to the ironmonger," I told Avi. "Will you go with me to his shop?"

Her face grew hard, cold. "The Latium is not one of us. He settled here two years ago."

Curiosity piqued, I felt more determined than ever to speak to him. "I will not go to the ironmonger's house" she said. "Your trail leads across the river, up that hill and through the next valley. You will not need directions."

"I learned so much from Rudy," I urged, feeling it a sort of apology. "I would like to see if this fashioner of iron has something to teach, something I may relate to my friend the next time I see him. Why don't you like him Avi? Don't you sing to the beat of his hammer on the anvil? Isn't he part of your music?"

"He hammers at the time of our morning's greetings to the sun," she said. "I have no choice. I must sing to his rhythm. He will not pound to ours."

Then she surprised me by wrapping her arms about my neck and squeezing. Quickly pulling away, she touched her fingers to my forehead. "You will always be welcome here, Wallis of Epirus, you and your friends," then she turned away, and I knew it was her good-bye. I wanted to bring her back. *I want to stay here!* I felt like shouting. I said nothing, but watched her retreating figure.

"She knows you," said Fedei. "She knows you from many lives before, and she would like it that you'd remember her, too."

I could not believe this. How could I have lived other lives? "I remember no such lives," I said. "Why wouldn't I remember?"

"Your head is too small," he said. He did not laugh, nor did he explain.

"When you return to the south, there is a better way than the route you came," Fedei continued. "It is a beautiful journey, and this time of the spring is especially beautiful. You go by boat most of the way."

"I hate boats," I said. "Is there also a trail?"

"The mountain sides are too steep for a trail, but the river journey is easy. You will like it. Just take the main road. You won't get lost."

Of course I would get lost. I always got lost.

Palo and I packed the cart with food and supplies, Keltoi jewelry, and a bowl of amber collected from the stream running through the village, a commodity more valuable than gold in the far south. Palo harnessed Spitter.

Except for Avi, all of Amber came to see us off–even Land, wrapped in his fur collar, though he never left Rork's side. Keer, Whist, Reed, Ovie, Shal, Palo and I carried rocks to drop into the deeper washes of the creek, for the water flowed strong enough, now, to be called a river, and much of the road had been washed away. Even Doss and Veil tried to help, though they splashed in the water more than anything else.

When Palo and I stood safely on dry banks, we looked back before going on, watching the others returning to the village side, some slipping from rocks, laughing, getting up soaked and continuing their return.

"You may stay, if you like, Palo," I said. "Spitter and I will be all right. The people of Amber will find a place for you, just as they have the others."

He hesitated, and I thought he might return. "No-o.., I'll go with you," he said, smiling when Doss slipped again. "You'll need help handling the merchandise."

Then I found myself thinking of the road ahead and wondering at the laces binding me to these people. Blessing my good fortune in meeting them, I, too, stood looking back.

And there, long white beard blowing in the wind, standing on the creek bank with the other villagers was the old man I had seen at the tannery back in Three Rivers. Where had he come from? He saw me looking and waved. Suddenly I felt release from the spell that bound me in this place. The villagers lived in a charmed existence somehow disconnected from the rest of the world, the real world, and the magic holding me here began to fade. Somehow relieved, I sighed, released from a tether.

"Besides," Palo added, "those folks are weird."

I laughed a great guffaw that startled Spitter into looking around at me. "You're right, Palo. I really couldn't get along without you."

"What are you laughing at?" he said, frowning.

What indeed, I wondered.

12

Three vultures circled just above the trees, dark blots on the cloudless, blue-white sky of morning. Broad wings outspread, tipping the wind in haughty indifference, they slowly marked the ground just forward and to the right of us for their next meal.

Curious, Palo and I left Spitter and the cart and pushed through the brush lining the road. We emerged into a shadowed pine wood, and trailed a path made by small animals.

A vulture blocked our way. Pinning us in its one-eyed glare, it placed a proprietary claw on a formless bundle heaped beneath pine needles. Even as we approached, the vulture tore flesh. Tossing its head to flip the carrion upward, it stabbed the air and swallowed in one convulsive gulp.

"Hi-yhii!" Palo yelled, running at the creature.

Grabbing and dragging along an entrail, the great bird lifted, beat the air to rise to the branches of a tall pine tree, and sat, downing the rest of an interrupted meal.

I shoved the needles away from the pile with my walking stick, a long stick with a crook on the end, that I had traded for in Amber. It dragged against something metal. I bent and pushed away the rest of the needles with my hand, and Palo and I found the remains of a small animal, caught and killed in an iron trap.

It must have been here more than a day, for despite the cool, spring weather, the carcass had begun to smell. The eyes popped out of the black-nosed face and the tongue thrust between its teeth. The vultures had ignored the bloody fur, all four black feet, and the bushy red tail peppered with longer, stiffer black hairs. It gorged where the reward was greatest–the creature's white belly.

"A red fox," I said, "a vixen. Look, the teats on its skin are still extended."

"You think she had babies somewhere around here?" asked Palo. "They'll be hungry."

"If they are here we'll never find them," I said. "The mother trains them to stay in their holes till she calls them out."

"I know how to make a fox call," he said. "I used to talk to the foxes when I lived in the woods. Before you came."

"Oh, you do, do you? So how does a fox sound?"

"It sounds like a baby crying," he said. "I used to hear them. At first I thought there was a baby lost somewhere in the woods, but I looked and didn't find anything. They sound like this," he said, and cried. "Aanh, haanh, haanh. Aa-a-a-nh, hanh."

"Well how about that?" I said. "You sure that was a fox?"

"I saw one running away one day, but I didn't see him when he was crying. So I figured that's what it was."

"We can't do this one any good," I said. "Might as well let the big birds eat."

So we headed back toward the cart. At the last moment, Palo looked back. "Wallis. " he whispered. "Look."

I looked. A little gray furball huddled near the carcass trying to knead milk from the dead vixen's belly.

"We can't leave it," Palo said.

"Palo, we have no milk, no way to look after it. He's better off here, in the woods."

Starting back toward the kit, he called softly, so not to scare it, "He's all alone, Wallis, and he's hungry." I sighed, waited, and watched. My thought was that the kit would scamper away when Palo approached, but he didn't. Palo picked him up, cuddled him in his arms, and brought him to me. I recalled a rag tag boy I had once found in the woods of Spiros staring at me through an eye too big for his face, a face as dirty as this kit's dusky fur. I protested no further.

"We'll make him a bed," I said. I moved a box of jewelry, placed it on the bottom of the cart, near the back where the sides were higher, and piled blankets and furs on top, where I could get them easily. "We can't give it our blankets if we hope to ever use them again. Better get something we can throw away. How about pine needles? Palo shoved the kit into my arms and hurried back to the pinewood. When he returned, he carried the vixen's tail on top of the needles.

"You brought the tail?"

"The baby will miss his mother. Maybe if he smells this..." Palo piled his needles in the corner, just behind the seat of the cart, hollowed them out with his hands, took the fox from me, and laid him inside. Then he arranged the tail so it wrapped around the kit.

"What can we feed him, Wallis? He was so hungry."

"All we have is dried fish, dried fruit and old cheese," I said. "See if he can chew it."

Palo broke off a piece of meat and found a dried fig. The fox smelled the fish and sniffed, held it firm with his claws, and began to gnaw. It moistened and the kit sucked. He abandoned the meat and started on the fig. That went a little better. Finally so tired he couldn't hold up his head, he fell asleep. I stroked his head and examined a bloody place on his ear. A notch had been torn out of it where it joined the skull, and a scab had formed.

"He's been marked," I said, and showed Palo. "It is almost healed." Palo touched it. The fox stretched, laid his paw atop the torn skin and went back to sleep. "It's still sore," Palo said. "Is there something you can put on it?"

"He's all right, just doesn't want us playing with his ear right now."

Just past the place where we found the kit and halfway up the next hill, we saw smoke rising from a hut. "Must be the ironmonger," I said. "The one who disturbs Avi when he hammers. Guess he built that trap. We'll stop by, tell him he caught something, but it's too late to save the fox pelt. You'd think he would have checked his traps before now. Maybe he's sick." I mentally reviewed my stock of herbs. Avi had packed a bag for me, wrapping each herb separately in clean linen squares. Better than a fortune in gold and silver, to me.

So we climbed the short hill to the house, the scent of baking bread drawing us along the way. The woman met us in the clearing and invited us to sit beneath the shelter at the side of the house that served as her summer kitchen. "I have fresh bread," she said, and rolled away the stone that served as the outside door of the oven to see if it was done. The domed, clay oven joined the walls of the mud-daub house, and, as I could see through the low-cut window, it also opened to the inside. The outer door, I supposed, to use in the summer, the inner in the winter.

The woman broke open a rounded loaf. The steam rose in a wavy tendril and brushed her face. She sniffed the air, smiled approval, and handed the pieces to Palo and me. She sat beside me on the bench, folded the towel she had been holding, laid it on her knee, and smoothed it with her fingers.

Her pale face and hair marked her as one of the woods people, but her prominent nose, beginning high between her brows, and her height, less than my own, recalled to me the travelers I had met coming from the coasts of Italy. Her eyes, a silver grey, settled on my face. She tipped her head to one side, a question unvoiced.

"I have seen you in the village," I said, "but didn't know you were the ironmonger's wife. We came by to tell your husband the vultures are getting his catch."

"Kato is working," she said, then paused. "But it is time to eat. He'll be home soon."

"Is his shop nearby?"

She looked aside. "Kato is very secretive about the location of his shop. He fears the theft of his knowledge. Are you here to steal, Daneion?"

I had hoped to learn something of his craft. That could be considered theft, by one who had such fears. I made a note to ask no questions of the man, Kato. I lifted the bread to take a bite, and my sleeve fell back.

"Your bracelet is beautiful," she said. "May I see it?"

"It's a gift for a friend. I'm just wearing it until I give it to her." I removed it from my wrist and she turned it over and over in her hands. "It shows the sacred rivers. That marks you as a Student of the Mysteries. Avi, from the village, said you had climbed the tree, and that you had made the vow of truth when you drank from the well. Have you seen the wizard?"

"The wizard? We saw an old man with a long white beard, both in Three Rivers and just as we crossed the stream leaving the village," I said. "Was that the wizard? The villagers told me something about a wizard, but I haven't met him."

"The One Who Remembers," she nodded. "Some call him the Watcher."

"Have you met him, *mylitta*?"

"No," she answered, "but I have seen him. He visits an uncle of mine, Miangl. He lives in Manching just west of here. My uncle sometimes tends the Weeping Tree. The Watcher goes to sit beneath its branches."

"Why would he sit beneath the tree?" I asked, intrigued despite my better judgment.

"It is the third step in the path of knowledge," she said. "First there is the Oak of Tannin, then the Well of the Truly Spoken...."

"And now the Weeping Tree," I finished. And if I chose not to sit beneath the tree? I wondered. Had I any choice? Perhaps not. Perhaps the "wizard" had placed a spell on me. "Would they allow me there?" I asked.

"Anyone may visit the tree," she said. "I have sat beneath it many times."

"Betha!" roared the ironmonger from around the corner of the house. I felt the ground shake as he approached. Short and blocky, arms long and muscular, shirt drawn forward between his legs and looped over his girdle, he threw his body forward, one solid step at the time.

He came from the shadows and sunlight struck his head. My heart almost stopped. He looked like Philip. No. Not quite like Philip. Philip stood tall, straight. Regal. Even on the field of battle, the king's skin, tanned from the sun, gleamed with sweet oils. The muscular shoulders of this, shorter, man, sloped from his jaw to his elbows—a result of long hours spent over a forge, lifting and pounding with heavy iron hammers. His skin, as dark as a Nubian's, stank from the oils of black smoke over which he worked. Black hair curled around his ears and joined in waves of black beard cut square at the level of his collarbone, all shrouding his face like oily, gray-black clouds hanging heavy before a thunder storm.

My eyes burned as he neared, his scent recalling my days near the smelting furnaces at H'stok. He eyed Palo, Spitter and her cart, and then looked at me, squinting. His mouth curled downward. Just like Philip's when he was angry.

"What nonsense is she spouting to you?" he charged, continuing without awaiting an answer. "You're the stranger from the village. Pay no attention to the woman's nonsense. They're all superstitious fools. Betha, be quiet. I'll not have visitors thinking we're part of that foolishness."

"You are Latium, Kato, and you have not yet learned our ways. The tree is well-known in my home village," she continued, looking at me.

"The caretakers will make you welcome there." Not changing her quiet, even tone, she said, "The traveler has information about one of your traps."

"Ah, caught something, did it?"

"A fox," I said. "But you're too late to collect the pelt. The vultures have gotten to it."

"Pelts. I care nothing for the pelts. I set the trap to get rid of the pests. They invade my chicken yard, rob me blind. I'll clean them out. Every god-cursed one of them. When I'm done there won't be a thieving pest left anywhere in the woods. I leave them in their traps to scare the others away." He roared with laughter, voice vibrating the air. Made my feet itch.

Palo rose and went back toward the cart. He carried a bit of the bread in his hands and I knew he went to try to feed the little one. I wondered if the kit would eat bread.

"Do you have a milking goat, *mylitta*?" I asked. "Perhaps, if you have more milk than you need for yourselves, we could buy some from you, to ease our thirst along the way?"

She nodded. "I'll get it for you."

"Betha," called Kato. "Wait up." Then in a loud whisper, I heard him tell her, "This is a peddler from the south. He has lots of money. Charge him well."

And she, in a normal voice, answered. "Woods people don't sell their milk to strangers on the road, Kato. When will you learn our hospitality?"

"And when will you learn to live in the real world, woman? We must have money to buy flour for next winter."

"The flour is taken care of, Kato. I dig herbs for Avi, and the woods people supply our flour." Her voice faded as she entered the spring house to get milk. Kato entered with her, and came out still arguing.

"You should charge the healer for those herbs. They're worth a lot more than the price of flour."

Betha returned with a full bag of milk. "If you leave the milk in the goat's belly skin for a while, it will harden," she said. "Then when it has turned to cheese, add some salt to the whey. That'll keep it from spoiling. The Keltoi know that makes the best cheese."

I crossed my arms on my chest and dipped my head. I had seen Ton do that for thanks, and she nodded, smiling. "You are welcome in my house, friend," she said, the traditional response.

"This is MY house," Kato bellowed, "and I will say who is welcome here." He glared at me.

I backed away. I might have offered coin for the milk, or returned it, but I saw Betha's faint frown, and smiled, ducking my head again. And, I excused myself, the kit needed milk, which it would have had, if the ironmonger hadn't killed its mother.

"How far to the Weeping Tree?" I asked.

"One day's wal…"

Kato exploded. "There is no weeping tree."

Betha held up a thumb, meaning one. She held it close to her breast where Kato could not see. "I was mistaken," she said. "There is no weeping tree," but, even as Kato grasped her hair and jerked her toward the house, her eyes glanced west. Whether or not Kato approved, Betha had told me, one day's walk to the west.

"I'll lock you in where you'll never tell your lies again."

I didn't see a rough ironmonger disciplining his wife. I saw a certain arrogant king of the Makedoné, preparing to beat my little bird. In a blinded fog of rage, I followed, seeing nothing but the door closing in front of me. I banged my hands on the door. They came away bloodied from loose splinters. Palo pushed in between me and the door. I shoved him aside, continued pounding. The door opened. Betha looked out. "Shh!" she warned, whispering. "He'll kill you. He's gone for his blade. I'll be all right. I'll offer him bread. His anger does not compare to his hunger. Go away. I'm all right."

I backed away. This woman, so fair of hair it gleamed in the sun, was not Olympias, and the crude ironmonger was not Philip. I stumbled back toward the cart, flipped a thumb at Palo. He and Spitter followed.

Out of sight of the hut, the fox kit jumped onto my back. Startled, I tucked him beneath the folds of my cloak. We walked like that for a long time. When I was certain he slept, I put him back into his bed, and wiped my face with my sleeve. My nose still stung from the scent of the forge.

13

The next day we found the encampment of the people who tended the Weeping Tree. We had descended a long, winding trail most of the morning, and before noon, began passing tents pitched in a thinning wood. In the midst of the tents, beside a small, mist-shrouded lake, a shelter had been built, and two attendants, hoods thrown back to enjoy the sunlight, greeted us.

"Betha sent us," I said in greeting. "She said you would tell us about the Weeping Tree."

"My niece. Betha is a fine person," said a man of about fifty years of age, rising, dipping his head in greeting.

"Then you are Miangl?"

He acknowledged the name with a nod and a wave of his hand toward a stand of velvety green moss, and seated himself, facing me. "Betha is a child of the wood. But I can't say the same for her husband. Foreigner. Friend of Betha's mother. Betha's mother came from the south, from the Latium people. She's gone on, now, to her rest. I think Betha has been here several times to talk with her, but maybe not. What visitors see and who they talk to is their business. So long as they don't get caught in the underworld."

I said. "The underworld."

"This is a spirit tree," he said. "Didn't Betha tell you?"

"No. She only said that I was a student of the mysteries and that I should stop here."

Miangl chuckled. "Betha didn't have much time to tell you anything, did she? Kato sees to that."

"He was there," I said.

"Um-hmm. The tree is well known in the lands of the Virunum. People come here from all directions to speak with their ancestors. The call of the underworld is especially strong here, under the tree."

My first concern was for Palo. His was an uncomplicated, trusting mind. I wouldn't want his spirit lured away, leaving him to a somnalistic idiocy. I began to look around, to suggest that we prepare to be on our way.

Palo stood at my back, the fox kit in his arms. "Can I sit under the tree?" he asked.

Miangl looked at him, saw him fondling the kit. He smiled. "I would say you're just about the right age to sit under the tree," he said. "Of course, if you were younger it wouldn't be safe. How old are you, about fourteen?"

"I don't know," said Palo.

Miangl nodded. "You'll have to wait till the others finish. There is only enough room for two or three. And they must sit apart, not touching, so the tree will have space to weep upon their backs and shoulders and heads."

The tree grew downhill between the shelter and the lake. Upper branches and shining leaves sparkled in sunlight, but the lower half, glimpsed through layers of cloud shrouding the lake and the surrounding bowl-like valley, seemed a many-legged creature arising from the Underworld.

"The lake is a hot spring?" I asked, longing for a bath.

Miangl nodded. "The spring keeps the ground warm. The tree likes it. She's the last of her kind around here. The old stories tell of weeping trees that filled the valleys, before the sun went south, when gods walked with man."

I had seen a tree something like this once, in a holy shrine across the Aegean, just south of where we had gone to live with my sister and her husband. That tree had also grown near a hot spring, but no one mentioned it weeping.

Smooth root-like growths drooped downward from the branches. Where the growths touched, they mated with earth and penetrated, eager to return to their beginnings. A sacred grove, but a single tree.

Within the grove, in little alcoves the caretakers had cleared by tying away the ropy tendrils before they mated with Earth, three dark blots marked the bodies of seekers. They looked like bugs caught in the web of a giant spider. The enclosures might have been chambers prepared for visitors—or traps set to catch the unwary.

"We think maybe she gets lonely for the Earth Mother, so lonely she stretches out her fingers to caress her," said Miangl. "She likes to have people come to sit beneath her branches and talk over old times."

The tree's desire to return to earth—could it impart that same desire to the visitors? I didn't want Palo pulled into any underworld. I said, "Hmmm. Dangerous."

Miangl thought and then continued. "Not really, so long as the caretakers sit on watch."

"And if they don't?"

"Well, the seekers could stay there till they die, or even if not, they could lose their souls there. The attraction of the underworld is quite strong here. Sometimes we have to pull them out from under the tree."

Palo laid a hand on my shoulder, squeezed. How could I refuse him? But I vowed not to sit under the tree with him. I'd wait with the watchers. Three sets of eyes would be better than two, just in case the others went to sleep. "All right," I said to Palo. "We must pitch our tent. You can sit under the tree tomorrow." I looked the question at the caretakers.

"First dawn tomorrow," Miangl agreed. "Most of the visitors say it's better to bathe first then sit beneath the branches naked. There's a good place on the hill for your tent. The ditches for body wastes are there," he pointed, "just behind that ridge."

I rose to leave, aware, suddenly, of how quietly we had been talking. The kit, asleep till now, stretched and yawned. Palo put him on the ground, and he vanished into the mists of the lake. Palo started after him and Miangl called.

"Oh he'll be back. Now that you've fed him he's bound to you forever." He chuckled. "A bondage you may regret."

That evening, currying Spitter and cleaning her hooves with a hoof pick, I considered the tree. We had camped but a short distance from her, so close I could scent her leaves, cool and airy, but her scent somehow conveyed an animal musk sweetness. There was no denying her attraction; I felt totally right, calling the tree a "her." And it was true—I felt her loneliness, her call. I pitied her—the last of her kind.

That night I dreamed of Yiayia. "You too, must sit beneath the tree," she said. "This is why you have come." She felt my protest, and I felt her smile. Yiayia was like that. She never argued. She made statements.

֎֎֎

The next morning, Palo and I bathed in the spring, our figures merging with the morning's pink mists. A curious quietness permeated me, enclosing me in my own private world, neither longing for company nor feeling crowded, just content to be where I was, when I was. And when I was done, I felt complete. Prepared. In a single movement Palo and I rose from the water to approach the tree.

We sat near, but not touching, as the caretaker had instructed, and waited. It was not uncomfortable beneath the tree. Sitting naked on soft, green moss, I leaned against a springy web of tendrils stretching from upper branches to earth. The earth and air, lazily warm, drained away any sense of urgency, any fear. I felt cradled, comforted.

The caretaker had said I could call anyone from the spirit world I chose. I thought of calling Yiayia, but it hardly seemed necessary. Didn't my grandmother hover somewhere near me every waking moment? And she had visited me. During the night.

So who? How Olympias would love to be here. She could talk to her mother. Ask her questions. Tell her how much she had missed her after her mother had been killed.

"Wallis," a voice whispered. Alerted, I listened, jerking my head to find anyone who could have called my name. "Wallis," again the whisper. "I am Tanya, Olympias' mother. I am glad Olympias has you for a friend," she said. The voice hushed, but a sense of someone nearby invaded me, drenched me so completely that I found it difficult to breathe. I felt a love so complete I wanted to weep. The feeling lasted only a moment, but for that moment I felt the certainty of truth, of wholeness beyond anything I had ever before known.

That awareness faded and another replaced it.

"I am Alexandros," said the voice, so controlled, carrying such a weight of power that I shrank, retreating to the inward core of myself– where I go when I feel unprepared to face life. Where could I find the courage to respond? I, a coward.

"Alexandros?" I answered, my mind a roaring hum. "Alexandros?"

"I am Alexandros," he said, softening the presence to a bearable degree, "he, spoken of by the People of the Trees." I sensed the presence softening, a willed and generous gesture, giving my own being space to breathe. It was not a retreat, just a lowering of the strength of his presence for my sake. Gratefully, I emerged from my private guarded space.

"Olympias' unborn son?" I asked.

"Yes," he whispered, quieter still. I emerged further, far enough to be able to think.

"You will not trust me at first," he said, "but later we will become very close. I will need your help. A great task lies before me. You must help me gather support from the people. My time will be short. I won't have long to accomplish my goals, and the window is narrow through which I must slip."

"Window?"

"I am part of a greater plan," he said. "The maps have been drawn. Now the paths must be walked."

"What are these plans?" I asked, doubting.

"Earth and its peoples are entering a time of causes," he said. "I prepare the way for another, who will adjust the cause and effect spectrum. It will mean a new awareness for the child we call Man."

I understood nothing of what he said. I waited, longing for more, uncertain of what to say. I could not let him go. Not yet. "The people of Amber spoke of you," I said. "They called you the Son of the Bracelet." I held out the bracelet for the spirit to see. My arm tingled, and power generated by the bracelet raced through my arm into my torso, down into my legs and upward through my neck and shoulders.

I saw a child, a fair-haired boy, leaning against the breast of a woman. The woman wore white with purple and blue embroidered border. A bracelet of the white iron worked with wavy lines of blue and fitted with polished white stones, a coin sized medallion in the center. The bracelet encircled her upper arm, gleaming. She cradled the boy's forehead with her hand, crooning, willing the boy to fight, fight to breathe. The boy's breath came in whistling whispers. In. Gasp. Out...Forcing. And in again, laboring, straining to breathe. Age three, four, five, I saw, written in the air above their heads.

Then, into the rounded plane of sight came a figure. A man, red beard and hair peppered with white, lithe, muscular, eyes the color of autumn moss, a man darkened by long hours in the sun. The man carried a bowl of liquid. He spooned the liquid, dribbling it between the boy's lips, stroking the boy's throat to make him swallow. One spoonful, another, another, until the bowl was empty, then the man laid coals in the fire of an iron stove, a stove decorated with enameled figures of deer and a hunter with bow and arrow. In a pot of water simmering on the stove, the man dropped a handful of herbs and stirred the mixture with a wooden spoon. He lifted the boy and held his head near the steam.

The man nodded, permitted a half smile as the boy inhaled the vapors, a strained breath in, a forced breath out. All the while the boy struggled to breathe, the man grunted words in a rhythmic, cracked voice, a feeble effort toward a song. These were the words taught me by Yiayia, my grandmother. I was that man.

The boy's breathing grew easier, drops of moisture from the steam and from his own body sweat joined, streamed down his face and moistened pale brown curls turned gold from the sun. The man raked the moisture from the boy's face with his finger, inserted it into the boy's mouth. Finally the boy opened round, sensitive eyes, and the man studied them—left eye two colors, half green, half brown, the right eye hazel. As he watched, the boy's left eye changed colors, lightening in the white of his mother's dress, darkening when she moved away. A child of the mists

A force gripped me, pulled me away from the images and I approached another sphere of light, entered and waited, hanging in space above the figure of a man, seated before a tent on a folding stool. Many people milled the area, standing, talking, awaiting their turns to speak to the man. Money, much money, passed from the hands of the people into the hands of a man who stood beside the seated man. The receiver of the moneys counted coins and dropped them into a huge earthen jar decorated with figures of gold and silver and many colors. It was the store of a very rich man. Above the figure of the seated man, I saw, painted on the air, the shape of another man, huge, somehow inimical, directing the movements of the two below him.

The people who paid the money went away grumbling, counting their few remaining coins, and turning various items of merchandise over to boys who loaded it into carts and into baskets fitted onto the backs of mules. One of the people who walked away was the man with the red hair, red beard. Myself.

After the people left, I watched the seated man stand, pat his generous belly as though having completed a satisfying meal. The man said, "The barbarian queen will be murderous when she learns the prices she has been forced to pay." He laughed and his belly shook, up and down, up and down, joggling the colorful many-folded fabrics overlying loose pantaloons. Ornate sandals laced up to his knees, covering the fabric. A Persian. A eunuch. The man clapped his money changer on the shoulder and went away talking, laughing as the man's bearers rolled the heavy urn onto a flat cart that hugged the ground, and pulled it away, one pulling, one pushing.

The money changer said. "She will come after us, you know; it isn't like her to ignore a proper fleecing."

The man who had sold merchandise said, "The barbarian queen will not live past the fall harvests. My assassins will see to that." And in the air above the two men's heads I saw the queen. She wore the bracelet of blue rivers, the white stones and the medallion. Olympias. Again I was pulled away from the images and could see a glowing, white sphere, a sphere of light which drifted farther and farther behind as I floated in quiet darkness.

My back arched, spasmed. My voice erupted from my throat in a strangled call. "Ah-eee!" My arm dragged against a tendril of the tree joined firmly with earth.

Suddenly terrified, I tried to stand. My body refused to respond and I realized that I had not screamed, only thought it.

"Remember," said the voice, fading. "A child who will early become a man, early die." The presence vanished, leaving me with questions unanswered, an empty longing unfulfilled, and a terror of an unknown thing, waiting just beyond my understanding.

Away into the darkness I floated, a bit of driftwood pulled along in a soundless current. I drifted toward another sphere of light, toward it... into it.

I knew where I was. I walked in the body of a man, a man with a silver coated donkey, a boy, and a cart loaded with bits of treasure, gathered here, gathered there. Pots of herbs grew, jostling with the movement of the swaying cart. In the corner slept a tiny furry gray ball. A fox–the kit we had rescued. I felt aligned with the figure of the man, yet floated a handbreadth away. A woman floated nearby. She smiled and then looked sad. "A long, long journey, Tadpole, a hard way to go, but I will be with you. For every step." I fought to merge with the figure of the man, but again I was pulled away, and into the flow of the black stream.

Another being approached. This being did not invade, but rather attached itself to me as a shadow attaches itself to an object. I felt suddenly wise, learned, beyond my wildest reckoning. And I remembered, as an actor remembers a studied part, as a scholar remembers a favorite history.

I remembered walking the earth in the body of a little girl, a beggar in the streets of the City of Beggars on the Bosporus. I remembered a brother who begged alongside me, near the gates of the city. I remembered hunger, beatings, and the kind hand of a physician who brought me bread. I remembered a sister, a little two-year-old girl sold for money to pay for food...

and...

I remembered debarking a great ship, stepping foot on new land in the body of a woman. Others with me, all clothed in many-colored dresses that swept the earth.

and...

I remembered a tribe of brown people living in the hills of a dry country. My mother ground corn (what is corn?) in a great hollowed stone bowl. And I remembered leaving that tribe when still a child.

and...

I remembered standing on a shore, watching a flying ship. On the rocks nearby, a tower stood alone, a light flashing, flashing, flashing–circling within a room at the top of the tower. On the shore stood a woman with family, protected, loved. The watcher remembered. The watcher wrote about it.

I awoke, drenched with sweat and resin from the tree.

Palo spoke aloud. "You shouldn't have abandoned me. Wallis has been more mother and father to me than you ever were."

How was it possible? I heard an answer from the one to whom he spoke. "I am sorry, my son. I was sick. I knew I was dying, but I should have found you a home. I'll do better next time."

Next time? What next time, I wondered–and heard in many voices answers to my question.

"We are Self. Self grows. Self remembers. Self believes in future. Self searches for Self. Self loves all. And self forgives Self for separation." The voices joined in a spectral symphony carefully arranged and orchestrated...and then faded.

Palo aroused with a mighty indrawn breath, as though he had never breathed before.

"Palo," I said. "Are you all right?"

"It was my mother, Wallis. She said she was sorry she left me. But she should have taken me to her family first. I will never forgive her."

"Oh no, no, little brother," I said, remembering the great ships and later the great flying barges. "Never is a long, long time."

We walked away from the tree, and where my arm raked my hip, it stuck in damp, sticky resin. The tree's 'tears,' I supposed.

※ ※ ※

Again we bathed in the springs, using moss that grew everywhere on the nearby grounds to rake the resin from our skin. All the time, I longed for such a tree as this to grow where I could visit often. What a marvel. An impenetrable gap between worlds could be crossed without effort, with only a peaceful afternoon's rest. But Miangl had said this was the last of her kind. Then, perhaps I could gather drops of the resin. I would spread a blanket beneath the tree, catch the drops, let them harden and roll them into little pills to take whenever I wished to communicate with the spirits. Would the tears work the same if taken internally? I would ask.

"You would never awaken," said Miangl. "Others have tried. They all died."

He looked at me a long time, not speaking, and I began thinking of other things to do. Finally he continued. "But a child of the tree could perhaps survive if placed in the proper environment. She is sacred, you know. And she is vulnerable. Non believers seem to hate her, and seek to destroy her. You must not voice abroad what you have learned here."

I remembered Kato's reaction to the tree. "Some already know," I said. "Betha's husband is an unbeliever. He hates the tree, or at least, he hates what it represents. He calls such things superstition."

"Ah, yes. Kato." Miangl nodded. "The Watcher keeps a sharp eye on him." And then he laughed aloud. "Kato cannot find us. He has tried time and again. Kirri always leads him astray. He finally became convinced that Betha is delusional. She lets him think what he wishes. Safer that way."

"Then there really is a watcher? And his name is Kirri?"

Miangl smiled, closed his eyes and nodded slowly. When he raised his head he glanced at Palo, beside me on the blanket, again cuddling the fox.

"Foxes eat pears," said Miangl, rising to enter the hut. "I just might have one in my basket." He returned bringing a basket of pears, grapes and apples and set it in on the moss beside us. "Eat what you like. Bathers always come from the springs hungry. Wonder why that is?" He turned away from me, reaching for a basket of bread, cheese and mushrooms on the blanket behind him. I couldn't see his face, but I could feel his knowing smile.

Palo and I had sat under the tree for six hours, from day break until noon, and that, without breakfast. I had simply forgotten to eat, and I suppose, so had Palo.

"Will you answer a question for me?" I asked.

"If I can," he said.

"I seem to remember one who called himself Alexandros. He spoke to me. Under the tree."

"Yes?"

"You don't seem surprised."

"No…, not really," he said, "though Alexandros seldom speaks. Do you remember what he said?"

"He said that this is a time of causes…" I flushed. This sounded so silly.

"And?"

"That he must enter a window. And then he said that he must prepare for another who will also come," I shrugged, decided to follow the thought. "Through the window."

Miangl smiled. Laughed, and the laughter grew until he rolled over on the moss, sides shaking, and finally pushed himself erect and wiped his eyes with his sleeve. The laughter erupted again, and again he fell over. This time he didn't get up, but propped his head on his arm and looked at me, eyes so full of mischief that I wondered how he had managed to become a Caretaker of the Tree.

I am accustomed to being an object of humor. People laugh at me for various things all the time. But now, I wanted only to stand and run.

Miangl sat up and placed his hand on my arm. When he touched me, the bracelet tingled. Astonished, I paused, waiting.

"The window is…is a space of time," he explained. "Time is fluid, like the water in the spring. We mortals float on that water, sometimes going somewhere, sometimes circling aimlessly—like leaves caught in a whirlpool."

Miangl looked away, across the fogs above the springs and farther, it seemed, until a hill, blue and misty in the distance, stopped his gaze. "Then we come to a waterfall, and the current carries us over the edge and we are dashed to the bottom of the falls.

"During the dash, it is anyone's guess which way we will float when we hit the surface. We may be caught in another eddy and circle for days, or we may be carried beneath the waters never to arise again. But we may find a log, or a rock, to stop us."

This he said while gazing at the mountains. He looked back at me. "But sometimes...sometimes one of us will lead the way, will carve a wake through the waters. All who are captured in the tow of this one will go together, to land and to form a reef. And on that reef others will light. The reef will build, become an island. A haven for those lost in the currents. To pull themselves from the water. To find soil to grow, to make a home."

He looked away again. "To become, together, like the airborne roots of the Weeping Tree, clinging to Earth Mother for love of her and her children yet embracing the sky, the sun, the stars, for which she will forever yearn."

He said nothing for a while, attention fled elsewhere.

"And the window?" I asked. "There is no real window?"

Miangl smiled again, this time as remembering a dear friend, "Alexandros always prefers to speak in metaphor. It requires a certain leap of imagination to understand him, but he is quite appreciative of those who make the effort."

I understood the word, metaphor. Greek scholars liked to use it all the time. It meant using one object to explain, to identify another. Sometimes concepts could only be understood by such a tactic. "I understand," I said. "When he uses it I will know."

"You plan to sit beneath the tree again tomorrow?"

"Oh, no," I said, "I mean when I talk to him, when he comes."

Alexandros is coming?" This time I heard joy, surprise, in his voice.

"He said I wouldn't trust him at first, but...."

Miangl stood, yelled for the other caretaker. "Alexandros is coming!" He called. "When!?" he snapped at me.

"When?"

"When, man! When will Alexandros be born?"

"He didn't say. Could be soon. He will be born to Olympias. She was married this spring."

"It must not be too soon. The stars must be in alignment." He wailed, slapping his face. "Another two cycles. And we must prepare. You must convince Olympias to wait. Who is the father?"

"Philip of Makedonia," I said, wondering. "Why?"

Miangl put one hand on his hip and stroked his beard with the other.

"Philip," he mumbled. "Why Philip? Not good. Philip is a young soul. He will need training. Where were they married?"

"At Samothrakè."

Miangl nodded. "Then the priests of Sitos, Dionysus and Orpheus have already pledged him. We need only prepare him."

Too bewildered to speak, I watched the man stride here and there, on the sands, the moss, the rocky ground, and the sands again. He circled my place on the moss, reversed his direction, and circled again as a leaf caught in the fickle currents of a dust storm. "Good. Philip is a warrior. Alexandros will be trained in the arts of war."

Good? I doubted that. The man had no honor. I worried that he might hurt the little bird, perhaps even this Alexandros.

"That means that the place where Esu–the One Who Comes After– must be prepared." He jerked to a stop, grabbing my shoulder, pinning me, as though he expected me to bolt.

Where!" he thundered. Again the bracelet tingled. "Where will Esu be born?"

I'll never know where the words came from, but I answered, "Beyond the Aegean, in the land of Canaan."

"Where?" With both hands locked on my shoulders, he shook me, bobbing my chin, forward and back. "Where!"

"A...Aphrath," I managed to say.

Miangl stood still. "In the lands of Zarathustra," he said, wonderingly. "The home of the Magi. Of course." Again he took his place on the moss. "The way has already been prepared for him. We have now only to alert the Persian king. And if he proves intractable?" he considered, a question addressed only to himself. "Then we'll have to conquer the armies of the Persians," he answered.

'Conquer the armies of the Persians,' the man says. Who does he think he is? Only to conquer the Persians.

"Conquer the Persians?" I asked, but Miangl seemed totally deaf and dumb, unaware that I was even here, sitting beside him in the sun.

ᄆᄆᄆ

Miangl helped me find a seedling, very rare, for the tree seldom bloomed to form seeds. She spread by inserting the tentacles hanging from her limbs into the earth below. We dug the little tree, leaving the roots embedded in its soil, and carefully placed her in one of Ana's jars, that one my friend had given me when I left Athens, the one she had intended for carrying water.

Miangl held the little tree up to the sky. "You will travel far, little one," he said. "And you will taste the soil of a foreign place, but you must not grieve for your mother. Daneion will prepare a place for you, and you will grow, be strong, and unite the spirits of that place." Then he raised the little tree to the four directions and again toward the south. This is the way you will go. Your mother will know where to find you.

"You must keep her moist," he said, turning to me, "and warm. Not too much sun, and when you plant her, a shelter beneath an arbor of grapes would be good for her first years, near a source of warm water, as you see here."

I knew of such a place, on the coast not far from Makedonia. Hot springs like these flowed in abundance. Trembling, I took the pot from Miangl, and spit on the soil. The tree received its first moisture.

Spitter had been turned loose to forage, and had found some of her special lichen growing on banks far up the hillside from the lake. I whistled for her, watched to see her lift her head, reach for another bite then begin her return. Our road ran near that patch so I determined to stop to gather more before we left the area. Palo and I packed our cart, leaving room for the pots of plants at the top, and the bed for the fox, though the kit was nowhere to be found. Palo went looking while I finished the packing.

Miangl brought a basket of pears and laid them on top. "You'd better put those where that fox can't get to them."

"Looks like the fox has decided to stay here," I said.

"I wouldn't count on it," he answered. "He knows where a good meal can be found. He'll be back."

But when Palo, Spitter and I pulled out, the fox hadn't returned. Palo kept looking, peering into the bush on either side of the road for a long way, and his drooping shoulders told me of his disappointment.

Then, a short way up the road, Spitter slowed to a shuffle and stopped. A gray blur shot from the wood on the left, climbed the wheel, jumped into the cart, and burrowed beneath the fox tail. Two glittery rusty-gray eyes peered over the edge. Palo looked at me, stunned. "Wow. Did you see that? I never saw anything move so fast. He flew." He scooped the fox into his arms and rubbed behind its furry, round, black ears, swallowing hard, trying not to cry and having a rough time of it. "That's what I'll call you. Fly."

The kit lifted his head and we saw the tip of a tail of a field mouse hanging from his lips. He squirmed out of Palo's fingers and vanished into his sleeve. Palo clutched at the weight, gripping Fly against his body. "He tickles." He giggled.

Spitter snuffed, and moved out again. Palo hurried ahead, and I walked beside Spitter's head, murmuring, whistling to her as I sometimes do. "You knew Fly was out there didn't you girl? How do you know these things?"

Rested and fed, body and spirit, I embraced my little caravan, the road, the trees, the snakes, the rabbits, the gnats and mosquitoes humming about my ears, and even the vultures circling wide and high, far away in the blue sky. Enthralled in harmony, moving to the beat of the remembered, symphonic rhythm of a cosmos united, glorying in the humming vibrations racing through my body, I paced a rhythmic beat. Spitter shattered the spell. "Ha-onh ahonh, ahonh, ahonh."

14

Our road snaked through steaming bogs crowded with lichen-bearded trees, a quiet journey for few traveled this narrow, sunless route. Vaporous rain enveloped us, soaking our clothes. Palo and I removed our boots and pants, tied up our long shirts, pulled the tails forward between our legs and tucked them in at our girdled waists.

When trees broke to sunlight, we shaded our eyes with our hands and saw before us a sea of shimmering, long-bladed bog grass, painted with silver strokes by the giant fingers of whimsical breezes.

No hills were visible, no protection from any unexpected rise in water where we might safely pitch a tent should there be rain during the night, so we just hurried on, eating away the distance step by monotonous step.

Fly alternated between his place in the cart and the folds of Palo's sleeve. Older now, the kit disappeared from time to time, returning with whatever kill he could make, grasshoppers, mostly, but once the feather of a water bird clung to the fur of his white collar. We no longer worried about feeding him, and I wondered when he would stop returning to us.

Once, startled by a movement beside me, I found the fox on Spitter's back, perched atop her load. From here he watched the terrain, aware of the movement of every bird, every snake, and every grasshopper. Eyes squinted, he allowed his head to rest on a lump in the pack. I caught him watching me before he closed his eyes, feigning sleep.

Maybe it is true that gods sometimes inhabit the bodies of animals. I found myself prepared to believe anything after our stay with the People of the Trees.

Some few, their chosen ones, decorated their forearms with a tattoo of a tree—an oak like the one I had climbed to find The Green Man and to hear and to be shaken by the voice of their god, Tannin. Ton once saw me admiring the tattoo, and asked me if I'd like to have one like that.

"Only your chosen ones wear the tree," I said. "I am a foreigner." So I declined, knowing that the tattoo would be the final joining—in spirit and mind—a joining of mission.

"I must go," I said. I promised my grandmother I would seek my kinsmen."

"You seek much more than that, Pelos Daneion of far away Athens."

I had seen the powers of Ton and his students, but still I needed to ask, to be assured. "How do you know what it is I seek?"

"I was born knowing. Sometimes knowing is a burden, but with you, I have found joy and reason for life."

"Tell me what it is you see. It would help me to avoid the trials of travel." I teased, a response born of a lifelong need to practice a code of disbelief in the supernormal. The code had kept me sane when things happened that did not make sense to me. Yet, isolated from my own world, that code no longer served. I knew what he said to be true.

"It is not wise to reveal too much to those who have chosen not to know their futures," he said. "Lessons learned the hard way are not forgotten. You have many lessons to learn."

So I did not dismiss Fly's lingering gaze. Perhaps I was truly being observed by one other than a fox kit. I watched him watching me, and it seemed that I saw myself through his eyes, like one of the visions I had witnessed as I sat beneath the Weeping Tree. Sometimes when I allowed my mind to wander, those visions still flashed before my mind, glimpses of other places, other times, held up for viewing.

One image now presented itself full blown. I watched a man, the same man I had seen before, the man on the horse called Bukephalus. This man had suffered a wound in the head, and I tended it. Captured by this man's nightmare images, I fought to contain the sense of them, forcing them back again and again to the scene most continuous. Each time I led him back, he grasped my hand, pulled it to his chest, and I knew his gratitude. Weary, so weary I had come near fainting, still I was as fresh as morning dew compared to this old companion of mine. Alexandros. Alexandros, my son. What have I done to you?

Again I saw myself walking beside the cart, tears streaming down my face.

I handed Fly a nut I carried in my shoulder pouch. He grasped it between his paws, sniffed it, then caught it in his teeth and disappeared into the cart to hide it as though he thought I might try to take it back. Returning, he yawned, stretched, leapt from the cart and caught up with Palo. He tried to climb Palo's bare leg; Palo picked him up, and he disappeared into Palo's sleeve, riding, watching the trail through a part in the fold. Palo, hand tucked into his waist girdle, walked for miles without disturbing the kit's rest.

Two days later, after riding a crowded ferry down the River Main, we stood on a hill overlooking the Rhine. Huge flat boats traveled the river, those heading north floating with the current, and those heading south being towed by oxen, with pole men lining the sides of the boat, shoving the boat away from the banks. Ships of home depended on sails when there was wind, on oars when there was not. This way seemed exhausting and primitive.

Clean, refreshed from soaking in one of the hot springs that seemed everywhere in this country, comfortably sated with stew and fresh-baked bread, I walked out on a dock to watch the boats float by. Pelicans perched on pilings, lazing in the sun, necks folded, heads tucked into breasts. Sea birds wheeled and screamed overhead, and the gusting river breeze tossed my hair and parted my beard.

My waking dreams had shown the bracelet adorned with gleaming moon-white stones—stones mined in the North, downriver, in Herne. If I boarded one of these boats I would be there by noon. But then I would have to travel upriver again, and that would take another day and a half. I leaned against a post, startling one of the pelicans. She shifted her feet and stretched out her neck for balance, then tucked it back in, closed her eyes and slept. If I were this bird, I thought, I could carry the rocks in my throat pouch. Flying, I could be in Pella in just a few days.

Buoyed by the inspiration of flying, and imagining placing the bracelet on Olympias' arm, I straightened, preparing to hail one of the ships I saw carrying passengers.

Then I saw the wizard. He stood on the path between me and the boat landing. Straight, despite his age, he stood still, resting his right hand on a staff longer than he was tall. I rather imagined that he could block my path if he chose, and that I would have been unable to pass, were that my intention. The old man said nothing, just stood there, wispy beard flowing out beside him, and looked at me.

Something passed between us. I knew him, from somewhere, sometime. Yet I was certain we had never spoken. I must not go downriver, he is saying. I must...I must return to Olympias. Trouble? A sense of urgency washed over me. The little Bird was in danger? Yes, but from what? Then the wizard turned and walked away, leading us south.

"Never mind the stones, Palo. We're going home."

THREE

WITHOUT HONOR

Kirri, The Watcher

Miangle, lost in reverie, entwined within the tentacles of the Weeping Tree, spoke, but his lips did not move and his eyes were closed.
"The peddler was here, Watcher, but he blocked my knowledge of his thoughts even while sitting beneath the tree."
"He is well trained. He blocks his thoughts even from himself."
"He does not know?"
"He does not allow himself to know. If he knew, he could not do the things he must."
"How will we track him when he goes? Should I follow?"
"You must not leave your post."
"We will lose him. Iskander will arrive without assistance. The translation will be too much for him. His spirit will shatter. We cannot risk that."
"Do you suppose your view of this pattern to be unique? Nearness to the tree blinds you."
Rebuked, Miangle shriveled into a tiny image of himself. How had he dared question the decision of the great one? "I have failed you. I am not worthy of your trust."
"Dismiss humility, Miangle. It is false, and it borrows despair."

"How is one not to feel humble in your presence? To deny that I feel humility is to deny truth."

"There are many truths. Choose which you will serve. All others fade away."

"I cannot. I am ignorant."

"Consider the tree. She will feel your remorse. She will grieve. Listen, watch. Learn. When the Records pass to you my Watcher in Waiting and when you wear the Mantle, if you are not prepared you will be consumed in humility. Humility and its brother, Conceit, are two of the great destroyers. But for now, be content in your ignorance. Other eyes lend us assistance. Even animals."

"The fox?"

"The fox, yes, but he will not travel to the far south. I will send others—one will remain with the peddler for as long as he is needed. Daneion will name him 'Singer.'"

"And Iskander. All the plans of our ancestors to bring harmony to this world depend on him. Will he comply?"

"Comply? Iskander's road has not yet been walked. He will act in his own time, in his own way. The question is, Will we comply with *him*? Watch and see. Wait and learn."

"But if the old ones from the south interfere, Iskander may be defeated."

"No one defeats Iskander...no one, except, possibly, Iskander himself."

1

"Only a two-day journey," the shopkeeper on the Rhine said. "The boats are large and comfortable and cliffs are unbelievably beautiful. Just take that road south out of here. Safe enough, no bandits have been reported for more than two weeks."

Safe enough for him, perhaps. I doubted he'd ever taken the trip except in his dreams. The part about the bandits rang true, so I checked my cache in the pouch beneath the cart. If bandits hadn't been seen in two weeks, it was about time for them to be out again.

About three days journey across wilderness we came to a river. We fished and cooked, then went swimming–so pleasant on this warm, late spring day.

"Look! The old man," said Palo. Beaming, he stood on a rock to get a better view and waved his hat as high as he could reach. A flat boat with three men passed by, a small sail filled with wind opposing the current from up stream. Kirri's beard, layering on the wind, pointed the way ahead. "As old as he is, he sure does get around."

My palms itched. That old man showed up too often. A spirit of the trees? A wraith? Couldn't be if Palo saw him too.

"Knows his territory too cursed well."

"What?" asked Palo.

"Where is their wind?" I said, then louder, "I don't feel any wind."

On the fifth day, about noon, we broke through a dense copse of wood into a village. People sat on the ground or on benches, just passing the time of day in a clearing near a spring, a rolling mound of water emerging from earth. Gathering into a pool captured inside banks of moss-choked rock, it broke through and tumbled downhill–the headwaters of the Danube, as the shopkeeper had promised. "Best cross there, at Ulm," he had said. "You won't get another chance. The river gets wider, deeper farther down. No ferries, not with the current like it is this time of year."

I found a seat on a log not far from the spring and fanned gnats from my face with my hat. Palo drew water for Spitter, and then wandered over to a small group of laughing people. A young man shuffled shells back and forth, and Palo watched.

"That one!" A girl yelled, and the young man lifted the nut, made a wry face, reached into a jar beside him and gave her a handful of nuts. Onlookers laughed, and one said, "Let me try." Then the game began again.

I wiped my face with my sleeve. Spitter sounded off, "Ahonh!" and Palo went to draw water for her. He came back a few minutes later, set her water jar before her, and handed me a dripping cloth. I wiped my face and massaged the dust from my beard, dragging the cloth across my head from face to the neckline, squeezing the water out and wiping again, all the time murmuring thanks to Palo, who wasn't listening, but watched the nutshell game.

A small boy, six or eight years old, limped through the clearing. He sat near the nutshell game, but didn't watch. He seemed in pain, and desolate with worry.

The fox kit jumped from the cart, climbed Palo's leg and darted into his shirt. "Palo," I said. "Uncover Fly's head, so that boy over there can see him."

Palo pulled the little fox forward till his head stuck out, and rubbed behind his ears. From where I sat, the kit's throaty, guttural voice sounded like the purring of a cat. Palo turned toward the boy and pulled Fly farther out of his sleeve.

The boy came over to get a better look, and I watched him walk, limping. It looked like a deformity. "Want to show me that foot?" I asked, pulled him onto my knee, and helped him remove the soft leather boot. If the boy were deformed, he would need help finding a trade. Perhaps Avi and Ton could help, but how would I get him back to them?

No. Not deformed, only a nasty infection. "Palo, get my medicines from the cart and bring some more water, will you?" I washed the boy's foot with my laundry liquid and saw that he had stepped on something sharp, making a small, deep hole in his heel. The heel had swelled to the point of bursting. I set him on the log, propped his foot on an upturned bucket, and drew out my surgeon's knife.

Brows drawn into wrinkles, the boy tensed and closed his eyes, not moving, never once grunting nor whimpering as I opened the wound, probed and drained it. When he opened his eyes and looked, he relaxed. I drenched it with strong wine, sprinkled it with green copper dust, wrapped a bandage around it and helped him put his shoe back on.

"I could have done that," he said. "My father has a knife. He would let me use it."

"Didn't it hurt?" I asked. "Wouldn't you have been afraid to cut yourself?"

He shrugged. "It hurt before you cut it. It doesn't hurt now. Felt good when you let the white stuff out. I don't have any money to pay you, but I have this." He showed me a pretty pebble, and, catching a gleam of pale green, I held it up to the light. I saw nothing unusual, spat on it, rubbed it on my shirt and held it up again. By all the gods, this looked like an emerald.

"Oh no, fellow, I can't take your rock. You keep it. You owe me nothing."

"No," he said. "You made my foot quit hurting. I want you to take it." He shrugged. "There's lots of them, just lying on the ground over there, see?" He pointed toward two carts set away from the others, and grabbing my hand, pulled me in their direction. He grunted, wincing with pain and falling to his knee, not so brave now. I lifted him and carried him toward the carts.

"Have you been named?" I asked.

"My father calls me Kev," he said. "There he is over there. His name is Devi."

A man, half sitting, half leaning on a high stool beside a cart and donkey, spooned warm tallow into lamps, and a woman waited for her lamps to be filled. "He had an accident and had to have one of his legs cut off," said Kev. "The healer said if he'd seen it earlier he could have saved the leg. Then when my foot got sore I thought I would have to cut it off." He grinned. "But you fixed it."

The boy had thought I meant to cut off his leg, yet he had held still, not a sound.

He wanted down. I set him on his feet near the carts, and he dropped to his hands and knees, looking for pebbles around the cart that had fallen as the peddler filled sacks and took coin or barter. Grinning, he held up a white one to show me, and stuffed it into his underarm pouch.

One of the carts had large jars filled with rough, uncut stones, each jar holding a different color rock. I bought a bag full of mixed stones and moved to the next cart. This peddler also sold stones, but these had been collected in woven grass sacks, sides of the fabric pressed down for display.

Many had been cut and polished. Stunned, I gazed at what must have been several rich men's fortunes in precious stones, just lying open to view in a humble peddler's cart. I bought a large bag full, one that took two hands to lift, knowing that they would sell to the first jeweler I saw, and paid with gold stamped in Athens.

I added the bags to my merchandise in the cart and again sat on the log beside Spitter. The boy had come back with me grinning, still limping, but walking carefully on his toes. "See? I told you." I agreed, and made a place for him between Palo and me.

"Where have you been?" he asked. "Do you travel all the time? What do you do? Are you a peddler? How do you know about fixing sore feet?"

When he hushed, I answered the last question first. "My grandmother was a physician. She taught me how to fix feet, and I am also a peddler. It's a good way to see the world and meet people like you. Sell merchandise and fix feet. Yes, that's what I do."

"I want to be a physician when I grow up," he said. "Where can I learn how to do that?"

"Go to a healer," I said. "Ask. If they like you they'll teach you how to do it. Is there an herb doctor around here?"

"Yes," he said. "There she is, by the spring, drawing water. And there's one of the ladies who gathers herbs and roots for her."

"Where?"

"Over there."

An older lady, swathed from head to foot in fabrics dyed with earth colors—rose, yellow, and brown—sat talking to a man I could not identify, for people hid him from my view. The woman poked him on the arm, joshing, laughing. The crowd, gathered to hear him speak, parted and I saw that it was the old man who had stopped us from traveling farther north, sending us home. Ton had called him Kirri. Here? In

this lost village? Intrigued, I stopped fanning.
"You see? You see the old man?" asked Palo.
"I see. He made it here before us."
Palo stood, craned his head this way and that trying to get a better view. Finally he stood on the log so he could see over the people's heads.
I handed him my cup. "Why don't you take him a cup of water?" I said. "Talking is thirsty business."
Palo hurried toward the group.
In all the times we had seen the old man, never had we spoken, and Palo's curiosity had been burning him alive. He nudged between the people to get near Kirri, gave him the cup of water, and found a seat on the ground, as near him as possible. The circle closed in again, and I could no longer see either Palo or the old man.
"Do you know him?" I asked Kev.
"That's Kirri," he said. "He guards the sacred sites."
"Ah. You mean like the wells and the weeping tree?"
"You know about the sacred grove? The tree that looks like many but is just one?"
"I've been there," I said. "But I never spoke to Kirri . Does he come here often?"
"No. I've only seen him once before. Today is special. Someone is coming through from the north, the one who wears the bracelet. Kirri is escorting him through the lands of the willows..." He glanced down at my wrist. "You are wearing a bracelet." He paused, suddenly understanding, and said, "Are you him? Are you the special visitor?"
I had traveled across the great alpine mountains with this bracelet given to me as a gift for Olympias, the elfin girl who had captured their hearts by my story. In the village of the People of the Trees, the carpenter had told stories about her, and he had blessed the bracelet, endowing it with strange qualities.
"Ah-hmm," I cleared my throat. "Yes, this is probably the bracelet you heard about."
"Really?" He jumped up and hop-ran-hopped to the huddled group. "There's the man!" He yelled, pointing back at me. "The man with the bracelet for the princess Olympias. See! I talked to him. He made my foot well. It feels just fine now. He is a wizard."
Before I knew what had happened, people gathered around me, all talking at once, all wanting to see the bracelet. I heard murmurs of "...blessed by the Tree..." and "...spoke to the king..." and "...advisor to

Olympias..." and "...great physician..."

"My foot doesn't hurt now. Not much, anyhow. He didn't cut off my leg." He burrowed through the people now surrounding me as though my proud owner.

Then the group hushed, and a woman joined them. The woman drawing water from the spring. Hardly past puberty, lips and cheeks as pink and sweet looking as cherries, and a waistline I could have grasped between two hands, she said, "One at a time, my friends. We will bless the bracelet."

So they lined up behind her, each coming forward, kneeling to kiss the bracelet, taking a deep breath of air, breathing on it and murmuring a few words, none of which I could hear, nor certainly remember. Embarrassed, I tried to take the bracelet off to pass it around, but the healer stopped me.

"Allow our people to show their love," she said. "Their blessings are as much for you as for the bracelet." So I just sat there, holding up my arm till each had passed.

The old man was not among them and when I looked around, I could see him nowhere.

Food had been prepared for a feast and I was pulled into the crowd and near the tables. Groups of people sang, played music and danced. Palo joined in the songs of the wood folk as though born to them. Lonely, haunting melodies, they were, like echoes of the Weeping Tree. Longing for something, somewhere, just out of reach.

The village healer came to sit beside me to eat and I told her about Kev. "He wants to be a healer," I said. "Can you teach him?"

"The kind of healing I do can't be taught," she smiled. "It was a gift from my grandfather, passed on at his death, but I also studied with a man in the north and west, across the Rhine. Rober, of Galli. I'll tell him about Kev. I've been watching the boy, wondering where his talents would direct him. I'm glad he wants to be a healer. It'll help his family, too. They don't have much money."

We stayed the night, but slept little, for the people kept me talking about home and Athens until nearly dawn. Before the sun broke free of the trees, that time before the birds awaken, when even the river runs quiet, we prepared to leave. We awoke to piles of gifts, brought to us by the villagers. Palo and I packed boxes and jars and sacks onto the cart so high it threatened to tip, and we started out.

The Danube flowed, not wide, here, but strong. Rushing waters carved deep chasms into the earth, sometimes low, but higher in any of the bends. A suspension bridge, too narrow for our donkey and cart, crossed it. A ramp dug from rock banks down to the river, provided access for loading and unloading wagons and carts, and a rectangular ferry boat with slightly rounded bottom, waited on a landing, a gated end hinged and laid to the ground to provide a ramp for boarding.

Large enough for perhaps fifteen people, Spitter and our cart filled most of the space, but a man and woman found places near the leading side to watch the crossing. The woman seemed ill, covered from head to toe in clothing, even in this warm weather. She sat on a keg as soon as she boarded. The man, older but more able, stood beside her, blocking her from my view.

A rope spanned the river and, on the side facing the current, the rope threaded through iron rings set along the rim of the sides. Palo, Fly swinging in the pouch of his sleeve, hitched Spitter's halter to the side of the boat and stood watching the water, hoping to see fish, and the man with the woman tossed bread crumbs up for wheeling, diving seabirds.

One of the two ferrymen tugged on the rope, and we began the crossing.

"For gods' sake, Munk, give me a hand here!" yelled the first, who seemed by a few years the younger.

"Oh, too much for you farm boy?" laughed the other. "Used to having oxen do the hard work for you, that's all." But, grinning, he stood and grasped the rope just behind Munk and tugged on the line.

"I can pull it just fine," said Munk, "as good as you. It's just that I use my left hand and you use your right."

"Nonsense. What does it matter which hand I prefer? I still have to use both hands. It's the same thing."

"How would you know it's the same? I always pull it on the way back; you sit down."

"Well, you act like you want to do the pulling, so I just let you."

Munk sighed, exasperated. "Artur, you're pulling the boat coming back this time. Just wait till you see how different it is."

Artur laughed again, but took his place beside the rope and, wind whipping blond curls across his face, bulging arm and leg muscles matted with blond hair, pulled. The ferry picked up speed.

I paid Artur and Munk, laying a coin in each hand, noting as I did that Artur held out his right hand, Munk, his left. Both put their coins in pouches, Munk's hanging from the left side, Artur's from his right. I don't think either of them noticed the difference.

I remembered Olympias talking about Phaistos, the horned priest of Kreté. "He used both his hands equally." I rubbed my two hands together. No one else knew, but I used both equally, too. Did that make me a demon?

Our return journey through the mountains proved uneventful. One evening, near the fire of a band of wool sellers, we camped on a rolling green pastureland at the top of the world. Shepherds and their flocks surrounded us. Many fires sent ropy tendrils of smoke into the quiet heavens. All sat gazing at a golden mountain to the north east. The colors shimmered and shifted, pale gray to pale yellow, then golden red, finally softening to the pale violet shadows of starry, moonlit night. Stark and treeless, it alone seemed real, all else consigned to fantasy.

I wrapped myself in my blanket and lay watching it, at peace with the mountains, with my fellow spirits in human form, and the four-footed creatures of all the earth, who for the length of the changing of the colors, seemed frozen in their usual pathways. I dozed off to sleep to the sound of Palo's whittling as he carved a new whistle from the stem of an elderberry bush. The next day, Palo sent shrieks of sound across valleys, and we paused to hear returning echoes. If Fly had heard them, surely he would have returned.

2

Our trail down the south side of the mountains overlooked a vast lake, shining white in morning light. We began the descent with Palo looking backward most of the way, searching for the fox.

I had seen the wandering looks Fly had thrown at various wooded copses along the way, knowing he would be leaving us sooner or later, but I had put it out of mind. I enjoyed the flash of orange as he erupted from the brush to leap into the cart to bury his catch, and then come to ask to be lifted and carried or to burrow into the cart to nap.

"He may show up at the boat, Palo. If he doesn't, we'll have to leave him here, you know." Personally, if he didn't show, I couldn't blame the fox. I hated the thought of boarding a boat, too, though the woolen merchants we had met along the trail assured me it would be a pleasant ride.

Palo ducked his head, concurring, though he continued to scan the countryside as we followed the trail downward, on a slope that grew ever more easy to walk.

The laughter and hustle and bustle at the boat landing helped me dismiss lingering thought of the willows people and their dark magic. Finally able to rationalize our account, I believed myself to have been charmed, drawn into their superstitious fantasies. The great divide of the mountains now placed them forever beyond a wall, leaving me free, once again to pursue my own interests far away from their murmurings and songs.

The visions beneath the Weeping Tree had been drug induced, its resin putting to sleep my more-responsible nature. I touched the soil of the little tree growing happily in its jar, and considered a place to plant it, a reminder of the foolishness of man. I thought of the perfect place in Ana's garden. Ana would love it. Not beside a warm pool of water as Miangl, the watcher of the tree had directed, but it would have to do.

The round, blue eyes of the child, Veil, of the People of the Trees, haunted me. In the dreams she said were dreamed by her doll, Te, she had seen my grandmother. How could she know of Yiayia, if she hadn't seen her? Chiding myself for my simplicity, I drew a great breath and expelled it. Why didn't that bring relief?

෴෴෴

The lake lay open to the sky, awaking to the shattering rays of first morning sun. Many boats, already far from shores on either side of the lake, winked in shining color. Others, small fishing boats clustering around the dock, bumping, dipping and swaying, awaited their master's release to take flight.

Palo and I squinted, glorying in the warmth, reluctant to wear hats. I sighed, breathed deeply. Morning scents.

A ship's mate tried to loop a lead rope around Spitter's neck. She pulled back. I waved him off. Palo and I walked up the ramp onto the boat, and Spitter followed.

I loosed her from her cart, and she stepped forward to the prow. "We'll have to secure her against the waves," he said. "It gets pretty choppy mid way. He went aft and brought ropes and a blanket. Then, as Palo held her harness and talked to her, the mate ran the ropes through rings set in the side of the boat, knotted each with one corner of the blanket, spread the blanket beneath Spitter's belly, then did the same with the ends on the other side, pulling them snug against her. She seemed to like it, relaxing first one foot then the other and allowing the blanket to support her weight.

"Haw-e-e," she called, meaning, I think, "Let's get moving." Only then did I release her harness.

The captain, a swarthy man in his mid-thirties, I guessed, directed the activity, gesturing with his right hand to have them move boxes and cages of birds so we could board. With his left hand, he held a cloth against his jaw. It smelled of mint. Later, when I sat beside him near enough to smell his breath, I understood.

Several people milled around, distressing both the captain and the sailors, and an older couple, a man and a woman, found seats on boards. A younger man, dressed in a flowing, hunter-green cloak and boots laced high around the calves of his legs, stood near his trunk, rounded and inscribed on the top. One of the boys sat on the trunk, hoping to go unnoticed and get a ride, payment for his work in moving boxes, but the young man told him not to sit there. The boy got up, and the captain, gesturing one-handed, shooed him off the boat.

Sailors lengthened or shortened the lines to the mainsail, bringing the boat about and into the wind. Oarsmen, two on either side of the boat, dragged their paddles in the water to slow the turn, or, on the opposite side, to pull to increase it.

A banner, a gold figure on a blue sea, fitted above the mainsail. It lifted, caught the wind and stretched out before us.

Where was Palo during all this fuss? Resting his chin on his arm laid across the rail at the stern, looking back at the mountain. He must have been tired. He had not slept when we camped on the great plain atop the mountain. All night he had worked, whittling and carving his new whistle.

I picked up my medicine bag from the cart and moved to sit beside the Captain amidships. He propped his chin, and rubbed absently on his jaw. "Would you like me to look at your tooth?" I asked. "I have something to ease the pain."

He nodded, opened his mouth, groaned with the pain caused by the cooler air, and pointed to the tooth.

"It has to come out," I said. "Would you like me to pull it?"

"Either that or just kill me," he grunted.

I gave him a tiny crystal of opium poppy resin, waited a few minutes while he chewed. The strained look went off his face. "Open up," I said, and clamped the shell of decayed molar with my pliers. Standing in front of him, I pulled. The tooth popped out and went flying across the deck.

I gave him wine to rinse his mouth, the vile kind I carry for cleansing wounds. Experience had taught me that good wine would be swallowed. Opium mixed with wine, would have put him to sleep, and I wanted to make certain our captain stayed awake to sail the ship. Then I gave him a small tear of Myrrh. "Chew it," I said. "It'll ward against the sickness." And sweeten your breath, I thought, but didn't say.

"Are you all right now?" I asked.

He explored the hole with his tongue and grinned. "S'fine now," he said. "How muth?"

"Oh, nothing. Nothing at all," I said, "except maybe you can tell me something about the country."

"Mostly swamp," he said, "especially south and east of here, though there are villages built on poles down near the sea. You know the Adriatic?"

"Born there," I said, "Epirus."

"Ah, from the east. Well, you should be all right going that way, but I wouldn't advise you to head south and west. Ulvoin country."

"Why not the Ulvoins?"

"They'll rob you blind. That's how they live. Every traveler who goes that way comes out poor."

"We plan to head east anyway. Back to Athens. You know Attica?"

"Same as Athenai? Yes, been there a few times. Son goes to school there. I think that's where that young man with the big trunk is headed. To study at one of the temples."

I looked where the Captain nodded. The young man stood beside his trunk, holding the rail, riding the swells and staring upward at the mountains.

"How's the pain. Need more medicine?"

"Sounds good," he said, and held out a hand so callused from handling raw hempen line that I wondered he could feel anything at all.

"Just chew it. Don't drink any wine with it. Water maybe, if you have some clean enough. If not, I have plenty."

He nodded. "Never drink wine anyway, mead's my drink."

"Keltoi?" I asked.

"My mother."

"But your father, Latium?"

"Yes, how'd you know?"

Laman's black eyes squinted against the sun, teeth white against leathery sunburned skin.

"Just a guess. I've been in Keltoi country for the last four months. Learned to like their fermented honey drink. But I'm glad to be going home. And by the way," I added, just to make certain, for I wanted to get across this lake without mishap, "Don't drink any mead either. Just water."

"Mate!" The captain called, "Let's roll the mainsail. That wind will break our pole." He rose to untie a line and pull it taut, and I walked toward the stern, where the young man with the trunk still stood by the rail.

"The captain tells me you're headed for Athens," I said. "That's where I'm from."

He took his eyes from the mountains long enough to size me up. Apparently he wasn't impressed, and looked away again. "My mother's idea," he said. "She wants me to study with the masters."

"You aren't interested?"

"I didn't want to leave a girl. We should have married; I should have brought her with me. I care nothing for learning what stodgy priests can teach me. I've already read everything in my father's library. I can teach myself if I need it."

His profile, sharp, high nose and chiseled forehead and jaw suggested haughty birth. I waited, saying nothing, expecting nothing more.

"I'd rather study with Plato. He's a philosopher, has a school in Athens."

"Hmm. Yes. I've heard of him," I said. "Socrates, his teacher, was a friend of my grandmother's."

"Do you know Plato?"

"I've heard him speak."

"What did he talk about?"

"Nothing, mostly. Just asked questions. The students did most of the talking."

"I've heard that he is very wise."

I shrugged. "Probably is. Most learned men keep their mouths shut most of the time. At any rate, when he speaks, he speaks very softly. It's a trick of his, making people quieten and come nearer, to hear."

"Know anything about the temple in Athenai?"

"I know a priest there. Family where I live. Ana and Dimitri, son of Thiusi, live there. They call the priest Vitos. If you see him before I do, tell him Daneion sent you. That is back in Athené's country."

"You believe in Athena?"

"In Athens it's smart to believe in Athena."

"I see," he said, warming. "I am Willem, son of Roget. My father is a merchant of wines." Willem laughed. "In fact, my father is a merchant of anything that pays well. He owns a tavern in the *ossida*, beside the lake. You can see the roof tops from here. Ours is that one." He pointed toward houses clustered on the side of the mountain. "It's the largest, the one near the water. The white building with a red-tiled roof." In the water, the building's white reflection dominated the jumbled effects of the others.

"You aren't interested in following your father's trade?"

"Selling wine is all right; I worked in my father's tavern for a few years..." He looked away toward the mountains again. "My father has never been away from the *ossida*, but I saw the people who passed through our tavern, and heard their stories. Mother had some grand idea that I should become a priest. I want to travel the world. Learn about the people across the Adriatic, the Aegean. I want to see where the spices, the silks come from."

"Babylon, Persis, India," I said.

"Yes. Have you visited them?"

"Not all," I said. "My family moved to Lesvos, an island across the Aegean, when I was a lad. I grew up there. My heart brought me back to the land of Hellene."

Willem and I talked until dusk, he telling me of the influx of Keltoi into his *ossida*. He didn't like Keltoi. I didn't mention the origin of the mother of our captain.

Palo squatted near the two cages of pigeons, and poked oats through the bars for them to eat from his hands. The old man and woman gave them fresh water and smiled at Palo, but neither were much for talking. Mostly they just looked and listened.

We sailed until dusk, arriving at the docks and tying up in the midst of fishing boats being unloaded onto carts, children on the docks being called in for the evening meal, smoke streaming from chimneys, and songs erupting from a nearby tavern.

The mate untied the ropes of the blanket supporting Spitter, and Spitter sat down on the deck. Palo and I pulled and I whistled, all to no avail. The boat emptied, and I shouted at Willem before he faded into the crowd. "Look for Dimitri and Ana in Athens, they'll help you." The old man and woman with the pigeons disembarked. Anchor dropped, sails furled and neat, dusk overtook us. Still Spitter sat.

"Are you Daneion?" asked a young man emerging from a jumble of people on the docks. "I am Tomaso."

Spitter looked up at him, heaved to her feet, and proceeded down the ramp, then backed into the shafts of her cart as though we had been the ones delaying matters.

"Well would you look at that," said Palo, then looked at the young man. "Did you do something to make her get up?"

"Oh, no," he said. "I was just coming to talk. They told me to watch for you. They said the man I was to meet knew about medicine."

"Who told you to watch for us?" I asked.

"Raben. Fedei told him you would come help my brother. Raben gave me this." Tomaso handed me a letter, written on vellum with vegetable dye. I recognized Fedei's writing. It was the same as the names of the herbs on Avi's herb boxes.

"Raben?" I said, unrolling the vellum. "The only Raben I've heard of is a peddler across the Danube."

"Yes, that's him," the boy said. "It's for my brother, Dah'n. He's sick."

"How did you know me, Tomaso?"

"Raben said Fedei told him your donkey would sit down on the boat and wouldn't get up. I just watched for a boat with a donkey, and then watched to see if it was sitting down."

"Tomaso, I never saw the peddler named Raben, and how could Fedei know Spitter would sit down on the boat and not get up?"

Tomaso shrugged. "That's just Fedei. He knows things. See." The note was written to me. I read. "These are friends of ours. We would be grateful if you would see Dah'n, the son of Ozhio."

I felt a heavy weight descending across my shoulders, my back, the thighs of my legs. Suddenly it seemed a major task even to think of taking a step. I had left those people far behind. Hadn't I? Purely, simply, they had tricked me. Tricked. Probably the whole clan. By Fedei and Kirri, certainly, but also perhaps by Ton, by Avi, and by all those who had ever heard stories told about Olympias, about me.

I am not your agent, I wanted to scream. I am a free man! A herm at the lightening struck tree where we had stopped to give offering before we crossed the mountains on the return trip to ask for blessings on our journey had warned me, and justly. But its warning came too late. Someone should have placed it beside the door where I left Leon's tavern, all the way back in Athens. I had been captured as though a fleeting bird–captured by these people and made to obey their commands. Would I ever again be free? But a worrying thought came to me. Before the woods people, there was Yiayia. My grandmother. She had sent me to find the Wise Ones. Had I ever–ever in my whole life–been free? Yiayia? Yiayia had forced me onto this path? No. Not Yiayia. Still her words returned to me, replete with all the power her image commanded, that day when we confronted the weeping tree and I decided not to sit there.

"You too, must sit beneath the tree. This is why you have come."

Caring nothing for the sights, the sound, the smells, I followed the others, too dazed to find my own way. Finally, forcing past my anger, I found voice.

"What's wrong with your brother?"

"He has seizures," he said.

"I have no cure for seizures. You must see other doctors."

"We did, but they don't help. Fedei sent you. He wouldn't send anyone unless he knew they would help."

"He didn't send..." I hushed. Tomaso would believe what Tomaso wanted to believe.

Tomaso led us toward a wagon. The driver waited, holding the reins in his hands. Another man on a black horse fought to control his mount. "Where do you live, Tomaso? Is it east? Perhaps I can see your brother on my way home."

"West," he said, "About a day and a half trip."

I stopped in the middle of the street. "West. Sorry. I'm headed east."

"But Fedei said you'd help, and we've been here waiting for you for two days."

"Fedei shouldn't have promised..." I began, but Tomaso's forehead began to wrinkle and his eyes glistened with a fervor I could only associate with certain religions.

"You were sent by the Gods." Tomaso grasped my wrist, gently but insistently. "You must come."

The gods. Always the gods. I sighed, weary of wide-eyed primitives. I longed for the cynics of the streets of Athens. It seemed these holy people of the north were as power hungry as the priests in the rest of the world.

And what of Olympias? Hadn't the elusive old man in the long white beard indicated that I should hurry home? Wasn't Olympias in danger?

Not in danger. Now I understood. I had been tricked to see the boy, Dah'n. And I couldn't even help him. Seizures. The bane of my life. And mystics.

Tomaso climbed into the back of the wagon, leaving the seat beside the driver for me.

"Later," I said, standing my ground, feet firmly planted in the middle of the street. "I'm stopping here to rest, to eat. To sleep in a real bed. We'll talk tomorrow."

I started forward again toward the tavern, carefully placing my feet one ahead of the other, for the ground moved as though I were still on the water.

Tomaso laughed. "You wouldn't want those beds, Daneion. They're full of bugs."

Bugs. I hated bugs. I paused. Tomaso waited. "Then I'll walk," I said. "If I can get the road to be still."

3

Spitter would take no position but lead regardless of the majesty of the company. I knew that, Palo knew that, but the black horse, the pick of the Ozhio stables, did not know that.

Nose and tail high, impatient to be off, the black immediately pushed toward the front.

Palo looked at me and winked. As one, we stepped off the road, well clear of the donkey. Spitter passed the wagon and oxen, eased up behind the black, nipped him in the rear and hopped to the side. I hadn't known she could move so fast.

The black reared, came down hard, and kicked. At emptiness. The guard toppled from his seat. The horse ran, fleeing the flat countryside like a bushrabbit from a forest fire, heading for the faint gray line of mountains bordering the plains.

Serene, virtuous, Spitter moved ahead and continued at the steady, ground-covering pace she preferred.

"Wonder what got into that horse?" asked the man, picking himself up and brushing dirt off his face and out of his hair. "He never acted that way before."

"Maybe he saw a snake," the driver of the wagon said.

Shaking his head, the unseated rider climbed into the wagon. "Ozhio'll kill me if that horse doesn't come home."

"There is a god of justice," I mumbled. Whatever ill fortune any of them received, provided just payment for troubling me, lengthening my miles from home. 'From home.' My mind supplied the words, but my longing painted the image. It was not Athens I saw, but the face of a girl. A girl lost to me. I could not return to her, regardless of my weariness from the journey.

Fedei had no right to make promises for me, promises I might not keep. I should have said no.

But I couldn't have said no to Tomas, not while looking into the blazing light of faith in his eyes. "I can't help your brother, Tomas," I said. "My family has fought the shaking sickness for as long as any of us remembers, without a cure."

"Do you have the shaking sickness?" he asked, startled eyes searching my face.

"No, not I, but I dare not have children. Sometimes the curse skips a generation."

"The local doctors say that, too, but Fedei said…"

"Fedei." The man had taken charge of my life as certainly as a warring conqueror. "How do you know Fedei?"

"He and Avi visit Dah'n whenever they can. And when Raben brings crafts to sell from the People of the Trees, he comes by our house."

"They come here often, then."

"Well, not too often, maybe once a year. They came by on their way home two months ago. They visit the Keltoi village in Bononia, farther south. Father wanted them to take Dah'n home with them to see if they could heal him. They said they had no cure, but they would send someone, another physician, to look at him."

"And that would be me." Two months ago, neither Fedei nor Avi knew me. How could they know I—or anyone matching their needs—would come this way?

"Yes." he grinned. "And you came."

"Humph."

Fields of grain to my left swept across the rolling green distance and olive groves spilled from foothills into valleys beneath peaks of snow-capped mountains on my right, Overwhelmed in noble grandeur, feeling my fury slipping, I braced my will, clung to my anger, and sucked from the remains every possible perverse joy.

"We'll stop at the doma just ahead." Tomaso pointed toward a white-plastered house beside the road. "That's where my cousin, Davidé and his family live. There is a hot spring nearby." He made a curvy gesture with his hand. "And Davidé has a pretty maid who gives good foot massages."

Tomaso shouldn't have said that. This, the final provocateur undid me. My anger slipped away like mist in the sunshine. I could almost feel the steam rising, drawing the sweat from my body and the strain from my muscles. Perhaps the curvy maid would massage my callused feet. I could not dislike this young man who had climbed down from his place in the wagon and now walked beside me with such springy steps, swinging a stick, slapping the air and missing a passing grasshopper. I sighed, surrendering. Might as well accept it. Life would be handed me, a day at the time.

We dipped lamb stew from a pot hanging over a fire that night, spread olive oil on hot bread, and sat with Davidé and his family on benches beneath the trees to eat. None of us wore coats. Palo had removed his pants and boots. Later, after a bath in the spring, the maid, Alinna, did indeed massage my tired feet. Then I slept in a real bed, in a real house, on a goose-down mattress large enough for both Alinna and me.

꒰꒰꒰

"That used to be marsh," said Tomas. Threading through rocky outcrops at the edge of the mountains, the road beyond Davidé's house overlooked a vast delta to the south. "Father said when he was a boy, this road flooded in the spring. Anyone who lived in the foothills of the mountains had to travel by boat if they wanted to get out. My grampa built his house on stilts. No one wanted to live out here, then. Rocky mountains on one side, covered with ice most of the year, and marsh lands on the other. Grampa and his people dug ditches across the valley to drain it, and the land filled in with dirt from the mountains. The ditches became rivers draining into the great River Po. Now the land is so rich everyone wants to own it. People come from across the mountains on both the north and the south. My grandfather told settlers that if they'd help him with roads, they could have the land. But too many came. Now they steal our sheep and our goats. We have to keep the horses in fences to keep them from wandering away where they'll be stolen."

The black horse had come into the barn at Davidé's during the night. The guard repeatedly nudged him with a heel in his belly, but he refused to take the lead, stepping to the side, or well behind Spitter.

Warm air chilled as cool winds descended the mountain slopes.

Palo walked by my side, watching the sky.

"Weather." I said. A cylindrical cloud rolled in a horizontal line across the sky, thick, dark. The air chilled, and the earth vibrated with nearing claps of thunder. I whistled for Spitter to hurry. Again. A third time. I moved up to her head. Looked her in the eye. "Don't you see that cloud forming? Rain is coming. You hate the rain. We'll get soaked. Our only hope of shelter is that grove of trees ahead. Hurry." She looked at me, raised her head, surveyed the sky, and continued her pace.

From out of nowhere came a blizzard of balled white ice, pelting our heads, our shoulders and arms with stinging fury. The driver of the wagon laid the whip on his mule, and as with one mind, we all ran for the copse of trees.

Everyone but Spitter. "Ha-onh. Ahonh ahonh ahonh," she screamed, surely heard back at Davidé's house.

Safe beneath the dense thicket of trees, I looked back to see her. Through the white, ice-filled air, spread-legged she stood, anchored to the spot, desolate, alone, backed up as closely as she could to the cart, head tucked between her legs.

As suddenly as it had started, the hail stopped. We looked out onto a glittering, white prairie. Nowhere across the clear and sunny sky, was there a sign of the black cloud.

Crunching ice pellets beneath our feet, we descended the slight hill toward the road. When we reached the cart, Palo dug out his boots, pulled them on and wrapped the leather strings around the calves of his legs.

"Ha-onh," bellowed the aggrieved donkey once more, shook her head till her harness rattled, and again took the lead, head drooping.

She looked sideways at me, accusing. "I didn't cause the hail storm," I said, "Don't blame me. Maybe this is payment for biting the horse. But he sure jumped, didn't he? Whoo-ee."

She glared. "Oh, I know you're embarrassed. But if you had run with the rest of us, you'd have missed most of the hail."

She bared her teeth. Glared. Looked away.

"You've been through worse than that. Remember? In the mountains when you kept me from falling into the ice?" Still no forgiveness, she did whuff, to clear her throat.

I felt Tomaso staring, watching first me, then Spitter.

"Ahem," I looked toward the mountains. "Does that snow ever melt?" Tomaso didn't answer. The look in his eyes made me nervous. It was not one of doubt, but of awe. I switched the brush along the trail with my staff and stopped to trim a branch, smelled it tasted it. Agh. Now the boy would believe I ate bushes. This one looked and tasted like what Yiayia had used for blood in the issue. I cut more.

📿📿📿

Sheer-sided, ice-crowned peaks closed us in. Spilling through the mouth of the valley, four houses and outbuildings climbed the south side of a rounded knoll. The Ozhio home, welcoming us in sunlit warmth, overlooked trees and vines heavy with unripe fruit. Gardens crowded every open space, and grapevines climbed the sides of houses and shaded pavilions.

We followed the road upward, winding through fieldworker's cottages. People waved and shouted, happy to see Tomaso home. Each in turn examined me, and bobbed a head in respect. Three boys stopped their play, came running and climbed onto the wagon. The oldest took the reins and drove the rest of the way uphill.

I walked behind Palo and Tomaso, as Tomaso told us of the garden terraces on either side of the valley. He pointed to a waterfall hardly visible in the distant shadows between the cliffs, and motioned to show that its waters had been channeled toward the gardens by ditches reinforced with walls of rock. No raw earth. Old construction.

Someone in the house screamed. "Dah'n." Tomaso started running.

Palo laid a hand on Spitter's neck to stay her, and I hurried after Tomas, past a fountain in the center of a black-tiled plaza. We ducked into an alleyway between stone-walled houses, climbed a stairway, and burst through a doorway opening from a stoop above. I trailed him through a maze of dark hallways and rooms, and through aisles lined with musty-smelling, heavy wooden chests to emerge into a large room almost dark with heavily-draped windows.

A boy with fishy white skin thrashed about on a small, high bed. His jerking shook the floor beneath us. A man, short and heavy, black hair balding on top, round face drawn in worry, held one of the boy's arms against the mattress, while a woman across the bed held the other. The boy shoved his hips high in the air, dropped, again, again. His tongue protruded, blood streamed across his cheeks, chin, and neck, soaking his pillow.

"Don't hold him," I said. "You could bruise him. Just stand beside him to make sure he doesn't fall off the bed. Stuff his mouth, Tomaso; he's chewing his tongue. Watch him. If he vomits he could choke. We'll have to turn his head." Tomaso grabbed the sheet and poked it around the boy's tongue. Vomit surged forth into Tomaso's fingers. He grasped D'ahn's head to turn it to the side.

"He isn't breathing, Tomas, loosen the sheet. See how gray his face looks? Like ashes. Raise his shoulders a little so his head falls back."

Immediately D'ahn drew a great, hoarse and wracking breath. The woman who had stood beside the bed handed Tomaso a stick, raw with tooth marks. I nodded, and when Dah'n opened his spasm-hardened jaw, I stuck it between his teeth.

I could give nothing by mouth during the seizure, but Yiayia had found with Uncle Davos that smoke from the burning of certain herbs made the shaking less severe. "Watch the stick, would you please?" I said to the woman. "I have something in my bags that may help." Luckily I had brought leaves of dried hemp from Thraké. It came in handy for calming, and sometimes when bargaining grew tense.

Palo had dumped new-cut barley hay for Spitter and the mule. Spitter looked up at me as I approached, then nosed into the hay. She had forgiven me. Some things work out right.

I grabbed a bag of leaves and ran up the stairs, through the outer door, down the halls of dark and antiquated clutter, and emerged again into Dah'n's room. Still he jerked. Where did the strength come from? So frail, surely he was now burning away the last thread of life.

"A brazier, for the herb," I said, speaking quietly as Yiayia had done in emergencies. The greater the tension, the quieter became her voice. The woman handed me a pottery bowl brazier, used to break the chill on cold winter evenings. She brought a coal from the fire in the hearth and laid charcoal around it in the bowl. I tossed the leaves onto the winking charcoal and a spark of flame darkened the end of a stem. A tendril of smoke rose, and a cloying scent wafted through the mildewed room. The fire blazed. I spit on the flames, smothering them to a steady stream of smoke.

The thrashing slowed, but the eyes still rolled, showing only the whites. I held the brazier nearer Dah'n, careful to keep it outside the spastic jerking of his arms. Slowly the tension left his body. He collapsed. His breathing evened, he groaned and then drifted off into a shallow-breathed sleep.

Ozhio blubbered, reached for a towel to wipe his eyes, to blow his nose. Then he took D'ahn's hand, dropped to his knees beside the boy's bed and laid his head on the mattress. "Goddess of Healing, thank you for sending us this holy man."

The woman dipped a cloth in the water basin, squeezed it and patted the blood, the sputum and phlegm from the boy's face, then rinsed the cloth again and laid it across his brow.

"Never have I seen him recover so quickly," she said. "But he will be sore from his bruises. I am Myrna." She glanced at me. "I've been with the family since before the death of D'ahn's and Tomaso's mother."

"Thank you Myrna," I said, beginning to suffer the weakness that always invaded my senses after witnessing a seizure. I sank to the side of the bed. "I have comfrey for the bruises," I said. "I'll get it." I started to rise, dropped back. Determined not to show strain before these troubled people, I rose again, crossed to Ozhio's side of the bed, and put my hand on his shoulder. "He'll be all right, at least for a while, my friend. You must rest."

"I'll get his medicine," said the woman. "When he wakes I'll give it to him."

"What is the herb?" I asked.

"I don't know. The physician didn't say."

She took a small clay pot from a table beside the bed and handed it to me.

I opened the cork and smelled it. "Mugwort," I said, nodding. "Good. It will relax him and then stimulate him to eat."

"After the potion he will sleep," she said. "He won't wake to eat till late evening. He needs a lot of sleep, the physicians said. Then after he sleeps and eats I have to give him more."

Evening? Too long. "Halve the dosage," I said. "He must wake to eat, and exercise to gain strength." I stayed by Dah'n's side as Myrna prepared the potion.

"You can tell what the medicine is by smelling it?" asked Ozhio. "None of the other physicians can do that."

"I don't hear so well," I chuckled, "but my nose can smell a mouse in a hay barn." Ozhio attempted a smile. Failed. "He'll be all right, Ozhio," I comforted. "Now let's take a look at you."

"Oh, I'm fine, I'm fine," said the fat man, rising from his knees, gasping with effort. He heaved a great sigh when back on his feet, and laughed. "I am just too big."

He walked with me out to the cart and leaned against the side as I opened my medicine box, laid aside my surgical tools, and found my bag of dried comfrey root. "Never have I seen my son shake so before. I feared he would die. Yet he recovered faster this time than ever before." He waited for me to speak. I nodded, understanding, saying nothing. He continued. "You knew the shaking sickness? You have seen it before?"

"Many times. My uncle, Davos." I lifted the little pot with the plant I had dug beneath the great oak tree, carried it to the fountain and held it submerged up to the rim. Worry for Dah'n increased in me as I waited for the soil to moisten.

"You must plant this herb beneath an oak," I said, handing it to Ozhio. "When it grows, its family will spring up from roots that run beneath the surface of the ground. Pick it and dry the leaves. Then crush them and make Dah'n a tea. Give it to him daily. It may lessen future seizures. I found it in the lands of the Willows People beneath one of their sacred trees. They called it rumark."

I lifted a leaf with my finger. Paler, less firm and sturdy, it missed its home. But the berry, standing tall and proud remained, dry enough to pick. I will take the berry and plant it in the garden where I live with friends in Athens."

"You would give the plant to my son? Someone you have just met?"

I looked away, remembering, trying to remove from mind the many scenes of my uncle shaking, chewing his tongue, vomiting. I had intended the plant for Davos, but my uncle was old, the threads of his life coming to their ends.

"Dah'n is young. I know of no cure for the seizures, only something for relief. He has a lifetime of sorrow ahead of him. I must relieve that sorrow if I can."

That afternoon, a room full of well-wishers gathered around Dah'n's bed. Myrna propped him up, leaning against pillows. He asked for his clothes. "No, no, you must rest." said Ozhio. Myrna entered with a thick, rich stew of meat and broth and half a loaf of oiled bread. Dah'n turned away. Saliva drooled from the corners of his lips.

"Eat, grow strong," she said, but her voice betrayed her belief that her favorite would ever again be strong.

I cringed at the thought of the boy's tender digestion assaulted by this rich diet. "Perhaps a fruit would be easier for him to swallow," I said. "His tongue is swollen. Sore. Are your figs ripe yet?"

"Yes," said Tomas. "I saw a few on the trees only today."

He darted away to pick them, and I saw from a window that Palo followed.

"Give me my clothes," said Dah'n, voice slurred as he spoke around his swollen tongue.

"Give him his clothes, Myrna," said Ozhio. "He'll see he's too weak to get up."

"I can do it," he whined, as Myrna held his shirt ready to slip over his head. The poultices of comfrey Myrna had applied to his bruises had been removed. The blue marks had faded somewhat from his wrists and ankles where he had been held. They would be gone by the first light of day.

When he tried to stand, I held out my hand for support, smiling, encouraging. His legs collapsed. I caught him and started to put him back into bed. "No. I want to go outside."

"How long has it been since he was out?" I asked.

Ozhio shook his head. "I don't remember. Many months."

"Then outside we shall go. It's a beautiful, warm day. The sunlight and fresh air will do you good." As it will for the rest of us, I thought. Despite Ozhio's and Myrna's looks of concern, I lifted the boy. Easily, too easily, he came into my arms, fragile bones protruding from his flesh, flexing beneath my fingers. "Sunlight is what he needs now," I said, pushing past Myrna as she tried to help, and Ozhio, wringing his hands. Ozhio followed me through the dark rooms, a hand laid protectively on Dah'n's arm where it lay across my shoulder.

We found benches beneath a grape arbor beside the plaza, and I set him beside me. His head lolled onto my shoulder. I held my arm around him, and supported his head with my hand.

"Who are you?" he asked, struggling to force the words past his bitten, swollen tongue.

"My father named me Daneion," I said. "It means borrowed." I laid my chin against his forehead, to feel his heat. It felt cool, drained. "Sounds a little like your name, don't you think? Dah'n, Daneion?"

"No-o," he answered, trying to smile.

Tomaso brought sugary ripe figs for all of us. The first of the crop. I peeled one for Dah'n, and put it in his hand, hoping he would be strong enough to lift it to his mouth. The effort of dressing had left him totally drained of strength. His fingers clasped the fig, raised it to his lips and sucked. Before he could finish one, I had eaten three.

We stayed four days with Ozhio's family, and Dah'n grew stronger.

Tomaso helped him to their goat cart, and pulled blankets around his thin shoulders. They followed us as we walked the hills. Our procession gathered more people who saw us out, all come to congratulate Dah'n; each in turn looked at me thanking me with teary smiles.

"You remind me of my uncle," Ozhio said one day. "He was a peddler too. He traveled all across the country, and he adopted young orphans, just as Palo tells me you adopted him."

"Palo's growing up. Wants to be a farmer." I scratched my chin then dragged my fingers through my beard. "I move around a lot. Don't know what I'll do without him, but when we get home, he'll stay with our friends in Athens. They own a large farm."

Ozhio's gardens, especially those in the terraces, raged with health. "We ship our goods across the seas," he said, circling the land with a wave of his arm. "Our wagons travel throughout Galli and our ships as far away as Byzantium, beyond the Propontis. We also bring back silks and spices to sell to the people across the mountains.

I remembered the scent of spices in the village, Ulm. That must have been part of Ozhio's commerce. This then, should surely be a very rich man. Yet he and his family still lived simply in the humble house of his fathers, though the stilts had long been replaced with stone for storage rooms built below.

"I've never been outside this valley, Daneion. Why did you come north, from Athens?"

Running away, I thought. "Searching for family," I said, "hoping to find someone who knew something to cure the shaking disease. I want to help my uncle and his daughter. Dah'n is the first case I've seen."

"I have family in Bononia, just west of Ravenna," he said. "The story was that one of them, a distant cousin, suffered the seizures. Do you suppose you and I could be related? Our family came from Epirus, near the city-state of Neoptolemus. We are descendants of Molossis, son of Achilles."

It seemed the progeny of Achilles had peopled the earth. "Then you would be related to Olympias of Epirus, daughter of Neoptolemus. She is Olympias of Makedonia, now," I said. "She has married Philip II, son of Amyntas III and Eurydice."

"Ah. Then her road will not be an easy one. Philip marries often; he takes his women's dowries and their power. Then they seem to disappear from the face of the earth."

Ozhio spread maps across a table on the garden patio, maps drawn on precious vellum by his ancestor, the one who had done much to drain the swamps of the savanna surrounded by mountains and sea. "If the Ulvoins see you, they'll take that beautiful donkey for taxes," he said. "You'll have to swing wide to the South, travel through the heart of the grasslands, and into the swamps along the coast of the Adriatic."

He threw up an arm and hailed a man returning from the bath house and waste ditch. "I have people going to Ravenna with a shipment of goods to Athens. They'll go along with you. You'll be safe with them."

I tried to protest. I liked to travel alone.

"No, no. The drivers will enjoy your company." Ozhio would not be denied. "Fieros," he called. "This is Daneion. He will be traveling tomorrow, to the sea. Take good care of him."

Fieros, naked except for a cloth slung across his middle and twisted shut with a stick, came toward us, tall, muscular, chest, back and arms so choked with hair he truly needed no shirt. Shiny white teeth spread wide beneath a black mustache as he reached out to take my hand.

"No need to trouble yourself," I said.

"No trouble at all, at all. Some of us will stay with you as long as you need us. The road goes all the way through the grasslands to the sea." Voice booming, this man alone would crowd all outdoors. "A merchant ship is waiting for us. You can return to Athens with us."

"I have to pick up a friend in Tergesté. I'll head north after Bononia." Perhaps I said it a bit too sharply. Palo shrugged, muttered, "Boats. He hates boats." He turned his face away, but I saw his shoulders shake and knew he was laughing.

◩◩◩

The high road to the sea laid by Ozhio's ancestors to keep their cart wheels from miring in grassy swamp land, now served to guide our feet through a swirling sea of mist. A low-hanging sky, gnarled and dingy, drooped above our heads. Palo and I waded through layers of gray fog that muffled even the rattle and squeak of wheels and the sudden, erupting screech of birds disturbed from their nesting places. Camouflaged with dust, Spitter and her silvery-gray cart became specters born of fog.

Palo wore only string sandals and breechcloth, and I wore a ragged shirt and patched breeches, clothed as a vagrant beggar when traveling lest some highwayman become attracted. We walked, my fingers resting on the cart rail smoothed by many years of travel. The touch provided an intimacy with the road, telling me of every bump and incline, leaving my mind free to wander. In my right hand, my shepherd's crook measured the miles one jab at the time. I flipped the crook from right hand to left, and stripped a dried seed pod from a tall plant beside the road. I stopped, opened it, examined the silky white interior, and released the seeds, tracking the path of airy puffs as they merged with mythos.

    I flexed my shoulders, spread moist arms to the sky and bonded with this magic quietude, my only regret being that my early departure would have been noted, and that those who had proclaimed themselves my protectors would, by now, have loaded their wagons, hurrying to overtake us.

    We crossed a vaulted stone bridge high across the Padua River, stopped to see hazy outlines of a mud hut with smoke streaming from a fire in the yard and a woman and a boy pulling weeds from a garden strip along the river. Aboard a flat boat, a man and his family of three slipped below the bridge.

    "Birds," said Palo. "See. Beneath that blanket. One is pecking at the straw in the woman's mat."

    The woman from the boat looked back and saw us standing on the bridge. The man waved and grinned, fine white teeth parting between a heavy brush of brown mustache and beard. I waved back. Farmers. Taking their birds to market, maybe. Before they disappeared around the bend, a bird flew from the boat, circled, and disappeared into cloud.

    "One got away," said Palo. "Must have been the one I saw pecking the straw."

    No great loss, I thought, but heaviness in my chest kept me silent. Too much greasy food from Ozhio's tables, probably. We left the bridge, and I stripped a stem of mint leaves as I passed, thrust one into my mouth, and chewed. I needed to eat, but the only thing we had brought from Ozhio's in Mittland was more greasy meat and soft bread. I spit out the mint, dug oats from Spitter's bag, and lapped the hardened grains from my open palm.

    A day and a half of travel, Ozhio had said, before we reached Felsina. If we kept walking we could stay ahead of the merchant wagons, but the mists grew heavy, and my shoulders became soaked. We would have to stop, find shelter. The rains were coming. Who knew how high the river could rise?

    We left the lowlands and climbed a gentle grade toward deeper shades of greenish blue. It seemed we would soon be in the mountains, but the road continued, hugging the foothills on our right.

The sky lowered behind us. Black mist smeared the lines between sky and earth dragging vertical streaks of dark. Distant rumbling shattered the quiet, and the first, heavy drops of rain stung our heads and shoulders. Water beaded and rolled from Palo's sunburned, oiled back. A surge of wind tugged at my hat, and I anchored it with my hand. I had no whistle signals to hurry Spitter along. I whacked her across the rump with my staff, knowing it wouldn't work, and it didn't. She stopped. The squeaking of wheels and the plop plop of footsteps silenced. I raised my hand to strike again, determined to get her attention.

Voices. Immediately tense, I reprimanded myself for my negligence. An ambush? I turned my good ear toward the sound. Prepared to hurry on, I heard the squealing of children and the sudden laughter of a woman. Without further hesitation, Spitter pulled toward an outcropping of rock and continued on. Through a hole. Into a cave.

The cart jammed the opening.

"A donkey is coming in." shrieked a child. "And a cart. And some people."

"Push it back out," said the woman, "so they can come in."

"Ha-onh. Ahonh, ahonh, ahonh" screamed Spitter.

Then a man with gravelly voice said, "Here, little lady, you're blocking the door, let's back out, there, now. Back. No, you don't have room to turn around. Back."

But when Spitter moved she only adjusted her hind legs to brace against the man's weight.

I climbed over a wheel, pushed past her and plunged into darkness. "Sorry, folks," I said. "She won't move. You don't know stubborn till you've met my donkey."

"Look, Pa, it's a little man."

I knew I'd spend the next hours being called Little Man. I was wet, I was tired, my throat burned with last night's dinner, and now I had to share a cramped cave with strangers and this demented donkey.

"I'm called Daneion," I said.

Palo climbed over the wheel and pushed in beside me. "And this is Palo."

"It's dark in here," said Palo. Why don't they build a fire?"

"We tried," said the woman, but couldn't get one started."

"No dry kindling," added the man.

"I brought some," said Palo. He climbed back out over the wheel, rolled the canvas, dug out dry wood, tossed it into the cave, and then returned, bringing the tinder box.

Two men, a woman and two children waited inside. "I'm Meed'n, this is Venda," said the man. "We stopped when we saw the rain coming, but all the wood we found was wet."

Palo scratched a light from the tinder box and lit a splinter. Meed'n stood with bent back, head grazing the ceiling. Dark holes indicated further passages in the cave, and Palo led the way to find larger rooms in the back. He called, and, by Palo's meager light, the two children and a young man gathered the kindling and wood and carried it deeper into the cave.

"Hello. There inside the cave," came a call, the voice of one of the men traveling with the merchant wagons. "You in there, Daneion? Your cart is blocking the door."

I heard all kinds of struggles and curses as each in turn tried to pull the cart out of the door. Spitter dropped her head and braced herself harder.

"Hold on," I yelled above their racket. "Spitter hates the rain. I'll unhitch the cart so you can pull it back."

Loosed from her harness, Spitter snuffed, nudged my arm, and swung her neck from side to side looking around for her feed bucket. She was unhitched, right? So it was time to be fed and watered. It didn't matter how inconvenient it was for me. "Zeus" I grumbled. "How'd I ever get roped to you?"

"Ha-onh," she called, and Palo appeared from the back, bobbing his head beneath a low hanging ceiling. I left her to Palo. He grabbed her harness, pulled her through the opening and followed the others down a grade into the cave. "I see she has you trained," I said, calling back. "No need for me...." I slipped on wet rock, fell, and slid on my back along a rounded grade downward—as graceful as a leg of lamb. I picked myself up and walked toward a feebly glowing fire, embarrassed, but prepared to grin and laugh.

Venda poured water into a pot readying it for the fire, Meed'n spread blankets for us to sit on, and the children chased each other around the fire, giggling. A boy not much older than Palo unpacked bowls for supper. Palo and the merchants had been settling Spitter's cart outside the cave. No one had even seen me fall. I was wet, miserable. My stomach burned. Despite the crowd, the noise and activity, I was alone—unnoticed by anyone, living or dead. Suddenly I didn't want to be alone.

回回回

The cave opened out, both higher and broader. The floor, slick with moisture, slanted toward a hole tunneling through rock. I eased up to the hole from the side and tried to see into the darkness. I saw nothing, but heard an insistent plink, plink, plink of water falling somewhere far below. Remembering my fall on the slick floor, I eased back from the opening, willing my heart to slow its beat. Returning, I gave the hole a wide berth.

"Come, friend," said the man. "Get warm and share our food. We'll bless the goddess together."

Goddess? Not Gods? Despite my ill disposition, my curiosity quickened. "Are you from the north?"

"My wife, Venda, was born across the big mountains, among the trees. That's where I found her. Her family welcomed me, a stranger, and their priestess married us. The boy was born and then the girl, but as soon as they were old enough to travel we decided to come south, to live by the sea, where life would be easier. Here, have a bowl. Venda has made soup. Her family were farmers, but I've always been a fisherman."

I glanced at the young man, surely too old to be a son of this young couple. "That's my brother, Kosti," said Venda. He wanted to travel, to see the sea."

"Where do you come from, Daneion?" asked Kosti, and even in this dim light I recognized the glitter of intelligence in his nut-brown eyes. "Do you come from the place where there is no winter?"

I took the bowl from Venda. It smelled like weak bean water with a hint of goat meat. No greasy lamb stew for these people. Kosti broke a piece of hard bread and handed me half. "Palo will be hungry, too." These people had little to spare, but they offered what was, perhaps, the last of their food.

At that moment the noisy crowd of merchants filed through the narrow open space where I had slid down, and circled our fire. "Ah. Good, you have a nice fire going," said Fieros. "Look. We have brought food. Enough for us all." The wagon master's voice filled the cave, spilled into unknown places in the blackness, and echoed back to us in mind-rattling thunder. Who needed a storm? We had our very own. Right here.

"Soup?" asked Venda, handing Fieros a bowl.

The wagon master quieted, took the bowl, and bowed low above it, whether to scent its aroma, or to see what he was being served, I never knew, but he said, "Your kindness is gratefully appreciated, mistress. Like my own mother you are, to care so for strangers," then he dropped the bag he had been carrying, and a bounty of food these people had seldom witnessed, spilled onto the floor. The others quickly filled their bowls, but I, stomach praising Venda's weak soup, let it lie.

Three men gathered around the fire with us, Fieros the merchant and his two assistants, Giorgio and Tito. Damp wood sputtered and popped, and its dancing flames cast giant shadows against rounded walls. I doubt that anyone but I even noticed the shadows, so bent were the merchants on cramming food into their mouths and decrying their hardships, claiming Meed'n and his family's respectful attention.

Hardly the giant of which Tito's name implied—at least not yet, for he could still have grown the height of two of my hands—Tito was in love.

"We'll be married in two years," he said, tossing bread into his mouth and wiping greasy fingers on his leather boots. "Her father owns the copper mines of Populonia, and he'll get me on the Mining Directorate. Before this time two years hence you will all be coming to me for trading permission. But—" he said, swallowing, turning up his wine bowl and draining it—"I'll remember you. While all Tuscany awaits my sanction I'll set aside the shiploads of copper intended for my Greek friends. Mark my word."

Giorgio, the elder by at least four years, whooped and slapped his knee. "You think old Stefano will let you have his daughter? You're a plebe, Tito, and Finna is patrician. You'll be right here with us, trying to beg permission to trade just like us Hellenes."

"Careful, Tito," said Fieros. "The Praefecti of Rome have their eyes set on those mines. The Tuscans will be defending their property with every slave and pubescent farmer that they can conscript. Don't be a hero. Stay out of combat. The Romans will win."

Tito laughed, somewhat forced, I thought, and said, "Finna loves me. Old Stefano can deny her nothing. And don't put too much trust in the auspices of diviners. Those charlatans can read anything they want into the signs they say they find in the liver of a lamb."

"It doesn't take a telling to know the power of the Romans. While you and your people are farming and building roads they are busy organizing their armies."

"Don't put us Etruscans on the losing side yet. We're smarter than the Romans. All we have to do is send word and farmers will hammer their plow shares into hatchets and spears. We have been bred to strength, and our hearts are as brave as lions. The Romans don't dare try to confiscate our property."

"Our property?" scoffed Giorgio. "The last time I looked you were asking Fieros to lend you a shekel for a necklace for Finna. As I recall, he said he'd pay you when the ship docked in Athens." He grinned and tossed a bone to the back of the cave.

Tito leapt up, shoved Giorgio to the ground. In an instant they were rolling, rolling. Slipping. Sliding toward blackness.

I'll never know what moved me. I grabbed Tito's hair, and stopped his fall. Giorgio continued sliding, but caught Tito's ankle and hung, legs dangling in darkness, one hand, palm outspread, trying to grasp a rock floor made smooth by ancient, flowing waters. The fingers, digging at a shallow furrow, gave way even as I tried to edge Tito higher.

All three of us slid toward the hole.

"Agh." I gasped. Fieros and Meed'n both leapt to grab for Tito. Giorgio's hand on Tito's ankle slipped. He clutched a pant leg, and we heard a rip as fragile cloth gave way to Giorgio's weight. Palo snatched my crook from where I had laid it beside my place and handed it to me. I grabbed it with one hand, waving it, not knowing what to do with it, holding Tito's hair with the other, but bracing my leg against the opening to pull. Meed'n grabbed me under the arms to drag me back. Fieros snatched the stick from me and held it out to Giorgio. Giorgio grabbed the crook, releasing Tito's pant leg. Suddenly freed of Giorgio's weight, Tito, Meed'n and I fell backward, shoving Venda, who had been watching, screaming at full timbre, onto the pile of food. A jar of wine broke and sprayed across greasy lamb and hard-crust bread, splashing across the floor and dousing the hot coals.

We plunged into darkness.

I heard scrapes that told me the men had continued to drag Giorgio upward. Retching stink of vomit filled the cave.

Time and motion froze. The ringing in my ears, vibrating from the steady stream of screams from Venda, Kosti, and the children, filled the gap. Impressive. They had put the booming, echoing yells of Fieros and Meed'n to shame. The cave became as silent as a tomb. I sat shaking, hearing scraping noises. The faint light of a hot coal illuminated Palo's face as he blew the coal alive. Searching the rock floor with wide spread hands, he located scattered sticks of wood.

Fieros and his group hurried away as soon as the rain slowed, saying they needed to reach the sea before light to get a good start traveling, but I knew they needed to be gone, to escape their embarrassment. Palo lay on his mat beside his fire, exhausted, lidded eyes closing in sleep. In an air acrid with the smell of vomit, I spread my own blanket. Who cared how soon the sun would rise. In the cave, darkness reigned.

֎֎֎

The mists of yesterday vanished, burned away by sun. Not even dew remained on hurtfully green grass, pushing away the dried stems of winter. Had there ever been such a thing as winter? I pulled my hat lower onto my forehead, shielding my eyes from morning sun. Today we could see the massive lava rocks of the road. Black, intense, worn silky smooth by countless others such as we, the stones asserted eternal permanence.

"Arf, arf," barked Kosti, dancing around the cart, bending his elbows forward, dangling his hands like the paws of a dog, sometimes reaching to touch the ground. Small and quick, Kosti would never be a big man, though his high forehead and wise eyes promised much. His strength would all be in his mind, and his ready wit would smooth his way.

From high atop the seat of the cart, Boy laughed. "No. You can't ride with us."

"Arf, arf," Kosti insisted, and Girl tossed a bit of bread toward his mouth. Valiantly, Kosti snapped at the air, trying to catch it in his teeth. Venda and Meed'n laughed, having seen this act many times, it seemed.

Kosti tried to jump aboard, failed, of course, and continued barking. Grinning, he stopped; Girl raised her arms, and Kosti helped her down. Boy claimed the seat for himself, lifted the rein and pretended to be driving Spitter. "Get up," he called, slapping the rope across Spitter's rump. Spitter hopped, ha-onh, a-honhed, and actually walked a little faster.

Kosti held Girl's hand, pointing out to her the mountains on our right and smoke trails from a polis. His voice kept a steady murmur and sometimes Girl laughed, winding her arms around his neck. Palo walked beside me, taking no part. A wistful smile shadowed his cheek.

"We could use some music, Palo," I said, touching his shoulder.

He took his flute from the pack hooked across his back, and began to play. Kosti and Girl dropped back to walk with him, and Kosti did a hopping dance in time to the music. Girl laughed, tried the dance herself and bumped into Palo, tripping him. Together, they collapsed in a heap, Kosti helped them up, and Palo began again.

I hurried forward to walk near Meed'n and Venda.

"Where will you go?"

"I have kin in Ravenna," said Meed'n. "We'll stay with them until we find a place, any place by the sea," voice heavy with longing, recalling to me my own youth in Phoenikia. "My brother owns a fishing fleet. My father used to say 'If we earn nothing, at least we'll not go hungry.' And food from the sea raised big strong boys to pull the heavy nets." He laughed, then sobered. "There were many days when that was all we ate." Yet, said with love, the words held no hint of hardship.

"And Kosti?" The youth's arms and legs and knife-blade thin shoulders seemed hardly able to hold his large head erect; how would he pull nets?

"Venda has taught him the tallies. They will work them together. Venda and Kosti are from the old line. Smart."

Old line? The Wise Ones, perhaps? I held my silence, not really wanting to know, hoping I had left the wizard people behind forever. Too much talent, too much knowledge. Frightening, what they could do, should they decide to use their powers. If Avi and Ton possessed no capacity for corruption, I wasn't too certain about Fedei. I still simmered from his tricks.

"I have friends in Athens. Ana enjoys looking after people. She'd feed Kosti until he cried for mercy. He would be welcome there. Dimitri owns land, a farm, goats, sheep, vineyards and orchards. He'd have plenty for Kosti to do, to earn his keep. Your little brother could study at one of the universities."

Venda clutched Meed'n's arm and pulled his head toward her, whispering in his ear. They looked at me, Venda smiling broadly. "We're grateful for your offer, Daneion," said Meed'n. "We'll talk to Kosti."

"Tell him to look for Dimitri. Anyone will know him."

囗囗囗

Meed'n, Venda, Kosti and the children left us in Felsina. Meed'n said he was eager to get home, and no doubt that was true, but I suspected that they had no money to pay an innkeeper for lodging. They would sleep on the road, eating the remains of the food Fieros had left behind. I thought of my hoard of coins, gifts from Olympias, and money earned by trading, but I offered nothing. Proud people would have been offended.

Palo walked in silence, his flute again packed away, eyes downcast, noticing nothing of interest along the way. I had seen how he watched Kosti, the children, Venda and Meed'n. He envied Kosti his easy wit, his family.

"You wanted to go with them? To be a fisherman?"

Palo drew back his head, a denial. "No..." He looked away as though to see a distant farm house, sheep, goats, chickens. "I just want a family."

"Kosti has a family, Palo, but he isn't able to take care of himself like you do. All his life his sister and brother have told him what to do. But you, in an emergency, you act fast. Why, where would I be if you hadn't handed me my stick when you did. And Tito? And Giorgio? We'd all be at the bottom of that pit, probably."

Of an eye level now, for he had grown the length of a finger during the winter, Palo looked at me long, intensely, from a single soulful eye that had seen too much of the hardness of life. Brow furrowed, he tried to speak, but his throat choked.

I wrapped my arm about his shoulders. "You'll be all right, Palo. I'm certain of it. And you'll have your family one day. Why, you can get married and have your own children. How about that?"

🙰🙰🙰

Beyond Felsina, silvery blue bogs reflected mountains extending from north to south, stopping our gaze from the open sea, but it would take high mountains indeed to block the heady scent of salt sea air. Mud huts and some stone houses lined the roadway into Felsina, and with the huts came the smell of freshly turned earth and the scent of wood ash and meat fat boiling in a pot. We passed one stone house built so close to the road that we had to shoo chickens from our way.

A young girl saw us and ran inside. A moment later a man looked out the window, waved and ducked back inside. I considered hawking my wares—a good way to learn news of the city. A bird, a pigeon, fluttered upward from somewhere behind the house. I watched, saw it circling then level off to fly. North.

The village of the People of the Trees would be north. For an instant I thought of Whist and his love of birds, waving a hand through the air, saying "Whist. Whist." Could this be one of Whist's birds heading home? Why would it be down here? Across the mountains? Could birds be returning to the People of the Trees to tell their news? What news?

News about me. These people were sending news about me back to the tree people. To Whist. A chill shivered my skin. Whist? With evil thought against me? I remembered a child of seven, a clear, untroubled face, blue eyes wide and rounded. An innocent. No. Not Whist. Not even thinkable. We passed the house. I glanced behind me. The man and the girl had been joined on the steps by a woman. They waved again. I didn't wave back.

4

The inn bustled with frenzied activity. It sat on the intersection of crossroads, north to south and east to west. The stone floor, polished smooth with beeswax only last night as I slept, now lay heavy with the dusty prints of countless customers, suppliers and serving people.

Travelers from the south, dressed in short togas and shirts and sandals of varying styles, trembled in the cool morning weather, and those from the mountains, foreheads beading in sweat, quickly shed their extra cloaks and woolen hats. Farmers dressed in rough, unbleached linens and barefoot, coming to town to deliver food and supplies, stayed to drink and share their news. One woman and her daughter passed out freshly laundered linens, collected coins, dropped them into a leather drawstring bag tied around the woman's waist, and picked up a pile of dirty clothes as they passed out the door—quick, efficient, and probably expensive.

The scent of roast pig soaked in wine smoked the room, and Palo and I sat waiting for a serving maid to work her way down the long table to our end. It would be a while.

Palo reached for the pack on the floor at his feet and pulled out his flute. Music? In this racket?

He stood, leaned against the end of the table and began to play. The first notes drowned in cacophony. Undaunted he stepped out into the center of the floor and began the skipping dance he had learned from Kosti, even as he quickened the beat.

The innkeeper, a man so thin his toga hung like a sheet draped across a stick set in a field of millet to keep away the magpies, glanced his way and frowned. Florid of face from standing before the cooking fires, he wiped his hands on a huge rag and advanced on the boy. I stood, intending to warn Palo before the man arrived, but others gathered between Palo and me, blocking my way. The innkeeper stopped, waiting for the music to end. The general noise lessened and some began clapping in beat to the rhythm. Passers-by craned their necks to see inside the window and door, and some came inside, looking for seats at a table.

Soon no seats could be found, and listeners gathered to lean against the walls. Palo played and danced on. A serving girl reached our places, and, paying scant attention to what she was doing, filled our plates so full the juices of the meat ran onto the table. As an afterthought, she dropped bread atop the meat and moved on, all the while searching to see the head of the musician through the crowd.

Oblivious to the commotion he had caused, Palo came back to the table. "Our food here yet?" He slung a leg across the long bench, and stabbed the pig with his knife point. The blade caught the mid morning light from the window behind our table and flashed across the room. Several men who had been trying to come nearer, hung back, whether in respect for Palo's music or the sharpness of his knife, I never knew.

Those who had come to hear Palo play stayed to eat. Noises quieted except for calls from the kitchen servants, the rattle of eating utensils, and the chewing, spitting and slurping of customers. We saw no more of the innkeeper that morning except for brief flashes of his bald head as he dipped barley gruel from a huge kettle hung before the fire.

Yells came from the open window behind me, and I turned to watch. A woman banged on the door of a hut just across the alley way behind the tavern.

"Rofe," she called. "Wake up, you sorry excuse for a surgeon and let us in."

A boy pulled the short handles of a flat cart with low sides, and a man lay inside it, groaning.

"My man has been hurt. Rofe! Rofe!"

I left a plate still full of food, but crammed the rest of the bread in my mouth as I hurried from the tavern. "Pay the girl, Palo," I said, in passing. "I'll be out back."

I reached the cart before the surgeon opened his door. "What happened?" I asked.

"He fell off the roof," the woman answered. "Broke his leg."

"I'm a physician. I'll take a look," I said. The man's ankle lay at an odd angle to his knee. I touched it and he screamed. A sliver of bone peered through purple skin.

"He never complains," said the woman, "but I knew he was sick this morning when he woke up. He said he had to get the roof thatched before it rained again. I told him to let Pio help, but he won't trust the boy to do anything. Lucky Pio was there with him though, I was down in the pasture, milking the goats. I would never have known he was hurt. I don't know what I'll do if Bruno loses his leg. Who'll break the land, who'll turn the wheel to grind the wheat? Or fix the roof, for the god's sake."

"No need for him to lose his leg," I said. "But he'll be off it a while." I considered how I could lay him flat on the cart to set the bone. I had left Spitter and the cart in the shelter beside the inn. I'd have to go get my medicines.

"Is it always this hard to raise the surgeon?"

"It is when he drinks all night," she said. "He's a good man when he's sober, but it's hard to find him that way. Sometimes we have to get his father to come and wake him. He's back there in the tavern, the owner. Pio, go get Rienzi. Tell him we need to wake Rofe."

Pio wavered between going and staying. "Go!" shouted his mother.

"But..," said Pio, looking at me.

"For god's sake, Pio, this man's all right. He's a physician, didn't you hear him?" Pio left, but not without looking back over his shoulder.

"I have to get my medicines," I said. "Keep banging on the door. We must lay your man out flat, and we need to do it fast. Look at that swelling."

I found my bag and box of surgical instruments and hurried back to the alley. The innkeeper, Rienzi, had arrived. He inserted a key in the lock, turned the handle and shoved.

"I'm coming. I'm coming," the man inside said, and howled as the door rubbed across the top of his foot. "Oww! How do you expect me to take care of anybody if I can't walk? Get him in here, lay him on the table. What in Hades happened to you Bruno?"

Bruno rolled his eyes and grabbed at his leg, groaning.

"Now why did you do that, leg?" Rofe asked. "Bruno has been taking care of you, hasn't he? Giving you plenty to eat? Bathing you when you're dirty? How have you failed him? Let this be a lesson to you. Legs have to be steady, to keep a man from falling off his own roof." So he had heard every word we had said, as we waited outside. On and on he went, talking as he shifted Bruno on the table and dropped a knife into a bowl of wine. I smelled no sourness of breath that would betray an evening spent with alcohol, but his hair and clothes showed signs of sleep, and his eyes were rimmed with red.

"A good man is up and about this time of day," said the woman. It's just too convenient having a tavern next door, and that owned by your father, too." She glanced sideways at Rienzi, who drew back as though personally accosted.

"Too bad I can't just boil you, leg, to get the poisons out; I'll have to wash you with this sour wine. Now lay still, leg, we have work to do."

"You just don't know how hard it is to keep things going on a farm, Bruno," said Bruno's wife. "You think you do all the work, but I'm the one who has to make sure there's food on the table, and clothes to wear and tell you when the sheep need shearing."

"I...I'll just get back to the tavern." Rienzi turned, headed for the door. "Lots of customers. I'll see you later, son, I'll send somebody with food if you run too long on Bruno. Glad you were here, traveler, to help with the lifting..." Rienzi looked at me. "Aren't you the one who was sitting with that musician? Good boy. How long are you going to be in town?"

"I've made no certain plans, as yet," I said, trying to hold Bruno's good leg still. He kept trying to turn over, first one way then the other.

"Well, just forget about the cost of food and lodging; long as that boy plays and dances, you pay nothing."

"I'll need more wine to clean this wound, Pa, thanks." The door slammed behind Rienzi.

"You went and did yourself in good, leg, broke clean through the skin, now why'd you wanta do that? I'll have to patch you up good. And I'll bet you're going to throw poor Bruno into a fit when I try to pull you straight. That right Bruno? Think you can hold this ornery leg still while I fix it?"

"O-h-h" moaned Bruno.

"He's just a farmer, Rofe," said Bruno's wife. "What do you think he knows about how to act when he has a broken leg? He's never been hurt before."

"Unnhh. Last year," groaned Bruno, and held up a hand missing a joint in a little finger.

"Oh, that." said the woman. "Over in a flash. You just tied a rag around it and went right back to work."

Pio stuck his head in the door. "I got the wine, Rofe."

"Fine, fine, Pio, just set those jugs right here next to me so I can get to them easy. That's a boy."

Rofe lifted a jug, poured a bowl full and held it for Bruno to drink. "A little wine will help make that leg stay still, Bruno." He poured most of what was left over the leg, paused, looked at the remains, and then turned it up and drank it himself. "Helps my hands do their work," he explained, to no one in particular.

"That better Bruno?" He touched the foot.

Bruno howled. "The foot's fine, Bruno," said the physician. Just the leg that's hurt." Bruno groaned, shook his head. "Foot," said Rofe, "you're not hurt. See, your skin's not even broken. He touched the big toe. You're not even near the break. That's half way up the leg, almost to the knee. See?" He squeezed the toe. "Doesn't hurt a bit does it?"

"Agh," grunted Bruno and tried to pull away from Rofe's hand.

"Well maybe a bit more wine, that'll help the leg stay still, eh Bruno?" He poured another bowl of wine, held Bruno's head up and pressed it to his lips. "Good wine, eh friend? Go right straight to that leg and help it be still." Again he finished the last swallow, himself. "Yes, good wine. Father sent you his best."

He touched the toe again. Bruno almost sat up on the table trying to pull away from Rofe's touch.

"My god, Bruno. Be still," said the woman. "You'd think nobody ever had a broke leg before. Worse than Pio. Act like a man."

Bruno groaned, subsided, whimpered. A tear rolled down his cheek.

The calf of the leg continued to swell, and if it were not set soon it would never again be straight. I had to do something. Bruno's leg, it appeared, had become immune to the consoling effects of Rienzi's wine. I drew the pouch of opium crystals from my bag, taking care to lift out a white grain while hiding it with my body. Opium, the juice of the stems and seed pods of the poppy, was not something to play around with.

"I have something that leg will appreciate, Bruno." I crushed the white crystal with my mortar and pestle, and raked it into the wine bowl. "Added to your wine this potion would tame a tornado. That leg will be happy to have us straighten it."

Rofe poured wine into the bowl, stirred it with his finger, lifted

Bruno's head and held the wine to his lips. Again he left a few swallows in the bowl and prepared to drink it himself. "Uh, better pour that on the leg, Rofe."

Rofe sighed, but drained the bowl over the wound.

The woman watched Bruno's face, quiet for once. His lids drooped, and the tension went out of his body. He sighed, and the woman smiled. "Finally. Now I can get back to my work. The pigs need slopping. Pio. Come on boy, there's work to be done at home."

Did I imagine sighs from Rofe and Bruno? I felt like sighing myself. I wondered where Palo was. When I worked, I could usually find him at my elbow, watching.

Bruno chuckled. "That leg's being still, Rofe," and continued babbling, humming, he broke out in song. Something about a neighbor's daughter. He made moves as though dancing. I held him on the table.

"Yes, yes, Bruno, that's it. Now the dance is over. Sit and talk a bit. Um hum. Summer is here. Apples will be ripe soon. Yes, apple pies, dumplings..."

I held Bruno under the arms and Rofe pulled on the leg. Pulled again. Jerked. The bone clicked.

"There. That does it," he said, leaving the leg to pour the wine off the instruments then lift one with a clean cloth and wave it in the air. In passing, he looked longingly at the jug holding the new wine, but continued toward his patient. "We have to get the pieces of bone out of you, leg, so you can heal right. There's one. Another. My, you're full of splinters. Bone, why have you let yourself get so out of shape? You should be strong and hard, and here you are letting yourself get brittle, easy to break. Now when you get home, you remember, have Bruno eat some of that white clay down by the creek, it'll come straight from Bruno's mouth to you. Make you strong. If Bruno falls again, you won't break so easily. There. That's the last of the bone I can see. Just a minute let me feel...yes, I think that's all, now another little bath in that beautiful wine and we'll just tie up. You'll be helping Bruno walk about the farm in no time. You'll even be helping him dance with that pretty neighbor girl next to your farm.

"Fasteners, traveler, in my bag. What's your name anyway? Where are you from?"

"Daneion," I said, "From Phoenikia, Epirus. North of Athens on the Adriatic."

"Never heard of it," said Rofe. "Never been to Epirus; never been to

Athens. Lived here all my life. This house used to be my father's house. He gave it to me when he enlarged the inn. He and my dead mother's sister sleep above the kitchen. Says he can smell when the bread is done that way." He drew dried ant pincers from his bag, attached them in the skin and pulled the openings shut. When he finished he washed his hands, then dipped the rag into another bowl of wine and smeared it onto Bruno's leg.

Bruno snored.

"Good wine. Good wine." Rofe poured another bowl, took a swallow, found a chair, pulled it out for me in front of the fire and sat in another beside it. Sighing he offered the bowl to me. I declined; he finished the bowl and rose to pour another.

"What was that stuff you gave me for Bruno? Worked like magic. I wish I had more of it. The only thing I have to sedate my patient is wine. The trouble is, I can't be around wine without drinking it, and sometimes I risk getting too drunk to work on my patient. If I had some of that stuff you used I'd get the job done faster. Wouldn't drink so much myself. Still have to clean the wound with wine though. Don't know any way around that."

"Sorry, Rofe, I only have a little, and I have to make it last till I get back home. I know a dealer in Athens who has it shipped in from somewhere beyond Persis." I looked away as I spoke, certain that he would detect the lie. Actually I had gathered the juice for the crystals myself. The flowers could be found almost anywhere along the roadside, if one knew where to look, and Ana grew them for me in her garden. Pretty little white flower.

Ah, but as addled as Rofe had become, he was still alert enough to sense my hesitation. "You're afraid I'll get into it myself, aren't you? Well, you may be right. I probably would. It's my nature. Given me by the gods. No use fighting it. I was born to drink wine, and take anything else that I could get my hands on, I guess. Decreed by the fates."

The same old story. I felt an anger building inside me, an explosive anger. The fate of the gods. Even were it true that mankind possessed no self-will, how could it be that a supreme being could just build in a weakness, one that could not be overcome. I didn't believe it. Man had to be free to choose.

Palo came in the door, saw us, pulled up a stool and sat before the fireplace, laid only with ashes now, for Rofe had added no new wood. Palo had brought bread and meat from the tavern and he handed it to us, keeping a healthy portion for himself.

"It's free," he said. "Innkeeper liked my music. Said it brought in customers. Wants me to play tomorrow, if we're still here."

"Where have you been?"

"I went back to see the birds, there where we saw one fly away last time. The man keeps dozens. They live in a cage on his roof. He let one out. It flew around a while then came back. I asked him if that one we saw yesterday had come back. He didn't say. I saw Fly."

"You saw the fox? Not possible, Palo. He'd be much too far away from home. Must have been some other red fox."

"He watched me, and came up close before he ran away."

Curiosity grabbed hold of me. "Which way did he run?"

"North. He stopped and looked back at me just like Fly used to do when he wanted us to follow him, then he ran till I couldn't see him. He went up a path that leads around the village."

"It runs into the trail that goes past the tavern heading north," said Rofe. "Bad road, but passable, they say. I wouldn't know. I've never been farther than a day's walking distance from here. This is my home. My fate."

Fate. A position against which no argument worked. I'd had enough of the besotted surgeon. "Let's go, Palo. Show me where you saw the fox."

Rofe took another swallow of wine. "He was probably after Ozhio's birds."

Ozhio? I stopped and looked back, intrigued despite myself. "Does this Ozhio have kin who suffer seizures?" My words fell on deaf ears. Rofe, the man with magic in his fingertips, sat with head rolled back, snoring.

൹൹൹

Once Spitter saw which way Palo and I were headed, she moved out in front.

"Didn't have to make a big deal of it," Palo said, "bringing the cart. It's just a little way down the road."

"Um hum," I agreed, not explaining. Some things you do by habit. You do those things because you have found that they work. You don't even have to think about them any more. Like waiting till you're out of sight before you put money in the secret compartment beneath the cart.

I whistled for Spitter to stop, and felt beneath the cart for the money bag. Good boy, the stock handler. Nice eyes. I trusted the look in a man's eyes. Men, not boys. Never knew what a boy might do. I pulled the pouch from its hiding place and glanced inside. All there. I poked it back under, and we started up again.

A cart approached, meeting us from the opposite direction. He had seen me squatting, reaching under the cart in front of the wheels to put the coin purse back into the secret pouch.

Probably not a thief. Sitting high on the seat of his blue and white cart, he rode like royalty, caressing the reins in a familiar way. Easy wealth, I decided. The donkey, surely not far from his stable, pulled easily. Too smooth for a thief, still something about the man was wrong. Something out of place. My back stiffened. The hairs on my arms rose. I stood beside Spitter, waiting.

Jakardos

Thin, wiry, he darts here and there with hawk-eyed grace. A weakling I might believe him to be, seeing him at rest, yet no effete could support that fiery brush of mane and beard, nor sprout muscles from every limb like apples on a tree. Ton calls him Wallis, this Daneion Pelos, grandson of Sivya, the Bei. Scarcely taller than the boy he is, the boy named Palo.

"He will not trust you," said Ton, "and that will be his saving. He must stay by his caution for now and as long as he lives. His life—and our hope—depend on it.

"He will help you if you are hurt, and that is the best way to gain his trust, for in compassion his defenses sleep."

So what am I to do? Wound myself? I think not. As for illness, I have spent not a single day of my life abed. Perhaps another need. The wheel of my cart could break? It's a new cart. My donkey could sicken? Pharo glows with good health. What then?

He sees me. Too late. I must proceed.

5

The driver pulled the cart to a stop, as I feared he would. He made no move to step down.
"Is there room in the tavern?" he asked–no apologies, no introduction. He assumed I stood waiting his approach to serve his needs. "I have heard that Rienzi of Bononia keeps a clean inn." He smiled when he spoke, a genial smile, a too-broad smile. Too many white and even teeth erupted from beneath a smutty mustache, cutting a gleaming gash in the square-jawed, swarthy face. The voice projected as though from a stage. Tonal. Melodious.

Stunned, I fought instant resentment of this too-bold stranger and managed an answer. "The food is good." I regretted my words even as I spoke. My voice, never melodious, now seemed crass and unpolished. Yet, I assured myself, I was no backwoods pagan. I cleared my throat. "There were more beds when I was there. They may still be empty."

"I trust the stables are also stocked?"

"When we were there, my donkey was well cared for," I said, "but she is unaccustomed to coddling."

I must have glanced at the man's donkey, for he answered, "Neither is my old mare, but Pharo here is borrowed from a friend, and I must take care of him."

A lie. The donkey responded too easily to his master's touch. "You are fortunate to have such a generous friend," I said.

His eyes never wavered. A good liar. "Perhaps I'll see you again. Do you plan to stay another night in the tavern?" Where I slept was none of his concern. If given the option I would put much distance between us.

I whistled. Spitter lifted her head from the roadside grass she had been nibbling, looked at me, looked at the stranger, and pulled forward. "My plans are never definite, not even to the direction of my travel," I said, unwilling to commit myself for the least of his questions. Without further word, yet somewhat reluctantly, I thought, he allowed me passage then continued on toward the village.

Palo pointed to a sandy, gutted trail leading away from the road. "Here. This is where I saw Fly."

I stooped above a tiny foot print, sniffed the dirt, and detected the musty odor of fox. I glanced up the path. Early-summer grasses fell away to either side of the trail. Someone had dug trenches for drainage. The trail led somewhere but no one had traveled this way lately. Not since the rain.

"Here's another one," Palo said. "Looks like he's following the road."

Hardly a road. I glanced at my wheels, dreading repair should one break. Spitter brayed; eager to be moving. The house where we had seen the pigeons lay just ahead. It would be easy to stop back by after we checked the tracks.

Palo said he had seen the fox sitting beside the trail farther along the path. "He's leading us somewhere, just like he used to do," he said.

We followed the trail till late in the day where it joined the main road. 'Patavium,' read the stone marker, the road we would need for our journey north. We had traveled too far to turn back, just for the night. I rolled back the canvas on the cart to check our supplies. The stock man had loaded dried fish and lamb, cheese and wine and bread, courtesy of Rienzi, saying Palo's entertainment and my help with the injured man more than paid for our room and food. No need to return except to talk with the man with the pigeons. I considered returning. I really wanted to know about those birds, and the man could have been the relatives Ozhio spoke of. Still, such a long way, for only one night. As though listening to my thought, Spitter jerked to a start, somewhat nervously, I thought. Animals could sometimes sense things lost to humans. I moved up to her head.

"What is it girl? What's wrong?"

She rolled her eyes around at me, shuddered, rippled the silver hairs across her shoulders and whuffed, but continued walking. Something ahead, I supposed, a disturbing scent. "Watch for thieves, Palo. If they jump us out here we'll never be heard of again. I untied the ropes holding the canvas, ran my fingers down the inside wall of the cart, past the bag of oats, touched the long knife. I laid it on top and pulled the canvas over it. I checked again, adjusting it so my fingers would close on the handle. Nothing more I could do.

The land turned marshy, no place to set up a tent offside, so Palo and I built our fire and spread our blankets on the trail. We caught frogs for our dinner, lazy frogs as big as rabbits. I cut off their legs and dressed them as Palo walked along the road looking for paw prints. Sometimes he stopped, staring out over miles of flat saw grass bog as though expecting the fox to stand up and wave to him. Beyond the bogs, rolling lowlands of stunted trees, saltbush, and celery grass gave way to a string of low mountains—sentinels between land and sea.

The moon rose, turning the bogs into poured silver. Palo returned, took a roast frog leg and ate, all the time scanning the bogs with his one, keen eye. I left him to his solitude, rolled into my blanket, and lay watching lights hover over the marsh, flashing bright and then fading—on, off, fiery wraiths that formed dancing, fantasy figures across the surface. Swamp gas. Cracking, popping, it seeped upward, exploded into free air. Swamp gas could kill, but it kept to the low places. Safe enough here, I decided. The popping gas joined a rising, falling chorus of the croaking of frogs. Spitter beside me still hitched to the cart, mummered, snuffed, stomped, and was quiet.

I closed my eyes, opened my mind, and blended with the night, memory retracing events of my journeys, attempting to draw meaning from the loss of control of my actions. I didn't like what I saw.

The smoke of a wet bogwood fire and the aroma of hot barley soup pulled me out of troubled dreams. I sat up. Barely sunrise. Palo was certainly eager to renew his search. But Palo was not there. Instead, in Palo's place across the fire, sat a man. For a moment the world spun and I thought I was still dreaming. A nightmare. I rose, stretched, ran my hand beneath the canvas.

The man grinned at me. "I got an early start today. Hope you don't mind my taking advantage of your coals for a fire." It was the man with the blue and white cart. His white teeth tore at the frog leg I had left hanging above the fire.

My fingers closed on the knife. "Where is Palo?"

"Palo? The boy?" he asked.

"What have you done to him?" Slowly, I drew the knife to the edge of the cover.

"You were alone when I rode in. Is the boy lost? He wouldn't go into the bogs, would he?"

I dropped the knife.

"Fly," I said.

"Fly?"

"Fly. A fox."

"He's gone fox hunting?"

"Listen!" I interrupted. "What is that?"

"Fox." he said. "Coming from over there, where the ground rises."

As one, we scrambled to our feet. Whipping aside saw grass with my staff, feet sinking in ooze, I entered the bogs, the stranger close behind. The land smelled of salt water, oppressive in the odor of decaying vegetation. I followed a disappearing trail of bent weeds.

"There." The stranger pointed. I saw nothing but tall grass. I tried to leap high enough to see but muck sucked at my feet.

"What is it?" I asked, hating that I must ask this taller man. He pushed past me in that direction, but stopped with the first cut by sharp grass. He stood aside and I again took the lead, pressing away the grass with my staff, laboring for every soggy step.

We emerged onto a slight rise, passing shrubs I had never before seen, some with buds and blooms of yellow and lavender just catching the light of morning sun. I would have marked them for further study, had I been able to mark. Lost in this bewildering, suffocating ooze, I moved blindly, placing one foot before the other. I tried to scent the trail, but smelled nothing but swamp, felt nothing but the slick ooze of rotting vegetation. My feet slipped, skidded. I sat on the edge of a shallow basin of chalky mud and rotted weed. Sunlight wavered, shimmered, dissolved. A dark spot colored the ooze ahead of me. I fought to see through sun bright and shadowed grass.

Palo. Head downward, face half mired in milky liquid. He would drown in poison water.

I grabbed an ankle and began pulling. A tangle of vines bound his arm, resisting my pull. I tore them away and pulled again. The white soup flowed, seeping into the cavity made by his fall. The land wavered, blurred; I strained toward action, struggled for meaning. As though in a dream, I saw a stranger bend, lift Palo into his arms, begin a slippery climb to higher ground. I stumbled, recovered and followed, the movement pulling time into focus. The stranger laid Palo on a turf of moss, and I dropped down beside him. Habit pulled my fingers to Palo's wrist, found his pulse. Reedy. Fast. I felt around on his body. Cuts and scratches from the saw grass, but no breaks. I lifted his head, brushed milky moisture from between drooling lips. I had seen this happen once, in a hole where offal had been dumped. A lamb had wandered in. Dead in moments. I coughed. Grabbing for anything I could lay hand on, I clutched a mound of moss, ripped it from the earth, and scrubbed at Palo's face, eyes, nose, between his lips. I grabbed more moss, wiped around the ears, the neck, the hands, the arms.

All the while, I mumbled. "Palo. We have to get your hair trimmed. It's growing out. Need to shorten it around the shoulders. What will Delos say when we get back to Athens? Why, he'll laugh till his sides burst and point at your hair. We'll get it cut at the next village, a straight cut across the back, maybe, something to give you a more worldly look..." Words drooled to mush in my mouth. My tongue swelled past my lips. Light faded.

Water splashed over my head. I looked up into dark eyes, as wide open as sky on a moonless night. Sinking, sliding into their depths, I welcomed their control, giving myself to this quiet power. My spirit returned to Yiayia's cottage. I lay watching stars from my window, knowing I would never again see the sun. A prickle of regret, and...

I returned.

The eyes above me wavered, blurred. Something grabbed me under the arms, pulled me to my feet, slung an arm across a shoulder and pulled me, stumbling, up a hill. I dropped onto moist and spongy turf, blanked, again was jerked to my feet to lurch forward one step, two, three. My legs struggled to remember their pattern. Failed. I fell again.

I awoke, aching, every part of me thundering in pain-radiating sheets. My head lay cradled on a blanket roll. Spitter ha-onh, a honhed and Palo moaned. A hawk circled above me, screaming, welcoming me into the land of dreams. Not today, Hunter. It seems I must continue. At least for a while. The stranger watched from across a fire, rubbing his eyes with the heel of one hand, holding the last of the frog legs, drooping, uneaten, with the other.

𐅂𐅂𐅂

Jakardos was his name. Called Jak, he said, by his friends. Without him, Palo and I would still be back there, melting to mush in a death dance with the rotting weeds. Then why did I hate him? Why didn't I trust him? Something about his manner still rang false. He was too smooth, too even, too open. People so practiced in artlessness surely had something to hide. Deception lived behind that mask of innocence. I knew it. Yet, now, I could not send him away, and Jakardos showed no signs of planning to leave.

Jakardos, not Jak, I called him, a gesture of defiance and denial. Jakardos, he was to me, as long as I knew him, and that turned out to be a very long time.

Jakardos, son of Etruscan nobility. His parents were people of wealth from grain mills scattered across the lands of Italy.

"Wherever there is grain to be milled," Jakardos said, "the family of Medoros mills it, but I will be no miller, and I told my mother so." The man had not stopped talking since we packed the carts and started our journey. Wanting, needing solitude to recover from this damnable headache, I moved forward. He followed. I climbed into the cart. He climbed in beside me. "And that was fine by my mother," he continued, hardly drawing a breath. "She has wanted to travel the lands all the days of her life. "You will see the world, Jak, she said. You must tell me of what you find.'

"So I took, uh, borrowed Pharo from the stables. Mother gave me a bag of coins; I bought this cart, and started down the road. That was two weeks ago, and till I found you I had almost decided to head for home. Now I see that it really can be done. I can travel the countryside, go where I want to go," he laughed, "and see the world my mother wanted me to see."

"With that new cart and highborn donkey, you'll be taken by thieves before you get more than a few miles from home," I said, hoping he'd give up and go home.

"That's why I need to travel with you," he paused from his narrative to answer. "You know how to travel. I need to learn things like that."

There was more, but the words became like flies buzzing in my ear, meaningless, fading in and out, and I smelled lemons. I massaged my forehead, my eyes, willing away the pain. I had taken the powder of the fungus in my tea, so far without result. Palo rode Jakardos' almost empty cart, leaning against the side, bundled into his blanket, breath labored, face pale. I stepped down from the cart, walked alongside him. I checked his pulse, felt his forehead. He shrugged me away, needing to search for a small red ball of fur along the weedy plains on either side of the road.

He would be all right. Just needed time and fresh air to recover. I should have warned him about the swamp gas. Such a cocky, bold little man; he followed my way only because it suited his own. But he knew little of the dangers of travel, and nothing of bogs. I should have warned him.

"...just passed my sixteenth birth year when my mother's father died, leaving the mills and all the wealth to her." Jakardos, again, now walking beside me.

My head hurt. And why did I smell lemons? I carried no lemons in my cart, and they didn't grow around here. The only place I knew of lemons was in Mysia, across the Aegean near the home of my mother and my sister and her family. I had never smelled them elsewhere. The bog gas must have messed up my nose. Tense, uncertain, I began to sniff for smells around me. Away from the bogs now, I detected the familiar odors of animals and humans just as always.

"I didn't have to work, we had enough servants to care for a kingdom, but I liked the stables, the horses, the donkeys, the goats. One time when a mare was in foal I found that just talking to her eased her labor, so after that I practiced and practiced. I talked to all the animals, and soon, just hearing my voice they did whatever I wanted them to do."

I stopped, right there in the middle of the road. "And just what was it you wanted them to do?"

"Oh, anything—turn left, turn right, back up, hurry..." He stopped walking, looked back at me and continued, gesturing dramatically with his hands. "Once I even told a stallion which mare I wanted him to mount and he did. Oh, I know, you'd say it was the stallion that made that decision, but the mare was in a pasture with at least ten others, all in season. That stallion picked her out like a blazing house afire, and gave her a fine colt. It looked just like him."

"Maybe you could teach this ornery ass of mine to obey. That would be a real trick."

Jakardos missed my sarcasm. He kept talking, leaving me free to do my thinking. His voice stopped, startling me to awareness. Something he had said. The bracelet. I answered to shut him up, if but for a moment. "A gift for a lady."

"I know of a jeweler in Patavium, just ahead. He can put jewels in it for her. His shop is just off Meduacus River. Everything happens there. You can buy anything in the shops. Artisans everywhere, not too expensive, either....." The chatter continued, who knows what he talked about. Did I hear something about dancing girls? And how did he know I planned to have an artisan put stones in the bracelet? I hadn't told him.

※※※

We crossed the Padua River, then the Athesis, but we hardly noticed that these were rivers; it seemed only that the swamp grasses cleared to open water, flowing, filling and soaking an already saturated land.

The voice of the people changed. Commerce with Athens had kept the language of the Greek settlement, Bononia, pure. Here, my unaccustomed ear struggled to put meaning to the words of these people. Jakardos, however, moved through the dialects as easily as he crossed the road.

Palo and I watched as he procured passage for us on flatboat ferries, haggled for fares and exchanged news of the river and the roads. I caught a few of Jakardos' words and marveled that our journey had been so fraught with terror. How had we ever survived? We had been accosted by bandits, fought our way through snake pits, and–only slightly–delayed by spirits of the dead taking life from creeping swamp gas. I, one of the heroes of his myth, listened, astounded. He mentioned nothing of nearly losing Palo in the swamps, nothing of his aid in saving him, and nothing of our illness. Where is the heroism in headaches?

Eventually, the ferriers pulled us across, no charge, having been well paid by his storytelling wizardry. Jakardos learned, in turn, a route to avoid the tax gatherers who were now charging twice their usual amount, hoping to build a road south and east from Vicetia to Patavium and through the swamps to the land of Seven Lakes. Some rich Roman needed a faster route to a fortress on the mountain overlooking both the lakes and the sea.

Our self-appointed guide moved us swiftly through Patavium to a tavern, an ancient stone house, the roof a sun deck overlooking the streets of old town. A thatch-roofed pen for Spitter and Pharo hung off the side. The sleeping loft, upstairs and half as large as the tavern, overhung the gardens where street noises and smells faded to a subdued background.

Promising foods more delicious than either of us had ever tasted, Jakardos directed us through village traffic. Houses lined the walkways, some as much as three stories high. How jauntily we walked the sun-laden, mud-brick streets trailed by the scent of potted flowers on flat-topped roof patios. Mind-destroying swamps quite forgotten in the welcoming shades of massive chestnut trees in market square, we followed Jakardos–praising the sights of the city, pulling Palo and me along with the force of his enthusiastic charm. I hardly paused to wonder...how did the patrician who professed to know nothing of traveling, know so well this polis and this language of strangers?

Jakardos cut a path through pens of goats and feeding donkeys, pausing in his running patter only for a fit of convulsive sneezing when we passed cages of chickens and geese. Abashed, dabbing with shirt sleeve at tears streaming down his face, he led us on through milling traders, shoppers and children, dragging Palo by an elbow when he stopped too long to watch a street entertainer with snakes.

In a lull from his chatter, I thought to wonder that I would allow a man I so mistrusted to lead me about–I, who had traveled with ease the world and all its major cities from Athens to Byzantium to Lesvos. Yet Jakardos' world was not the world I usually traversed. Jakardos' world burst with color, tastes, emotions, stuffed to the limits with exotic activity...not an unreal world, just bigger than real, a world made brighter by his fire.

We stopped before the jeweler's shed. A man, wizened, bald except for a white fringe around his scalp, hammered gold into a clasp meant for some worthy lady. He looked up through eyes so blue I thought I'd drown in them. He nodded. Every part of his face, from wrinkled forehead to chin smiled–everything except his lips. They closed tightly on gold wires that he pulled one by one from his mouth to lay against the clasp and wind into intricate design. He looked at us, waiting.

Jakardos stepped forward. "We have a piece of jewelry we'd like you to see," he said, and turned to me.

Suddenly shy, I hesitated between giving the smith the bracelet and turning to run. Yet I could hardly move my hands, and my feet seemed turned to stone. "I have a bracelet," I said. "It is for a queen."

The smith held out a hand, and I placed the bracelet in it. He turned it around and around, touching the waved blue lines, fingering the clasps, and finally holding it up to the sun. Polished metal turned to white fire. He nodded, and removed the wires from between his lips. "It is good. I will work on it. Come back tomorrow." Not, what do you want me to do with it, not how much it would cost. Just, come back tomorrow.

Dismissed, I turned away, obeying. I'd still have been there today, had that smith willed it. I know.

I looked back at the shed, but the ancient had disappeared. For a few moments Jakardos remained silent, and I thanked whatever gods there be for it. Tomorrow we would return, for sure. The man had Bird's bracelet.

The market thinned in the early afternoon, and merchants began to spread cloths across their wares, preparing for afternoon siesta. Palo stopped at a tent to look at knives and Jakardos and I moved on, he to buy a leather belt and I to examine good used clothing. One robe caught my eye, too long, yet short enough to clear the ground when I walked if caught up with a girdle. I liked the way the pale yellow fabric shone in the sun. Bordered in blue, it seemed a fitting garment, within the means and manner of a simple peddler. I would wear it when I visited Bird.

Jakardos finished his purchase and came to join me, commenting on the robe, saying the yellow would enhance the red of my hair and beard. Flattered, I tried to ignore him. Still, my thoughts turned to the picture I would make in Bird's eyes, red hair, yellow robe; I would stand just so, allowing sun light to fall on me, just as when the colors of the robe first caught my eye. Again, the sheer power of the man's voice had drawn me into his special world, his expanded universe.

It wasn't until I found Palo going to Jakardos for direction that I came up for air.

"Good choice," he said, as Palo showed him a knife he was considering buying. "It will make a fine statement when you visit the ladies. See, the scroll on the red handle and the sheen of the polish of the blade. A fine choice, indeed."

"No," I said. "The knife will be useless for anything more than show. Test the blade with your thumb."

Palo brushed his thumb across the blade. "It's dull," he said. "It won't even cut. Jak, do you suppose I could whet it to an edge?" Longing weighed his voice.

"Well," Jakardos hesitated, looking at me.

I resented being made the villain in this story. The knife would be useless. If the blade began with no edge it meant that it would hold none. I told him so, but I added, "The knife is for show. There could come a time when it could serve for that, but it would impress no one of importance, for they would see in an instant that it is neither a serious weapon nor tool. However, it is your money, your decision. You decide."

Palo weighed my words even as he weighed the knife for balance.

"It's no good for throwing, either; see how it drops on the blade side when I hold my finger under the middle?"

"Who showed you that?" I asked, impressed.

"Ton," he said. "Ton taught me to throw a knife. He said you never know when you'll have to kill a snake."

Two surprises in one. Ton used a throwing knife? To kill a snake? The gentle dreamer, a fighter? An incongruous combination.

Palo returned the knife and looked at others, this time weighing them, dragging his thumb across the blade, polishing them on his sleeve.

I sought the reason for my disquiet, and found it. Palo had not come first to me with his questions.

Leave the boy alone, I wanted to say to Jakardos, immediately recognizing the folly of such a statement. Jealousy seemed strange to me, like shoes that do not fit. I held my tongue, yet vowed to study this man. Why did I distrust him? Mentally I set him aside, vowing to listen no more to his fantastic tales in that commanding, entrancing voice.

The tavern echoed with emptiness that night. Even so, delicious smells met us at the door. The innkeeper sat on a three-legged stool staring out an open window. A breeze ruffled his long, curly brown hair and beard. A scroll lay loose on his knees. He looked as the wise old scholars of Athens must have looked when they were younger, when they could be seen without a crowd of admirers surrounding them. We might have been shadows on the wind, for all the attention paid us by that innkeeper.

We found places at a table and waited for the maid to serve us. Between the innkeeper and the door hung a picture painted on wood and framed in cowhide. I recognized the Oak of Tannin, the tree tattooed on Ton's forearm. I would have approached to ask him about it, but I hesitated to break into his reverie. Beside me, Jakardos told Palo about how this used to be the innkeeper's house, and his wife had insisted he turn it into a tavern, since most of his drinking friends wound up here anyway. Of course, she built another house, adjoining the gardens, for this is where her flowers grew. How did Jakardos know the history of the inn? Perhaps he made it up as he went along. Yet I would not confront him for affirmation. He could probably prove it. People told him things, though I don't know how they managed to find an opening. I considered when I had told him things. Not much. Yet he managed to spin an entire yarn from every inference. Sometimes he got it right.

All of a sudden he stopped talking and started sneezing. I looked around toward the sound of fluttering wings.

A pigeon dropped out of the sky and landed straight into the lap of the innkeeper, knocking the scroll from his hands. It snapped shut, slipped from his lap and rolled across the floor. I rose, collected the scroll, and returned it.

"Well, I think we have a friend here," the innkeeper chuckled. The pigeon huddled in the crook of the innkeeper's arm, sticking her head out and staring at me as I advanced with the scroll. Wrapped around the leg of the bird, something pale yellow showed from between the innkeepers fingers. A scrap of vellum, the same as the note sent to Tomaso from Fedei.

As the innkeeper stroked the bird, his sleeve slid up his arm to his elbow. There burned into the skin of his forearm I saw the tattoo of a tree. Startled, I blurted. "You are an agent of the woods people. They have sent you a message."

The innkeeper looked up, confusion in his face. He hadn't even heard us enter.

"Woods people?"

"I recognized the tree," I nodded toward his arm. "I was there."

"Yes," he sighed, accepting. This little friend comes from the gentle people of the land of trees. Ton said you'd learn about the birds sooner or later."

"The message? It is about me?"

He nodded, opened the vellum and read. They want to know if you have seen the jeweler. They ask if he completed the piece and dedicated it for you."

"They know about the jeweler?" I grabbed the innkeeper's shoulder to steady myself. "What else do they know?"

It must have seemed a command, my grabbing his shoulder and shaking it, for he answered truthfully. "We have seen your future, but please, it is forbidden that I speak."

"If it is about me I have a right to know." I had held my suspicions about the forest people too long inside, and I pressed him. "What have your seers seen?"

For long and long he stared into my eyes, struggling to speak, choking it back. "To know the future is to change it, especially if one is the prime mover. The future of our world would be cracked, perhaps disintegrated, should you know the reading of the record. I am forbidden." He looked again at the note. "Avi asks about your health. She sings for you."

Bewildered, I stumbled to my seat on the bench. Jakardos still sneezed, and Palo stroked the blade of his new knife across his shirt tail, back and forth, saying nothing, saying everything.

I would have challenged Palo for information, but Jakardos would hear. Later, I thought, when I go with him to get Spitter ready for the night. But it did not happen. Jakardos also went along, and as we cleaned and brushed Spitter, he cleaned and brushed Pharo–talking nonstop the entire time. Done with chores, Palo rolled into his blanket on the straw near the donkeys. Envying him his peace, I went inside with Jakardos and climbed the ladder to the loft. Gratefully I eased into quiet sleep, as the voice of the Etruscan faded. He did not snore.

回回回

Something woke me before dawn. I lay on my stuffed mattress, listening. A sound came again, and I realized I had been hearing it for some time. I glanced toward the other bed, thinking Jakardos had been talking in his sleep. The bed was empty.

I rose, went to the window and looked out over the gardens. Jakardos stood facing the east. The last light of moon and a lightening of sky from a still unseen sun defined his face, his black hair and beard, his shoulders and flowing white robe. In a voice that sent shivers down my spine, Jakardos sang. He sang of wind, of sun, of water. He sang of newborn babies and purple flowers. I had heard that song before, the morning song in the village of Avi and Ton. When he finished I wiped my tears. A wizard. By my heart, the man was one of the wizard people, and his voice held his magic.

"I know who you are," I said, when he returned to the loft. "And it does not matter. But if you travel with me you will learn to keep your mouth shut."

He grinned, and those impossibly white teeth flashed in so disarming a manner, I almost relented. "Not a word," I cautioned, glaring, gathering my things and preparing to descend the ladder. He obeyed.

回回回

I would not have returned to the jeweler had I not left the bracelet with him. He scared me spitless. I was just not ready for another such encounter. But again we threaded through the crowds of market, passed the animal pens, this time taking a wide berth around the chickens and geese and settled ourselves before the shed of the jeweler.

Could this be the same man we had seen yesterday? Such an inofficious gentleman. Again, lips compressed, he smiled, welcoming customers. But though just as blue, his eyes compelled me not at all, and he waited cheerfully as I showed him the stones I wanted in the bracelet. Three stones, I considered, to balance across the front, maybe one large one in the center and two smaller on either side. Then my gaze fell on a circlet carved from horn in a piece meant for securing a robe across the shoulder. In the outside center, sculpted in gold and laid in a square background of pooled and hammered silver a coin gleamed, an Athenian tetradra with the profile of Athené's face. She wore a helmet. I examined the inside of the ring. An owl.

"Athena?" I asked. The jeweler smiled—everything but the mouth—though, now his lips held no gold wires. I wondered how he accomplished such a thing, and vowed to try it in private to discover the particular muscles he used.

"Can you put it on the bracelet?"

"In the center," said Palo.

Jakardos, looking the apology at me, added, "With two stones on either side, two large nearest the medallion." I agreed, my edict for his silence overlooked. The man could be useful.

"Of course, of course," smiled the jeweler, and at once popped the coin out of the circlet and held it before the bracelet. "Like this?"

"Perfect." I removed the bag of stones from my belt and handed them to him. He spilled them into his hand and quickly picked out two large cubes of calcite, dismissing emeralds and rubies and amber as though worthy of mere bangles.

"White with ice-blue highlights when polished," he said, "In honor of the goddess."

On our third day in Patavium we returned for the bracelet. With cupped hands the jeweler extended it toward me. Inserted through holes and secured beneath, two perfectly faceted stones, polished till they caught the light in winking brilliance, were fitted on either side of the coin. I looked underneath, inside the bracelet. The owl met me eye for eye. When I saw the owl, I sought to praise the jeweler for his skill. Paralyzed, I found myself drowning in eyes which had once again become twin seas, compelling. My head swam. My knees gave way. I dropped.

Embarrassed, I stood, preparing to make my excuses. I had tripped. Lame. I had bent over to pick up a rock. False.

When I rose the man had disappeared, and Jakardos and Palo stood watching me.

"He would take only a ruby for his pay," said Palo. "I gave him one from your bag." How long had I been on my knees?

"Your lady must be very special, for a gift like this," said Jakardos. Too choked to speak, I tried to fasten the bracelet on my arm. "Why don't you wear it over your heart," he said, "now that it has been dedicated?"

Dedicated. Yes. It seemed right. The bracelet, now complete, heavier by far with the added weight, seemed as light as air. My body raced with energy as I held it in my fingers. I would not be able to think of my duty with this around my wrist. I looped it through a silver chain the jeweler had left with Jacardos, hung it about my neck and shoved it beneath my robe. It made a bulky lump on my chest, but it felt good there. We turned to leave. My feet danced across the smooth gray stones of the market place. Palo and Jakardos walked on either side of me, and when I glanced their way, they both wore smiles too insistent to fade. Were they laughing at me? No. Their eyes held only wonder, and something more, almost like love. It was a sense of camaraderie, a union of common mission.

6

In our journey around the northernmost part of the Adriatic, the road kept to the foothills, never taking us through the marsh, though trails branched away and down toward thatched roof villages built on stilts and boarded piers, and extending into the sea on flat boats. Days we inhaled steamy, salt air laden with the redolence of drying sea fare, and in late afternoon and night, shivered in cool drafts rushing down from the mountain peaks.

Chores completed, mats and blankets lying open to unclouded skies, we sat watching the colors of the grass change from purple/yellow to gray, with the setting of the sun, as Jakardos sang to Palo's music. Away to the east a pinpoint of light from some large fire sparkled. In that direction lay the village of Tergesté, the chiefdom of Tharros.

What could I do about Ena? She would not abandon her daughter to the ministrations of Thera, her dead husband's sister, a woman who hated her and her Athenian manners. No. She would stay, to serve as Thera's servant if necessary–anything to protect Thelana. I would be forced to return to Athens with an empty cart. I dreaded telling Leon of his daughter's plight. Even now I could imagine his grief. He would blame me for his loss.

Bizarre alternatives flooded my mind. I could steal Ena and Thelana away under cover of night. Our company, dressed in dark hoods, would seek the shadows, rushing to clear the pass before Tharros and his guards could catch us, enlisting the aid of the robbers to ambush Tharros' guards nipping at our heels. In my vision, their shouts rode the nightwinds, up and down hills and across the water in flatboats. Still we raced, hiding behind rocks, in abandoned huts, in caves hidden by frantically collected brush. Almost I could feel the earth shudder, pounded by the feet and horses of Tharros, always chasing, never catching.

Now *there* would be a story for Jakardos to tell. I laughed, stuffed a blanket roll beneath my head, and turned onto my side to sleep.

The next day about noon, fire erupted in the marsh just off the road, catching quickly and spreading across the grasses. Pharo screamed, reared, fell sideways across a shaft, smashing his cart. A wheel rolled drunkenly down a bank and into the inferno. On and on it rolled, catching fire, picking up speed, bumping over stones and jumping ditches. Finally, slowing, wobbling like a wounded bull, it dropped.

"Ha-onh, ahonh" Spitter called, frozen into place despite the flames only a few feet away. Pharo raised a head, looked at her, then jerked to his feet, snuffing. He rubbed his head against his foreleg, and his cheek came away bloodied. I looked for healing liniment as Jakardos and Palo worked to right the cart.

"Leave it," I said. "The shaft's broken. The wheel's gone and you didn't bring a spare. Pack your goods on Pharo's back. You shouldn't have brought that cart anyway. Too rich. Too attractive. You can see that blue and white paint for miles. I rubbed liniment on Pharo's foreleg, wondering how the fire started.

"A piece of glass," said Jakardos, throwing a blanket across Pharo's back.

"What?"

"A piece of glass. The sun shone through a piece of glass and started the fire."

A chill gripped me. "I hadn't said anything. How did you know what I wanted to know?"

"Wasn't hard to figure out, I've seen fires like that before."

That wasn't what I had meant; I wanted to know how he knew what I was thinking. Little details began to add up. How did he know things he couldn't possibly know? My thoughts must be as transparent as water to him. Violated, my private thoughts spread to view like laundry drying on the bushes. How foolish, how simple I must seem to him. I whirled, ready to fight.

"Please," he urged, hardly whispering, eyes begging forgiveness, voice heavy with....pain? He touched his head, rubbed his temples.

He felt pain. Good. I wanted him to hurt. Such as he should not be permitted to live. An abomination. All the doubt I had felt about the man since the first time I saw him high on his shiny cart–that rich man's cart–fused into explosive anger.

"I'm sorry," he insisted, dropping to one knee. "If I had been talking, Pharo would not have bolted. Please, don't be angry."

What? Confused, I drew back. I had caused his pain? His apology made no sense. How could anything I did, short of pommel him with my fists bring him to his knees? The thought of beating him? My anger could cause him pain? My first impulse was of triumph. I wallowed in a sense of power. I could kill a man, just by thinking it. And where did I go from here? Should he be killed?

I plunged into waves of horror. What if I could kill a man with my anger? What if I couldn't control myself? What if?

And a sudden revelation. This is why Yiayia used to leave me when I felt anger, even though I said nothing.

I had no words for apology. I didn't understand what had just happened. His words repeated themselves in my ear. 'If I had been talking, Pharo would not have bolted.' My head roared in confusion.

"We'll find you another cart at Tergesté, one a bit less gaudy." I sought words, attempting to soothe us both. Color returned to Jakardos' face. With such powers now, what would this young man be when fully mature? Not angry now, but fear of both the powers of this man-boy and for my own capacity for violence, shook me.

"We'll get you a spare wheel. But stay out of my head, wizard. It'll go easier for both of us."

He brushed a hand across his forehead wiping away sweat, nodded, and stood.

"I can control myself when I'm talking," he explained, willing me to understand, though I could see he himself didn't understand.

'*What are you? It hasn't been easy for you, has it?*' I thought, wondering if he heard me. Jakardos turned away, unknowing, honoring his pledge. I no longer smelled the oil of lemons.

꧁꧁꧁

For two days and nights, the mysterious, winking light guided us across the miles, growing brighter in the evening of each day's travel. From the flat lands of grass and marsh we climbed a gentle slope toward

Tharros' mountains. The light finally resolved itself as a bonfire built in Tharros' pasture, a blaze as big as his stable. Lights from hundreds of candles and lamps lit all the windows of all the buildings. People milled around tents pitched on the terraced hillside, and open fires lit little groups hovering near the smoky scent of dripping meat. Horses and donkeys clustered in fences thrown up for temporary stock yards. Someone took Spitter's and Pharo's reins, and guards festooned with many-colored sashes escorted us to the main house. We climbed the outer stairway to the roof, following the sounds of music and laughter.

"You're here!" shrieked Ena, running to me just as she had as a child, clinging to me as though her very life depended on my presence. I knew better. This was just Ena's way when she was happy. "I thought you wouldn't get back in time, but Keo wouldn't wait."

"Wait? Wait for what?"

Keo looked through the open door, and hurried to Ena's side, grinning. "Our wedding." He grabbed her under her arms and slung her round and round, ending by collecting her to his chest and squeezing. "Ena has agreed to become my wife." He spoke only to Ena, gazing into her upturned face.

"Tomorrow, Daneion." Ena pushed Keo away far enough to speak. "We are to be married tomorrow. And Palo! And who is your friend?"

"I am Jakardos," Jakardos offered, "Or Jak if you prefer." He dipped his chin, bending his neck in the manner of one deeply honored. "Your friend was kind enough to allow me to tag along. He saved my life when we came through the marshes, and has taught me much about traveling through strange lands. But he did not tell me about you. And Keo?"

I saved his life? I would have corrected him, but he gave me no opportunity to speak. The master storyteller was off and running, explaining the perils of swamp ghosts, and the terrors of meeting the dead, face to face. Jakardos's circle grew, collecting anyone who came within sound of his voice. Palo, as rapt as anyone, hung on his every word. It was too much. Was I the only one in this house immune to his demon talents?

෴෴෴

Tharros stood on a terrace wall facing the gathering of people. Firelight splashed brilliance from gold threads in the borders of his floor-length blue robe as he raised his arms to welcome his guests.

"Thank you all for following the flames of our wedding fires. Some of you have come from across the sea, others from the mountain tops, and still many more from our very own Tergesté.

Today we welcome you to our home, to celebrate the wedding feast of my son, Keo, and his chosen bride, Ena." He raised his arms and the crowd broke out in cheers.

"Who have you chosen for premarital night, Tharros? Who will seal the Bond of Clans?" The call came from someone in the midst of the crowd. Everyone began calling out names, jostling against those they named and laughing hysterically.

Tharros raised his arms again, and everyone fell silent, waiting. They would joke, but those chosen for premarital night–a member of Keo's family and a member of Ena's–would bed together, consummating the wedding of families. It was a sacred pact, and one of highest honor.

"I have thought long and hard of this. I feared that such a union might not be possible. No one of Ena's blood is here to share our joy. So I have chosen her closest friend, one who has known her since before she could walk, to stand in for her father or brothers, one I have found completely worthy, in every way." He held out a hand and the sleeve swept a wide half circle, seeming to touch every guest in the crowd. "Pelos Daneion! Come forward!"

Nearly choking on the bread I had cozened out of the cook, I spit it out. Ah, I hated doing that. The cook had added preserved figs and fresh cream. I looked around, seeking some place to hide, but someone saw me and hands pushed me forward. I dropped the rest of my bread, swallowed again, coughed, and went forward.

Tharros wrapped his arms around me, nearly smothering me in fine blue cloth. I knew how fine. I had brought it with me from Athens, and before that from Byzantium.

Again facing the crowd, an arm as heavy as a barrel of oil across my shoulders, he squeezed and I coughed, worrying the last of my bread. As the representative of the Clan of Tharros the Bold, I give you–for one night only, mind you," and when the laughter of the crowd died down, he continued, "I give you my daughter."

Daughter? Thera!

"Tharros. Tharros. Tharros," the crowd cheered, and my knees gave way. I would have fallen from the terrace wall but that Tharros' arm held me firmly in place. He whispered in my ear, "Stay with me, friend, it's almost over."

Over? What could be over? My troubles had just begun. I couldn't sleep with Thera. Not after what she had done to Ena. Now I would have to run from Tharros' wrath, not because of Ena but because of Thera. Wildly, I began devising another escape.

Music and dancing began in the gardens, only one of the places musicians had gathered. Like butterflies dancing on air, the notes brushed our ears as we moved from the yard toward the fire pits where whole pigs roasted. Legs and mind numb, I sought a way of escape. Tharros never let go my arm, at times dragging me along when I slowed. Not only must I sleep with his daughter, I would be held captive until I did. Oh. Have I told you that I am a coward?

We passed Jakardos leaning against a door frame, foot propped on a stool. His eyes followed me in our progress, and I had presence enough of mind to wonder why he was alone, not in a group, telling some story. Then I smelled lemons. A tingle streaked through my limbs, like what I felt when touching something after I'd combed my hair and beard. Did I sense a question? Taking a chance, I answered, *'Help me man; get me out of here!'* He grinned, and I knew he had heard me. So his commitment to non-invasion had its limits. Prepared for anger, I felt only relief. I patted Tharros' hand and said, just loud enough for him to hear, "not so hard, my friend, my bones will break." Tharros looked at me and raised his brows, not releasing me, gesturing toward a group of tables and benches.

"Go, go, children," he said to a young couple who had followed us, waiting to serve us should we need something. "Young people need to dance."

Alone, attempting quiet, Tharros whispered, yet Tharros' whisper could call a dog from across a field. "You need not worry, little friend. No consummation of the marriage of the clans will be needed. That was done when Ena married my firstborn. It's all just ceremony. But don't tell Thera," he chuckled. "She needs to be reminded once in a while who is chief here." A trifle more seriously he added, "But if you choose, you may still honor my choice. She is a virgin. I know, for I have had her examined. Giving her away without her will is only just, for the way she has treated Ena." He shrugged. "She had cause for her behavior, I suppose. When Ena took her position as head of the house and servants, Thera was displaced. When Sata was killed, Thera forced Ena to step down. Ena stayed in her rooms to escape Thera's constant rebukes. Now that Ena, married to Keo, will again be the chief wife, Thera's hatred is all the more likely.

"You must still go to her tonight, be seen entering her tent. It will be set up in full view from the house and gardens. People will even be watching from up there." He pointed to smaller fires burning in the hills behind the house.

Was this meant to console me? Why didn't I feel relieved? I dreaded facing that woman, to be closeted with her. She could destroy a man with a glance. And I had no doubt that she concealed a knife beneath the flowing chiton.

回回回

At dusk, two effeminate male servants from Tharros' household came to bathe and dress me. I restrained myself from snatching back Bird's bracelet when they removed it from around my neck. Palo watched. Saying nothing, he took it from the hand of the servant, and placed it in his sleeve.

I minded not at all the tub of hot water and oil they brought to groom me, and I must admit that when the shirt and robe were fitted across my shoulders, I did look rather handsome. I didn't even mind the scented pine water they combed through my hair and beard, though it robbed me of the power to smell anything else. But when they would accompany me to the tent of Tharros' daughter, I faltered. They waited. "Go on," I croaked. "I'll follow. Soon." As soon as I could get my knees firmly locked beneath me.

"Good," said Jakardos, jerking me back away from the tent opening. "Quick, Palo, help me." Jakardos, naked, snatched my robe, then my cloak, and threw them around himself. Palo untied the laces of my sandals, and Jakardos stepped into them even as he fastened the cloak across his shoulder. I watched, too stunned to speak, my mouth, I fear, hanging open till it dripped.

"Shut the flap behind me, Palo," he said, striding through the opening as though on his way to the market, knowing that his cart held by far the more desirable merchandise. Wits finally surfacing, I snatched a girdle from a hook. "Here. Put this over your head."

Fully three strides past the opening, he turned, ducked back in, covered his head, grinned and left again. Hair still damp from the bath, I stood in a draft, chilling. Palo threw a robe across my shoulders. My dirty robe. "Ugh" I said, removed it and rummaged in my bag for another. I came up with the yellow robe I had bought in Patavium—the robe I planned to wear when I saw Bird. Hastily I stuffed it back in, went deeper and brought out a tan robe, one with fringe, wrapped it around me and tied it with a brass girdle. Not as fine as Tharros', but then it wasn't supposed to be. Before I left the tent I also threw a girdle over my head, wrapped it across my chin, and tossed a length over my shoulder, thereby hiding my sun bright, red hair and beard. I joined others watching the tent of Thera, as interested as anyone. Worrying. What if Jakardos were discovered? Someone passed me a bowl of wine and a sweetbread.

The shadows visible through the fabric of Thera's tent disappeared with the snuffing of the candle. As a single person, the crowds waited, silent, hardly breathing. The tradition followed that when the act had been consummated, the honored couple would step outside to be seen and cheered by the crowds, and the man would return to his household, in this case, mine. This time, the tent stayed dark so long the crowds gave up and went home to bed. "Zeus!" the man beside me muttered, rising, "Who would have believed that skinny little guy would last this long."

And that's how my reputation as a great lover originated.

What? You don't believe me?

༺༻༺༻༺༻

I woke to the singing of the morning hymn. Jakardos had not come in at all last night. Burning with curiosity, I rose, dressed, and wandered outside. He stood high on a rock bluff to the east overlooking the valley. The sun, finding him before it found me, illuminated his silhouette in liquid gold against a still dark sky.

For whatever pain and distress he had caused me in the past, at this moment, I forgave him. More than that, I would be grateful forever that he took my place last night. He had saved me from an uncertain humiliation, I am sure. Never could I have wrested desire for Thera from these spindly limbs. I dreaded the woman. Though Tharros had said I need not consummate the Bonding of Clans with her, I dreaded even entering her tent.

Ending his song, Jakardos saw me, waved, and came down from his high place leaping from rock to rock as though his feet had grown wings.

"Did you sleep well?" he asked, and winked.

"Well enough," I said, "and you?"

He grinned. "Not at all. Take my word for it Wallis; never enter the tent of a love-starved woman."

Well, had he enjoyed it or hadn't he? He clapped his hand on my shoulder and said, "I smell beer and hot bread, shall we go eat?"

◰◰◰

Again I dressed in the fringed robe and belted it with the bronze-linked girdle, preparing for the wedding ceremony of Ena and Keo. I washed Palo's hair and trimmed it with his new, keenly-whetted knife, leaving the top and sides long in the manner of young Athenian men. Jakardos dressed in a white robe of finest wool and cinched it at the waist with his new leather belt, and then I trimmed his hair even with his collar. Wetting his hands he pushed it back from his face and dragged his fingers through his beard, looking to me for approval. I nodded and dressed my own hair and beard in a similar manner, holding it down to my scalp with both hands until it obeyed.

◰◰◰

So stunned I forgot to breathe, I watched Ena descend the ancient stairway in the Hall of Skulls. A bride of some pagan god, she seemed, hair streaming in a black cloud about her shoulders, falling from beneath a hammered gold diadem studded with amber, my gift to the bride. An orange ribbon, the color of brides, knotted in an intricate bow and dragging the steps behind her, held the folds of the white dress tight beneath her breasts.

Her eyes found me, lit, then slid past me to a far part of the hall, and darkened. I turned to see what she had seen. Thera, scowling, stood a few paces from Jakardos, fingers brushing his hand. Jakardos moved away and came to stand beside Tharros, Palo and me.

Keo, resplendent in ivory and gold, waited for Ena at the foot of the stairs. Together, they walked across the hall down an aisle parted through the crowd, and stood before the hearth pit laid with wood for the ceremonial fire.

Tharros and I stepped forward. Tharros handed me a wooden key as large as my arm. I laid it across my two hands and held it out to Ena.

A key to the house, her badge of authority. Keo, armed with a live ember from the kitchen, touched fire to wood. It blazed with the first touch. The crowd whooped and cheered, formed a line and circled the hearthstones. This would be a successful marriage, blessed with wealth and many children.

Keo swept Ena into his arms and carried her up the stairway, disappearing into the dusky gloom, leaving a room that felt empty, deserted, despite the people packed shoulder to shoulder, laughing, singing, dancing around the hearth, arm in arm.

When the glaze disappeared from my eyes, I looked around to see Jakardos, looking uncomfortable. Thera stood beside him. Ah, funny.

The wedding celebration lasted three days, and during that time, every time I saw Jakardos he was attempting to hide from Thera. And failing.

回回回

Our donkeys and loaded carts waited on the road in front of the big house, Spitter and her cart, then Pharo and his second-hand cart, and Leo's donkey and cart. I hadn't realized we would be carrying so much. Even Leo's cart was filled. Our good-byes said, our promises to return, our messages to Leo from Ena memorized, Ena held Thelana's hand and leaned into Keo's embracing arm. Jakardos, standing beside Pharo, nervous, distressed. Did he dread to leave Thera? Had the woman managed to cage this young lion?

A commotion arose from one of the outbuildings, and another cart and two donkeys came out of a shed and lined up behind us. "Wait! Wait," a woman called. "I have some more." She and a man hurried down the steps from the big house, carrying a large basket between them. The woman rearranged the things in the new cart then added the large basket. The cart swelled with goods. "Kroté! Go get the other basket. It's beside Friise's bed. My little Friise will need more clothes than this."

Tharros and Thera came down the steps, Tharros scolding, handing Thera a huge money bag, and Thera beaming. I hadn't known she could smile. Tharros handed her up onto Leo's cart and she settled herself into place, tucking in her many scarves, waving to the friends and family and servants who stood nearby.

Thera? Now I was the one dismayed. I turned to Jakardos, waiting an explanation. "I had no choice," he said, defeated. "She would have told Tharros you were not the one to sleep with her. I told her I didn't want marriage, but she would not listen. She just would not listen."

I could not believe my ears. "Tharros thinks you will marry her?"

"No. He knows I don't want her. She still thinks I'll marry her, but I told Tharros that we would find her a husband. He understands. They are all glad to see her go, under any conditions. He has given her a fortune for a dowry."

The man called Kroté brought another large basket down from the house. "Where will I put it, Tass?" he said. "There's no more room on this cart, and the donkey can't carry any more."

Tass looked around, first at the bags, then her cart, then at mine. "There's room there," she pointed. "We'll put it on that one."

My cart? My carefully arranged cart? She would pile stuff on top? I stepped between Kroté and my cart, and waved him away. "There's no room here."

"Yes, there is," said Tass, hurrying up and shoving past me to my cart. "See, here, and here. We can move this box to the back, and that will give space here, next to the seat for the basket. Then Hom and I can ride this cart and look after my Friise's things. Kroté! Where is the bag? Run get it. Hurry, we don't have all day."

Do the Fates follow some perverted design? Do they conspire against me? I who would travel alone, preferring to go unnoticed, would now be traveling with a babbling woman, another so haughty she could harden water with a glance, and a caravan certain to be attacked by the first band of highwaymen we passed. Wildly I planned. Perhaps Palo, Spitter and I could slip away from the rest of the train wherever we camped during the night. But Thera's clothes were now packed in Leo's cart.

"Leave it," I ordered. I. Ordered. Yes I did. "Your mistress will have to get along without it. And you and your husband will have to walk."

"Walk. I can't walk all that way," Tass shrieked. "I am a house servant, not a field worker."

"Oh? Well now, you're a traveler. And travelers walk. You can carry the bag, if you like. See? We're all carrying packs."

She stood open mouthed. Slowly her lips drew into a scowl. She hurled the bag to the ground and jammed her hands on her hips. "We'll see who does the cooking, tonight."

"Ha-onh Ahonh," screamed Spitter, pulling out into the road. I walked, Palo walked, and all the rest followed.

7

Our carts bumped and rolled through the Canyon of Thieves. I scanned the peaks for smoke from breakfast fires. No smoke, but from a rock ledge not too high above our trail, I found the eyes and pale upper face of a girl peeking down on us. She could not have been as old as Palo, perhaps ten or twelve, and as we passed, a glimpse of yellow flashed through a break in rocks and shrubs. She climbed like a goat, toward a thicket growing on a ledge high above our trail. I waved in the direction of the thicket.

Six men rose. One of them pointed across the way. I looked and found three more, all as scrawny, as pale as the girl. I waved to them as well and whistled Spitter to a stop. Rummaging around in my cart, I pulled out a basket of food. Roast pig, bread, cheese and an amphora of wine. I set the entire basket on a flat rock beside the road, waved again and moved on.

"What was that for?" demanded Tass. She had moved her cart ahead of Jakardos' to follow mine, but hadn't seen the people high on the ridge. "Why are you leaving our food? If you are propitiating the gods, you are doing it with our supper."

"Not gods," I said, walking on, disinclined to explain. "Just hungry people."

"It's still our supper," she called from behind me. "You could have asked us first." Then she asked someone behind me, "Where are any hungry people?" I looked at the clearing above, and grinned. No people.

"Go back and get that food, Hom," she said. "It's foolish to leave it lying there."

"It's gone," Hom said, a minute or two later. "Something got it." I heard a sharp intake of breath and then blessed, peaceful quiet.

I spotted a valerian plant twice as tall as I. I whistled Spitter to a stop, and dug out my shovel. What a find! And the woman's herb, pennyroyal. All over the side of the hill.

The whole party came to a stop. I heard exclamations from all down the line, and looked to see everyone coming forward to locate the cause of the disturbance. My patience snapped.

"I'm a doctor! Doctors need medicines. There!" I pointed toward the valerian. "That's what I'm stopping for."

"The sleeping herb," said Tass. "Kroté. Get a digging tool and help him."

"I don't need...." I began, then hushed when I saw Kroté's tool. A no-nonsense affair of iron as sharp as a knife, designed for working. And as he passed, Tass handed him a basket. "Get that pennyroyal too, and that tall plant with the white bloom."

As it turned out, I didn't even need to dig. Kroté loaded the basket and handed it to me. Tass nodded as I passed by, Hom slapped Rocky's hind quarters, and we were moving. Walking alongside the cart, spreading the roots out on the seat, I mumbled curses. Angry, angry that I had begun to respect that impossible woman. Who would have guessed she'd know herbs?

From that moment on, it was Tass who spotted the herbs, Tass who called the caravan to a halt, and Kroté who dug them. Many of them I didn't recognize, but I'd cross the River Styx before I would ask that woman what they were. By the time we reached Narona, twelve days later, all three of the carts were spread with drying herbs.

"We'll set up in the agora," I said to Palo.

Beneath a spreading plane tree, big sheets of white bark peeling away and seed balls hanging heavy on the limbs, we found a place among the other peddlers and set up our boxes. The men and Palo and Thera went to examine the wares of the shops, and I laid a few items out for sale. Tass tied the stems of herb leaves into bundles to hang from a limb, and I cleaned and rinsed the roots we had gathered. As it turned out, I didn't have to ask her what they were; she talked to herself as she worked. I just listened.

Tass saw the seedling weeping tree. Grown to about the height of my knee, it had begun its eternal quest of return to self, drooping its tendrils to explore the dirt in the pot at its feet. She grew silent, staring. "Where did you find it?"

"North of the Alps, beyond the Danube," I said, "near a hot springs in a forest that stays warm all through winter."

She nodded. "I have heard of the place. My grandfather visited the mother tree when I was a child. He had visions. Did you sit beneath the tree?"

I looked away, reluctant to describe my experience. How could she understand?

She did not ask more, just nodded. "My grandfather would never tell what he saw either."

"What did you say that mullein was for?" I asked and Tass smiled, such a lovely smile, with dimples in wide, rounded cheeks.

"Sore throat," she answered, beginning a long streak of explanations about the other herbs. Many I knew, but said nothing, listening with half an ear, to see if her use differed from mine. Meanwhile I scrubbed roots and patted them dry, searching for faces among the crowd. Bodies parted momentarily, to reveal Jakardos speaking with a peddler. A peddler who looked like me.

A bit dizzied, feeling slightly displaced, I sought a clearer view. He stood leaning against his cart, cleaning his teeth with a straw, smiling and nodding at Jakardos, talking. Interested, I watched as long as I could, catching glimpses through the throngs of people. When they finished, Jakardos clapped him on the shoulder, much as he usually did me, and ambled off toward the water and a produce stand selling pomegranates, nuts, and melons.

Palo bought leather strings, and I wondered what he had in mind. Hom and Kroté with their heads together talking, drinking mead, and Thera searched through layer after layer of fabrics.

Not yet hungry, I walked through the plaza examining merchandise, found two pots I thought Ana would like, and returned to my roots. Tass sat on a box with her chin propped on her hand, watching children playing with plane tree seed balls. As it sometimes happens in times like these, images took on vibrant life, images that would stay with me forever—a flash of red, a ribbon someone had tied around the neck of a goat; a black and white bird sitting on a limb above our herbs, cleaning its wings; a mother nursing her baby, rocking back and forth on her stool and crooning. Could these be the fierce Illyri Olympias had warned me about? The ones who sent warriors to raid their stores every year following harvest?

What was the little bird doing now? Was she entertaining dignitaries from the Hellespont? Having drawings made for a sculpture? No. She hated posing. She said no artist she knew could sculpt or paint her as she thought she looked.

She lived in another world now, a world that, to me, seemed fashioned from fantasy—in any event, a world that did not include me. I pressed the bracelet against my chest. A gift for a queen, a toy for somebody else's wife. My stomach hollowed. I laid out smoked fish we had bought from a tradesman when we ferried across the clusters of islands yesterday. "Tass," I said, "are you hungry?"

▣▣▣

The second day out of Narona, we walked along a plateau of land near the water and watched the world come awake. Fisher boats loaded gear for their day, and smells of breakfast from the seafaring peoples rose with currents of air from the sea. Palo and Jakardos hurried away from the trail to buy fish and bread. We ate and walked, always with an eye toward the sea, the rocks, the sea birds, the sail boats—and the darkening skies. Half a day more should find us in Skodra where there would be shelter and supplies.

I stepped aside, waiting for Jakardos to catch up. "Isn't that peddler ahead of us one we saw in the agora at Narona?"

"I think that's his cart. You could pass for doubles. He's maybe a bit older."

"Do you know him?"

He glanced down at his sandals. "I've seen him around."

I sniffed that lemon scent again. My anger flashed. He winced.

"He told me he's headed for the gold fields," he said, a bit too fast, and without that peculiar resonance in his voice. "He wants to buy gold to trade with Philip. He expects to fill his cart with trade goods at Pella."

"What would Philip want with gold?"

"To pay mercenaries. He's rebuilding his army after the war at the lakes."

I wondered how to ask the question. "Did the peddler tell you all that, or did you..."

Jakardos glared. "He told me," he snapped, then shrugged. "People tell me things."

This man had more tricks than a circus juggler. People told him things, he says, just like that, as though it were the most unimportant thing in the world. They told him, whether with or without actual words. I doubted he even knew the difference. As an afterthought, I wondered what I had told him. Nothing much, I decided. First of all I detested his controlling voice, and second, I seemed able to keep him out of my head with my anger.

"Go on," I said. "What else did the peddler tell you?"

Jakardos grunted, a tiny sound, deep in his throat. I waited. "He knows of you," he said finally, reluctantly. "He passed through Amber soon after you."

Could this be Raben, the merchant who traded with the People of the Trees? Was he carrying birds? "Jakardos, does he keep birds?"

He avoided my eyes.

"There he is," he said. "Ask him." Why did I feel challenged?

⁙⁙⁙

No, I decided. Raben did not look like me. His hair was too long, and silver hair glinted from the red. One eye drooped as though half asleep, and the tip of his tongue peeked out the side of his mouth. His jaw extended like a pouch; he chewed something. He spat, just missing me. I eased up to walk beside him, to the left of his cart. His donkey needed brushing and I smelled month-old man sweat, even though he had just left Narona with its bath pools. But when he looked at me with that one fully opened eye, I sensed a crafty intellect that it would pay me to watch.

"Your donkey has a limp," I said, moving closer. "I noticed it from a short way back. I thought you might want to know." The donkey had no limp, but most drivers pay no such attention to the beast that pulls their cart.

"Been there all his life," he said, agreeing. "Limped when he first started walking, limps now, when he wants me to stop so he can graze." He patted his donkey's flank. Dust rose. "You look a little like me, you know, after I've cleaned up a bit. Don't waste much time washing when I'm on the road. Just get dirty again."

"I have some liniment I can rub on your donkey's leg, and check his hoof for you if you like, when you stop."

He chuckled. "Rub him all you like, but he'll still limp if he has a mind to."

"I have to warn you. My donkey is moving up on your rear. She doesn't like to follow. Never can tell what she'll do. Up the road a ways, she nipped a stallion who tried to lead, and he threw his rider."

Raben looked behind, glared at Spitter. She glared back. "Bring her around," he said. "Plenty room up front. Old Baldy won't mind. He's used to being treated like a donkey."

His inference stung. Spitter was no ordinary donkey. "I heard you've visited the palace in Pella. Make many sales?"

Spitter pulled to the lead and Palo and Jakardos moved up from behind. Raben noticed them, nodded. Jakardos sneezed. I looked around, but didn't see any birds. "Sold everything I had. Philip came out and looked at the merchandise himself. Didn't even ask a price, just bought it all. I was just up from Athens with a full load. Too expensive for most people. Not for him. Then when I totaled up, he sent somebody inside to get money." He laughed. "The boy told me later Olympias gave it to him. From her own pouch. She looked madder than a boar hog."

"Perhaps she didn't like using her dowry money to pay for his purchases."

"Dowry. You think that is her full worth? I've heard stories. She's rich. Not that it serves her much. The word is that Philip is already scouting new territory. She bores him. Maybe she's getting too old. He never sleeps with her."

"The queen is very beautiful. Did you see her?"

"Humph. No. These high and mighty women don't like to show themselves much. They send slaves out to do their bidding. She's some kind of priestess too. Maybe thinks she's too good for him. Maybe she is. He'll have her money spent the first year, if what he bought from me is any sign."

I felt a rush and knew Jakardos was questing again. I let him in. I don't know how I did it, I just didn't get angry. I needed his help.

"Women." Jakardos sneered. "Who understands them? Real men don't try. We just take what we want from them. Luckily the law backs our side."

"Jakardos," said Raben. "Didn't realize you were traveling with the peddler. Want to visit the gold fields with me? You can make your fortune in one trip."

Jakardos' face lit up like a child's at the sight of honey cakes. "Hey, that's not a bad idea. What could I trade?"

"They'll take anything. Food is good, and games and horses. That donkey of yours ought to bring a good price." He laughed. "Course those stupid miners might try to eat him." The two of them bent nearly double, laughing. It wasn't that funny. Eat Pharo? I couldn't believe what I was hearing.

Then the truth hit. They were laughing at me. At me! Finally, red in face, they hushed. Still grinning, Raben pulled a huge, dirty linen from his sleeve and blew his nose.

"I'd like to buy some of those birds you're carrying," I said.

Both Raben's eyes opened wide and the little pink tongue disappeared. He stared at Jakardos. "You told him?"

"No," said Jakardos, sneezing again. "He isn't stupid you know."

"No, guess not. You'll do just fine, Peddler." He uncovered a cage filled with pigeons, releasing a raucous chorus of coos and a spate of sneezing from Jakardos.

"I'll trade these for some of those leather goods you're carrying. If you need me, just wrap a message around the foot of one of those birds with the red thread and release it. It'll find me, wherever I am." He winked. "I keep their mates with me. They always know where home is." Raben lifted one of the cages, and Palo took it. Hurrying ahead to our cart, he coo-coo-cooed, set the cage on top of the canvas and slipped his hand inside to pet the birds.

"This is my road," said Raben, pulling left on his donkey's rein. He threw up a hand and called back over his shoulder, "When you give the queen her bracelet, tell her Danu and her people welcome her." He disappeared up the road. To this day I can hear the sound of his laughter fading in the distance. So he knew about the bracelet. Suddenly I hated him. Sly old devil. What else did he know? Could he read minds too? Or had Jakardos shared my business with a stranger? I began to feel like a chicken in a cage full of lions—not scared, exactly, but should I be?

Jakardos sneezed again and dropped back to walk with Thera, Kroté, and Hom. Tass had found a place lying on the seat of Leon's cart. She slept, gently snoring. The donkey would tire too easily with her added weight, but I said nothing. Tass was, after all, not a real traveler. Only a house servant.

8

At Skodra, the road forked. The way to the left led toward the lakes where Philip had met Bardyllis on the field of blood. I could not go that way. The ghosts of soldiers I could not save waited to haunt me. And over all, the specter of Philip, a powerhouse of frenzied energy, darting here, there, everywhere at once, and always beside him, his general, the straight-backed warrior with cold lips. Parmenion. I had looked into the eyes of that general when he rode by the tents to view the wounded, and when he had caught up with Palo and me to give us Philip's coins. Where Philip radiated heat, Parmenion chilled, gave order and direction, funneling the king's energy to devastating result. I dared not meet his eyes again for fear that he would remember me.

Uncle Davos lived near the west coast, very near the road we traveled. I would take that route. I had no healing herb to leave with him now, the sacred herb from the Tree of the Green Man. Ozhio's family had planted it in their garden, even before I left. That decided, I did no more than stop to refill our water jugs in Skodra and let the donkeys drink. We needed food but the street vendors of that mean little town of the tribe of the Labeaté were few, and those sold no food. The hollow-eyed stares of pinched-cheek women and children followed us, waiting in feral stealth to snatch anything left unwatched. None of our party complained our early leaving.

So this was the aftermath of Philip's and Bardyllis' great war. I dared not show sympathy. They had forgotten the impulse toward kindness, searching only for weakness. Here are your fierce Illyroi, Olympias. Starving. They won't bother you for a while, for they have eaten their war horses.

It was not until an hour past Skodra, past the fork in the road, past my point of choosing, that I could drop the pretense. The road turning left had led straight into Pella. To Olympias. With all my heart I wanted to go to her, yet just as surely dreaded to enter her presence. I would have to see her, I knew. She would call, and I would answer. Oh, had I the fortitude to deny her. I walked, not speaking for a long while, not seeing the restless waves dashing the rocks far below our path nor hearing the cries of feeding seabirds. Resting my hand on the side of the cart to guide my steps, I walked beneath a sky weighed with wind-smeared clouds. Like fingers of destiny, they all targeted me. Where could I go? Not even the lands of the Keltoi had obliterated Bird's image; rather had she followed me, staining my memories. I swallowed repeatedly, trying to relax the knot grown hard in my throat.

A bird landed on my hat, skewed it sideways, fell onto my shoulder and slid off. Before it hit the ground it soared back up and landed on my shoulder. "What?" I tried to dodge, then to brush it off, but it clung to my shirt with its talons. There I was, flinging my arms around trying to brush it off, but each time I succeeded, back it came, screeing and squawking. A pigeon from the cage. "Palo! Why did you let it out? It'll get lost."

Palo, racked with convulsive, silent laughter, doubled over beside Spitter, hanging onto her mane for support. Jakardos, attracted to the commotion hurried up from behind. Then, between sneezes, he began laughing too, all as I struggled to rid myself of the pesky bird. Jakardos pointed to my shoulder. I twisted my neck to see. There, hidden within the folds of the girdle tied around my neck, I found seeds. Seeds! How had they gotten...? "Palo." I reached for him, intending to teach him a lesson he'd never forget. He ran, looking back and laughing. He knew I'd never catch him, not in a thousand years.

I brushed the seeds off onto the ground, and two birds fell on them like buzzards on a sick jackel. I stood with hands on hips glaring at Palo and then at Jakardos. Jakardos quit laughing, and tried to look innocent. I relented, reached into Spitter's barley bag and drew out more seeds, sprinkling them along the ground as I walked. The birds, all out of the cage now, followed, pecking at the ground with every step. Palo opened the cage and all the other birds hopped in like a well-rehearsed acting crew. All but two. Those, the ones with the red thread tied around a foot, took to the air and headed north. To find Raben, of course. The world suddenly rushed in on me. I felt the air, cool and moist from the sea, and I smelled cheese in the saddle bags on Spitter's back. I noticed that my left foot had developed a blister. It all felt good, even the blister. For a few precious minutes, I had been distracted from brooding about Olympias.

🮰🮰🮰

Uncle Davos was past any need for herbs. His widow said he had died peacefully, in his sleep, and she gave me a box he had left for me. Inside, I found two rings. One I remembered seeing on my grandmother's hand, the other, a plain silver band Davos had fashioned for his little finger. I thanked her and left, sad that I had not told Davos good-bye, but knowing how glad he must be, now, free of seizures. Besides, I didn't even know if the herb could have helped.

A dust cloud as black as my mood glutted the city of Athens. It neither shifted nor settled all the time we watched, approaching. I chilled, despite the heat. The gates to the city hung open, and we entered unchallenged. Letting our caravan roll past me onto singed and dirty streets, I stopped to speak to Kalais, the guard at the gate, half-nude now, and wiping his bald head with a cloth. The cloth left grainy, dry streaks on his scalp and face.

"No rain, more than a month," Kalais said. "Wells are low, some gone dry. The soldiers are back from Boeotia. E'via is ours again. The Boeotians hadn't the heart to fight." He waved me through, and reached for the towel again. "Our war horses are pulling wagons now, bringing in water. Did you see any of them on the road?"

"No," I said, "Didn't see much of anything. Quiet. Too quiet."

"Not too quiet for the Makedoné your princess Olympias married. I hear he's traveling the country with troops, speaking to anybody who'll listen. 'Insulted,' he says. 'It is the citizens of Athens who have been insulted, and not by him.' I never heard how he thought we'd been insulted, just that he thinks we should fight, but people are listening. I'd like to know who he thinks will do the fighting. Not those highbrow demos, anyway, you can bet on that."

I trailed after our carts, leaving the guard ranting behind me. "No. It won't be those aristocrats. It'll be me, they send, that's who. I got nothing against Philip. He's a good soldier he is, drinks with the men. Downs as dark a wine as the best of them....."

This made no sense. Philip wanted the Athenians to fight? Against him? My head swam, and my eye lids scratched from the dust. Ana would have water. Her well never went dry. I would spill bucket loads over my head.

⁌⁌⁌

Dimitri's olive trees, growing along the road all the way from the gate to the house had suffered nothing from the drought. Branches grew thick and leaves clustered tight around olives. A picker saw us, yelled a greeting, threw down his rake and started running for the house. Before we neared the gates, I smelled water. A crowd of people carrying buckets hovered outside Ana's gates, but broke to allow us passage when Vitos motioned them aside. Servants hauled water from the fountain and filled buckets one by one, waving for the next. Delos came running out to take a dive at Palo, and Dimitri came from the shed wiping his face with a towel. I heard women shouting from within the house and a few moments later Ana stood at the door releasing waves of scent from hot bread and roast garlic.

"Come," she called, beckoning us inside out of the sun. Servants unhitched the carts and led our donkeys away to the watering troughs. Tass began fussing with Thera's hair to tuck in the strands of her braids, a hopeless effort. Dust crusted her body from head to foot.

"Never mind," I said, "Ana will understand. The servants inside will help you."

Thera tried to smile. I know it was an effort; nothing in her background had prepared her for the role she must now play, that of a spinster, at the mercy of the woman of the house. "Ana is nice," I urged. "You'll see. Don't worry."

"If you'd stopped at a river so we could bathe, we'd be presentable for strangers," Tass retorted, and snuffed.

"In what?" I asked. "The river was dry." Traveling with women was awkward. I vowed never to do it again.

Together, Palo and Delos pulled the cage of pigeons out of the cart, and a roar of bird coos erupted. Delos whooped with excitement. "I know where we can put them. In the shade in the courtyard."

"Delos! I called. "Don't let anyone wring their necks for dinner." Servants came to help unload and carry the boxes and bags into the house. "Upstairs," I called. "Don't clutter up the porch. I lifted the box containing the vases and headed for the house. I couldn't wait to show them to Ana, to surprise her.

Wiping flour from her hands with an apron, Ana tucked her hair behind her ear and held the door open for me. "Who are our guests?" She asked, smiling. She'd missed a spot of flour on her nose. I shifted the box to my left side to free a hand and brushed at her nose with a finger. She raised the apron edge and brushed at the spot. "A princess. A princess who thinks she can get Jakardos to marry her by following us down here," I grumbled. "She and her maid have been nothing but trouble all the way."

"Now Urval," she grinned. "What happened?"

"Urval," I said. The real Urval lived alone, away from the road, back in the fields near the wall. Ana sometimes gave him food and he always grumbled when he saw what it was. He never thanked her, and he always ate whatever she gave him. Then he took the jars to market to sell. I smiled, as she knew I would.

"Did you ever get your jar back? The pretty one with goats frolicking. You should give him food in plain jars. He never brings them back. Better than that, give him no food at all."

"He needs the money from the sale of the jars. But he's too proud to take it. This way at least he will have money for a shirt." A shirt. The man didn't buy shirts, he waited till the rags hung on him and some kind vendor gave him another. He bought wine with the money from the jars.

"Who is Jakardos?" she asked.

"It's a long story, little mother, and I don't know where to begin. He's the tall man talking to Vitos. He attached himself to us up the road a ways." I eased the complaint in my voice, not caring to be called Urval again. "He saved me and Palo from certain death." Her mouth rounded and her brows knit. "It's over, now, and we're none the worse for the trial. I'll tell you about it later, or better yet, get Jakardos to tell you. He's a much better story teller than I." He had also saved my skin when he took my place in Thera's tent, but I thought better about telling her that.

Ana hurried away to see to her guests without taking the box. I followed voices to the back, stepping into cool shadow beneath the shelter Dimitri had made for the courtyard. Thatching grass lay across six beams, shielding the court from the sun. A welcome draft of air brushed my hair and beard.

"Ours is one of the few springs in Athens that still flow," Vitos was saying. "I have to wear my temple vestments to command enough respect to keep the street people from overrunning the house and yards, just coming to get water."

Palo had set the infant weeping tree on the floor under the shelter. Vitos picked it up and examined it. "I've never seen anything like this," he said. "Think it'll grow here?" I shrugged, almost too tired to speak, set the box of vases beside a column, and collapsed on a marble bench, welcoming the chill.

I lay on the bench, pulled a blue and yellow pillow beneath my head, and closed my eyes. Vitos hurried away to settle a dispute at the gates, and Jakardos followed. The world and its noises receded. No longer did I hear words, only voices fading in and out, blending in an ambiance of home. Athens.

Ana woke me with a touch on my shoulder. I sat up. "Olympias sent a message for you," she said. "She wants you to come. Bendi will meet you at the tombs in Aegae and lead you to her camp."

Bird wanted to see me? Tingles swept up my spine. I looked away and struggled to speak past the knot in my throat. I failed. Swallowed

Ana touched a cool hand to my cheek "She is married, Toppi, only married. She's not dead."

☙❧☙

"It's all a game to Philip." Ana set fresh cream on the table for our breakfast. "Demosthenes and his Philippics are just spice to his sauce. Anytime Demosthenes gets all fired up with another oratory, Philip just laughs, pushing him further to see how far he'll go."

"What do you think Philip intends?" asked Jakardos, holding out his bowl, smiling at the servant. Blushing, she poured sweet curd and went back to the kitchen for more.

"Nothing," she said. "He intends nothing. He just delights in provoking Demosthenes."

"What he did with Argaios and his troops was decent," said Dimitri.

"Somebody want to tell me what's going on?" I asked. "I've been away, you know."

"There's nothing decent about that man," said Ana. "He just wants to drink and whore in the streets with boys."

"Now, Mother, you can't believe all the gossip you hear in the market. And anyway, the ways of a foreigner are different from ours. Sorry, Thera, I didn't mean you."

Thera's brows knit as though trying to understand the quick Athenian speech. Ana passed her more spiced apples, smiling.

"I don't listen to gossip, Dimitri," she chided. "Olympias sends messages. She's homesick."

"Well pardon my saying, dear, but you can't listen too much to Olympias, either. You know how headstrong she is."

Ana paused in her return to the kitchen, putting her hands on her hips. "And who should I listen to? You're away all day with your apples and plums and pears and cheese and goats and... You don't give a fig about politics anyway. It's all nonsense to you." She hurried away to the kitchen and came back with bread.

"What did that barbarian do?" I pressed. "Kill somebody?" The king's bloody image remained in my mind, and that is how he would always appear to me, regardless of any fine cloak he might choose to wear.

"No, he didn't kill somebody. That's what Demosthenes is all-fired up about," Ana said. "Argaios and about three thousand Athenians and mercenaries went to Aegae trying to get the royals to reseat him as king of Makedonia. The people just laughed at him. Philip caught Argaios sneaking away. Trapped him in the mountain passes. Didn't kill a single soldier. Sent them home. Even gave the Athenian citizens gold 'to pay them for their trouble,' is what he said."

Jakardos laughed. "He wanted them to know he could do with them what he would, and they could do nothing at all about it. It's a tactic used by the Keltoi warriors. Sometimes they fight with sticks. A touch and you're supposed to be dead. The losers go home sore, but still alive."

"So that's what Kalais, the gate guard was talking about," I mused. "Something Philip had said. That the Athenians had been insulted, all right, but not by him. I guess he meant Argaios had insulted them by not fighting, just surrendering."

"If one doesn't fight, one doesn't deserve the honor of being killed?" asked Ana. "Is that it? Men! What honor is there in being dead?"

"It makes a kind of sense," said Jakardos. "Philip's prestige is one of the weapons in his arsenal. He gained points in the minds of thousands by defeating Argaios' army, and all without losing a single Makedonian."

"You think he's a good tactician, then," I said. "That he can win wars with talk, not arrows."

"Sounds that way to me. Costs less too."

"He's not concerned with money," I said. "Spends it like pebbles tossed into water."

"It's Olympias' money anyway," said Vitos. "She's a careful spender. Philip wanted her to give all her money to him. Said he would know best where to spend it. I told her I'd keep it for her till she called for it. She gave him some, though. That's probably what he paid the Athenian soldiers with." His chin dimpled. "He probably thinks that's all she had. And she's not telling him any different."

"Be careful, Vitos," said Ana. "Philip is a dangerous man. He plays the fool, but he's cunning."

"I would do nothing, say nothing, to bring the princess harm, sister," he said. "You know that."

Delos and Palo burst in from where they had been eating outside. "Papa," said Delos. "We need some more cages for the birds. They're all crowded up in there. And we want to see them fly."

"You'll need to wait till they're hungry," said Jakardos. "Then release only one of a pair. Then they'll come back to eat, back where their mates are kept."

"Is that how it works?" I asked. "They return to their families?"

"Just like people," said Jakardos. He glanced at Thera.

"I will keep your secret," said Thera. "Tharros keeps pigeons too. I brought two to release when we arrived here. He will know we arrived safely."

We all stared at her. This woman had layers we had not plumbed. Not only had she understood our speech, she had kept her own secrets. I hadn't known she carried pigeons.

Jakardos burst out laughing. "So that's why I always sneezed when I came near your cart. I thought you had brought feather bedding."

"I sleep on a mat," she said. "The same as you." They shared a look that I could only guess about. I raised my brows and Jakardos flushed. When I went up to my room, I saw that Ana had put Jakardos in with me, and Thera, Tass and her guards in the rooms over the shed. Smart lady.

回回回

Palo and I started north toward Aegae early the next morning.

Outside the Thiusi walls people had already gathered to fill their water jars. As he often did, Dimitri walked with us through the groves to the city gates, attempting to share his last private thoughts with me, away from the business of the house.

"I'll start those cages for the birds right away," he said, and slapped my shoulder, then on second thought wrapped his arms around my neck, squeezing my head to his chest. "Give the princess my love, and tell her...tell her we are still her family."

"Family, yes," I said. "Still family."

He turned back at the gates, leaving Palo and me to our journey, using the light of the moon to guide our footsteps. Spitter Honh a honhed, an answer to the strains of Jakardos' morning song that floated out to us, his way of saying farewell, safe journey.

Was it coincidence that Palo's and my steps kept rhythm with his music? I wished I could sing like Jakardos or play a flute like Palo. A friend had taught me to play the lyre when I was younger than Palo, but I had never bought an instrument of my own. Too bulky to take onto the road. All I could do was whistle. So I whistled. It helped keep my mind off where I was going.

Olympias

Philip is not a man. He matches words with elegance, sometimes brilliance, but when the audience has retired to their expensive quarters in his doma, he is a ship at sea, awash without a rudder. Wandering in a cloud, spinning in a circle, he turns to shallow advisors waiting to spring. In treacherous flattery they lead him, all to their own ends. They lie in wait, offering boys for love and wine for comfort, even as they spend his gold robbed from his marriage bed. 'Celebrate life!' the false ones say, and then laugh behind their hands at their shallow king's fumblings.

So much could have been done for the people. Food for the starving in the winter time, shelter and protection for women and children without families. He would turn to me, for I am a rock projecting high above the waves, but his counselors block his view, ridiculing me as a barbarian ignorant of the needs of noble Makedonians—I, only a woman. I shame him. I am defeated.

'Sire a son' say his counselors. 'Without a proper heir your dynasty is condemned. Then, when they lead the king to me stumbling with drink, they watch, standing in full light, to see that I keep to my place, that I submit in silence.

But never has Philip's seed taken root in my womb. My son does not accept this mortal's offering. He refuses to be quickened in stupor.

I sit atop the mountain at the place of offerings where countless women have waited to speak with the ancestors. I watch the valley below. The physician appears. Bendi steps from the bushes to meet him, catches him under the arms, swings him wide, laughing. Bendi is a good judge of men. He loves Wallis. Bendi and Palo wait near the tents. I hear Wallis approaching, climbing the path below my watching place. The spirits of the ancestors call me, applauding. It is their doing that my old friend is here. Not mine. It is for them that I have come to Chau. Even as the old ones lay upon me their benediction, I dedicate to them my allegiance.

I stand, reach for Old Sun. It drowns me in warm approval, its colored rays beaming through clouded drapery. From out of a universe too great to contain, I sing my songs of anguish. My voice touches the sun-warmed stones, the burial places of the ancestors. This must be, I hear them call, for we have willed it.

And I have willed it. But Wallis will not offer. Never will he present himself. His *areté*, his honor, does not permit it.

I crumple to the rock. I allow my right leg to swing to the side. My foot does not touch the ground. I pull my left knee up to my breast and wrap it with my arms. I offer myself to the sun, to the Earth waiting since time began for this day, waiting for me to come to sit, to take my place. I relax, spread my legs and think: This man and no other shall father my son.

9

I slowed, breathing easy in this low mountain air, still strong from my journey into the high mountains of the Galli. I stopped some distance away to look at her, to remind myself that this was a real woman, not a goddess, for so she seemed to me. She sat on a rock poised between heaven and earth, her nose and the square of her chin above a bare shoulder profiled against the sky. She stood, held her arms out to the powers of earth and sky and turned—once, twice, eyes shut, chin lifted, offering herself to the wishes of the old ones, putting her life, her will into their hands. A single misstep and she would topple, plunging to her death among the trees, the rocks, the shrubs at the foot of the cliff. Back arched, arms raised high and spread wide, lifting her face to the parting sun, she began a trill, loo-loo-loo-loo, ah-h-h, ee-e-e, mmmm-m-m-n—so long, so long she called, not drawing a breath. So lonely, so sorrowful, the sound spilled into the winds to be carried across the land.

I stepped backward into the black shadows of the trees, not wishing her to see that I had witnessed her private moments, and waited for her return from communion, waited for her to rejoin a world peopled with mere mortals. With me.

Having spent her breath, she inhaled, drawing her arms inward to her heart. Then she crumpled, laying her face against the stone.

"Wallis, " she said, without looking. "I thought you'd never come."

I said nothing, too startled for reply. She turned, found me and smiled, though not the joyous smile I had rushed for miles to see. Again she sat, one leg turned toward me, the other caught up at the knee and held with her arm. Her unbound hair fluttered, and her gown, drenched in the orange and purple colors of the sunset, billowed in the rising winds. She tucked the chiton between her legs, sat on it, and pushed her hair behind her ear. "I saw you coming up the trail. See?" I moved nearer and looked where her hand pointed. Indeed, the path I had climbed crossed beneath her vantage point, beyond a narrow, bush-choked gorge. "I saw you and Bendi and Palo coming up the hill, past the tombs." She patted the rock beside her and I climbed up. "I ran up here to watch, to wait for you."

Searching for the words, willing me to understand, she curled her hand inside mine and leaned her head against my shoulder. I put my arm around her and pulled her head to my chest, content to be near her, to smell the flower scent of her hair, her skin, musky from running. Together we looked out over the cliff to the shining columns of the old palace turned golden in the last light of the day, and the remains of the tombs of the family of the Argeadai, somehow cleansed in the heat, the neutrality of time. We were two people alone, detached from the world, needing, wanting no others, neither of us daring to speak lest the spell be broken and we be plunged earthward, our moment stilled by the ordinary.

"He cares nothing for the land, the people," she said, finally. "He is not cruel, he is..."

"I know," I said, finally. "I saw him at the Battle of Ochrid. The dead and wounded lay around him like pebbles on the sand. He walked past them as though that is truly what they were. Pebbles. Rocks. He kills without conscience. Without remorse."

She pulled away, stood, wrapped her arms about herself. I gazed, weak with fantasy. "He cares more for his horses than he cares for me or anyone, and he uses the pages, the boys sent to him by the nobles, giving no thought to their feelings. Some of them love him. He has that ability, you know, to inspire love. He just doesn't feel it himself. He doesn't feel hate either. I have seen him argue. He fights with words as surely as swords; he bends the will, the thoughts of others as he would bend twigs, but his words do not touch himself. No wonder the spirits of the ancients do not approach him. He is hollow."

Not wanting to rush, dreading to leave this sacred, protected place, we yet began the descent, past old ashes on old cairns, timeworn evidence of sacrifices toward forgotten ends. Shadows lengthened, so enclosing the trail in darkness that we sought footing by touch and a kind of seeing that I imagine my blind old Yiayia would know. It was by that same perception that I knew she wept, for she made no sound. I stopped, gathered her in my arms and felt the sobs shake her body from the depths inside. "I wanted to be a good wife, a good queen." Her words choked in her throat. "I was willing to use my friends, my people, my gold to make this marriage work, so we could make things better for them. But it is killing me. I cannot bear the humiliation he heaps on me whenever I show my face among his companions. I am a princess of Molossis, the Bride of Dionysus! Not a s-slave girl."

I jerked her around to face me. "He offered you to his friends?"

"He dares not go that far, but he ridicules me when I speak. He says 'What would a woman know of these things?' His men and his boys and his women laugh, then ignore me."

"Welcome to the world, princess," I said. "And keep your dagger close at hand. Neither this man nor his friends can be trusted."

"I have something better than a dagger," she said. "I have the altar snakes. One sleeps in a jar at my feet, in the very urn you brought me from the cave of my ancestors. She would harm no one, and must be coaxed even to eat a mouse, but none of the court knows this. She terrifies them."

A convulsion of dread washed over me. The people in the village already distrusted her, a foreigner. The snakes would only add to her terrible mystique. "You must win the people, little bird, or they will turn against you."

"How can I do that? Philip's general, Antipatros, surrounds me and my attendants with guards whenever we go out. I never have a chance to speak with the villagers. These last three days I have been forbidden to show my face at court. Philip says 'go visit your friends, speak with the dead. See if they will act against me. And he laughs, but it is laughter without mirth, for he fears my powers as priestess.

"He does not know how I love this place, how I long for the peace known only by the spirits." This from the fiery princess with dogs so fierce my heart thundered when the great black looked my way.

She tripped, I reached to catch her, and my hand caught her breast. I moved it away, but she brought it back against her and pressed it there. How natural it seemed to me to draw her in, pressing her body against mine, dipping my face to bury against her neck. The scent, the overwhelming feminine scent of her.

Knees too weak to sustain me, I leaned onto her, and she pulled me down, down, to lie on freshly fallen leaves and soft mountain mosses. Wind soughed through the pine limbs overhead, and earth and wood smells enclosed us from any but our own senses, our feelings. With this surge of joy I realized that with the final breath of every night since I had fled north, I had held her just so in my heart. "Princess. Little Bird, I must not do this." I pulled away.

"It's all right, Wallis. Without you, without this...this touching, I will become as hollow as he is. Make me real, old friend. Make me whole, a woman. A real woman."

"You don't understand. Any child of mine will carry a curse. The shaking sickness. The seizures. I cannot do that to you."

"You cannot hurt me, Wallis. You could never hurt me." She paused and then blurted, "I am already pregnant."

"What? You bear a child? I have silphium. You can abort. You must not have a child right away. Wait a year or two until your rights have been established. Take charge of your army. Meet Philip as an equal. It is the only thing he respects." I had thought dead any ambition to return her to power, but seeing the discontent in her marriage aroused my dreams as fierce as ever.

I tried another approach. You will lose your birthright as priestess. Use the power you have to gain a measure of control. The child can come later—in its rightful time."

"There is power in motherhood, Wallis. Once, when I felt no reason to continue to live, you asked me if there was nothing I cared about. Not even having children. I need this baby, Wallis. I will shrivel and die without it." She pulled my hand between her legs. "I need you to touch the baby, to bleach the stain that man has left on me, on my skin, on my life. I need you to give my baby your spirit."

Even as I protested she bared herself to me and lifted my shirt. With the touch of her fingers, all will departed. I had no strength to resist her even if I would. Pushing me back, into the leaves, she straddled my body, one knee on either side of my hips. She guided me between her thighs and into warmth, into sweet moisture. Moving forward and back, forward and back, keeping rhythm to our breathing, a kind of humming growl rose from her chest. I convulsed, she cried out, and we lay still.

An owl hooted; something scrabbled in the dead leaves. I sat up, gave her a hand full of moss to clean herself, and pulled her to her feet. We continued down the hill, on the path canopied with pine and oak leaves, seeing with the night vision that comes after a time away from the light.

Olympias' people sat around their camp fires, talking in subdued voice. No one approached us when we appeared, and I knew they talked about us. Bird pulled me into her tent. Palo began a melody with his flute—soft and slow. The talking ceased, and Bird and I rested on her pallet, my arm beneath her head, allowing the music to lull us to sleep.

Light from a lamp awoke me, and I flexed my arm, numb from the weight of her head, to bring back the life. She sat looking at the bracelet I had laid on the mat between us. "What is this, Wallis?"

Turning it over and over, she held it to the light, catching the gleam of the metal, the stones, the coin. She polished the metal with the hem of her dress, and held it up again. "Do you like it?" I asked. "See, on the coin. It is Athené. And inside, her owl. You are Athena, and I am the owl, your eye to the world."

I thought to see joy in her eyes, but instead, I saw mystery. "It hums when I hold it," she said. "I feel it into the bones of my arms, my chest, my legs, my belly. What is it? Where did you get it?"

"Such a long story, princess. One you may not believe."

"I must know, Wallis. Something within me cries out to know. Tell me."

"This is a gift to you from the wise ones, the People of the Trees. They know all about you and told me stories even I hadn't heard. About your birth, about the death of your mother by the guards of Phaistos, about your rescue by a servant girl and your flight to the Selloi of Dodona. And they know the future. They say you will bear a son, a man like no one has ever known before. They say you are blessed among women."

Fingers trembling, she tried to open the clasp. "I'll show you," I said. I lifted the flap that secured the opening and fitted it around her arm above the elbow.

"Ah-e-e-e!" She yelped, and I thought I had pinched her. I reached to unlock the clasp.

"No. Oh no, my beloved. I will never take this circlet from my arm, for you have placed it there, and because...because I feel the heart beat of it." She clutched her belly. "And he feels it too."

I touched her belly. "He speaks to you?"

She laughed, that little three-noted laugh, the memory of which had followed me like a phantom wherever I went since first I had heard it. "Not like that. I don't hear voices, at least not most of the time. I hear...convictions. I just know. And his spirit is here. He has guided you to me."

Something cold gripped my heart. A thought occurred to me. "Princess, are you certain you were already pregnant?"

"Philip forced me the night before I left the palace. When he came to me, hot, stinking with sweat from drilling the warriors I brought from Molossis, he was on fire, not with passion for me but insane with dreams of glory. When he finished, he shoved me away and said, 'There, now. Make a son to keep you company while I am away, building my kingdom.'"

"Still..."

"It is done, my sweet friend. This is as the gods have decreed it. You said so yourself. The wise ones knew. They sent you, and our son came too."

A dread descended on me. If my seed lived in Bird, our son could suffer seizures. The tree people and their gods could be playing a monstrous joke on all of us.

"I'm sorry, Princess; I swore I'd never do this to you."

The camp awoke, horses neighed as handlers brought them water, a wisp of smoke from breakfast fires entered the tent, and our night was over.

回回回

At breakfast, Olympias showed her bracelet, and I pointed out the features. "The blue, wavy lines are the rivers, the life blood of the land. The stones are for the unseen spirits, for their protection. The face in the coin is Athené. The Tree People say she now lives in Olympias." I said nothing about the owl beneath, and Olympias and I exchanged a glance. Our secret.

Palo and Bendi came with us on our walk uphill, back to the shrine. Bendi asked, "How did the Tree People hear about the princess?"

Palo answered. "They knew all about her. They have received prophesy since before her birth. They tell stories about her around the camp fires at night. They say the King of the World, will be born to her. They call him Iskander."

"Iskander," said Olympias. "In Molossis that is Alexandros, the same name as my brother. It means leader of men. I will meditate on the name, here, among the trees. I will consult with the ancestors."

"I brought you something too, a gift, like Wallis. " Palo held out a whistle dangling from a leather string. "It's for when you are alone on the mountain. If you are in danger you can just blow the whistle, and someone can come to help." He tied it around her waist. "You must wear it always. And when you blow it, I will hear, even if I am far away."

We laughed, understanding his need to be part of the mystery. "So that is why you carved the whistle," I said, "and bought the string to hang it on. Bird, he carved that whistle in the heights of the great mountains, as near the gods as man may go."

As though she had been gifted with all the lands of Helené, Olympias placed her hands on the whistle and dipped her head. I will wear it in great honor and humility," she said, "remembering always the friend who gave it to me." Then she lifted the whistle to her lips and blew.

"Like this?" She laughed the three point chirrup I loved most about her, and blew again. Within minutes Diana and two guards burst into the glade where we stood. She saw them and laughed. "I guess it works. I will blow this whistle, this gift of my friend," she told the startled group, "whenever I am in danger."

Diana jammed hands still wet from laundry onto her hips. "Just see that when you blow it you are in real need. Else we may just ignore you."

She raised the whistle again and blew. "I have to practice."

Diana stopped her ears with her hands, turned and walked back down the trail. "Children."

"Is...Is there anything you need—money, land, a house?" she asked, hoarse, uncertain, shy—shamed in her abandon the previous evening. We had, after all, been the closest of friends before this, but only that. How could she know my heart? That I had desired her more than life itself? Such great pains had I taken to keep it hidden.

"Only one more night with you," I answered. For whatever mischief we had wrought, what was done was done. I lifted her tiny hands and kissed the fingers, then let my hand wander up her arm to the bracelet. "The first time was for you and for your son. I would spend one more night with you. For me."

༄༄༄

That night after dinner, Bendi and the other guards disappeared. "They are circling the camp," said Olympias, suddenly shy. Diana has prepared a bath for us in my tent. Bendi sent Houros to the point overlooking the trail from Pella. I must know if Philip or his messenger comes." She left the final thought unspoken, but we both knew. If Philip learned our secret he could kill me and imprison Olympias for the rest of her life.

"What will you tell him about the bracelet?"

She smiled as cunning a smile as ever I have seen. "He will know only that it is a gift from the People of the Trees, to honor me as a voice of the gods and the ancestors, and to bless the conception of a son." Thinking, she added with a glitter in her eye. "A son of Zeus."

"You play a dangerous game, little bird. Be very careful."

She sighed. "I will use any trick or deceit possible. Philip may not know it yet, but he and his Makedoné are building a kingdom for our...Alexandros. I will be queen and queen mother." Her voice trembled. Her words were meant to fortify herself, not to impress me nor anybody.

We went inside the tent and immersed ourselves in a great bronze tub of warm water. I rubbed her back, massaging muscles drawn as tight as bow strings until she relaxed, laying her head on my shoulder. "You will do what must be done, little Bird, but don't forget why you do it. It is for the sake of the people, and for the land. The boy, if there is a boy, comes not just to you but to everyone."

"I know. I am only a woman."

"But what a woman," I groaned, feeling her slick leg slide between my thighs, massaging my man part. I began a smooth, gentle, back and forward motion up and down her leg, and let my hands roam wherever they would. They cupped her breasts, nipples grown hard beneath my fingers, slid down her body to find her woman place. She moaned and grew limp. I lifted her from the tub, placed her on the mat and entered her, all the time crooning softly, and—as near as I have ever been able—coming to song. To ecstasy.

Afterward, near dawn, we lay naked across furs Diana had laid out for us, furs I had brought from Galli, gifts from the people of Ulm. Olympias lay dozing on my shoulder. How could I let her go back to a man who cared less for her than he did for his horses. But what could I do? A proud man, Philip and his generals would hunt us to the ground.

"I will come back, Bird. I promise. We will find a place where kings and priests don't rule, a place where your son will grow strong and free. It is the only way we can be together. If Philip learns of me he will kill us all, even his own unborn son, for he would believe him to be mine."

She stirred. "Our son, Wallis. Your son and mine." Last words no more than mumbled, she went back to sleep. Warmth from her kisses still on my lips, I placed them against her forehead, tasting salty moisture, and smiled. "Our son," I echoed. Let us dream while we could. The cold light of day would come all too soon. "I will be back for you Bird. We will go away, away where the long arms of priests and kings don't reach. I must make plans." I eased her head off my shoulder. I could not waste one more moment of precious time. I kissed her again, and rose to dress. Even now the sky gleamed with first light. I must be far and away from here before any of the king's men could be about. I leaned over our bed of love. "I will be back as soon as I can, my darling. Be ready for me."

凹凹凹

Did I feel more a man when I left Chau? Did I fear my manhood less? She was mine, Philip, at least in the heart, long before she was yours—if she ever was, ever could be yours. Still the ceremonies took place—the union between Philip II of Makedonia, of the blood of Heracles, and Olympias, Princess of Molossis, of the blood of Achilles, and—as daughter of the Chosen of Kreté—Bride of Dionysus.

What ceremony supported my union with the little bird? Only the ceremony of the heart, which, at least for me, bound more tightly than any incantation of any priest. Such bindings are not loosed, no matter the distance put between.

Ceremonies. Chains designed to instill obedience in the subjects of kings and priests. It was time the rules changed. I would not have her so stripped of dignity, so defeated. She was a daughter of gods, Speaker for Demeter, Bride of Dionysos. She was Athena Nike, goddess of victory. I would fight for her, I would take her away with me, I would take her to a place so far from Philip that he would never find us. I knew of places where women were honored, such women as Jakardos' mother who ruled her own family. Even Ana possessed more power than Bird. Perhaps we could go to the lands of Etruska. Never again would Bird be forced into a bed she did not choose, and her son would grow strong and free and proud.

A son. Alexandros would be our only child. I had vowed never to allow my seed to grow within any woman, but Bird and I would need no other children. We would have our son.

I passed a formation of rock on which someone had scrawled the words, *pan areté*. Travelers always left messages on rocks for those who came after, messages intended to be helpful guides across some dark crevice or flowing river. I hadn't seen this message before, though I had traveled this way many times. *Pan Areté.* All for Honor.

Jolted back to earth after scaling the cliffs of gods, I stood staring. Palo and Spitter continued down the winding road beside the rock-choked water. Soon the sound of a squeaky wheel of the cart merged that of the stream rushing toward the valley. The message drawn on the rock seemed only for me. *Pan Areté.* The enormity of what I had done flooded my body. Crumpling to a ledge washed sharp by water from a spring beside the path, I sat looking at the message. All for Honor. No longer would honor guide my path. What I had done had been without honor.

I found a soft white rock in the edge of the water. With shaking hands I lifted my arm toward the message. Heart choked to overflowing, I crossed out the word, "*Pan*," and wrote above it, "*Xoris.*" Without. I am without honor both for what I have done and for what I am about to do. Split asunder, my past life–all that I knew, all that I had been taught–jerked, sped away from me, dissolving into the mist of early morning. I stood watching as the Daneion Pelos I knew dissolved and scattered. Another–both many-named and nameless–would be leaving this place. This spirit belonged to Olympias. No longer possessing a will, no longer a master of my fates, Olympias beat the trail; I could only follow.

The winds carried an echo of my mother's voice. My mother, whose very name, Areté, meant honor. 'Walk away, whispered the wind. 'Find other trails. Marry another woman.' Another woman? There was no place in my heart, my life for any other. I dropped the soft white rock. It fell, rolling away to splash in the stream. Committed, resolute, I bent to lift my back pack. I gathered a great breath and let it go, firming my destiny to that of a rock-hard brick drying in the sun.

Honor indeed. "I'm sorry, mother, I have no choice. It is you who wear the badge of Areté. Not I. Again I sighed, a great burden lifted from my shoulders. I am not perfect. I smiled, practicing the thought. I am not perfect! Spirit freed, breaking the plaster of dust gathered on my face and on my spirit, I shifted my back pack higher. No longer bound by the need for perfection, a world of opportunity awaited me. New world, new rules. I thought of Philip without fear. Philip? Once beyond my need to satisfy my mother's command for *areté*, for honor, Philip no longer mattered. I could match him...I could *best* him. Now. Catching the cart in easy stride, I said, "Get us home, Spitter."

Characters

Olympias

Daneion Pelos	Wallis, the narrator, the first of many names given him
Palo	A boy Wallis finds in the woods and adopts.
Spitter	Wallis' donkey
Olympias, (Myrtale)	Princess of Epirus, later mother of Alexander the Great
Tanya, Regina	Olympias' dead mother
Diana	Servant and companion of Olympias
Neoptolemus	King of Epirus and Olympias' father
Bendi	Bendigeidfran. Captain of Olympias' guards.
Dimitri, son of Thiusi and Ana, wife of Dimitri	Friends of Olympias and Wallis. Wallis lives with them when in Athens
Delos	Ana and Dimitri's son
Yiayia (*Yaa Yah*)	Wallis' paternal grandmother
Harkos and Kaelos	Thieves
Thalia	Olympias' servant
Timotheus, Marina, and Thoron	Wallis meets them near the Cave of the Blue Light
Kaesa (*Saleme*) and Nada	Ghosts in the Cave of Blue Light
Havos	Ghost, Nada's husband
Plise	Olympias' sister
Havin d'Ru	Olympias' sister's lover
Altera	Sister of Havin d'Ru

Characters

Phaistos	High priest, Temple of Unseen Spirits in Crete
The Selloi (*Selli*)	Tribe of holy people of Dodona
Doll	Olympias' step mother
Tibbe Louios	Ship owner in Kasya, lower Peloponnesus
Mathisos	Tavern owner in Kyphanta Peloponesus
Acteon	Servant of Phaistos
Kiria	Greek for lady
Daphnei	Servant of Tibbelouios.
Mara	Wife of Tibbelouios
The Kaelas	Twin daughters of Tibbe Louios
Polydamus and Calais	Guards on the gate from Athens
Davos	Wallis' uncle

People of the Trees

Bardyllis	General of Illyria who leads an army against Philip
Parmenion	Philip's general
Euridice	Philip's mother
Amyntas	Philip's father
Ptolemaios	Euridice's lover, consort
Perdikkas	King of Macedonia, Philip's older brother
Euphraos	Perdikkas' teacher
Orvon	Goat herder Wallis meets on trail toward the War of the Lakes.
Gisesi	Grain seller hired by Philip to buy feed for his horses.
Kotys	King of Thrace
Pausanius	Philip's cousin, contender for the throne
Agis	A Paonian under Bardyllis

Characters

Korius	Philip's personal manservant
Leon	Tavern owner in Athens
Ena	Daughter of Leon, tavern owner in Athens
Thelana	Ena's daughter
Sata	Ena's dead husband
Tharros	Ena's father-in-law
Thera	Tharros' daughter
Carthies	Tharros' servant
Keo	Tharros' son
Rudy	Owner of iron foundry
Rufus	Rudy's son
Lehan	Iron monger who makes the bracelet
Ahner	Lehan's wife
Lilia	Daughter of Lehan
Shalot	Chief of the Clan of the Trees
Estra	Shalot's daughter
H'Ruso	Estra's betrothed
Yelli	Maker of tables in Shalot's village
Spiri	Girl Palo liked in Shalot's village
Kinari	Wife of Yelli
Tivol	Son of crazy woman
Avi	Healer of the People of the Trees
Ton	Teacher of the People of the Trees
Fedei	Ton's uncle
Land	Boy who is autistic
Rork	Goldsmith who looks after Land
Minna	Rork's wife
Veil	Child who speaks to her doll, Te
Doss	Youngest child among the People of the Trees
Neelis	Woman of the People of the Trees who has asthma
Reed	Young bard. Lives with Neelis.

Characters

Whist	Child of the People of the Trees who works magic with wood and feeds the birds
Ovie and Shal	Twins from People of the Trees who see the spirit of Yiayia
Keer	Works with beads making jewelry, the oldest child of the People of the Trees
Vahna	Maid who saved Olympias as a child
Arrybus	Olympias' uncle
Fly	An orphaned fox
Betha	Woman who tells Wallis about the Weeping Tree
Cato	Iron monger who killed the kit fox, Fly's, mother in a trap, Betha's husband
Miangle	Watcher of the Weeping Tree.
Kirri	The Watcher, the wizard

Without Honor

Kev	Boy with sore foot in Ulm
Devi	Kev's father
Rober of Galli,	A reputed physician and teacher
Munk and Artur	Men who pull a ferry across the Danube River
Willum, son of Roget	Tavernkeeper's son whom Wallis meets on the boat trip in Etruska
Raben	Peddler who sells to the People of the Trees.
Tomaso	Brother of child, D'ahn, who has epilepsy.
Ozhio	Tomas' and D'ahn's father

Characters

Myrna	Servant of Ozhio
Fieros	Trader who travels with Wallis in Etruska
Venda and Meed'n	People Wallis meets in cave in Etruska
Kosti	Brother of Venda
Georgio and Tito	Travel with Fieros
Rofe	Surgeon in Bononia
Bruno	Man with broken leg in Bononia
Pia	Bruno's son
Rienzi	Rofe's father, owner of a tavern in Bononia
Jakardos	Traveler who joins Wallis in Bononia
Tass	Servant and companion of Thera, daughter of Tharros
Hom	Servant of Thera and husband of Tass
Argaios	Contender for Philip's throne, backed by Athens
Epaminondas	General from Thebes
King Kotys	King of Thrace
Kornios	Philip's personal servant

Pronunciation of Names

Makedon (Macedonia) =Mack-a-don or Mack-a-don-i-a
Thrake (Thrace) = Thray-kee
E'via (Euboea) = E-vee-a
Elefsis (Eleusis) = E-lef-sis
(Eurodice) = Ever-y-dee-chee
(Palo) = Pal-o
Phaistos - Fes-tos

Bibliography

SOME OF THE SOURCES USED FOR BEFORE THE DAWN

Maps and atlases
    Shepherd, William R. *Shepherd's Historical Atlas*
    Houghton Mifflin *The International Geographic Encyclopedia and Atlas*
    Harper Collins, *Past World, Atlas of Archaeology*

Encyclopedias and technical reference
    Kiple, and Ornelas *The Cambridge World History of Food*
    Bragonier, Jr and Fisher, *What's What- A visual glossary of everyday objects from paper clips to passenger ships*
    Bowder, Diana, editor, *Who Was Who in the Greek World*
    Symons, *Costume Reference, Costume of Ancient Greece*
    Kohler, *A History of Costume*
    Baedeker, *Baedeker's Travel Guides, Greece*

Translations
    Arrian, Translated by de Selincourt and revised by Hamilton *The Campaigns of Alexander*
    Plutarch, translated by Scott-Kilvert *The Age of Alexander*
    Theophrastus, translated by Arthur Hort, *Theophrastus Enquiry Into Plants*
    Jouanna, Jacques *Hippocrates*

Other historical reference
    Ellis, J. R. *Philip II and Macedonian Imperialism* –
    Errington, R. Malcolm, *A History of Macedonia*
    Green, Peter, *Alexander of Macedon, 356-323 B. C. A Historical Biography*
    Majno, Guido, M. D. *The Healing Hand, Man and Wound in the Ancient World*
    Heckel, Waldemar *The Marshals of Alexander's Empire*
    Ekdotike Athenon, *Philip of Macedon*
    Fr. Funck-Brentano, *A History of Gaul, Celtic, Roman and Frankish Rule*

Bibliography

>Ellis, Peter Berresford, *The First Millennium of The Celtic Empire History* 1000 BC – AD 51
>Ellis, Peter Berresford, *The Druids*
>Jones and Pennick, *A History of Pagan Europe*
>Willletts, R. F. *The Civilization of Ancient Crete*
>Grambo, Rebecca L, *The World of the Fox*
>Provatakis, *Meteora, History of the Monasteries and Monasticism*
>Adkins and Adkins *Handbook to Life in Ancient Greece*
>Keuls, Eva C. *The Reign of the Phallus, Sexual Politics in Ancient Athens*
>Ekdotike Athenon, *The Olympic Games in Ancient Greece*
>Immanuel Velikovsky *Peoples of the Sea, A Reconstruction of Ancient History*

Articles
>Severy, Merle, *The Celts, National Geographic Society, Vol. 151, NO. 5, May 1977*

Second Book of the Series
Son of the Bracelet

BOOK ONE, CHAPTER ONE
DRY LAND, STORMY SEAS

"How many have we gathered, Kosti?" I didn't expect an answer; I just needed something to say, something to draw me from darker thoughts.

I leaned forward against my ladder and looked up into the olive tree. Kosti pulled from the tree next to mine. Despite his spare frame, he had matched me, blanket for blanket, emptying his when I emptied mine. We had worked all morning, but unpicked olives still blocked the sky from sight.

Olives were Dimitri's only harvest that summer. Dead and dying root and grain crops lined the road back to the doma. Passing the animal sheds following the wagons early this morning, I had strained to see through the dust to where goats, sheep and donkeys stood just beyond the gates bawling to be fed and watered. Surely the grain would soon be gone, and except for Ana's free-flowing well, so would the water. Her well had never failed before. Everyone prayed that this year would be no different. Except for its faithful flow, the pears and fig trees would surely now be dead. The chilling air brought winds, but no rain. We took turns drawing water from Ana's well, to keep the animals and the pear and fig trees alive. It seemed Ana's goats and Dimitri's horses and donkeys would survive, but blossoms, so full and rich in the spring had fallen from the trees. They would bear no fruit. The winds came crisp and sharp, yet still no rain fell.

Preparing to repeat my question, I saw that Kosti's lips moved. He paused long enough to answer.

"Five hundred times to pull the rake. Each rake pulls about ten olives..." He stopped speaking but his lips continued to move. "Your blanket was higher than mine, but I will count them the same. My blanket held five hundred olives without rolling off. I have emptied my blanket nineteen times. This will be the twentieth..."

The boy was tallying every olive! I had thought to tease him, asking him how many we had gathered.

"Kosti! You think you must count olives? Dimitri would never demand that of you."

"No. Dimitri doesn't know I'm here."

"Then why..."

"Ana has nothing for me to do." He shrugged. "I guess she got tired of me counting chickens, ducks, eggs, jars of water—anything. I like to count, so she sent me to the orchards. She said maybe Dimitri had something here for me to do."

What a waste. "Have you figured how long it takes you to gather a blanket load of olives?"

He looked away toward the setting sun. "I came to the orchard before sunrise. I have filled twenty blankets. At the rate I am pulling olives, by sunset I will have pulled..." Again his lips began moving, and he looked away and to his left.

"Never mind, Kosti. Whoa. I said never mind. It doesn't matter. No Greek counts time. It is more meaningful that time counts the Greek."

"What?"

"It's a saying we have. One Greek is worth ten thousand years."

Bewildered, his mouth dropped open. "Ten thousand.... I must figure a bit for that, but since I have been picking olives one day, then I must be worth..."

"Kosti! Your sister said you were good with numbers, but boy! You must know more than numbers to make your way through the schools of Athens."

"Oh, I won't be going to schools. He looked at the setting sun with a worried brow. "I must stay here and help Dimitri and Anna so I will be worth more than what I eat." Again his lips began to move.

I stepped across the short distance between us, gathered his thin shoulders with my hands. "Kosti. Kosti! Look at me. We will find something for you to do, something that will honor your gift for the philosophy of numbers. You certainly have no head for farming. Perhaps the school of Pythagoras will make a place for you."

"Pythagoras?"

"A teacher my old yiayia told me about. Her father and Pythagoras were friends. Pythagoras believed in the powers of numbers. He said everything was numbers. I think you and he would have been close friends."

"I must finish counting..."

"No more counting. Gather your blanket..."

"But it isn't full! I must fill it to tally the..."

"No more, Kosti. Ana does not like her people to be late to the table. It has been a good day, and there are many more olives to be picked. Tomorrow!" I pulled him along to the blankets, helping him tie the corners of his blanket to contain the olives.

"It is not full. I must tally three of four parts to add to the whole."

My words fell on deaf ears. I picked up the knotted blanket, and Kosti counted, lips moving as we walked. I shoved the bundle into his hands, but when he grasped the knot he stood still continuing counting. What was I to do with him? Palo would have lifted the load alone, and with powerful arms slung it into the wagon, all the time telling me stories of the day.

I had hoped Kosti, the boy Palo and I had met in the cave in Etruska, would become good friends, but their very natures kept them apart. Palo had tried welcoming Kosti, showing him the birds and letting him brush Spitter, but Kosti had no need for birds and donkeys. Apart from music and dancing, such as the dance he had taught Palo on the long walk toward Felsina in Etruska, Kosti lived only in his head.

Jakardos said Kosti was a descendant of the same tribe as Ton, though Kosti knew nothing of the mysterious people of the trees, north of the Danube. Ton would have been overjoyed to have Kosti as a student of the mysteries of the tree people. He would not care whether Kosti understood farming and taking care of animals. Ton only cared for excellence of the spirit and the mind.

So far, since Kosti had joined the household of Dimitri, only when he danced to Jakardos' song and Palo's flute did he seem to awaken from some undercurrent that kept him submerged from the world. One must physically pull him from any sojourn with the god Abraxas, Keeper of the Number of Days, even to eat.

卍卍卍

Dry Lands, Stormy Seas continued in Book Two,
Son of the Bracelet

Contact and Ordering Information:

Before the Dawn ISBN   0-9762500-0-4 Case Bound
                     ISBN   0-9762500-1-2 Perfect Bound

Ki-Eea Key Press
    Box No: 818
    Kingston, Tennessee, 37763-0818

http://ki-eea-key.com/

Quick Pick Distribution
    22167 C Street
    Winfield, Kansas, 67156
    fax: 620-229-8978

       Toll free Phone: 888-281-5170
                               800-214-8110